Readers Respond to BROTHERHOOD OF BETRAYAL

"I read prolifically. *Brotherhood of Betrayal* is absolutely the best book I have ever read, and that is the shared sentiment of others I've loaned the book to."

—J.T., Jacksonville, FL

"I have just turned the final page of *Brotherhood of Betrayal,* having read through solidly, neglecting all household chores! This is an amazing book. No wonder Amazon gives it five stars."

—G.H., Oslo, Norway

"It was so therapeutic to read *Brotherhood of Betrayal.* I was counseled to get a divorce, but since I read this book I could not do it. As a result, my husband finally came to brokenness and is now leading us spiritually."

—P.W.

"I am quite moved by *Brotherhood of Betrayal.* I understand how your character felt on every page, every paragraph. I've been there. I am thankful for this compassionate, realistic novel."

—J.N., Trenton, TN

"*Brotherhood of Betrayal* was such a life impacting book. I sat in my clothes closet with the light on (so my husband could sleep) till 3:00 A.M. the first time I read it! I'm a bookstore owner, and *Betrayal* is my all-time favorite work of fiction."

—E.K., Ontario, Canada

BROTHERHOOD OF BETRAYAL

BROTHERHOOD
OF BETRAYAL

RANDALL ARTHUR

Multnomah® Publishers *Sisters, Oregon*

BROTHERHOOD OF BETRAYAL
published by Multnomah Publishers, Inc.
© 1999, 2003 by Randall Arthur Dodd

A previous edition of this novel was published under the title *Betrayal*.

International Standard Book Number: 1-59052-258-3

Cover image by Nonstock
Interior design by Katherine Lloyd, The DESK, Bend, Oregon

Multnomah is a trademark of Multnomah Publishers, Inc.,
and is registered in the U.S. Patent and Trademark Office.
The colophon is a trademark of Multnomah Publishers, Inc.

Printed in the United States of America

For information:
MULTNOMAH PUBLISHERS, INC.
POST OFFICE BOX 1720
SISTERS, OREGON 97759

Library of Congress Cataloging-in-Publication Data

Arthur, Randall.
    Brotherhood of betrayal / by Randall Arthur.
        p. cm.
    ISBN 1-59052-258-3 (paperback)
    1. Runaway husbands--Fiction. 2. Missionaries--Fiction. Forgiveness--Fiction.
    4. Clergy--Fiction. I. Title.
    PS3551.R77B76 2004
    813'.54--dc 21
                                                    2003011438

03 04 05 06 07 08 09 10—10 9 8 7 6 5 4 3 2 1 0

To my dear brother in Christ, Ric G.,
and the thousands of Christian brothers and sisters
like him who have been cruelly and carelessly abandoned
by the organized church.
Some, like Ric, have survived and overcome.
Many have not.

To Terry D.,
who made a difference.

And to my son,
Cayden Jeremiah.

Acknowledgments

I want to thank the thirty-three test readers of the original manuscript, who gave me invaluable editing suggestions.

I want to thank the various experts in the fields of law, medicine, travel, and the banking industry for their helpful information.

I want to thank all those at the GIC in Berlin (1994–1998) for their personal support and encouragement. What a great adventure we shared!

And I want to offer up a heartfelt THANKS to the staff at Multnomah Publishers (including Rod Morris, senior editor) for their vision for *Brotherhood of Betrayal* and for their energetic and remarkable efforts to turn the vision into reality.

 # PART 1

SPRING 1989
STOCKHOLM, SWEDEN
APPROXIMATELY FIVE HUNDRED MILES
SOUTH OF THE ARCTIC CIRCLE

1

W akened by the jarring ring of the bedside phone, Rachel McCain jerked forward, propping herself on her elbows. She fumbled for the receiver on the nightstand and cleared her throat. "Hello."

"Rachel?"

"Yeah?" She looked at the small alarm clock on the nightstand. It was 6:15 A.M.

The spring days in Stockholm were growing noticeably longer with each twenty-four-hour period. The sun, already two hours high this far north, gave full illumination to the McCains' bedroom through the half-opened curtains.

Why would anyone be calling at this hour? What was supposed to be happening? Who was this?

"This is Eric," she heard the voice say in English with its distinct Scandinavian accent. "I'm calling from the church. I apologize for waking you up, but all the men are here except for Clay. We've been waiting for him for about forty-five minutes. I'm just calling to find out if he's on his way, or if there's perhaps been a problem of some kind."

Rachel rubbed her forehead. *Eric... Clay...the men's weekend retreat.* It suddenly came to her.

With the phone still in her hand, Rachel turned and looked at Clay's empty side of the bed. "Eric, he was supposed to have left here at about ten till five this morning. He was going to take the bus over to Humle Park and then walk from there to the church. I'm sure he's already left, but give me just a minute and I'll make sure."

Rachel rested the receiver on the nightstand and crawled out of bed. She walked to the upstairs bathroom and saw that it was empty, then headed downstairs.

It took only a couple of minutes of searching all the rooms in the big two-story wooden house to confirm that Clay was nowhere inside. She quickly checked the garage, detached from the house, to see if their 1981 Volvo station wagon was there. It was. So were all the bicycles.

She went back inside and picked up the downstairs phone next to the living room couch.

"Eric," she said, her voice still rough, "he *has* left the house. But I don't know if he got a late start, or what. Maybe the bus is running late; maybe it broke down somewhere."

"That's possible, I suppose," Eric responded slowly. "If he doesn't show up in the next few minutes, I'll ask a couple of the guys to drive over to the bus station at the park and if necessary trace the bus's route back to your house."

Rachel ran her hand through her shoulder-length wheat-blond hair. "I'll walk down to the corner to see if he's still at the bus stop here. And then I'll call you right back." But even as she hung up, she was certain that Clay wouldn't still be waiting for a delayed bus, not while fifteen or so men were at the church anxiously awaiting his arrival so they could get on the road.

Returning to the master bedroom and slipping into a pair of old faded jeans and a sweatshirt, Rachel was abruptly revisited by the paramount and unshakable stress that came with each new sunrise, a stress that had slowly been eating away at her for the last eight or nine months

"Just two more months," she told herself when she walked out into the nippy morning air and headed toward the bus stop. "When we're back in Atlanta, things will start to improve. They've just got to."

2

Within twelve minutes, Rachel had Eric Torleif, a leading elder in the church and a business consultant by trade, on the line again.

"He's not at the bus stop here, Eric," she said.

"He still hasn't shown up here either."

"So maybe the bus he took has had problems between here and there." Although Rachel heard herself repeat what seemed to be a logical idea, it still didn't *sound* right. The Swedish buses, maintained so exceptionally well as a vital part of Stockholm's extensive public transportation system, simply were not known for breaking down.

"Are you sure he took the bus?" Eric questioned. "Could he have left the house earlier and set out on foot? Are you sure he didn't take the car or the bike?"

"The bikes and the car are in the garage. I've already checked. But whether he decided to walk or not, I have no idea. I assume he would have taken the bus; that's what he planned."

"All right, I'll go ahead and send someone over to the Humle Park station to see if we can come up with anything on this end. And I'll call you back in a little bit."

Rachel walked into the kitchen and looked at the wall clock. The time was just 6:35. She decided to shower and then wake up nine-year-old Summer, the oldest of her three children, to start getting her ready for school.

Rachel was sure Eric or one of the other men would call her back shortly with the news of Clay's arrival.

She headed upstairs.

She was just entering the bathroom when halfway down the hallway she saw her two-year-old son, Justin, standing quietly and motionless, like a faded silhouette, in the doorway of his room. Clad only in his red polka-dotted sleeper, he was staring at her with probing eyes. Eyes of…uncertainty.

Before she could say anything, he broke into a run and threw himself against her, clutching his arms around her legs.

"Well, good morning, fellow." Rachel reached down past his matted hair to rub his back. "You sure are up early. Are you okay?"

Justin pressed his face to her leg. Rachel sat down in the bathroom doorway and gathered him into her lap, gently pulling his head to her chest.

"You want Mommy to lie back down with you for a little while?"

Justin leaned his head away from his mother's chest, stared her in the eyes, and nodded a slow yes.

"Can Daddy lay down wib us, too?" he asked softly in his early morning voice.

Rachel sighed and ran her hand through his hair. "Daddy's already gone, honey. Remember last night? We told you he was going on a camping trip for a couple of days with some of the other men in the church."

"Wib Peter's daddy?"

"And with Carl's daddy. And Magnus's daddy."

"When he coming home?"

"Not today or tomorrow, but the next day."

As if that was all he needed to hear, Justin stood up, took his mother by the hand, and led her to his room. Together they crawled under the comforter.

They had been lying down for about twenty-five minutes when Rachel, realizing it was time to wake Summer up, tried quietly to slip out of the bed. Her stocking feet had just touched the gray-carpeted floor when she heard someone knocking on the front door. Still in her jeans and sweatshirt, she brushed her fingers through her hair and headed down the stairs.

She was halfway down the stairway when she heard lightweight steps behind her. She turned and saw Justin with his arms outstretched. Rachel stopped and let him catch up, then lifted him into her arms and proceeded to the front door.

When she pulled the door open, she saw Bengt Wennergren and Sten Oestlund, two of the men of the church, standing there.

Bengt, a single thirty-year-old architect, was one of Clay's closest Swedish friends. Together he and Clay had occasionally spent days camping alone in the Swedish wilderness hunting for moose and fishing in the inland rivers for brown trout. Sten Oestlund was a married thirty-four-year-old high school history teacher. Both Bengt and Sten, as was typical of 70 percent of the country's population, were tall, fit, and blond.

"We just searched the entire bus route between here and the church," Bengt spoke up, his six-foot frame and rough voice adding authority to his words, "and we didn't see him anywhere."

Rachel shrugged her shoulders. "There's got to be a logical explanation of some kind," she stated flatly, feeling for the first time the initial twinges of serious concern.

"Do you mind if I call Eric?" Bengt said. "He's sitting in the church office waiting to hear if we found out anything."

"Of course I don't mind." Rachel nodded toward the living room phone and gestured for both men to come inside. "I have to go upstairs and wake Summer up so she can start getting ready for school. But go ahead and make yourselves at home. I'll be back down in a few minutes. If you want, there's some milk and juice in the refrigerator."

Climbing the stairs back up to the second floor, Rachel was bewildered that Clay hadn't shown up yet. Justin, still in her arms, was silent again, his head resting on her shoulder. She hoped he wouldn't start asking questions.

She carried him around while she awakened Summer. As normal, it took several minutes to arouse Summer out of her sleep.

Sweden, with its extremely comfortable and slow-paced lifestyle, had succeeded in turning them all into late sleepers. Fighting early mornings had gradually become a family distinctive.

As Summer squirmed from beneath the red-and-white animal-print comforter, Rachel spoke a few words of love to her and gave her the usual list of morning instructions. Holly, barely six, in a bed just three meters across the room, slept through the morning commotion as normal.

Once Summer was finally on her feet and moving toward the shower, Rachel, with Justin perched on her hip, returned downstairs and entered the living room.

Bengt had just gotten off the phone and was starting to say something to Sten.

"Well, what was decided?" Rachel interrupted.

"He still hasn't shown up at the church," Bengt turned and explained to her. "So Eric's going to call the main bus terminal downtown. He's going to try to find out if any of the buses on this route have been delayed or have had any problems this morning. As soon as he gets some answers, he's going to call us back."

Rachel paused for a moment, then spoke, trying not to sound nervous. "Well, while we wait, I've got to make breakfast for Summer and prepare her a lunch. Would either of you like some hot cereal or something to drink? Tea? Coffee?"

Both men consented to a cup of coffee.

Rachel strapped Justin into a highchair and gave him a half-peeled banana, and then went to work to prepare coffee for the men and oatmeal for Summer.

The conversation that followed among the three adults gravitated toward the retreat and the eagerness of the seventeen men to get away for the weekend. The direction of the conversation, Rachel knew, was a natural and lighthearted attempt to mask over any serious and possibly premature feelings they might be having about Clay's whereabouts or well-being.

In the middle of the small talk and coffee drinking, the phone rang. They all three moved quickly back to the living room. Rachel picked up the receiver.

It was Eric. He had just spoken with one of the officials at the downtown terminal. No, none of the buses had been delayed or had encountered any problems. The chief dispatcher reported that the ten buses that had served the route between the McCains' address and Humle Park since five o'clock this morning had been on time at each stop.

The news only confirmed their confusion.

Eric waited on the other end of the line while they all tried to decide what to do next.

Rachel gave Bengt the phone.

"Since the buses were on time," Bengt speculated to Eric, "then obviously something happened either between here and the corner stop, or between Humle Park and the church."

"But we just searched those areas," Sten interjected with a whisper.

Bengt relayed back to Eric what Sten was saying.

Rachel stood in silence trying to keep her imagination from running wild. It just wasn't conceivable that Clay could be a victim of foul play. Things like that didn't happen in Sweden. The country possessed one of the lowest crime rates in the world. She had lived here for nine years and had not heard one time of a mugging, burglary, or kidnapping.

"I don't know, maybe we should call the different hospitals to see if he's been admitted anywhere," Bengt offered. "Maybe he got sick or something. Maybe there's been an acci—" Bengt looked at Rachel and shook his head. "It's just an idea. What do you think?" His question was directed to all of them.

"If something like that had happened, wouldn't the admitting hospital have contacted me?" Rachel said. "They could easily trace me through his ID."

"Yeah, I'm almost certain that would be the normal procedure," Sten answered thoughtfully, "but it still wouldn't be out of line to call around and ask, just to make sure."

Rachel nodded her agreement.

Bengt told Eric they were going to call the city hospitals and find out if Clay had been admitted anywhere. He then paused and nodded a response to something Eric was telling him. The conversation between the two lasted a couple of minutes.

"Okay," Bengt said to Rachel and Sten when he hung up, "while we're calling the hospitals, Eric is going to call the bus terminal again. If Clay doesn't show up in the next two or three hours, Eric wants to meet with all the bus drivers who drove this route between five and six o'clock this morning. He wants us to give him a couple of photographs of Clay to show the drivers to see if any of them remember picking him up."

Rachel said that she could get the pictures.

Following Rachel and Bengt into the kitchen, Sten pressed a couple of fingers to his temple. "Why don't we tell the rest of the men to go ahead and go to the cabins without us?"

Rachel started to offer an apology for the awkwardness of the situation when Bengt spoke up and said, "According to Eric, they've already decided to hang out at the church. They want to be close by so they can offer their help if it's needed. Three or four of them have already started cruising all the possible foot routes between here and there." He paused for a second, then with an artificial pout tried to lighten the mood. "While the rest of them are waiting around at the building, they're going to go ahead and start the big chess tournament."

"They're just taking advantage of my absence," Sten volleyed with a competitive grin. "They know they wouldn't stand a chance if they waited for me."

Bengt returned the grin and rolled his eyes. He started to say something, but at that moment Summer, dressed for school, came bouncing into the room. She suddenly stopped when she saw Bengt and Sten standing there.

"You ready for breakfast, honey?" Rachel asked, transitioning to an upbeat tone to try to cover her emotional distraction. She was already spooning hot cereal from a pot on the stove into a small plastic bowl.

Summer, her eyes trying to absorb what was going on, nodded halfheartedly and proceeded to the table.

"Did you by chance happen to hear or see Daddy this morning before he left?" Rachel asked as she placed the bowl in front of Summer.

Summer's eyebrows lifted as she reached for her spoon. "How could I see Daddy when I was asleep?" she answered, sounding as if she were trying to be cute in Bengt's and Sten's company.

Rachel opened her mouth to clarify her question when Bengt interrupted.

"Rachel, can I speak with you alone in the living room for a moment?"

At the very moment Bengt posed his request, Summer spoke up again. "Did Daddy do something that was wrong this morning?"

"No, no," Rachel said. "Daddy didn't do anything wrong. It's just that he hasn't shown up at the church yet, and all the men are there waiting for him so they can start their trip. I was just going to ask if you had any idea of how long ago it was when he left the house, or if you remembered him saying anything to you."

Summer shrugged. "Maybe he went to the gym."

Rachel wondered why she hadn't already thought of that possibility. Going to the gym two to three times a week to work out had been a ritual of Clay's for the last thirteen years. Nothing had ever sidetracked his devotion to that ritual—not marriage, not

RANDALL ARTHUR ♦ 24

kids, not geographical location, not anything. Because of the ever-shifting responsibilities of his ministry and their effect on his daily scheduling, though, he had never managed to work out regularly on specific days or at any specific time of day. But through sheer discipline, he had relentlessly managed to interweave at least a couple of workouts somewhere into every seven-day stretch.

But would he be so selfish this morning that he would ruin everybody else's schedule and cause an upheaval of concern just to do a few bench presses and curls? And without telling anyone?

Rachel shook her head. "No, I don't think he would be training this morning, knowing that all the men are waiting for him."

Summer started to open her mouth to say something when Rachel impulsively added, "But who knows? Go ahead and say the blessing by yourself, and I'll go call just to make sure."

As Rachel retrieved the gym's phone number from a loose-leaf booklet kept by the phone, she noticed that Bengt had followed her and was standing a few feet away.

"What do you think?" she asked him.

"I personally don't think he's there," he replied, looking as if some new thought was suddenly disturbing him, "but I suppose you should call just to eliminate any doubts."

Rachel looked at him, wondered what he was thinking, and picked up the phone and dialed.

In less than a minute, one of the men working at the gym told her that Clay had not been there this morning.

When she hung up, she turned again to Bengt. "Well, wherever he is, he's not at the gym." She sighed, closed her eyes, and lightly squeezed the bridge of her nose. When she opened her eyes again, she saw Bengt staring at her.

"Can I talk openly with you?" he asked with a lowered voice. He was breathing deeper than normal.

After a short pause, Rachel responded with another sigh. "All right, if you believe it'll be beneficial."

Bengt looked around, then spoke quietly to her. "The whole church knows, of course, that Clay has been going through some kind of personal struggle. And it's obvious to those of us who know the two of you that it's putting a strain on your marriage, probably a greater strain than we suspect." He hesitated. "Being a typically reserved Swede, it's not easy for me to talk with you about your personal life. But you and Clay are special; I care about you. So do all the others in the church. Our lives have been changed because of you."

Rachel now locked eyes with him. The stress that in recent months had become part of her everyday life, once again rose to the forefront.

Over the last nine months or so, Clay—before the eyes of everyone—had digressed from a vibrant and highly focused husband, father, and missionary pastor to a half-living zombie struggling in his heart and mind with something he refused to talk about, something that had imprisoned his spirit and would not let him go.

For six months, Rachel had tried, with mounting frustration and embarrassment, to explain to the young Stockholm Independent Bible Church why Clay, their founding pastor, was withdrawing from them and acting more and more like a machine void of spirit and soul.

Rachel had wanted to reach out to her husband. She had tried many times, with all her heart. But each time, he had responded coldly and tensely, telling her it was something he had to work through on his own. He would then walk away in silence.

And now, in the last two or three months, he had reached the point where he hardly even wanted to be with her or touch her.

Hesitantly, with fear in her heart, she had asked him if he was sexually involved with another woman. It was no secret that women were attracted to him; they always had been. His taut jaw, thick sandy blond hair, and athletic physique still drew a lot of female attention, even at his current age of thirty-seven. Clay had retorted emphatically, however, that he was not seeing another woman. And she believed him.

Am I the problem then? she had wondered repeatedly. Clay had always, until recently, told her she was the most loving, attractive, and devoted companion a man could have. He had always been passionate about her and had constantly displayed that passion in both his words and behavior. Had she somehow in the last year become insensitive to his needs and done something to squelch his passion? Had she become a disappointment to him?

She was beginning to feel she was losing him, losing the man she had loved and trusted for thirteen years of marriage. And she didn't know why. All she knew was that she was deeply confused, afraid, and hurting.

"I guess what I'm trying to say," Bengt continued from his heart, "is that none of the men who have tried to reach out to Clay have been able to get through to him. It's almost as if he hasn't wanted any help; as if...he's wanted to be left alone."

A tear came to Rachel's eye.

For weeks she had wanted to call Pastor Frank Lovett of their home church, North Metro Church of the Bible in Atlanta,

Georgia, and inform him of what was happening. He was the one who had fathered and grounded them in their Christian faith, the one who had married them, and the one who had ordained Clay as a gospel minister. He was also one of the primary men, along with the directors of their mission board, to whom they were now accountable. Moreover, he was their biggest encourager and supporter. He always had been.

Rachel had desperately wanted to beg him to speak with Clay. She had even threatened Clay with that intention during one of her recent outbursts of frustration. Clay, in the privacy of their bedroom, had quickly turned on her and in a rare temper-filled moment told her harshly with heated eyes and a raised voice, "You will *not* call Pastor Lovett; do you understand?"

Clay had insisted that he was working on his problem, that he didn't need the home church or the mission board to get involved. He had stressed with underlying tones of bitterness that neither of the groups would understand or try to empathize with his inner struggle anyway, that they would simply order him to heal himself immediately and then treat him like a vile and despised pagan if he didn't.

"There's no instant recovery," he had told her. "It's going to take time. Just continue to be patient with me."

But, to date, she had heard only his persistent promises, his defensive words, and his excuses. She still had not seen any actual recovery.

Her desperate hope for some relief was only being sustained by the constant reminder that in July, just two months away, they would after nine years of service in Sweden be returning to the States for a full year of furlough. She kept telling herself that once they got back to the States, Clay would come to his senses and realize that his extreme fears and claims about the leaders of their mission board and home church were overly harsh and unrealistic. He would see, once he was in their company again, that they were sensitive and responsible men who truly cared about his well-being. She was certain he would open up and confide in them and ask for their counsel.

"Do you think it's possible," Bengt questioned, "that he might have just decided to go away for a few days and not tell anybody? To be by himself? To somehow try to work things out on his own?"

Rachel swallowed slow and hard and looked toward the large living room window. A couple of times in recent weeks, Clay had shouted that maybe he should just move away. Not just for a day. Or two. But for... Surely he had only been spewing empty words in the heat of the moment. He hadn't been serious. She hadn't even thought about the words again, until now.

She looked back at Bengt. "I...uh...there have been a few heavy arguments." New tears started to roll down her cheeks. "He's been so distant. I've tried to tell him that the children and I can't keep living with a ghost, that his withdrawal is crippling us emotionally." She wiped at the tears. "I don't know—maybe I've driven him away with my constant pleading. *Is* that possible?"

Bengt shook his head. "No, no, I wasn't making that kind of suggestion at all. If he's chosen to go away for a few hours, or even for a few days, you're definitely not the cause. No one would think that you were, not for a moment. If he's felt a need to be alone, then it's for some other reason, a reason he's not yet ready to talk about. Besides, maybe my question was way off track anyway. Maybe he'll show up at any minute with an explanation that will make us all laugh."

Rachel said nothing. In the grip of her new and sudden fear, she simply took a step sideways, looked into the kitchen at Justin and Summer, then looked again out the living room window. She prayed fervently that God would deliver her from her present thoughts.

Before noon, all the local hospitals and emergency centers had been contacted. Clay McCain had not been admitted to any of them.

During the midafternoon, Eric managed to talk face-to-face at the central bus terminal with three of the six bus drivers who had driven the morning route between the McCains' and Humle Park. None of the three, after examining the photographs of Clay, remembered seeing him during the morning run.

By four-thirty, Clay still had not shown up at the church or at the house. In spite of everyone's efforts, no clues had surfaced as to his whereabouts.

At seven, all the men who had been hanging out at the church, plus several of their wives, gathered at the McCains' house, crowding into the living room and kitchen with cups of hot coffee in hand, and prayed. They also brainstormed for any idea, no matter how remote, that might explain Clay's disappearance.

With Rachel's permission, Bengt shared with the group his personal gut feeling that Clay was just seeking solitude for a day or two.

Although many in the group conceded that Bengt could be right, it was still the voice of the majority that they should contact the police immediately and file a missing person's report.

As Eric made the call, Rachel prayed again, this time desperately, that the thought that was plaguing her would go away and never, *ever* enter her mind again, and that Clay would show up soon and just sit and hold her tightly in his arms.

3

The next morning at five-thirty, Rachel was tossing under the comforter. She had been asleep for only an hour and a half. She was dreaming that Clay was lying at her side, gently stroking the hair on her forehead. He was telling her for the third or fourth time how sorry he was that he had gotten on the wrong bus. He had tried to get off, but the driver had not permitted him to until the first official stop two hundred kilometers outside Stockholm. He had wanted to call her when they finally reached the stop, but the location had been at a remote lake where there were no towns, businesses, or telephones.

As Rachel heard him explain how the next bus back to Stockholm didn't show up until nine hours later, she felt his hand move tenderly to her shoulder.

Her happiness somehow felt hollow. She tried to tell him, "You're forgiven," but the words seemed to stick somewhere between her mind and her tongue. She kept trying with mounting frustration to vocalize the words, but no matter how hard she tried, she couldn't get her mouth to open. Her lips felt as if they were stuck together.

Then, Clay's words faded into indecipherable sounds. Rachel felt him tug softly at her shoulder. His whirlpool of words became muffled, as if being shouted from a great distance.

She strained to hear and understand. One word finally rose

out of the gibberish and became clear. *Mommy*.

Rachel squinted inside her mind. Why would Clay call her Mommy? It was both silly and confusing.

"Mommy? Mommy?" The words continued to hammer at the ears of her mind, causing her to feel uncomfortably light-headed.

Then Rachel's eyes sprang open. Her mind was sucked back to reality as she registered Holly lying at her side on top of the comforter, pulling at her shoulder.

Rachel closed her eyes again for a brief moment to try to clear her head.

"Mommy," she heard her name called one more time.

"Mommy's half asleep, honey," Rachel said, barely above a whisper, as she made eye contact with her youngest daughter now breathing in her face. "What do you want?"

"Do you think we'll find Daddy today?"

Rachel caught herself staring at the ceiling, her dream abruptly stolen by the nightmarish truth that her husband was still missing and no one knew why or how.

O God, help me, she pleaded again in her soul for the hundredth time. *I don't know what's happening... I'm scared... Please bring Clay home!*

Rachel knew that Holly's question, like Summer's and Justin's throughout yesterday evening, was coming from the heart of a child seeking some kind—any kind—of assurance that everything was going to be okay.

Rachel reached over and pulled Holly, in her cartoon-print pajamas, to her breast. "We're going to do everything we can, honey," she whispered. "And a lot of other people will be helping us." She swallowed to work the dryness out of her throat. "Why don't you and I pray together, and we can ask God to help us find him. Okay?"

Holly, with her curly brown hair tangled from a night's sleep, nodded with a slight expression of hope.

Rachel prayed aloud. When she finished, she held her youngest daughter in silence and tried to hold back the tears.

Although she had been taught to trust God and had exemplified a strong faith as a wife and missionary for many years, she couldn't, even with sincere praying, now let go of her fear.

She wanted to believe, like Bengt, that Clay was okay and that God was watching over him. But what if something bad had happened to him? What if he was lying somewhere hurt? What if he needed help? Or what if...? She tried not to dwell on the one scenario that persisted to haunt her. But she couldn't shake it. Not yesterday. Not today. It had overcome her and was sifting from her all the security she had ever known.

She had occasionally been anxious, discouraged, lonely, despondent, and even depressed. But never had she tasted real fear. Never, until now.

Staring past Holly's head toward the ceiling, she felt completely alone. Even God felt far away.

She wanted to call their home church in Atlanta and cry over the phone to Pastor Lovett. She wanted to tell him what was happening. She wanted to share with him her escalating fear, ask for his counsel, and have the church pray for her family.

But what would Pastor Lovett and the home church think? How would they react? They had always put her and Clay on a pedestal. Throughout the years, they had even touted them to teenagers and young couples as Christian role models.

What if the Atlanta congregation—middle class, large in

number, and piously conservative—knew the truth about the last nine months? And what if she did voice to them her present fear? Being entrusted with something so personal and so serious, wouldn't they rally around her with unconditional love and concern? Wouldn't they accept and stand behind her family, no matter what, especially under the present circumstances?

She wanted to tell them. She felt she had to tell them. She just couldn't hide the truth any longer. She needed their help and reassurance. She also wanted to have a clear conscience; she and Clay received a quarter of their income from North Metro.

Maybe now was also the time to talk to Pastor Lovett about her and Clay's heartfelt shift from some of the home church's "old-fashioned" beliefs and practices concerning clothing styles, the King James Version of the Bible, pop music, cards, dice, Hollywood movies, ministry associations, and a whole list of other items that she and Clay had come to realize were legalistic extremes. They had been waiting for the right opportunity, primarily because of Pastor Lovett's and the denomination's extreme sensitivity about those issues. But they had procrastinated long enough. Now perhaps was the chance they had been waiting for.

She twisted her head, trying not to disturb Holly, who was momentarily still and quiet, and looked at the clock. The sun was already bathing the outdoors with its warm spring rays, but the time was only 5:45 A.M. If she called Atlanta, she would have to do it later in the day. On America's East Coast, six time zones behind Sweden, the time would now be approaching midnight.

She quickly buried the notion of calling as her brain continued to speed from one restless thought to another.

She was wide awake, but at this hour there was nothing she

could do. Except try to stay afloat in her misery. And be on call as a mother.

Her only consolation—other than the hope that Clay would come walking back into the house at any moment or that someone would report his whereabouts—was the interview scheduled for ten this morning at the central police station and the official search that she hoped would begin thereafter.

4

W hat we can do," Lieutenant Nils Ekberg finally offered, "is recheck all the local hospitals and assist Mr. Torleif in questioning the last few bus drivers."

Rachel was sitting on the other side of Lieutenant Ekberg's desk on the third floor of the newly built metal-and-tinted-glass police headquarters. She had told the officer everything she knew about Clay's disappearance. She even endured the standard missing person's questions about her husband's possible illegal drug associations, enemy relationships, marital infidelity, mismanagement of investments, and physical and mental disorders possibly leading to extreme depression.

Listening to Lieutenant Ekberg's summation, Rachel struggled to remain composed. She understood that Ekberg was trying to establish a motive for why Clay might have been victimized or gone into hiding. Nevertheless, she felt disemboweled, as if the questions had been darkness personified, laughing hideously at her and Clay's long-established Christian testimony. She felt like she was going to be sick.

"Unless some kind of evidence of criminal activity or coercion surfaces," Lieutenant Ekberg continued with pen in hand, "the only other thing we can do is submit an official request to the major local newspapers to run a high-profile news article about your husband's disappearance, accompanied by a good photograph, and try to solicit some eyewitness knowledge of where he is or what has happened to him. However, before we take that course of action, we'll wait another forty-eight hours to first see if Mr. McCain shows up on his own."

"Please, I want you to help in every way you possibly can," Rachel pleaded.

Lieutenant Ekberg wrote down for her what his step-by-step course of action would be during the next three days. When the plan was understood and agreed upon, and when facts about Clay were compiled for a probable newspaper report, Rachel thanked Lieutenant Ekberg and left.

Bengt and two ladies from the church, Marie Blomqvist and Liv Munthe, who had met Rachel at the police station earlier, were waiting outside in the warm sunshine, a prized commodity due to Sweden's extremely short spring and summer seasons.

The two ladies were some of Rachel's dearest friends and part of a close-knit group of middle-aged wives and mothers.

Fighting to stay in control of her emotions, Rachel stood there on the curb of the busy city street and gave them a thorough account of the meeting, then expressed that she needed to be alone for a while. Only when she repeatedly assured them that she was going to be okay did Bengt, Marie, and Liv agree to comply with her request. After affirming that they would stay in touch throughout the day, they all departed in separate directions.

Rachel headed across the street toward an empty bench at the edge of one of the dozens of green and flowery inner-city parks. She felt suddenly dizzy and was sure she was going to vomit. Once seated, she managed to slowly fight back the nausea.

Five or six gray pigeons pecked invisible food from the ground a few feet away at the base of a concrete-anchored garbage can.

Rachel's mind paced.

More now than yesterday, she felt the need to inform Pastor Lovett of her present circumstances. Her emotions were crying out for supportive and objective feedback from the man who had established her in her conservative Christianity, the man who was still her official pastor.

She looked at her watch. The time in Atlanta, she quickly calculated, was 5:20 A.M. Feeling drawn to look for a pay phone, she stood up and started walking. Within a block and a half, she spotted a phone box.

When she finally stood with the receiver in her hand and a coin to insert for operator assistance, she suddenly broke into tears. The arm holding the phone went limp.

Maybe she was acting prematurely. Maybe she should give the situation a couple more days, at least until all the hospitals and bus drivers had been contacted.

She propped her head against the scratched and dirty Plexiglas partition and strained to regain her composure. After several deep breaths, she hung up the phone.

Walking back to her car, she nervously hastened her pace. She needed to get home to relieve the baby-sitter.

By six-thirty that evening, personal inquiries had again been made at all the hospitals in and around Stockholm. Clay McCain was not, and had not been, a patient at any of them.

Two of the three remaining bus drivers had also been reached. Neither of them remembered ever seeing the man in the photograph.

When Rachel heard the telephone reports from Eric, Bengt, and Lieutenant Ekberg, her hope suffered another blow. Immediately, she wanted to safeguard the children from the same devastation, yet she felt a need to be honest with them.

She seated them together around the kitchen table and gently passed along the report that their dad's whereabouts was still unknown. Justin scurried to her lap. Summer, with a look of deep confusion in her eyes, left the table and ran to her room. Holly replied softly, "But God is going to help us find him, isn't He, Mommy?"

Rachel emphasized to Holly and Justin that all of their friends, along with the policemen, were going to keep searching and that everybody was still praying.

She then followed Summer to her room. She found her staring into her small aquarium of goldfish. Rachel repeated to her the same assurances.

Later, when the kids were somewhat settled, Rachel dialed the number to her dad's house in Marietta, Georgia, a suburb north of Atlanta. She knew from years of disappointing experiences, however, not to expect any support from her dad, Billy Allen Ward, even if he was at home and received her call. As a long-haul trucker working for a major trucking company, he had never had a strong presence in her life. Even on those rare occasions during her youth when he managed to be home for a few hours, his conversations with her were never an exchange of thoughts and feelings but rather an issuance of opinions and instructions.

One of the few childhood memories she had of her dad was when occasionally on Sunday afternoons she would sit in silence in the shade of a giant oak tree in their backyard and watch him make homemade vanilla ice cream and listen as he rambled on about the trucking business and labor unions.

He was not a religious man, and his input into her life became even less when she became a zealous and legalistic Christian at the age of eighteen. She had tried regularly since she moved away from home to cultivate communication by sending cards and letters, but a meaningful relationship between them had just never developed.

Nevertheless, she now felt a natural obligation to let him know what was happening in her family's life. There was also an undying, deep-seated wish that he would somehow want to get more involved this time. After all, he was now her only parent. Her mother, an emotionally decimated wife due to the perpetual absence of the man she married, had died of cancer three years earlier.

When the number rang through, there was no answer. Rachel waited patiently before she hung up.

She then tried to reach Clay's parents, Lloyd and Hester McCain, both non-Christians who a year and a half ago moved from Atlanta, where they had lived all their lives, down to a retirement village in sunny St. Petersburg, Florida. They were both in their early seventies. Mr. McCain, because of a rare degenerative nerve disease, was now largely dependent on a walker for mobility.

Rachel felt her heart beating as she waited through the rings.

Her mother-in-law answered. Rachel, not wasting time on trivial pleasantries, asked her to get Clay's dad on the line with them. When her father-in-law picked up an extension line, Rachel told them of the events of the last two days.

Her mother-in-law started crying.

Rachel knew that due to Mr. McCain's health problems and

Mrs. McCain's need to be with him around the clock, there was nothing they could do to help. She simply tried to sound hopeful as she answered their questions and assured them that she would keep them informed.

When she hung up, she regretted that her and Clay's Christian legalism of the past—their excessive and self-righteous behavior, rules, and attitudes—had alienated his parents. She cringed with sorrow as she remembered the many times she and Clay, during their first four years of marriage in the States, had forbidden his mom to come into their home because she smoked. Rachel hoped intensely that she and Clay could some day mend that rift their blind adherence to such senseless rules had caused.

Now, however, she didn't feel strong enough to dwell on the issue.

Instead, sitting there by the phone, she felt the urge to call Pastor Lovett. Again, she decided to wait.

That night the kids slept with her in the master bedroom. Justin and Holly snuggled beside her in the bed. Summer, at her own insistence, lay in a sleeping bag in the corner of the room.

It took longer than usual for the kids to lose themselves in sleep.

Rachel lay awake till three in the morning and worried. It seemed that her only remaining hope, barring a miracle of some kind, would be the newspapers. If the newspaper companies printed the article that Lieutenant Ekberg described, surely a reader somewhere would come forth with helpful information.

O God...please, she begged with a new rush of tears.

She pleaded until she lost awareness of her surroundings and dozed.

◆   ◆   ◆

The next morning, as had been her motherly routine for seven years, Rachel assisted the children in getting ready for the Sunday morning worship service.

Two years after arriving in the country, she and Clay had learned to speak Swedish fluently, not as a necessity, since three-fourths of the Swedish population spoke English, but as a matter of principle and desire. Upon completing their language studies, Clay launched their ministry and organized the Stockholm Independent Bible Church in what the directors of the mission board claimed was record time. The charter membership of the church consisted of four families, for a total of fifteen people. With Rachel working alongside Clay, they had seen the congregation grow both numerically and spiritually every year since. The church now consisted of more than two hundred people. She and Clay were applauded in stateside mission circles for being one of the few successful missionary couples in northern Europe.

In light of the current crisis, Rachel fretted about their ministry. The eight elders of the church, however, had decided yesterday that all the regular church services would continue to take place in Clay's absence, according to schedule. Rolf Nyborg, a middle-aged and gifted teacher in the congregation, was scheduled to speak this morning in Clay's place.

Through the morning rush of serving bread, cheese, and boiled eggs for breakfast and helping the kids get dressed, Rachel tried to shake off the heavy realization that this was the first Sunday morning during all their years in Sweden that Clay had not been with his family.

When she eventually stood in front of the bedroom mirror and put on a pair of pearl earrings and matching necklace, she was overwhelmed with a feeling of sheer emptiness. The expensive earrings and necklace suddenly seemed vain and unimportant. Her "quality beauty," the phrase Clay had always used to describe her appearance, seemed equally cheap.

The only thing of any real importance now was her marriage. She just wanted Clay. She wanted him to come home, and she wanted to feel his impassioned love again.

Turning from the mirror, she tiredly removed the earrings and the necklace and left them lying strewn across the dresser top.

By the time she and the kids arrived by car at the church building—six hundred square meters of converted office space on the second floor of a low-rise multipurpose structure—she was wondering if attending church this morning was even appropriate. Shouldn't she instead be doing something to locate her husband?

The thought was still bothering her as she greeted people in the hallways. It continued to dominate her emotions as the congregation assembled in the auditorium and sang the opening hymn and as Eric Torleif stood to offer the official welcome.

"It would be a little awkward," she heard Eric begin as he looked out over the crowd of more than two hundred men, women, and children sitting in folding chairs, "for us to carry on this morning with a normal program and pretend that nothing out of the ordinary is happening in our church. So we're *not* going to pretend. Most of you already know what's going on. And for the few of you who don't, I feel a need to let you know immediately that our pastor has now been missing for more than forty-eight hours."

Whispers and sighs swept through the audience.

"The last time he was seen," Eric continued, "was in his home late Thursday night when he went to sleep. He left his house by foot sometime early Friday morning before his family got up. He was supposed to take the bus to Humle Park and rendezvous here at the church with the men for the two-day retreat. But he never showed up.

"The men who were participating in the retreat spent all of Friday morning and afternoon searching the streets and footpaths between his house and the church. On Friday afternoon, we even managed to speak with three of the six bus drivers who drove the morning route from the pastor's house to Humle Park. None of them, when looking at his photograph, remembered seeing him.

"In addition, we contacted all the hospitals and emergency clinics throughout the city to see if he had been admitted at any of them. The answer was a negative.

"Since then, a missing person's report has been filed with the police department." Eric paused to clear his throat. "During the last twenty-four hours, we have, with the police's help, been able to reach two more of the bus drivers and reestablish contact with all the hospitals. Still, no one has seen him.

"As you can understand, we're greatly concerned. As far as we know now, if he doesn't show up or isn't found by tomorrow at this time, some of the city newspapers will run a missing person's report, along with a photograph, and ask for the public's help."

Eric paused again, this time as if to adjust his seriousness to a greater intensity.

"However, I also need to let you know that the pastor has been undergoing some inner struggles during the last few months, struggles of a personal matter that he hasn't been willing to discuss. Some of you have already picked up on this.

"Because of these struggles, Bengt and a few others who have recently spent time with him feel it's possible that he has chosen to abandon all of his responsibilities for a few days in order to go into hiding and try to deal with his thoughts and his feelings. I share this with you only because..."

Rachel, sitting three rows from the front, reacted with a deep gulp when she heard the word *abandon*, a word she tried desperately to dismiss.

Marie Blomqvist, sitting at her side, placed an arm around her.

No, he wouldn't do what you're thinking; there's no reason! Rachel shouted at herself, berating her voice of inner fear. *He loves you. He loves the kids...remember!*

She was squeezing her fists in her lap.

"Of course, nobody right now is sure of anything concerning his whereabouts or his well-being," she heard Eric continue, "so there is still hope.

"It's because of this fact that I feel we should take time, while we're together this morning, to pray earnestly for his emotional, physical, and spiritual safety. And to pray for Rachel and the kids.

"I realize you probably have a lot of questions you would like for me or some of the other elders to address publicly, but let me assure you that the information I've shared with you is thorough. For the moment, it is all that we know."

Eric hesitated for emphasis, then continued.

"So I'm going to ask right now that we table our regular program and all kneel at our seats. And I would like to ask as many of you who will to pray out loud one at a time. I've already spoken with Rolf Nyborg, who will be teaching this morning in the pastor's place. He has agreed to let us take as much of his time as we need. So, with that in mind, let's all kneel and unite our hearts together in prayer."

Eric started to make an additional statement when one of the ladies in the congregation, a tall forty-eight-year-old divorcée, stood to her feet in the center of the crowd. "While we're praying," she said with a tone of hurt, "maybe we should pray for ourselves as well."

Everyone in the congregation ceased their initial movements.

"Maybe we've been negligent," she continued nervously, "in giving Pastor McCain the personal support and encouragement he needs. If Bengt is right and the pastor is off somewhere trying to cope with some kind of stress or doubt and felt that running away for a few days was the only solution to his problem, then maybe it's *our fault.* Maybe we've failed to show him how much we appreciate and need him. Maybe while we've expected him to be attuned to what's going on in our lives, we have failed to be sensitive to what's going on in his. I, for one, would hate to find out that he's alone somewhere suffering because of us." The lady sounded as if she might start to weep. "Personally, my son and I owe him too much. Without his persistent and compassionate effort to reach out to us, I'm sure neither one of us would be a Christian right now. I mean, on the day he helped me come to Christ, he literally rescued me from imminent suicide. And for two years now, my son and I have been able to rebuild our lives because of him. And it's not just my family; we *all* owe him. So maybe we should pray and ask God to forgive us and to help us, from now on, to be more sensitive. If

I'm out of line, please forgive me, but that's the way I feel." She then sat down.

A moment of awkward silence blanketed the group.

Before Eric could respond, a large arm suddenly rose high in the audience, on the left side near the rear. The bearded man who raised his hand was already standing by the time Eric acknowledged him.

"Maybe Lisa is right," the man spoke slowly and somberly as he motioned with his hand toward the divorcée. "Maybe, as a church, we've taken our pastor for granted. If that's the case, then he deserves better treatment from us. Ingrid and I," he said, glancing down at his wife, "owe him as much as anybody in this church. It's because of his patient counsel that we're still married." The man went momentarily silent. It was obvious to everyone that he was trying to keep from choking up. "He took a lot of walks with me," the man stated, exhaling deeply. "My family and I will be indebted to him for the rest of our lives. And like Lisa said, if we as a church have contributed to what's going on, I believe we should pray and ask God to forgive us. And going a step further, I want to suggest that when he returns—and I'm sure he will; I believe he's going to be protected, no matter where he is or what's happening to him— we have a special service and tell him how grateful we are for his life and ministry and remind him of the extent to which God has used him in our lives."

When the man sat down, several others stood in sequence and expressed their supportive heartfelt response.

As Rachel listened, she tried to find solace in the prevailing spirit of optimistic concern. As a lone tear escaped the corner of her eye, she reached over and squeezed Marie Blomqvist's hand.

When the people finished their impromptu sharing, Eric, bolstered by the group's united purpose, led the congregation into a time of fervent prayer.

One person after another prayed aloud, some standing while they prayed, others on their knees.

By the time the prayer session ended, only ten minutes remained in the church's Sunday morning program. Rolf was asked to hold his sermon till next Sunday, pending the pastor's return.

In closing, the music director, at Eric's request, led the congregation in the singing of a hymn about God's trustworthiness during troublesome times.

As the crowd broke up and divided into small pockets of conversation, an air of intense concern could be felt throughout the meeting hall.

Some of the men, led by Bengt and Sten, gathered at the front of the auditorium and decided they would spend the afternoon going from house to house in the McCains' neighborhood showing Clay's picture and trying to find someone who had seen Clay on Friday morning.

Marie Blomqvist and Liv Munthe, receiving Rachel's numbed consent, followed Rachel to her house and prepared a hot lunch for her and the kids.

The last of the six bus drivers was successfully reached by the early evening. The image in the photograph was a face the driver said he had never seen.

The men inquiring door-to-door near and around the

McCains' received only negative answers as well.

Upon hearing the grim message, Rachel tried again, in the privacy of her room, to call her dad in Marietta. When she heard him pick up on the other end, she burst into tears, explaining the news of Clay amid her hard swallows and sniffles.

Her dad responded awkwardly, not knowing what to say.

The phone call lasted for less than ten minutes. Her dad's basic reply was a well-meaning but empty, "You're a strong girl, honey; I'm sure everything's going to work out for you."

After the call, Rachel sobbed even more. She felt drained. In every way. By everything.

Stretching facedown on the bed, she promised herself she would try to call Pastor Lovett tomorrow.

5

D o you think he has been kidnapped?" Pastor Lovett asked, with all the seriousness of someone sharing the pain. Rachel was sitting in the solitude of her bedroom. Summer, Holly, and Justin sat in front of an animated television program where they had been told to stay while Mommy made an important call.

Hearing Pastor Lovett's voice, Rachel felt a certain amount of solace. She envisioned Pastor Lovett sitting at his desk in the church office in north Atlanta. His six-foot-one-inch, 220-pound frame in a dark, three-piece cotton suit. Close-cropped gray hair. A fifty-four-year-old fighter for Christianity. A domineering leader and personality. Her pastor. One of her only links with "security" right now.

"We just don't know," Rachel answered, trying with little success to curtail her emotion. "We're not ruling out anything at this point. All of us, the police included, are just hoping the newspaper article will flush out some kind of helpful information." Rachel dug at and pinched the fabric of her jeans with her free hand.

"And you say the article's going to be printed sometime in the next couple of days?"

"The police were told by a press agent this morning that the report would be published in tomorrow's paper, or in Wednesday's at the latest."

There was silence over the line for a couple of seconds. It seemed to Rachel that Lovett was maybe writing something down. "How are you personally coping?" he then asked.

Rachel responded slowly. "Just ask everyone there to pray for me. Some moments I think I'm doing okay. But mainly...I'm just fighting to stay sane. I...I never imagined in my wildest dreams that anything like this could happen to us."

"Listen, Rachel, you and Clay are one of our church's favorite couples. You always have been. The fact that Clay is missing has me reeling, too. The whole church here is going to be in shock. But I want you to know we're going to be with you all the way in this. We're going to commit ourselves to pray. And we're going to be optimistic. And if you agree to it, I want to ask a few of our people to fly over and be there with you for a few days to encourage you, to help with the children, to cook meals, to provide some general back-home support."

"I'm not sure what to say, except...that...I'd be more grateful than you can ever imagine." Rachel turned her face from the phone and used a tissue to wipe her eyes. Being truly loved and cared for by those who had spiritually parented her seemed to take away some of the heaviness she was carrying. She was thankful for her friends there in Stockholm and for the irreplaceable help they were giving her. They were her dearest friends in the entire world. But a forceful demonstration of love and support from her home church of seventeen years right now was overwhelmingly therapeutic. "Pardon me for crying," she told Pastor Lovett as she placed the receiver back to her head, "but—"

"That's okay. I understand. I just want you to know we love you and we're going to be there when our missionaries need us. And in a critical situation like this, the very least we can do is send some people over to be by your side. And to keep from being a burden, we'll reserve a hotel room for whoever we send."

Rachel started to reiterate her gratefulness but halted as Pastor Lovett continued.

"For the next few days, I want you to call us collect here at the church every morning at about this same time and give us an update. If Clay shows up and everything's okay, then, of course, we'll cancel our plans from this end. In the meantime, I'll start working on a flight schedule for a support team, and tomorrow I'll give you the detailed information about who will be coming and when."

Before the lengthy conversation ended two or three minutes later, Rachel managed again to offer her heartfelt thanks. She decided to postpone the discussion about the questionable extremes of their denomination.

When she hung up the phone, she made a mental register of the hour.

With a deep breath and a momentary emotional lift, she picked up the phone again and punched in the number for their mission board, Partnership of Christian Conservatives for Global Evangelism. It was the mission board of choice for most of the churches in her and Clay's Bible Belt denomination. It upheld the same "old-fashioned" convictions and rules as North Metro and all the other churches in their association. The office was located in Greenville, South Carolina. She and Clay had been accepted as missionary candidates by PCCGE eleven years ago, two years before they moved to Sweden. She had been twenty-four at the time; Clay had been twenty-six. After being officially approved by the board of directors, they had spent a mandatory three months undergoing special training at a large associated church in Greenville. After their orientation and training, they selected Sweden to be their place of service, primarily because of Clay's Swedish ancestry through his mother's side of the family and because of his burden to reach "his" people. It then took them a little over a year and a half to raise their financial support.

During their first four years in Sweden, a coastal country of lakes, forests, and mountains that they had fallen in love with, they were visited twice by the director of the mission board's church-planting council and once by the European director. The visits were accountability visits to make sure Clay and Rachel, as first-term missionaries, were performing according to PCCGE's rigid policies and standards.

After a long-term and successful integration into the Swedish culture, they returned to the States for a required four-month furlough in order to give a field report to their numerous supporters spread throughout an eight-state area. During that brief stateside visit, they stopped by the home office at least four times. Two of those meetings had been mandatory, for purposes of "official exposure" to the home office staff.

During their most recent four and a half years in Stockholm, however, the mission board had virtually ignored them—no further "accountability" visits, not even any checkup calls. The only communication had been via two or three letters between Clay and the European director. She and Clay had presumed that the lack of contact was for three reasons: First, the growing number of missionaries joining PCCGE during the past four years was requiring all the extra time the directors and their assistants had to give.

Second, her and Clay's unusual success as American missionaries in Scandinavia had earned them the confidence of the PCCGE directors. Third, none of their supporting pastors were lodging any complaints about them to the mission board officials.

It had been during these last four years that she and Clay had experienced the most drastic changes in their thinking about Christian legalism.

After three rings, Rachel heard the receptionist pick up on the other end, identify the mission agency and offer her assistance. Rachel greeted the lady and asked to be connected through to the European director. She explained that her call was somewhat of an emergency.

Less than two minutes later, Rachel was on the line with Dr. Ed Brighton, her and Clay's European representative at the mission headquarters.

Dr. Brighton had served with the PCCGE organization for twenty-eight years.

Among the mission board's constituents, Brighton, during the last thirteen years of serving in the high-profile role of European director, had become known nationwide as an uncompromising stalwart of the Christian faith, equaling the legalistic extremism of his older and more powerful superiors.

To now hear Brighton's authoritarian voice stirred mixed emotions in Rachel. She was suddenly nervous.

She told him straightforwardly, "I need to talk to you for a few minutes; we've got a...worrisome situation here that you need to know about." Her voice reverberated with slight tension.

"Okay, give me just a moment. Let me tell Evelyn to sidetrack any incoming calls or visitors."

A second later, Rachel heard him in the background issuing the instructions to his secretary.

Then he was back. "All right, you've got my attention."

Feeling suddenly very vulnerable, she began. She took fifteen to twenty minutes to explain in full all that had transpired during the last three and a half days. As she told him of Bengt's opinion about the disappearance, she revealed to him for the first time Clay's progressive withdrawal during the last several months.

Brighton sat in silence, listening without interrupting.

When it was finally his time to speak, he did. "First of all, Rachel," he stated somewhat forcefully, "I can't figure out why you've waited so long to tell me about this personal struggle that you say Clay is going through and why you didn't report his disappearance to us at least two days ago. But we'll talk about that later. What I want you to tell me now is your gut feeling about what's happening. You say no evidence has surfaced that supports any one explanation over another. But surely you must have some idea. I mean, do you agree with the view that he's seeking rest someplace? Or do you think he's being held in an unknown location against his will, or maybe even lying sick or injured somewhere? Surely, as his wife, you have some kind of a hunch."

Rachel fought through her shocked feelings to give a proper and truthful answer.

Brighton waited.

"I...uh...tend to suspect, or...at least hope," Rachel answered, on the verge of tears, "that Bengt is right and that Clay has chosen to distance himself from everybody for a while and is physically okay. But, of course...I...uh...could be viewing the situation way out of line from what might be really happening."

"Rachel, I don't mean to be nosy, but if your suspicion is right, what do you think would drive a man like Clay to run away and just shut down? Are we talking about fatigue? Overload? Burnout? Or have you and Clay possibly been undergoing some kind of marital conflict that could be provoking him to withdraw?"

Rachel stalled again.

Brighton broke the silence after only about five seconds, trying this time to reduce the sharpness of his tone. "Look, Rachel, to a certain degree you and Clay are under my supervision. If Clay has carelessly run away from his responsibilities due to some kind of emotional pressure, then I want to be prepared to confront him and make sure he gets help when he resurfaces. And, I hope it's not so tragic, but if the police find evidence showing he's been taken against his will or has been injured, then I want to be ready, in an official capacity, to offer the mission board's assistance."

You're moving too fast, Rachel wanted to shout into the phone. But Brighton's momentum was engulfing her too quickly to backpedal.

"No, I don't think his progressive withdrawal has been caused by burnout, fatigue, or marital tension," Rachel said. "It has certainly created some, though. To be honest, I have no idea what has caused his abnormal behavior. He has refused to talk about it."

"Rachel, is it possible that Clay...uh—never mind. Listen, you've done the right thing to report his disappearance to the police. And I'm glad your home church will be sending a delegation to give you needed support. As a matter of fact, when we finish this conversation I'm going to call Pastor Lovett's office. I want to talk with him. And naturally, you and I will stay in touch throughout the next few days."

Before Dr. Brighton ended the call, he requested the telephone number of the police department in Stockholm and the name of the lieutenant working on Clay's case.

He assured Rachel of the mission board's commitment to her family and of their prayers.

Hanging up, Rachel felt pangs of anger. She felt like an accident victim who had just been chided by an insensitive doctor. She lay back on the bed and tried to calm her not-so-pretty feelings, telling herself that Brighton had really not been as harsh and cold as she perceived.

He was just reacting to the shock of the moment, she tried explaining to herself. *It'll be different in a couple of months when we all sit down face-to-face in his office. I'm confident of it.*

The disturbing feelings, however, followed her throughout the rest of the afternoon and into the early evening.

As she prepared a makeshift dinner late in the day for herself and the kids, the adrenaline that had kept her alert during the last eighty-four hours started to dissipate. She now started to feel the crushing weight of everything combined: a missing husband, emotionally distraught children who needed special attention, frightened and hurting in-laws, needling doubts, a dying hope she was trying ardently to keep alive, and a mission board director who was acting like a heartless schoolmaster.

With an oncoming migraine, she thanked God for her supportive and beloved Swedish friends and for her understanding pastor. They were God's arms and hands reaching out to embrace and encourage her. Without them, she did not know how she would be able to cope.

She had just taken some medicine for her headache and sat

down with the kids to eat when the phone rang. It was Clay's parents.

"No," she had to tell them after listening to the broken voice of Clay's mom, "there's no more news. He's still missing." As she answered their few questions, she tried to sound positive, but she felt transparently pretentious. "Try not to worry about me and the kids right now, though. The church here is helping us in every way they can. And in the next few days North Metro will be sending us some extra help from their congregation."

Her mother-in-law cried, telling her how much she wanted to be there to help. At that point, Rachel broke down. The rest of their conversation was a string of choked-out words and sobs.

When Rachel finally hung up the phone, she saw Summer standing rigidly in the doorway between the living room and the kitchen silently shedding tears. Rachel got up out of her chair and went to her. And held her tightly.

That night the children once again slept with Rachel in the master bedroom.

6

There was no news through the night.

It was the first morning since Clay's disappearance four days earlier that Rachel didn't want to get out of bed. She wanted to keep sleeping and pretend that the mayhem descending upon her life was only a bad dream. But her role as a mother would not allow her that wished-for escape. She had to get up and help Summer get ready for school.

Crawling out of bed, she tried not to awaken Holly and Justin, who were snuggled against her on either side. But the attempt proved to be futile. Both children started coming out of their sleep.

Immediately the morning began to unfold in a way that sucked away at Rachel's patience.

She first had to change Justin's soaked diaper and then replace the damp bed sheet with a clean one. During the last three or four days Justin's progress at being toilet trained had completely halted. Maybe had even regressed. Up until yesterday, Rachel had been dressing him each morning in training pants. But two days ago, when he wet three pairs of pants in less than five hours, she reverted to the use of diapers.

Once the bed was made, she went into the girls' bedroom and started to help Summer select her clothes for the day. Summer, slowly unbuttoning her pajama top, solemnly asked, "What if we don't find Daddy and he never comes home again?"

Rachel looked up from the red drawer where she was digging through pants. "Honey, we're doing everything we can to help find him. We've just got to be—"

Suddenly with crossed arms, Summer announced, "I'm not going back to school until Daddy comes home!"

For the next forty minutes, Rachel labored between the whines, questions, and interruptions of Holly and Justin to get Summer out the door, finally convinced that Summer would obediently make the ten-minute walk straight to the school building.

When Summer disappeared across the grass of the front yard, Rachel wondered with nagging guilt if forcing Summer had been the appropriate thing to do. The thought that she had just abandoned her nine-year-old daughter quickly added to her burdensome load. She resolved, after only a few minutes, to seek out advice from some of the older mothers in the church as to what would be the most loving and productive way to deal with the situation should it arise again. But she would have to work on it later in the morning. Justin and Holly were clamoring for her attention right now.

It became poignantly clear to her that the hour-by-hour waiting for Clay's return or to hear vital information about his condition or whereabouts was going to challenge every inner resource she possessed. Her alien fears were growing deeper.

The first reprieve that came her way throughout the long morning was a phone call from Bengt.

"I'll be taking the day off from work," Bengt informed her after asking how she was doing and reassuring her of his steadfast support. "I've decided to find out who in the church Clay spent time with during the last two weeks. I want to arrange to talk with them during the next few days and determine if Clay said anything while in their company that might provide us with clues about his intentions."

Ten or twenty minutes after the call, Rachel was putting a load of children's clothes into the washing machine and still trying to squeeze hope out of Bengt's plan when the phone rang again. She rushed up from the basement to take the call in the living room.

On the line, Lieutenant Ekberg from the police station notified her that the four newspapers with the largest readership in Stockholm would be running the article about Clay's disappearance tomorrow morning, Wednesday, May 10. The lieutenant promised her that the police department was ready to follow up on any leads that the report might generate.

For the first time since the seriousness of the crisis was fully understood, Rachel felt her sinking optimism reverse its downward momentum.

Maybe, *just maybe,* the newspaper article would be her, and everybody else's, answer to prayer.

At two thirty in the afternoon, Rachel sat down in her bedroom chair and made a collect call to Pastor Lovett in Atlanta. Holly was watching Justin in the fenced-in backyard.

The secretary at North Metro Church of the Bible had Pastor Lovett on the line in less than thirty seconds. "Any news in the last twenty-four hours?" Lovett asked.

"No, no news about Clay," Rachel answered somberly. "But I received word this morning that the four leading newspapers in

Stockholm will be publishing the report about his disappearance tomorrow morning. We're just hoping that somebody, after reading the story, will come forth with key information."

Prompted by more of Lovett's questions, she discussed further the newspaper and her hopes. She also told about Bengt's latest effort.

"Well," Lovett finally promised her, "know that the church here is praying virtually around the clock for you. For you *and* the whole family. We've been praying, and are going to keep praying, that God will intervene in a supernatural way. Everyone here is trusting Him to do just that.

"In the meantime, I've got good news from this end. Bill and Nancy Reese and John and Rita Holcomb will be leaving Atlanta Friday afternoon and will be arriving in Stockholm Saturday morning. I've got the flight information sitting right here on my desk. If you've got paper and a pen, I'll give you their flight number and time of arrival."

"I've got a pencil in my hand," Rachel told him, her voice filled with appreciation.

Rachel had known the Holcombs, both in their late fifties, for nearly seventeen years. She first met them the year she became a member of North Metro. At the time, John Holcomb had just been elected as one of the church deacons. For the last six years, he had served as the chairman of the deacon board. Simple, generous, consistent, soft-spoken, but extremely provincial, he and his wife, Rita, earned their livelihood from a landscaping business they incorporated soon after their marriage. The couple was like an older aunt and uncle to her and Clay. Before moving to Sweden, she and Clay had eaten in the older couple's home three or four times. And they had carried on dozens of lighthearted and friendly conversations with the couple in past years.

On the other hand, she had met the Reeses on only two previous occasions. Those brief encounters had been a little more than four years ago when they had returned to the States for their brief furlough. Bill Reese had just joined the staff at North Metro as a full-time assistant pastor. Rachel remembered both Bill and his wife as being professionally cold and seemingly very proud.

At the moment, however, she was grateful that both couples were willing to sacrifice their time to fly over and provide her family with support. She just trusted that their company, especially the Reeses', would be as welcomed as their help.

"By the way," Lovett said, "they're all flying over with open-ended tickets. They're planning to stay at least eight or nine days and are prepared to stay longer if the situation deems it necessary."

As the conversation drew to a close, Pastor Lovett repeated that he and the whole church were trusting God to perform a miracle. He then prayed over the phone with her.

After the call, she sat in silence for a few seconds and stared at a framed portrait of Clay sitting on her dresser.

She strove to remind herself of a truth that Clay had taught throughout his many years of ministry, a truth that she had always accepted as a part of her fundamentalist belief system: Life for a Christian, no matter how out of control it might appear, is never truly out of control at all. God in His sovereignty is always holding the Christian's circumstances together in His loving and almighty grasp.

Cowering now in the dark shadows of life's adversity, she wondered for the first time if that belief was based on reality or just on her denomination's theological wishing. She squinted hard with frustration.

Focusing again on the picture of Clay, she tried to compel the long-held doctrine that God has everything under control to transfer from her wavering mind to her struggling heart. But the attempt was ill fated. Her feelings of fear, now greater than she wanted to admit, loomed as an insurmountable blockade.

"Lord, forgive me!" she erupted tearfully into her hands. "I'm falling apart. I don't understand what's happening. Please! Just be merciful with me."

She continued to pray in silence. But the outpouring of her soul didn't bring any relief. Finally composing herself, she nervously picked up the phone and made her appointed call to Dr. Ed Brighton in South Carolina.

She knew that the rest of the day, like the previous four, would be nothing more than a tumultuous waiting game.

7

Following the advice of a couple of ladies in the church, Rachel got up earlier than normal the next morning. She spent an extra thirty minutes with Summer to try to provide a pressure-free time of mother—daughter camaraderie and heart-to-heart dialogue about their family's situation before sending her off to school.

The time proved to be helpful for both Rachel and Summer. Summer went to school, reluctantly but without fussing. Rachel, realizing the value of her and Summer's time together, was thankful for the wise counsel. Her present state of mind just was not allowing her to be a strong-thinking and creative mother on her own.

To the contrary, she felt she was approaching the edge of panic. Clay's prolonged silence, whether voluntary or involuntary, and the uncertainty of his well-being had become almost unbearable.

The sole thought on her mind after seeing Summer leave the house was to dress Holly and Justin, get to the local kiosk, and buy copies of the morning newspapers. The published report and plea for help put into the hands of four or five hundred thousand people was still her strongest hope. She wanted to see the article with her own eyes. She wanted to make sure it was truly there.

◆   ◆   ◆

Rachel was shaking when she handed the coins to the man behind the counter and picked up six of the city's most popular newspapers.

She had never seen the middle-aged vendor, a dark Pakistani, at the kiosk before. He stared at her as he handed back her change. Rachel didn't know if he was noticing her looks or her nervousness.

Feeling uncomfortably self-conscious, she took Justin by the hand, called to Holly playing a few feet to the side, and headed home. She clutched the papers under her arm as if they were life preservers.

Within two or three minutes of entering the house, she brushed the kids aside and spread the newspapers across the kitchen table. She quickly found what she was looking for. As she had been told, only four papers published the report.

The two papers with the biggest circulation, the *Dagens Nyheter* and the *Svenska Dagbladet,* had run the piece on page three. One of the two remaining papers had also placed it on page three. The fourth paper had printed it on page two. Accompanying the reports was the photograph of Clay that she had given to Lieutenant Ekberg. It was a close-up shot of Clay's face that had been candidly taken at the church's anniversary banquet in February.

Rachel tried to squelch the hurtful memories of her and Clay's cold interaction during that event as she scanned the titles of the four articles.

The bold letters all proclaimed a similar message: *Mystiskt Forsvinnande,* or Mysterious Disappearance.

She hurriedly read the reports in their entirety. Though slightly different, each paper's version covered all the primary facts.

The *Svenska Dagbladet* edition, which gave Clay's picture the most space, read:

> *Thirty-seven-year-old American pastor Clay McCain of the Stockholm Independent Bible Church has been missing since Friday morning, May 5. Reverend McCain was scheduled to lead a two-day men's retreat near Uppsala over the weekend. McCain left his house Friday morning between 4:30 and 6:00 to rendezvous with his group at their rented church building on Linne gatan, near Humle Park, and has not been seen since.*
>
> *Reverend McCain, 1.85 m and 80 kg, is believed to have been carrying a large, navy blue backpack.*
>
> *His congregation is asking anyone who has seen him since last Friday morning or who can offer any information leading to his whereabouts to please contact the central police department immediately.*
>
> *The police, unwilling to say if foul play might be a factor in the disappearance, have extended help to McCain's family and church by questioning drivers of the city's buses, subways, and trains and by inquiring at hospital emergency wards. The search for possible clues and eyewitnesses has up till now been fruitless.*
>
> *McCain, a devoted family man, has two daughters and a son. McCain and his wife, Rachel, founded their church seven years ago in downtown Stockholm. With an active membership of over two hundred local Swedes, the church has a larger attendance than 90 percent of the city's state churches.*

A special phone number to the police department was listed.

Rachel laid the paper down and fought back tears. Almost immediately, two small hands were holding her forearm. Looking up, her eyes met Holly's.

"Don't cry, Mommy," Holly pleaded, staring into her mother's face. "God will help us find Daddy through the paper. Okay?"

That evening, in the church's regular midweek Bible study, Eric read the newspaper article to a group of approximately sixty people and then spoke for about fifteen minutes on the topic "God, Our Helper and Sustainer." The rest of the meeting was devoted to group prayer and discussion about their missing pastor.

The elders tried to encourage everyone to believe in prayer and not to abandon hope.

8

On Friday afternoon, police lieutenant Nils Ekberg was sitting at his computer terminal compiling a character reference for a young police sergeant being arraigned for allegedly roughing up a middle-aged wife at the scene of an apartment brawl.

He leaned back in his swivel chair and stretched his arms. It was another unusually warm spring afternoon, and his thoughts quickly switched to the canoeing trip planned for the weekend with friends and family. He was lost in a world of tents, streams, and campfires when a female coworker walked over to his desk.

He looked up and made eye contact with the short-haired, pregnant sergeant. "Lieutenant," the young lady said, "there's someone here responding to the newspaper piece about Reverend Clay McCain. Sounds like they might know something."

"All right. Send him on over to my desk."

"Uh...sir, it's not a him; it's a her."

"Okay," Ekberg paused, "send *her* over." He brought out a pad of notepaper and penned the date and time in the upper left-hand corner.

He quickly printed a hard copy of the unfinished letter displayed on his computer monitor. He coded and saved the file to finish later.

Out of his peripheral vision he detected the return of his

coworker. He looked in her direction and saw her stop a few feet away and gesture the visitor toward him.

Even here in Sweden, where eye-grabbing beauty was the rule and not the exception, there were still a few women who were so intensely attractive that no man alive could see them and remain unmoved. One of those ladies was now standing in front of him. She looked to be in her late twenties or early thirties.

Lieutenant Ekberg stood and cleared his throat. He was looking into the most brilliant emerald green eyes he had ever seen. The lady's tanned face, more captivating than any model's face he had ever viewed, exuded pure sensuality and was made even more breathtaking by the blond hair that hung thick and free to the lower part of her back. Her neck-twisting figure—complemented by her designer jeans and skin-hugging pink T-shirt—radiated sheer eroticism.

"Lieutenant Nils Ekberg," the lieutenant introduced himself, extending his hand.

"Anna Gessle," the lady replied in a mellow voice, shaking his hand briefly. There was no smile.

Ekberg, enjoying the sudden whiff of expensive perfume, motioned for her to take the chair at the side of his desk. He sat down after she was seated.

"So, the sergeant says you know something about Reverend Clay McCain," Ekberg began, recording her name on his notepad.

"Before I talk," Anna Gessle said, "I want someone here to promise me that my name will be kept confidential."

Ekberg noticed a slight nervousness in the lady's voice. He spoke gently. "I'm the lead officer in the case, and I'm in direct contact with Mr. McCain's wife. So unless you talk to somebody else, I can guarantee from my end of things, at least, that your identity will remain a secret. *If* you're not directly or indirectly responsible for Mr. McCain's disappearance, that is."

"I didn't know anything about his disappearance until I read about it in the paper two days ago."

"Okay, your name is off the record. I'm listening."

Anna Gessle shifted her eyes from Lieutenant Ekberg's to the pad of paper.

Ekberg scratched lines through her name and laid his pen to the side. He then looked at her in silence and lifted his eyebrows.

Anna closed her eyes. "I met Clay three and a half years ago," she began, opening her eyes and looking at Ekberg. "We met in a fitness studio here in the city. Clay was already a member there when I joined. Since we both train two or three times a week, we've seen each other in the gym on a regular basis ever since."

"So, you're in no way associated with his church?"

"No. I, uh...didn't even know he was part of a church until I read it in the newspaper," Anna explained, trying to control her nervousness. "He always told me he was a teacher, but he would never give details. I never thought—"

"He 'always' told you? Pardon me if I'm stepping out of line here, but are you implying that you and Mr. McCain had some kind of ongoing friendship?"

There was new strain in Anna's face. "We were more than just friends. Up until three months ago, Clay and I were involved in a sexual affair that lasted for nearly three years."

Ekberg, having never met Clay, nevertheless understood how easy it would be for a pastor, or any man, to become physically involved with the female now sitting before him. She was one of those rare women who looked as if she were created just for carnal pleasure. And knew it.

"So," Ekberg asked slowly, "what is it you know, or think you know, about his disappearance?"

Anna folded one leg over the other and began picking at the edge of the desk with her nails. "I think...I'm pretty certain...he has left the country with one of my friends." She hesitated, as if she expected a question.

Ekberg signaled with his eyes for her to proceed.

"It's a lady I introduced to Clay about six months ago. She became emotionally attached to him in a strong way. Clay was equally drawn to her. When I saw what was happening, I slowly stepped out of the picture. The last few times I spoke with my friend, she told me that she and Clay were planning to run away together. She sounded serious, and I knew she loved him, but I never believed they would carry out such a plan."

"Her name and address?" Ekberg queried, picking up his pen again.

Anna shook her head.

"Just for verification."

"For personal reasons, I can't. I won't."

"How do I know you're telling me the truth then?"

Anna half shrugged as if not expecting to be disbelieved. "She's got long dark hair; she's single; she's rich," she stated, as if such a knowing description would be sufficient to establish her credibility as a witness.

"Then *where* do you think I can tell Mrs. McCain she might find her husband?"

"I don't really know. Possibly anywhere. My friend's parents are both dead and were extremely wealthy. They left behind several houses. Two are on the Mediterranean; one is in the States; another is in the Caribbean."

"I don't suppose you have any addresses?"

Anna shook her head again.

"I'm just curious. Why have you come forward to tell me all this?"

Anna paused as if in deep thought. "Maybe it's guilt," she answered with sincerity.

Lieutenant Ekberg picked up his pen and tapped it a couple of times on his pad. "With the exception of your name, I'll be passing along the information you've given me to Mrs. McCain. I trust you understand?"

Anna nodded that she did.

"Just one more question," Ekberg asked as he rose to his feet. "Did you know Reverend McCain was married and had children before you read those facts in the paper?"

Anna Gessle gathered her purse in silence and stood. She looked Lieutenant Ekberg in the eye and with the sound of shame told him, "Yes, I knew he was married and had children. I knew for three years...just as he knew the same about me."

Within the hour, Lieutenant Ekberg contacted Eric Torleif through the church and retrieved the name of the health studio where Clay trained.

With one call to the health club, Ekberg confirmed that Anna Gessle had been a member of the same club for the last three and a half years. She had also been seen leaving the club many times with Clay McCain.

9

Lena Torleif, Eric's wife, was in the McCains' basement helping Rachel with the laundry. Lena, a childless house-wife and part-time kindergarten helper, was ironing while Rachel finished folding a load of clean socks, T-shirts, and underwear.

The Reeses and the Holcombs from Rachel's home church in Atlanta would be arriving in Stockholm tomorrow morning at ten-thirty.

Yesterday evening in a telephone conversation, Rachel had told Lena of her need to have the house and everything in it clean and orderly before the couples arrived. Lena knew that Rachel was not trying to solicit help but was just voicing her concerns. It sounded to Lena, however, as if Rachel felt overly obligated to have everything in tiptop appearance.

"Your personal needs are far more important right now than housework," Lena had responded. "And considering the present circumstances, I assure you the two couples will understand if your house is a little unkempt. So, if I were you, I wouldn't put myself through the extra work. I just wouldn't worry about it."

"It's something I've needed to do anyway," Rachel had said.

Caring deeply for Rachel, Lena had simply showed up at Rachel's door a few hours ago, around noon, and said, "I thought maybe you could use an extra pair of hands."

Rachel, with stress etched all over her face, had welcomed the extra help.

It was now a little after four-thirty. Lena had helped vacuum, mop, and clean the kitchen and was nearly finished with the ironing. She had hoped to touch hearts with Rachel, to offer encouragement, and to be a helpful listener to whom Rachel could open up and express her worries and fears.

However, the only words that had passed between them all day, in spite of Lena's efforts to initiate something meaningful, were statements and questions about the housework.

Lena had decided not to push. It grated at her heart, but it was clear to her that Rachel didn't want to talk, that she was trying instead to distract herself from her threatening feelings by burying herself under a mound of work.

Summer, Holly, and Justin were not even around to help break up the subdued atmosphere. Liv Munthe was keeping them at her house for the afternoon.

Lena had decided, however, that she would at least ask Rachel if she could pray with her, if she could stand by her side and hold her and petition God to demonstrate His well-known ability to intervene in hopeless-looking situations.

The right moment finally presented itself when Rachel headed up the stairs with a clothes basket of folded clothes.

Lena turned the iron off, gathered the ironed clothes on their hangers, and followed.

Lena was halfway up the basement stairs when she heard the phone ringing. By the time she topped the steps, she saw Rachel picking up the receiver in the living room.

Lena heard Rachel acknowledge Lieutenant Ekberg on the

other end of the line, and stopped and prayed that it was good news. She unconsciously slowed her breathing and fixed her eyes toward Rachel. She hoped at any second to see her friend come alive with joyous relief. "O God, let it be," she whispered.

Rachel put the basket of clothes on the floor and slowly sat down in the cushioned armchair with the receiver to her ear. Lena saw her go deathly quiet, then close her eyes and swallow hard.

Lena stood motionless. She watched as the color in Rachel's face drained to a sickening pale. Everything inside her nudged her to go to her. She hesitated.

Rachel was suddenly nodding her head in silence. Tears appeared in her eyes. As the tears started moving down her face, her free hand raked through the hair above her forehead. Her entire body started heaving with convulsive crying.

Lena suddenly felt a sick feeling in her stomach. She moved quickly into the room and deposited her armload of clothes onto the couch, then ran to Rachel's side.

Rachel was now rocking back and forth. She still held the phone, listening intensely. Her free hand was fisted in her lap.

Lena placed her hands on Rachel's shoulders. She was caught by surprise when Rachel shrugged her away.

Fear hit Lena from every angle. Was Clay hurt? Was he dead? Is that what Ekberg was telling Rachel? *No, God! Please!* she silently pleaded.

Another minute or so passed before Rachel hung up. She focused on the carpet two or three feet in front of her and just stared through her tears. Her body had gone inordinately still.

"Rachel?" Lena asked, feeling herself start to sob.

Rachel didn't answer. She seemed to be unaware of her

surroundings.

Lena once again extended a hand to touch her.

With no forewarning, Rachel erupted with a groan of agony so loud it took Lena's breath away. As Lena jerked backward, Rachel leaped out of her seat with her arms flailing. The wooden lamp on the telephone table crashed to the floor, the lampshade careening into the wall. The light bulb popped into a thousand pieces.

Rachel ran out the front door.

Lena ran out of the house and across the yard after her.

Rachel was halfway down the block, past three or four of the neighbors' houses, when Lena caught up with her. "Whatever's happening, Rachel," Lena shouted. "I'm here for you... The whole church is here for you... You've got to—"

"Just leave me alone!" Rachel screamed without stopping or even turning her head in Lena's direction.

It was the first time Lena had ever heard Rachel aggressively raise her voice. She stopped and let her go. She stood for a moment to catch her breath, then ran back to the house to call Eric.

When she couldn't run anymore, Rachel, her chest heaving, threw herself onto the freshly cut grass at the edge of an empty soccer field. On her hands and knees, she stared at the ground as she gasped for air.

Ekberg had to be lying to her. Or had to be misinformed. What he had told her wasn't conceivable! It couldn't—

She barely managed to sweep her hair to the side before she threw up.

She tried after a minute or two to sit up, but her crying started again so strongly that she collapsed onto her side.

Mindless of her surroundings, she closed her eyes and screamed as loud as she could. Then she tried to will herself into nonexistence.

10

After half an hour or so, Rachel found herself staggering back up the street toward her house. Beyond the brightness of the sunshine, she saw Lena and Eric rushing down the sidewalk toward her, seemingly in slow motion, their mouths moving at the same pace as the rest of their bodies.

Only when she felt the strong touch of Lena's tearful embrace did she register the sound of words.

It was Eric speaking from somewhere at her side. "I've spoken with Lieutenant Ekberg," he said breathlessly. "I'm sorry, Rachel. I'm really sorry."

"We're here for you, all right?" Lena whispered through a tight throat.

Rachel, laying her head heavily on Lena's shoulder, nodded.

The next couple of hours passed in a whirlwind of commotion. A group of six ladies from the church—some of Rachel's closest friends, including Marie Blomqvist—gathered at the house to pray for her. The prayer time lasted more than an hour.

Summer, Holly, and Justin remained at Liv Munthe's during the meeting. Rachel, stricken by a migraine headache and a loss of orientation, agreed with a mere nod to accept the ladies' counsel to wait a few days before telling the children the dark news, "to see if Clay will contact you and inform you of his intentions."

Merlene Bildt and Ingela Sunneborn, two of the six ladies who convened for the prayer meeting, stayed behind, along with Lena Torleif, and prepared dinner for the children when they were returned to the house.

Merlene and Ingela stayed just long enough after dinner to clean up the kitchen and help get Summer, Holly, and Justin bathed and settled into their beds. They left with aching hearts after praying with the kids at their bedsides.

Lena Torleif decided to stay through the night, to keep an eye on Rachel and be available for her at any hour.

Around eight that evening the elders, plus a few other male leaders in the congregation, met at the church building to discuss the afternoon's disclosure and the future of their church.

A little before ten, when the meeting was over, Eric called Lena at the McCains'. He reported that Rolf Nyborg and two other good Bible teachers in the congregation had been asked to preach in Clay's place for the next two months until the McCains' furlough replacement family, the Kendalls, arrived. The elders made no other major decisions and probably would not for several weeks. "It's the mutual conclusion of the men," Eric emphasized from the heart, "that there are simply no facts to prove the allegation. As far as we're concerned, the case is still open. It's not impossible that the anonymous lady for some reason made up the story. We're just going to wait and pray."

Lena, after hanging up, sat for a few seconds to digest what Eric had said. She then went to relay the news to Rachel.

◆   ◆   ◆

Rachel, bathed and dressed in her nightgown, reached into Clay's closet and removed the small security box in which their family's important documents were kept. She unlocked the box and looked for Clay's passport. It wasn't there.

She felt a gripping sensation in her chest, as if her heart were cramping. *Where's he planning to go?* she screamed inwardly. *Why? Why is he doing this?*

Tottering, she ran out onto the porch that extended from their bedroom. She gripped her chest with both hands and tried to stifle the pain. She looked out over the backyard and saw the cherry trees with their springtime leaves and new buds. She thought of how hard Clay had worked to cultivate and groom their yard and how proud he was of his work.

Her eyes clamped shut as tears forced their way through. *He couldn't have abandoned us! He couldn't have just walked away! It's not possible! Not Clay!*

Stormed by her thoughts, she barely heard the knocks at her bedroom door. By the time she turned, Lena was already in the room.

With pain anchored in her eyes, Rachel listened to the report that had just come from the church meeting. She then asked to be left alone.

She locked the door and retrieved her wedding album from the small bedroom bookshelf. Trembling, she sat in her chair and focused on the album's cover. Her head flooded with a hundred memories.

With the album resting on her lap, she hesitated, then gradually lifted the gilded cover and turned to the first picture. It was a single photograph of herself standing in a Chantilly lace gown at the North Metro Church altar. She had been a twenty-two-year-old bride and a Christian of four years, innocently hoping and trusting God for a lifelong marriage of love and happiness.

Four years earlier she had been the beauty queen of her high school, the captain of the varsity cheerleading squad, the salutatorian of her graduating class, and, according to a school vote, "the most popular girl on campus." There had been a constant parade of boys vying for her attention. All her girlfriends had envied her. It seemed that every door in life had been an open invitation to her.

She possessed "everything," according to her peers, but below the surface she had sensed the shallowness of it all—the beauty, the popularity, the vain attention. She had felt empty, had felt that way for several years. Maybe it was due to her painful family life caused by an absent father and an emotionally dead mother. Whatever the cause, the emptiness couldn't be chased away.

Until Clay came into her life.

With two weeks left in her senior year, she had seen on the school bulletin board a poster announcing a week-long Christian youth conference at North Metro Church of the Bible. The featured speaker was a "nationally known" youth evangelist who would be "addressing the social issues of America's teens" and "giving hope-filled answers for some of life's biggest questions." Teaming up with him for the conference was a thirty-voice choral group from a Christian university in Anderson, South Carolina. More than a hundred teenagers were expected to attend each night.

Being a nonchurchgoer, Rachel had never heard of the evangelist, the choral group, or the university. And the only thing she knew about North Metro Church of the Bible was its name. Anything related to church, any church, was beyond her realm of knowledge.

She decided out of curiosity and out of her determination to find "something more in life" to go to one of the meetings and hear what the evangelist had to say.

The subtle fear of graduating and facing life as an independent adult, combined with the elation of reaching the end of twelve years of school, anesthetized her to the unpopularity of the decision.

She attended on the Friday night before the conference concluded on Sunday.

There were indeed at least a hundred teenagers, probably far more, crowded into the church auditorium. The atmosphere was charged with anticipation and excitement.

By the end of the service, Rachel was profoundly moved. Not by the choral group. Not by the evangelist or his message. But by a twenty-year-old college sophomore who gave a ten-minute testimonial about a living relationship with Jesus Christ, about being converted out of an "empty" life of drugs, pressurized sports, and scholastic achievements. With the sound of discovery ringing in his voice, he cheerfully announced just before he sat down that in the fall he would be transferring from the Atlanta technical school he was attending to the Christian university in South Carolina represented by the visiting choral group. "I want to give the rest of my life to the service of Christ," he proclaimed.

The young man had been introduced as Clay McCain, "one of North Metro's newest members."

Rachel was moved, not by the young man's tall and attractive physique, but by his unusual joy, certainty, and purpose and by his passionate claim of "finally finding something that filled the void" in his life.

For the first time ever, Rachel glimpsed the spirited and life-changing side of Christianity, the side that pointed to a living Savior who could radically fill one's life with meaning.

Wanting to learn more, she found Clay after the meeting. For more than an hour they sat on one of the pews at the front of the auditorium and talked about the Bible and the concept of God taking up residence inside the hearts of those who choose to be His followers.

Rachel attended the conference the remaining two nights, talked further with Clay, Pastor Frank Lovett, and others, and felt herself being drawn irresistibly and unexpectedly to the Christ of Christianity.

Within three days, to the dismay of her friends and her parents, she decided in an act of sincere and exuberant faith to give her life to Jesus, to be born again. Pastor Lovett was the one who prayed with her.

Her transformation was immediate. The emptiness that had plagued her for most of her teenage years vanished overnight. Her life was suddenly full and new, from the overwhelming peace in her heart to the enlightened and humble way she started viewing her everyday surroundings.

Rachel soon joined the church and began attending all the services. Her faith grew quickly, along with her hearty allegiance to all of North Metro's old-fashioned standards.

She spent much of her free time that summer with Clay and the other young single adults from the church. During those weeks of serious discussions and innocent fun, her friendship with Clay deepened to the point of admiration, respect, and blossoming love.

He was like no other guy she had ever met. It was obvious to her by the way he behaved in her presence that he had strong feelings for her. He even told her so one night on a miniature golf outing. But he also made clear to her that God was the foremost love in his life, and if God wanted him to, he would serve Him for the rest of his life as a single adult, like the apostle Paul. He revealed the strength of his sincerity by refusing to pursue her and by resisting the unusual number of girls who tried aggressively to lure him into relationships.

She was the only girl in whom he showed any interest. But his interest in her was only verbal. He never touched her. His dedication to God and to a life of moral integrity, especially in the light of his amoral background, only enhanced her attraction to him and challenged her constantly in her own spiritual development.

By the middle of the summer, her friendship with Clay and the church had persuaded her to pursue her college education at the same Christian university Clay would be attending. That university was one of only two Christian colleges in America Pastor Lovett approved of. The other school was in Indiana, much farther away and more expensive.

When she received her matriculation letter from the university a few weeks later, Clay's excitement seemed to equal her own. Pastor Lovett and the congregation at North Metro were already claiming her proudly as one of their own, calling her an "exemplary Christian teen."

Her old group of high school friends, however, shook their heads in disbelief, saying she was foolish to attend a Christian university. They thought she should be grooming herself at a "real" university for unlimited success in any prestigious and lucrative career she wanted.

Ignoring the opposition, she moved to Anderson, South Carolina, in late August, a week or so after Clay, and began her freshman year at the Christian university.

During their first month of classes, she and Clay joined an evangelistic team that every weekend reached out to the poor kids of the city with snacks, Bible lessons, flannelgraph stories, puppet shows, and music.

As often as the school rules would permit, they met together during the week for meals, church services, sporting events, school concerts, and to just walk and converse. Clay virtually ignored every other girl on campus. By Christmas break, she and Clay had become almost inseparable. By the end of the school year, their friendship had turned into a deep love that consumed them both.

During the final week of school, Clay shared for the first time his impassioned desire to marry her. Would she want him for her husband? And if so, was she convinced in her heart that their marriage would be God's will?

They were sitting in his car, parked at a large picnic area on the shoreline of Lake Hartwell. "Yes!" she remembered answering with a smile big enough to set a world record. "Yes! Yes, I want you. There's no one else in the whole world I'd rather spend the rest of my life with. And I have all the peace in the world that it's God's will." And she had meant it.

Even after all these passing years, she still felt the same.

She blinked away the tears hanging on the edge of her eyelids and proceeded to turn the pages of the album.

After much prayer, discussion, and counsel, she and Clay had decided to plan their wedding date for the month after her college graduation.

She reflected on the three long years of waiting that followed. The three longest years of her life. The anticipations and dreams, filled with glorious promise, had nearly been too much to carry for so long.

Every aspect of their relationship, with strict limitations on the physical, grew deeper and richer by the month, making their wait that much harder.

When the June wedding finally arrived on a hot and humid day in Atlanta, it turned out to be everything and more than they had imagined.

The ceremony itself was uniquely merged with North Metro's regular Sunday evening worship service. More than seven hundred people attended the event, one of the most talked about Sunday evening services during the months that followed. Intense jubilation permeated the crowd from the beginning of the official welcome through the moment of her and Clay's vows, all the way through to the cutting of the cake at the grandiose outdoor reception.

It was the happiest moment of Rachel's life.

The savored honeymoon on Jekyll Island off Georgia's Atlantic coastline, the unforgettable physical consummation, and the years of blissful union and companionship that had followed were echoes of their love and of their willful and joyful vow to be committed to one another until "parted by death."

Rachel slowly lifted her eyes from the photographs. She caught herself breathing forcefully through a tight throat.

Her mind sought for answers.

She knew Clay. She knew his love for her and for the children. She knew his inner strength; he was the strongest and most disciplined man she had ever known. If what the anonymous lady was reporting to Lieutenant Ekberg was true, then Clay had to be a victim, not a perpetrator.

And if a victim, then in a matter of days he would come to his senses. And come back to his family. Wouldn't he?

She focused again on the pictures.

Thirteen years together. The tightness in her throat started to choke her. What had gone wrong? Their beginning had been nearly perfect. Their marriage, unlike most marriages they had seen through the years, had for more than a decade been one of undying passion. Physically, emotionally, and mentally. Nearly heaven on earth. Their bond had been...indestructible.

Hadn't they guaranteed that? Hadn't their loyalty to God and their insistence on allowing Him to be the hub of their marriage guarded them from this kind of betrayal?

Rachel cradled the wedding album in her lap and dropped her head to her knees. She didn't understand. How could Clay lie to her when she had asked him point-blank if he was seeing another woman, if that was what had been causing his emotional withdrawal from her and the kids?

Had he been lying to her for *three* years, according to the anonymous lady's account? In the name of all that their marriage had stood for, how could that be possible?

If it was even remotely possible, then why hadn't Clay been able to tell her what he was struggling with? Had his silence somehow been her fault? Had she done something to make him think he couldn't trust her anymore?

She shook her head, trying to dislodge all the hideous thoughts. But the anonymous lady's story wouldn't even begin to fade.

A mistress! she cried out inside her soul. *A married woman! A married woman with children! For three years! And recently a second woman he had reportedly run away with!*

Rachel leaned back in the chair and let the wedding album slide out of her lap onto the floor.

She sat motionless, but her mind kept pacing. Had all this happened because of their philosophical shift from the far right? Had they strayed too far from their old position to be spiritually safe? But didn't people entrenched in religious legalism experience moral failures too?

She felt her hands clasp the ends of the chair arms. *How? How could he have done it? Why?*

No! Maybe it is all a lie. Like Erik said, maybe the whole story has been fabricated. There is no evidence. No one can prove anything.

Feeling suddenly dirty, she stood up and wiped earnestly at her arms.

She started moving toward the bathroom. In midstride, as if ambushed by an assailant, she dropped to her knees. She gripped the throw carpet in her fists and burst into tears.

It was over, wasn't it? Their life, their ministry, their future, their family—all destroyed by one short and profane phone call.

Falling prostrate, she curled up into a fetal position on her side. She wanted to stop hurting. For the first time in her life, she wanted to die.

11

P erhaps I should make a visit to the health club," Bengt said to Eric as they sat in Eric's car outside the church building, "and try to meet some of the people who know Clay. To see if any of them can verify the woman's story." Bengt's conversations with people in the church had not produced any new revelations. He had explained this to the church leaders in the emergency session just minutes ago.

"Yeah," Eric replied as they sat there in the quiet twilight of the long Nordic evening. "I suppose that's something that should be done." His pessimism and fatigue were no longer hidden.

Both men wanted to share their deepest thoughts and feelings with the other. But ultimately they chose to fight their inner turmoil alone.

When Eric walked into his house around ten-thirty that night, he switched on the lights and walked straight to the hallway phone. He removed his billfold and retrieved a business card. He flipped the card over to the backside and stared at Pastor Frank Lovett's phone number in Atlanta. Earlier in the evening, Rachel had given him the number and asked him if he would call Pastor Lovett and convey Lieutenant Ekberg's report. "I don't think I can talk to him today," she told him. Eric had promised to make the call.

He knew that the Reeses and the Holcombs would be leaving for the Atlanta airport in less than an hour. He suspected that Pastor Lovett would tell them the news before they boarded the plane. Perhaps that would be best. The two couples would then have the entire flight to absorb the shock and to think about their choice of action.

He whispered a small prayer for Rachel and for everybody involved as he lifted the phone and dialed.

Through the years he had heard much about Pastor Lovett from Clay and Rachel. But only once had he ever spoken with the man. That conversation had taken place two years ago over the phone. They had talked briefly about some promotional ideas regarding a Bible conference Clay had invited Pastor Lovett to conduct for their church in Stockholm. The conference never took place, however, due to the death of one of Pastor Lovett's older sisters.

Eric heard the phone ring on the other side of the Atlantic. He shifted his weight from one leg to the other and tried to suppress his unease. But how was it possible to make such a telephone call without feeling unsettled by all the potential repercussions?

"Good afternoon. North Metro Church of the Bible," a cheery female voice answered.

"Yes, this is Eric Torleif. I am a friend of Clay and Rachel McCain. I'm calling long-distance from Stockholm, Sweden, to speak with Pastor Frank Lovett."

"Okay. Hold just a moment, please."

In the protracted silence, Eric prayed again. This time he prayed for Clay.

"Hello, this is Pastor Lovett," a deep voice suddenly

announced.

Eric breathed deeply. "Pastor Lovett, this is Eric Torleif, one of the elders in Clay McCain's church here in Stockholm. I don't know if you remember, but I spoke with you once about two years ago when we were planning the Bible conference."

"Yes, Eric, I remember," Lovett said.

Eric sighed. "There's something I need to share with you. It's something you'll probably want to pass along to the Reeses and Holcombs before they board their plane."

"All right," came a weighty response.

Eric relayed the anonymous lady's story reported through Lieutenant Ekberg. He then took a few minutes to tell about the meeting of the church leaders, their unsettled opinion, and their ongoing investigation.

Pastor Lovett remained silent during Eric's entire briefing. Eric normally would have assumed the line had gone dead, but he could feel Lovett's presence on the other end. The silence was piercing.

At the end of the call, Pastor Lovett's only reply, given in a cold voice, was, "I will contact Dr. Ed Brighton at the mission board."

When Eric hung up, he realized he was sweating. Had Pastor Lovett really become so disrespectful to the McCains after hearing something so dreadfully unexpected about them? Or was it just Eric's imagination?

Readying himself for bed, Eric was unable to dismiss the telephone call from his thoughts.

When he was finally lying still under his lightweight comforter, absorbing a night breeze through the open window, a nearly forgotten story surfaced through the maze of seldom-used memories. It was a story he had heard Clay share with a small group of men four or five years ago on a ski trip in the mountains of central Sweden. The story was about Pastor Frank Lovett.

At the time the story took place, Lovett had been the pastor of North Metro Church of the Bible for less than two years. Clay was home for the summer holidays between his first and second years at the Christian university. As Lovett stood to lead the opening prayer for a worship service one Sunday morning, he surprised the whole church by angrily calling out the names of two deacons who were seated with their families near the front of the auditorium. He publicly emphasized that the two men, when elected to serve as deacons, had been entrusted with the sacred responsibility of setting a leadership example for the church in both wisdom and moral fortitude but had, he recently discovered, proved they were not trustworthy. The two men had just returned with their families from a joint vacation in Panama City, Florida, where they had been spotted swimming at a popular beach crowded with hundreds of "naked" sunbathers.

"These men know that such activity is lewd and is contrary to the convictions of our church. They've defied God. They've betrayed our trust," Lovett had proclaimed.

In the presence of the entire congregation, he asked them to resign immediately from their elected position. Publicly humili-ated, both men abdicated their position and soon withdrew from the membership of the church.

Clay, in the heat of a blazing fireplace, had told the story to Eric and the men one evening to explain the type of Christian background he came from and to illustrate Pastor Lovett's propensity toward authoritarian leadership. A propensity "common among most of the pastors in my denomination," Clay had revealed with obvious frustration.

Eric remembered being repulsed by the story. Through the years, he had seen Clay struggle to overcome the legalistic training he had received from his Christian university, his home church, and his mission board.

Eric had often wondered after hearing similar stories about Pastor Lovett, the university, and the mission board why Clay did not sever his connections with those groups and build a different network of stateside constituents. The few times he had raised the subject in Clay's presence, however, Clay had said, "It's just not that simple," and had steered the conversation in other directions.

Eric stared at the shadowy ceiling and felt his heart aching. For both Clay and Rachel.

If Clay was guilty as accused, how would he be dealt with by Pastor Lovett and the mission board? In a firm and loving manner that would lead to healing and restoration? Or would he be treated like the two North Metro deacons, cut off without mercy and forgiveness? And what kind of emotional support, if any, would be provided for Rachel and the children?

Eric rolled over on his stomach and sighed. He did not feel comfortable with the prospects.

12

Standing in the master bedroom, Rachel handed Justin to Lena Torleif.

"I want Mommy," Justin hollered as Lena took him in her arms.

"It's okay. Holly and Summer are going to stay here with us," Lena tried to console him. "Mommy will only be gone for a little while."

Rachel opened her closet to look for a comfortable dress to change into. Eric and Bengt were downstairs waiting for her. The two men had borrowed a nine-passenger van from one of the families in the church to drive her to the airport to pick up the Reeses and the Holcombs. The Scandinavian Airline flight from New York was scheduled to land at Stockholm's Arlanda International Airport in less than an hour.

As Rachel took a yellow summer dress from its hanger, she suddenly felt that she was being absurd. Her husband was missing. Her children were in the midst of an emotional maelstrom. Her life was disintegrating. And here she was, feeling the pressure to take off her jeans and put on a dress to keep from offending the Reeses and the Holcombs, to give the appearance of being in harmony with her home church's conviction that it was immodest and unspiritual for a Christian woman to wear pants.

There should be no reason for this, she wanted to scream. Her and

Clay's growing disagreement with the legalistic standards preached by North Metro and the other stateside churches in their ecclesiastical camp should have been made known to Pastor Lovett and Dr. Brighton two or three years ago. Why had Clay repeatedly postponed this discussion with Lovett and Brighton? Why had he insisted that...? She closed her eyes, leaned her head against the closet door, and tried to prevent an outburst of emotion.

Lena started to say something to her when the doorbell rang. The unexpected visitor at the door attracted the attention of the whole household.

Rachel soon heard voices at the front door. She decided to ignore the distraction and started to unsnap her jeans and change. But almost instantly, Eric called for her. Before she could answer, she heard him call again, sounding this time as if he were halfway up the staircase. Rachel sighed and walked quickly out of the bedroom to the head of the stairs.

"It's an officer from the police department," Eric explained as soon as their eyes met. "He says he needs to talk to you for a moment." He rolled his eyes and inhaled as if to say he was unsure of what they should do about the time element.

Rachel ran her fingers through her hair, made sure her jeans were snapped, and followed Eric down to the living room.

"Mrs. Rachel McCain?" the police officer asked when Rachel entered the room.

A dozen desperate questions detonated in Rachel's mind. "Yes, I'm Mrs. McCain." She felt a chill run through her body as she waited for the officer's next words.

"Can I speak with you in private, please?" The officer's eyes revealed the seriousness of the request.

Rachel looked slowly around the room. Eric and Bengt were staring at her, waiting for her to give her consent. Summer and Holly stood side by side in the kitchen doorway. The emotional disturbance of the last eight days hung miserably on their faces.

"We...uh...were just getting ready to leave. We have to pick someone up at the airport," Rachel stated as she turned to face the officer again.

"I only need about ten minutes of your time," the officer informed her.

Rachel slowly nodded her agreement.

Bengt was the first to move. Gently, but assertively, he began escorting Summer and Holly upstairs.

"I'll wait outside," Eric told Rachel. "Don't worry about the time. If we leave in the next fifteen minutes, we can still get there before they clear their luggage through customs."

Rachel turned and gestured for the officer to take a seat. She sat down across from him. Before the officer spoke, Rachel overheard Summer asking Bengt if the policeman was here because of Daddy.

Rachel felt a surge of pain, one that was no longer new or unfamiliar, rip through her heart.

"Mrs. McCain," the officer suddenly began, "my name is Lieutenant Andersson. Normally, Lieutenant Ekberg would be the one speaking with you, but he's off duty this weekend. So I'm here on his behalf." Andersson scooted to the edge of his seat. "A telephone call relating to your husband's disappearance was received at Lieutenant Ekberg's office about two hours ago. The call was forwarded to me. It was from a gas station clerk in Pershagen, a small township south of Stockholm. The caller was a man who was responding to Wednesday's newspaper article. I collected the information he gave and was going to leave it on Lieutenant Ekberg's desk so he would find it Monday morning. Ironically, about five or six minutes after the call, Lieutenant Ekberg phoned the office for a personal matter. I told him about the gas station clerk's call. We talked about the content of the call and the legitimacy of the caller. When he was satisfied that the call was credible, he asked me to contact you and pass along the caller's information."

Rachel felt every muscle in her body grow taut.

"The clerk claims," Andersson reported, "that on Friday morning of last week, sometime between six and seven, a man matching the photograph of your husband stopped at the station. He bought gas, used the toilet facilities, and bought some drinks and some snack foods." Andersson hesitated then proceeded with emphasis. "He was with a woman. The clerk says he remembers both of them because they were so affectionate. And also because they were driving one of his personal dream cars, a new Ferrari."

Rachel tried to control herself, but her eyes squinted and remained shut. Something inside her broke.

Andersson cleared his throat, then continued. "Lieutenant Ekberg and I are persuaded the man's telling the truth. For four reasons. To begin with, he says the lady had long black hair, a physical feature that matches the description given by the other witness." Andersson paused until Rachel made eye contact with him again.

"Second, unless your husband had the money or the means to buy or lease a new Ferrari—which we're assuming is not the case— then the car most likely is the property of the dark-haired lady. This again harmonizes with the other witness's testimony that the woman possesses substantial wealth.

"Then there is the time element. The clerk says he opened the station at five-thirty and remembers serving the lady and the man within his first hour and a half of business. The time of this sighting, when we consider the distance between your house and the Pershagen gas station, is consistent with the approximate time your husband reportedly left the house.

"And finally, there's what we call the independent testimony factor. This simply means that the gas station clerk, independent of any published reports or general public knowledge, gave information he thought was exclusive, such as the lady's physical description and her wealth, which is supported independently by one or more unrelated witnesses."

Rachel saw Lieutenant Andersson become quiet, waiting for some kind of response. Rachel wanted to ask questions, but her thoughts refused to be harnessed long enough to think analytically. All she could manage to do was to keep focusing on the lieutenant and keep breathing.

"Anyway," Lieutenant Andersson said after a few seconds of silence, "the gas station clerk has never heard the name of the lady who is our primary witness. So, unless evidence surfaces to the contrary, we're dismissing the idea that there was any collaboration of testimonies. As things now stand, we have two independent witnesses whose claims are consistent with each other." Andersson hesitated one more time. The tone of his voice changed from sounding professional to sounding sympathetic. "It seems, Mrs. McCain, according to all indications, that...what we have here is a case of...abandonment."

Lieutenant Andersson continued talking. Rachel could see his lips moving. But the darkness that rushed into her soul overpow-ered her sense of hearing. She strove desperately to fight the life-stealing blackness. She tried again to deny the betrayal it rep-resented. But the effort was in vain. In a matter of seconds, everything good she had ever believed in vanished. The blackness, she realized, had won.

Eric and Bengt, seeing Rachel's condition, asked Lieutenant Andersson to explain to them what was happening.

Rachel interrupted with a whispered request to be taken upstairs.

Eric and Bengt, deciding that the Holcombs and the Reeses would just have to wait, helped Rachel to her room. They asked Lena to keep the kids upstairs, then returned downstairs where they stood nervously and listened to Lieutenant Andersson recap his report.

Almost immediately, Eric and Bengt could hear Rachel's groans coming from the upper floor. The sounds became muted when they heard the bathroom door slam and the shower blasting at full force. Both men felt despair overtake them. The despair was compounded as they heard Lieutenant Andersson unfold the newest revelation. For the first time since Clay's disappearance, they accepted the evidence that their pastor and friend had indeed abandoned his wife and children for another woman. Their hearts were pierced.

"Please reiterate to Mrs. McCain," Lieutenant Andersson urged, "that Lieutenant Ekberg will keep the case open for a while longer. He wants her to understand, however, that at this point the only thing he can legally do is process the testimonies of new witnesses. He can't do more than that unless new evidence comes forth showing that the other two witnesses are mistaken about their claims and that Mr. McCain is indeed the victim of some kind of criminal activity."

"Can we talk with the gas station clerk?" Bengt wanted to know. "We would like to ask him a few questions."

Lieutenant Andersson contemplated the request. "According to standard procedure, I'm not authorized to divulge the names of case witnesses. But I'll discuss it with Lieutenant Ekberg. Perhaps we can talk with our captain."

When the lieutenant left the house, Eric and Bengt hurried upstairs.

Rachel was still in the bathroom with the door locked and the shower running, engulfed in a world of wailing anguish. She didn't respond to any of the knocks on the door or the pleading inquiries.

Summer, Holly, and Justin were in the master bedroom with Lena. They were beside themselves and in tears. Lena, looking haggard, was cradling Justin in her arms.

"Where's my daddy?" Holly wanted to know when she saw Eric and Bengt enter the room. She was standing at the edge of the bed, shaking with fright.

Eric looked at Holly then at his wife. The sickening feeling in his heart showed on his countenance. He looked back at Holly. "That's what we're trying to find out, honey." He knelt in front of her and pulled her into an embrace. "That's what we're trying to find out."

Eric saw Summer standing by one of the windows. She was

RANDALL ARTHUR ♦ 102

looking at him, her eyes marked with dried tears. Eric motioned for her to come and share in the embrace. She turned instead and sat on the floor beneath the window. She propped her elbows on her knees and placed her small hands over her chin.

Eric thought he saw suppressed rage on her face. He tried to expel the thought of this innocent nine-year-old being driven to emotional disaster. He made lingering eye contact with his wife, then shifted his gaze to Bengt.

"Bengt, can you take the children downstairs and get them something to drink? I need to talk to Lena for just a moment before you and I leave for the airport."

Bengt, feigning lightheartedness, gathered the kids and led them down to the kitchen.

As soon as the children were out of the bedroom and down the steps, Eric turned his eyes to Lena and repeated in four or five sentences Lieutenant Andersson's newest information. With Lena right behind him, he then moved down the hallway to the bathroom. The door was still locked. Rachel's groans, though somewhat quieter, were still distinguishable beyond the sound of the shower.

Eric knocked. Then knocked again.

"Go away! Leave me alone!" Rachel cried, her voice breaking.

"Rachel, will you please unlock the door?" Lena said. "We just want to make sure you're going to be okay."

"Pleeeease, I just want to be alooone!" Rachel pleaded.

Eric and Lena turned and stared at each other. Eric saw that the fatigue in Lena's eyes had changed to sheer heaviness.

Eric listened through the bathroom door for a few more seconds. When he ascertained that Rachel was not foolishly trying to endanger herself, he said to Lena, "Bengt and I need to go. Just stay close by and keep trying to get her to talk."

"How is she going to tell the children?" Lena asked under her breath.

Eric didn't try to answer. He simply pulled Lena's head to his chest and gave her a kiss. "Thanks for at least being here for her." As he held her in his arms, he told her he would call Merlene and Ingela and find out if they could come back this morning and give a few more hours of help.

Lena tightened her arms around him and nodded.

Within minutes, Merlene and Ingela were en route to the McCains'.

"Are you sure you don't want us to wait here till they arrive?" Eric asked Lena for the third time. Lena was sitting on the living room couch holding Justin in her lap, softly singing to him. Holly was nestled tightly against Lena's side. Summer was outdoors sitting alone in the backyard swing.

"I think we're going to be okay here," Lena replied quietly. "In just a few minutes I'm going to make us an early lunch. I'll try to encourage Rachel to come down and eat a bite with us. By that time, Merlene and Ingela should be here. Besides, you guys shouldn't be any later than you already are."

Eric looked at Bengt, who was standing by the front door. "Let's do it then."

En route to the airport, Eric brokenheartedly thought about all the positive reinforcement needed by Rachel and the children. He hoped and prayed amid his nagging doubts that the Holcombs and the Reeses would prove, contrary to their legalistic background, to be exceptionally sensitive and loving.

13

The Reeses and the Holcombs were standing along one of the main corridors, just outside the customs checkpoint of the Arlanda International Airport. Their numerous pieces of luggage were grouped all around them on baggage carts.

Bill Reese looked at his watch again. "We've waited for thirty minutes; I think that's long enough," he said impatiently to the other three. "I'm going to go get some Swedish money from one of the exchange banks, then find a phone and call the McCains' number. I want to know why there was no one here to meet us."

John Holcomb was disturbed by Bill Reese's attitude, especially considering the orientation of their mission. Since late yesterday afternoon, when Pastor Lovett broke the news of Clay's reputed long-term extramarital affair, Bill had seemingly pushed aside all concern and sensitivity for the McCains' crisis.

John felt pressed to challenge him, but he hesitated to voice his feelings. He disliked himself for being afraid to speak out. But to justify his reluctance, he reasoned that Bill's insensitivity might not be intentional. Maybe the man's conduct was simply due to fatigue. None of them had been able to sleep on the transatlantic flight. They had been awake for nearly twenty-four hours.

John decided, as chairman of North Metro's deacon board, that he shouldn't draw battle lines with one of his leaders over something that was possibly not as clear as it appeared. He watched as Bill strode off to find an airport bank.

Bengt spotted them first. Like most U.S. citizens traveling in Europe, the Reeses and the Holcombs were easily identifiable as middle-class Americans: the distinctive style and color of the clothes; the hairstyles—tapered and short for the men, sprayed stiff for the ladies; the overweight size of one of the couples; the heavy makeup on the women; the excessive number of suitcases that matched and looked relatively new; and the loudness of the voices. In addition, the two couples were standing idly in one location, looking as if they were waiting for someone.

"There," Bengt said to Eric and pointed in the couples' direction.

Eric nodded his agreement and took the lead.

"Whoever designed the pay phones in this country is an idiot!" one of the men, the average-sized one in the suit and tie, said angrily to the other three people in the group as Eric and Bengt approached.

"Excuse me," Eric interrupted in English. "Are you the Reese family and the Holcomb family from Atlanta, Georgia?"

The four pairs of American eyes turned and focused on Eric. There was a full second of silence.

"Uh, yes, that's us," the heavyset man said, trying to hide his embarrassment over his companion's unpleasant behavior.

"My name is Eric Torleif, and this is Bengt Wennergren." Eric extended his hand to the man who had spoken and then to the man in the suit. "We're from Clay McCain's church."

"I'm Bill Reese, the assistant pastor at North Metro Church of the Bible," Reese said coldly as he shook Eric's and Bengt's hands. "This is my wife, Nancy."

Nancy shook hands.

Eric felt an immediate transfer of tension from the Reeses. He pretended not to notice. He was sure Bengt felt it as well.

The heavy man introduced himself as John Holcomb, then introduced his wife, Rita.

"I apologize that we're late," Eric told them. "We had planned to meet you here with Rachel, but as we were getting ready to leave her house, one of the police lieutenants assisting with Clay's case dropped by unannounced." Eric suddenly did not want to divulge the rest of the news to these people. But at this point, how could he justify any type of deceit? "I'm assuming Pastor Lovett has already conveyed to you the report about the anonymous lady?"

"He told us shortly before we boarded the plane," Bill Reese said, looking as if he would rather be any place in the world except where he was.

"Well, what the lieutenant shared with us this morning simply builds on the report you've already heard. I'll give you the details when we're all seated in the van. Again," he clarified, "Rachel had planned to be here to greet you, but after hearing the lieutenant's update this morning, she felt the need to be alone for a while."

"How are the children holding up under all this?" Rita Holcomb asked. Her voice was pitched with slight nervousness yet at the same time possessed warmth. Her immense, olive green dress hung to her knees, camouflaging her enormous size as much as a dress possibly could.

"They're extremely insecure right now," Bengt answered.

"They haven't been told yet *why* their dad is gone. They just know he's missing and that a lot of people, including the police, have been looking for him. Rachel is trying to decide how and when she should break the news to them."

"Is there anyone helping her with the children?" Rita questioned.

Bengt nodded. "The ladies in the church have been doing everything they can. Especially during the last couple of days—almost around the clock for the last twenty-four hours. Three ladies are there at the house now."

In the awkward quietness that followed, Eric took hold of one of the luggage carts and started heading them toward the van. "Is this your first time to travel overseas?"

"This is the first time Rita and I have been out of the States," John Holcomb confessed, maneuvering one of the other loaded carts. "We both feel a little out of our league. But we just felt strongly that God wanted us to be here."

Nancy Reese spoke up for the first time. "Bill and I have been traveling internationally for fifteen years. He's preached in Canada so many times we've lost count. We've been to Mexico three times. And last year we were in Israel. So we're not novices, if that's what you're wanting to know."

"No, I didn't mean to sound discourteous or condescending," Eric stated. "I just wanted to know if you are familiar with jet lag. I was going to—"

"We're familiar with jet lag," Nancy interrupted. "And we've already told John and Rita all about it. And to fight it, we're all planning to go to bed this evening around seven or eight to try to catch up on as much sleep as we can before tomorrow."

Eric, quite sure he had not said anything to provoke such defensiveness, simply looked at Nancy and acknowledged her statement with a gentle nod. When they broke eye contact, Eric looked at Bengt with raised eyebrows.

John Holcomb nervously cleared his throat. "How come you both speak English so well?" he asked as they passed a large group of Japanese businessmen laden with cameras and briefcases.

"English is a second language for our country," Bengt responded, feeling that Eric might be grateful for a minute of reprieve. "Our own language is one of the smallest language groups in Europe. So in order for our country to compete in the international marketplace—and there's really no choice if we want to maintain a high standard of living—we have to carry the burden of communication. The Germans, the English, and the French aren't going to take time to learn Swedish, so in our schools we learn to speak their languages. English, though, is given the greatest priority. We start learning it in the fourth grade. Consequently, about 75 percent of our people speak English quite fluently."

Bengt paused long enough for them to exit with the carts through the outside doors.

Once they were out of the building, Bengt explained that there were many American and British programs on Swedish television and that all of them were broadcast with the original English soundtrack. "This gives everybody plenty of exposure. Plus, Eric and I speak English about half the time with Clay, Rachel, and the girls. So we get to use our English regularly."

By the time Bengt answered a couple more of John's questions about the Swedish culture, they were in the parking lot loading the suitcases into the back of the van.

When the luggage was in place and everybody was seated, Bill Reese looked at Eric in the front passenger's seat. "So, what's this latest report all about, Eric?" His voice didn't hide his feelings of being an assumed judge in the situation.

Eric cringed inwardly at the man's curtness. He turned slowly to face everyone in the rear of the van. He inhaled deeply and quietly. "There's been another eyewitness," he told them.

The Reeses and the Holcombs sat motionless as Eric told about Lieutenant Andersson's visit, the gas station clerk's sighting of Clay and the dark-haired lady with the Ferrari, the reason Lieutenant Ekberg and Lieutenant Andersson believed the report to be credible, and the official conclusion of abandonment by both lieutenants.

When Eric finished, Bill Reese shook his head in disgust. Rubbing his tired eyes, he mumbled sharply, "North Metro gives him thousands of dollars through the years, and this is what we get in return! Deception! And perversion!" Bill sighed gruffly. "I wonder if the man is even a Christian."

Bengt started to react, but Bill Reese continued.

"Pastor Lovett is going to need to hear about this as soon as possible. He'll want to call Dr. Brighton in Greenville, and I'm sure they'll want to make some kind of immediate decision." Bill looked at his watch. "I'll plan to call about three hours from now, around two-thirty. That should be about eight-thirty in the morning their time." Bill looked at Eric for a confirmation on the time.

Eric offered a hesitant shake of the head. He now understood that the news of Clay's moral collapse would soon be spread cheaply around the world like prime gossip. It would be chewed, savored, and then piously vomited up by all the people at North Metro, the mission board, the Bible college, and each of the McCains' supporting churches up and down the East Coast of America.

Eric's hopes that North Metro's delegation would try to be objective and patient and try to work sensitively to contain the overall damage now seemed foolishly naive. The dreariness of soul that he felt was almost sickening.

"I think we should just go on to the hotel instead of going to their house," Nancy Reese said. "This whole thing is repulsive; it makes me feel dirty. We can call Pastor Lovett from our room. We can eat lunch, or something, while we wait for him to call back with his decision. And then if it's necessary we can go to the house later this evening."

Bill Reese placed a hand on his wife's knee. "I agree." He then looked back at Eric. "Just go ahead and take us to the hotel." Before anyone had a chance to respond, he said, "You did reserve a second room, I hope."

Eric felt anger rise in his throat. He suppressed it. "It's waiting for you, according to Pastor Lovett's request," Eric said, trying to keep coldness out of his voice.

He started to turn and look at Bengt when he heard Rita speak up from the backseat. "If it's okay with everybody, I'd like to be dropped off at Rachel's."

A moment of uncertain tenseness permeated the van.

"I'll take you there after I stop at the hotel," Bengt broke the silence from the driver's seat. "I'm sure Rachel will be grateful for any help that's offered to her."

"Well, I sure hope she will," Bill quickly added, "because this trip is costing a lot of people a lot of money."

A thick silence hung in the air again.

Eric looked over at Bengt. He could tell that Bengt, like himself, was trying diligently to temper his feelings. Bengt cranked the van and pulled away.

The only words spoken en route to the hotel were between John and Rita and between Bill and Nancy.

Eric and Bengt focused straight ahead. Their thoughts and their prayers were running wild.

14

Less than half an hour after dropping off the Reeses and John Holcomb at the hotel and taking Rita Holcomb and Eric to the McCains', Bengt was standing in the trophy-filled office of the health studio where Clay had regularly trained and reputedly met the lady with whom he had his initial affair.

Facing Bengt behind the large metal desk was the club manager, dressed in sweatpants and a tank top and sporting a flattop. He was one of the biggest and most muscular men Bengt had ever seen. Bengt was sure, as he stared at the man, that he was the winner of many of the trophies displayed in the room.

"Look," the man was telling him in a hefty voice that matched the physique, "the lady you're wanting to know about is a friend of mine. She's married and has a couple of kids. I refuse to give you her name and have you or anyone else going to her with a lot of questions that might reveal things to her husband that he doesn't want to know. You understand?"

Bengt nodded and sighed with frustration. "So, you're at least confirming that Clay was a part of this lady's secret life?"

"All that I'm confirming is that she and Clay were friends and spent a lot of time together. What they did or didn't do in privacy is nobody's business. Not mine. Not yours."

It was clear that the man was not going to admit anything more. As Bengt walked out of the studio, with men and women pumping iron all around him, the confusion that had weighed on his mind for the last nineteen to twenty hours turned to deep melancholy.

The reason for Clay's antisocial behavior during the last several months was now clear. But why in the name of friendship had Clay not been able to confide in him? Or in the elders? Why had he insisted on struggling in secret with something so destructive when his friends had tried to reach out to him and had been ready to help him?

The whole concept of Christian brotherhood, which for Bengt had always held a strong place of wonderment and excitement, suddenly seemed like a monumental and deceptive facade.

As he got in the van and drove away, he felt a darkness descend on him that he had never experienced before. He inserted a tape of Christian music into the cassette deck and turned it up loud. But the faith-prompting lyrics lost their persuasive power. Finally, Bengt turned off the music and just drove.

"'Mr. LaRoyToy spent every day of that winter carving in his workshop.'" Rita Holcomb was reading the final page of the children's picture storybook to Holly, who was nestled in her thick arms and lap. They were sitting on the edge of Holly's bed. Rita could feel herself sweating in the non-air-conditioned house. "'In the springtime, when the sun returned to Guess What village, Mr. LaRoyToy did something that surprised the whole town. He invited everybody to a big party in his backyard. He especially invited the little orphan girl who no one had ever loved. At the party, he uncovered the biggest and the finest wooden toy horse he had ever made. Everybody gasped at how magnificent it was. With a strange gentleness, Mr. LaRoyToy gave the horse to the dirty little orphan girl. "Thank you," he told her, "for helping me see my selfish heart. From now on, I want to be different. I want to be your friend. I want to be everybody's friend." And guess what the people of Guess-What village saw on Mr. LaRoyToy's face for the first time in years? It was a smile. A big, big smile.'" Rita Holcomb closed the book slowly. "The end," she said.

Holly looked up thoughtfully from the book into Rita's eyes. "Am I going to be an orphan, too?" she whispered in her tiny voice. She stared as she waited for an answer.

As a mother of four and grandmother of seven, Rita pulled Holly snugly to her breast. As thoughts of Clay flashed through her head, she said, "I don't understand, child, what's happened to your father. But you're not an orphan. And you're not going to be. Your mother loves you very much. And she's not going anywhere. She's going to be right here for you. And she always will."

With her little brown curls matted against Rita's breast, Holly responded with stillness.

Rita just held her there.

Rachel was barely picking at the steamed vegetables and baked fish that Lena and Merlene had prepared for everybody. She hadn't eaten anything all day. Yet, she still wasn't hungry.

The only reason she was at the dining room table was that the ladies insisted she try to eat something. Plus, she had hoped that by coming down and being with everybody, her mind might be sidetracked from its unrelenting questions—*Why? When? How? How often? How long? Was it my fault?*—questions that seemed every second to steal entire years from her existence.

But there was no relief. She tried to feel consoled by the company of Lena, Merlene, Ingela, Rita Holcomb, and her own children. Yet she felt utterly alone.

Eric's phone call from the hotel forty minutes ago had not helped matters. He had sounded so unlike himself. Nervous. Almost angry. "It seems that Pastor Lovett and Dr. Brighton have made a decision," he told her. He explained that he was not free to say more than that. He would be leaving at any moment to drive the Reeses and John Holcomb over to the house, where Bill Reese would inform her of the decision.

Avoiding eye contact with anyone, Rachel again looked up from her plate and took notice of the clock. It was nearly six. Eric should have already arrived. For the first time in her life, Rachel caught herself nervously bouncing her leg up and down.

What decision had Lovett and Brighton made? Could she dare afford to be hopeful? For herself? And for her children? Or was she simply playing a mind game to believe that hope of any kind still existed?

She bit down on her lower lip and willed her leg to be still.

The questions spewing through her mind refused to be brought under control.

As she battled to maintain a semblance of sanity, she forced herself to pick up another unwanted piece of fish. She started to put it in her mouth just as the front doorbell rang.

There was instant movement all around the table. Merlene and Rita spoke to the kids and kept them in their seats. Lena got up to answer the door. Rita slid her chair halfway out from the table in preparation to welcome her husband.

Rachel felt her heartbeat accelerate. Within seconds, she heard Eric's voice at the front door, followed by an apparent round of introductions.

As the group made their way into the dining room, Rachel and the ladies around the table stood up.

The introductions, mainly led by Eric, were serious and soft-spoken.

John Holcomb, after hugging his wife and meeting Merlene and Ingela, moved directly to Rachel. Nervously, he hugged her. Rachel returned the hug. She felt her eyes watering. John told her how sorry he was and promised her that he was praying hard for her whole family. He then stepped aside to make way for Bill and Nancy, who walked up behind him.

Bill Reese, dressed in a dark suit and tie, looked into Rachel's eyes. "Rachel," he acknowledged, conceding her presence with a slight nod then extending his hand. His handshake was minuscule.

Nancy Reese, hardly able to make eye contact with Rachel, barely nodded. She chose to neither speak nor offer her hand. She simply stood at Bill's side.

"I'm afraid I'm the bearer of some complicated news." Bill paused to let the words sink in. "It's needful that I go ahead and share it with you. So, if you prefer, we perhaps should move into another room where we can have some privacy."

The thoughts buzzing inside Rachel's brain precluded her from registering Nancy Reese's deliberate aloofness. "Okay, we can...uh...go into the living room then." She motioned back to the room through which the Reeses had just come. She started to move in that direction, then stopped. "Do you mind if Eric joins us?"

"Sure, that's fine," Bill stated coldly. "As the leading elder in your church, he's already been told about the decision anyway. For ethical and official reasons."

Rachel glanced around at Eric and noticed for the first time his troubled countenance. In sudden trepidation, she turned and walked into the living room.

She sat down on the sofa with Eric. Bill Reese sat in the love seat facing them from the other side of the coffee table. Rachel felt paleness spread across her body.

"I want my mommy," she heard Justin crying in the kitchen, with the ladies trying to calm him. She clenched her hands together in her lap.

"Okay," she said, signaling for Bill to start.

"First, I'm just curious—how long have the pants been a part of your wardrobe?"

Rachel, in her current state of mind, was totally unprepared for such a question. The morning visit from Lieutenant Andersson had completely banished the pants issue from her thoughts. Fighting to give a rational response, she spoke softly, barely above a whisper. "It's...something "

"We'll save it till later," Reese cut her short. "Right now, I think you should hear the decision of your mission board and home church."

Rachel just stared at the man.

"As you already know, I called Pastor Lovett from the hotel room about five hours ago, after confirming everything with Lieutenant Andersson, and informed him of the latest report. Pastor Lovett, in return, spent his entire morning discussing the situation with his deacons and with Dr. Brighton and the directors of the mission board. All the men have concluded—very strongly, I want to add—that the evidence against Clay has become too incriminating and too sickening to justify keeping you here with support money while we wait to see if he's going to return. Pastor Lovett will be confirming it over the phone with you later this evening, but he wants you to permanently deal with your household goods and move back to Georgia within the next seven weeks, at the time of your originally planned furlough. He—"

Rachel felt her whole body jerk. "Permanently? But—"

"Listen, Rachel! Your ministry here is over."

"But you don't—"

"Don't understand? What I understand is that there has been an ongoing, shameless lifestyle of gross immorality in this family. A family that has been trusted by thousands of Christian people across America. I also understand that some of God's choicest men, like Pastor Lovett and Dr. Brighton, will be tainted by this travesty. And I understand that those men should be admired for making a quick and responsible decision that will honor Christ and His church."

Rachel saw her leg bouncing up and down again. With a concentrated effort, she made the leg stop. She slowly leaned forward in her seat, her hair falling to the front of her face. She felt a tear fall to her forearm. "Can't we...uh...take more time, maybe move a little slower? Can't—"

"*Time* is not the problem," Reese rebounded. "Sin and deception are the problems. Moving slower would proclaim to our people and to God that we don't take sin seriously. And that's not a message we're going to propagate."

Rachel sniffled and pushed on her knees. She wanted to

scream a dozen statements and questions at Reese, but the words stuck in her throat.

"I don't think you understand the magnitude of what's happened here," Reese continued. "Even if Clay showed up in the next hour and crawled in on his hands and knees begging for forgiveness, the disciplinary decision wouldn't change. The point is: Your family is now disqualified for ministry. As soon as you get back to the States, the mission board will start your resignation process. In the meantime, Eric has assured me that your church here will give you any kind of help you need during the next seven weeks. John and Rita have also volunteered to stay as long as you need them. Nancy and I will be flying back the day after tomorrow. At your church tomorrow morning, I'll extend an official apology to your congregation and assure them that the replacement pastor and his family will arrive on schedule and will do everything possible to provide strong leadership and ensure a smooth transition."

Rachel felt as if she were breathing air too heavy to inhale. As she forced her next breath, she looked over at Eric. He looked distraught and beaten. His eyes were bloodshot.

Rachel looked back at Bill Reese. She wanted to stand up in his face and bellow out her pain. She closed her eyes and tried to think. When she opened them again a moment later, Bill Reese was already getting up to leave the room.

"Seven weeks. Not one day more," Reese ordered as he turned and walked away.

Rachel squeezed her eyes shut again. She wanted to scream out to God in prayer. But for the first time in her life, God no longer seemed to exist.

15

Bill and Nancy Reese flew out of Sweden early Monday morning.

Later that morning, Eric Torleif received a phone call from Lieutenant Ekberg at his downtown consulting office.

"I'm calling," Ekberg explained, "in regard to Lieutenant Andersson's promise to try to get permission from the captain to pass along the name of the Pershagen clerk. I spoke with the captain about an hour ago. He said it would be okay to give you the clerk's name, providing the clerk himself did not object. I just got off the phone with the clerk; he says he doesn't mind. So, if you're ready with a pencil, I can give you the man's name and address."

"I'm ready," Eric replied as he grabbed a pen from his desk.

"The man's name is Axel Bjorkman. He works at the Statoil gas station on Highway E4, about a kilometer south of the town center." Ekberg paused long enough for Eric to write down the information then added, "I can give you a phone number, too, if you would like."

"Yeah, let me have it."

Eric penned the number, then thanked the lieutenant for his help.

Without putting the phone down, Eric waited for a new dial tone and punched in the number to the McCains'. One of the church ladies answered the call. Eric asked to speak with Rachel.

When Rachel came on the line, Eric told her that Lieutenant Ekberg had just given him the Pershagen clerk's name and number. "I'm going to try to make an appointment to meet with the man this evening. I'm wondering if I can come by in a couple of hours and pick up four or five pictures that show Clay at different angles. I want the clerk to see them. I want to find out if he's certain the man he saw with the dark-haired lady was really Clay."

When Rachel finally responded, all she said was, "Yeah...I'll have them ready." Her voice was an empty monotone.

Eric, trying to be sensitive, ended the call. The lifelessness in her voice complicated his concern for her. But as much as he tried, he could not think of any additional ways that he or the church could help lessen her pain or make her life any easier.

He was realizing more and more that the McCains and everyone close to them were caught inescapably in a whirlpool of life-changing consequences. The fear and pain were not going to go away. Endurance was now their only hope.

Yet, he felt it was impossible not to contact the Pershagen clerk and hope beyond reason that the man had somehow mistaken Clay's identity. Acting more out of fantasy than logic, Eric rang through to the Statoil gas station.

Bjorkman answered. He said he was expecting Eric's call.

Within five minutes, Eric had arranged to meet the man between four-thirty and five o'clock.

Eric then called Bengt at his architectural firm and asked if he could clock out early and go with him. It took only a few seconds for Bengt to confirm that he could go.

◆ ◆ ◆

Eric and Bengt's thirty-minute drive to Pershagen was virtually without conversation. On most any other occasion, the short, scenic trip would have been pleasant.

A little before five o'clock Eric pulled the car into the Statoil lot and parked at the side of the building. The station looked almost new. As he and Bengt got out and closed the doors behind them, Eric could not help but envision Clay, the Ferrari, and the dark-haired lady parked on the premises.

Could it really have been? he wondered with a deep sigh. This place. His pastor. A mysterious mistress. A forgotten moment in their hidden rush toward some kind of sexually fueled fantasy. Eric tried to dispel the picture from his thoughts.

He and Bengt entered the station and waited for a couple of people in the checkout line to be served, then asked the young man working the cash register if they could speak with Mr. Axel Bjorkman.

The young man, dressed in a red pullover shirt with a Statoil monogram, extended his hand. "I'm Axel Bjorkman. One of you must be the Mr. Torleif who called from Stockholm this morning."

Eric was surprised. The young man shaking their hand was barely out of his teens. Eric was expecting the man to be older, probably because of the conclusive value the police had placed on his testimony. "Yeah, I'm Mr. Torleif," Eric told him as he removed the photographs from the inside pocket of his jacket.

"So, you want me to look at the snapshots and identify the man who passed through with the knockout lady and the new

Ferrari about eleven days ago?" Bjorkman asked lightheartedly.

"That's right," Eric said, looking the guy in the eye. "But I want you to do it without rushing. I want you to make sure that your conclusions, if any, are certain. If you have any doubts, no matter how minimal, I want to know."

The smile on Bjorkman's face turned to sobriety. "Sure," he said.

Eric handed the first photo to him. The picture was of three couples posing together at a church banquet.

Bjorkman examined the colored photograph carefully. Eric studied Bjorkman's eyes gazing down at the picture. Eric expected to see a look of either recognition or doubt. He saw neither.

When Bjorkman looked up from the picture, Eric gave him the next one. The photo showed eight men sitting around a food-laden picnic table at a lakeside camp. Bjorkman's response was the same: silent and neutral.

Against all odds, Eric wondered tensely if the young man indeed might be having second thoughts.

Eric let him see the third picture: a trio of men singing happily together in a Sunday morning church service.

Then the fourth and final one: two men and five children playing kickball in a grassy backyard.

Bjorkman's expression, as he scrutinized the last photo, was still impassive.

Eric started to ask him what he was remembering, or *not* remembering, when Bjorkman laid all four pictures on the counter facing Eric and Bengt and proclaimed, "This is the man. Here. Here. Here."

Eric saw the young man point to the image of Clay in photos

one, two, and four. Clay was not in the photo of the singing trio; Eric had planted the snapshot to create possible confusion and to demonstrate that Bjorkman possessed a less-than-certain memory.

Eric exhaled his last breath of hope. "Are you sure?"

"Look, the couple was exceptionally good-looking. Plus, the lady was all over him, couldn't keep her hands off of him. I couldn't help but stare. When they finally crawled into their Ferrari and drove away, I kept thinking, that's one lucky guy." Bjorkman looked toward the snapshots. "Am I sure this is the same man? I'm positive."

Eric couldn't find any words.

"Which direction were they headed when they left?" Bengt asked.

"South," Bjorkman said without hesitation. He snickered. "They wound out the Ferrari in first and second gear as if they were trying to make up for lost time, as if they were running late for an appointment or something."

"I don't guess you noticed the license plate number?" Bengt asked.

Bjorkman snickered again, this time with questioning eyes. "I'm afraid that detail got by me."

The only other information Eric and Bengt were able to reap was that the new-model Ferrari was the standard red and that the dark-haired lady looked to be five to ten years younger than Clay.

For both Eric and Bengt, the drive back to Stockholm was excruciatingly lonely.

The next morning at work, Eric called the two Ferrari dealerships listed in the Stockholm business directory and spoke to the managers. From his cluttered desk, he told them an abbreviated version of the McCain situation and asked if they remembered selling one of their cars to an attractive thirtyish-looking, dark-haired lady during the last eighteen months. And if so, was it possible to acquire the lady's name as a link to learning Clay's whereabouts?

Both men sympathized but would not violate company policy and give him such information.

Before lunch, Eric passed along all his information to the two other lead elders in the church.

That evening, the senior elders summoned all the leaders of the Stockholm Independent Bible Church to another emergency session, this time at the Torleifs'. Eric shared the latest reports. It was officially accepted that Clay McCain was guilty of abandoning his family, his Christian responsibilities, and his church for reasons pertaining to infidelity. And it was acknowledged, to the heartbreak of all, that he would not be permitted to return to his position as their pastor.

The major portion of the meeting was spent on bent knees praying. Praying for Clay, wherever he was, that he would come to his senses and find healing and restoration. Praying for Rachel, Summer, Holly, and Justin, that by God's supportive grace they would endure the crushing blow with their sanity intact. Praying for the church, that it would remain levelheaded and rightly focused amid the painful upheaval. And praying for themselves as church leaders, that they, with a vulnerability equal to Clay's, would always find the needed strength to resist the many different forms of sexual misconduct.

The meeting ended early. Along with a lot of personal illusions and dreams.

16

Rachel sat in the master bedroom with her children. She roughly exhaled a puff of air. The children faced her, seated silently side by side along the edge of the bed.

With fear in their eyes, the children waited for her to tell them "some sad news" about Daddy. Holly held Justin's hand. Summer sat detached from her younger sister and brother, her stare boring a hole into her mom.

Rachel's arms lay stiffly in her lap. She felt the muscles in her neck clinch. How was she going to manage this?

"First of all," she began, trying to sound strong, "I want you to know that Mother loves each of you more than anything else in the whole world. And I'm going to be here for you. Please don't ever doubt that." She wanted to add that God was going to be there for them as well, but she could no longer say it without questioning whether it was true.

"What I'm about to tell you isn't going to be easy to understand." She paused, not for the kids' sake, but for her own. When she felt she could keep her heart from exploding, she continued with a strained voice. "The policemen have learned...that Daddy decided to move away from us for a while and that it might be...a long, long time before we ever see him again."

Rachel's words hung in the air as she took a deep breath.

In that instant, Summer jumped off the bed and stood,

looking as if she were going to run.

Rachel reached out and took her by the arm, holding her firmly in her spot. "I know this doesn't make any sense, but you've got to listen to me. All three of you. Daddy's not hurt. And nobody is forcing him to do something he doesn't want to do. For his own reasons—and I don't understand them either—he's decided that he wants to live somewhere else, with...with different people." Rachel pulled Summer into her arms. "We don't know where he is. We just know that someone saw him the other day and that he's okay."

Looking over Summer's shoulder, Rachel saw the bewilderment in Holly's eyes. Rachel's protective spirit as a mother felt like it had just been crucified. She reached out and grasped Holly's hand. "Somehow during the next few weeks we're going to have to be strong for each other. Mrs. Holcomb will be here to help us. And so will some of the ladies from the church. And then, when all of our things are packed, we're going to move back to America like we've been talking about."

"I'm not moving back to America!" Summer cried out, trying to jerk herself from her mother's hold. "I'm not going anywhere! I'm going to stay here and wait for Daddy!"

Rachel barely managed to maintain her arm lock around Summer's waist. "I don't want to move back without Daddy either," Rachel said with all her heart, "but we don't have a choice. The mission board and the church in America, the ones who give us our money every month, have told us we've got to come back."

Anguish and disbelief filled Holly's little brown eyes. And then her voice. "Doesn't Daddy love us anymore, Mommy?"

Rachel withdrew her arms from Summer and Holly and

cupped her hands over her face. She broke into a stifled cry.

Within the few seconds it took Rachel to regain control, Holly slid off the bed and embraced her tightly around the leg. Justin followed.

Rachel lifted Justin onto her lap. Summer stood rigidly to the side.

"I'm sure...Daddy...loves us," Rachel tried to answer through muted gasps. "I believe he's...just confused...right now." But even as she offered up her answer, she wondered if it was possible for Clay to truly love them, even to a minimal degree, and do the heartless and heinous thing he had done. She wanted to believe it was possible, but every feeling she possessed was screaming bitter denials.

"I want Daddy come home duhday," Justin whimpered.

Rachel reached out and ran her hand desperately through his hair. "I want him to come home today, too, honey. I want him to come home more than anything in all the world."

"Did Summer and I do something bad that made Daddy want to go away and live somewhere else?" Holly said in a whisper.

Rachel's bottom lip quivered out of control. She bit down hard on the lip until she could finally speak. "Listen to me!" she pleaded, sweeping her eyes from one child to the next. "Don't *ever* tell yourself, not for *one* moment, that Daddy went away because of you or because of something you did or did not do. You are not the reason he went away. Whatever his reason was, it had nothing to do with any of you."

Holly's sadness turned into a soft cry. She put her small arms around Rachel's neck and pulled herself into a protective clutch.

Rachel was pulled forward. With her head leaning between

Justin's and Holly's, she closed her eyes and started to sob. "All of you are a gift from God. Don't ever, *ever* forget that."

After a few seconds of purging her tears, Rachel looked up to beckon Summer.

But Summer was no longer in the room.

"Let me key in your account number, and I'll check for you," the bank teller replied across the counter with a smile. The lady, one who had helped Rachel many times before, focused on Rachel's bankcard and started punching number keys at the computer.

Rachel, standing alone at the high golden-oak counter, tried with great effort to conceal her trepidation. Needing a reason, any reason, to be by herself for a while, she had decided to make the present inquiry based on a question Bengt had asked her over the phone yesterday evening.

As she waited for the teller to pull up the requested information, she tried to resist fidgeting with her hands.

In less than a minute, which seemed an arduous wait, Rachel watched the teller write a number on a piece of scratch paper and place it on the counter. "This is the balance that's showing in the account," she announced.

Rachel scrutinized the number as she picked up the paper. "Thanks," she said. She stuffed the paper into her purse and wove her way through six or seven waiting customers and left the premises.

Rachel walked two blocks to a small city plaza and sat on a concrete bench facing a graffiti-covered statue fountain. She pulled from her purse the bank teller's note, along with the checkbooks for their Swedish and American bank accounts and their family's credit cards.

Rachel looked again at the balance written on the piece of paper from the bank: 16,126 Swedish kronor, approximately 2,635 U.S. dollars.

Rachel then took the Swedish checkbook and turned to the balance page. The latest recorded balance, in Clay's handwriting, was...the same. The last transactions in the account had all been made on the same day over two weeks ago, on May 2, three days before Clay vanished.

After transferring money into the Swedish account from the States, Clay, as usual, had written a check to pay their monthly rent. He had written another check to pay a phone bill and another check for 2,500 kronor cash.

The 2,500 was stashed away at the house. Rachel purchased groceries, postage stamps, and miscellaneous items from this monthly cash budget.

Rachel looked from the balance column to the check-number column. The number of the last check used, for the 2,500 cash withdrawal, had been noted. She flipped to the unused checks. No checks were missing. All previous checks for the last two months were accounted for. The same was true for the American checkbook. And she was holding the only two credit cards she and Clay possessed.

She could come to only one conclusion: Clay had left without taking any money.

For some reason, she started crying.

Was such a selfless decision on Clay's part an amends for shameful guilt? A final apology? Or was it the mark of his residual and struggling love, a love whose deep commitment of the past had protected and nurtured her as a woman for thirteen irreplaceable years? Or was the money simply needless to him, since his mistress was reputedly wealthy enough to take care of them both?

The checkbook slipped from her hand into her lap as her thoughts took her hostage.

Did leaving with no money imply intentions of an imminent return? Or no return?

She buckled over and threw her hands across her face.

Had she been such a disappointment to him that he hadn't even been able to leave a farewell note to explain what he was doing...or why? In the name of reason, what had been going through his mind? Didn't he realize the unbearable pain he was inflicting? Didn't he even care?

She dug the toe of her shoes into the asphalt. For the first time in her life, she felt hatred rise out of her heart toward him.

"Is there anything we can do as a church to convince you to stay?" Eric questioned Rachel earnestly. He, Rachel, and Lena were sitting in plastic chairs on Rachel's back porch, taking advantage of an early afternoon breeze. "I'm sure the congregation would stand behind any recommendation the board of elders put before them." His eye contact with Rachel was intense. He and Lena had spent the last half-hour brainstorming out loud for housing and financial options that could be implemented if Rachel chose to remain in Stockholm.

The weight of the decision had pushed Rachel to the depths of exhaustion. She sighed miserably.

Even if Eric and the church staff could quickly find another house for the interim pastor and his family, Rachel felt it would be an extreme risk, both financially and politically, for her to stay put.

First would be the political risk. North Metro Church of the Bible represented the core of her social and support network in the States. Even though she no longer believed in the rules that North Metro preached, North Metro was still her base of identity. It was where her roots were. She could not afford to agitate or defy Pastor Lovett in the present situation. She needed North Metro's acceptance and help, as demonstrated by Rita Holcomb, more than ever.

The financial risk would be equally undesirable. As things now stood, she was going to lose North Metro's monetary support. She would assuredly lose the income from her other supporting churches as well. Acquiring employment in Sweden to replace that income was not likely. During the last decade, she had known more than a dozen American missionaries in Sweden who had applied for work permits in order to obtain part-time employment with Swedish companies. All of them had been denied. Why should she be an exception?

Even if the Swedish congregation, as Eric was proposing, voted to support her monetarily in the event she decided to stay, could they realistically add the heavy expense to their already-pressed budget? If so, how long could they support her while she did nothing but wait? And would the interim pastor, Mr. Kendall, being a PCCGE missionary, endorse the decision or fight it?

The risks, Rachel decided, were just too many. And for naught. Even if she managed to wait in Stockholm and Clay came back, she and Clay would have to eventually return to the States for employment and for some kind of marital help.

And there was another key point that lingered above everything else: Would she be able to forgive him?

She shared her thoughts with Eric. Then added, "I know you're sincere when you say you'd try to give me all the assistance I need. That alone means more than you can imagine. But I think it's probably best for everybody involved if I simply cooperate with Pastor Lovett's decision and move back." Rachel paused and hung her head in shame. "Besides, like Bill Reese said, our ministry here is finished. There's nothing anybody can say or do that will change that."

Lena moved to Rachel's side and gently placed an arm of undying friendship around her shoulder.

The outdoor breeze died. The stillness around them was palpable. So was the pain.

That night Rachel phoned her landlord, a spry eighty-year-old man who had grown up there in the house. Rachel informed him, without explanation, that her family would not be moving back into the house after their year of furlough as originally planned.

"If things work out," she offered, "maybe the Kendalls will choose to stay longer than twelve months and will want to renew the rental contract for three or four more years."

Rachel thanked the elderly man for his past helpfulness and apologized for the abrupt change of plans.

After the call, Rachel went to the bathroom and took a couple of aspirins. She then returned to the phone and called her dad's number in Marietta, Georgia. After counting twelve or thirteen rings, she started to hang up when she heard a breathless hello on the other end.

She responded with numbed relief.

Upon hearing her greeting, her dad said, "I had just walked out the door. I'm getting ready to make a haul to Orlando. What's up?"

Rachel would have paid almost anything to hear her dad say: "I've been concerned about you. I've been wanting to call. Has Clay shown up? Is he okay? Are you receiving all the help you need from your friends?"

She sat down on the bed.

"Clay's still missing, Dad." With a faltering voice she told him how the situation had grown more complicated by the day. But even in her brokenness, it took her a while to build up to the confession, "The police investigators feel sure that he's momentarily...abandoned us."

Yet, she couldn't bring herself, no matter how hard she tried, to tell him that Clay's abandonment had been spurred by adultery.

"I think I'm going to need your help," she finally said in desperation. "The mission board is asking me to bring the children and return to the States, to wait things out over there." She added that they would be flying back in about seven weeks, the same time as their original furlough plans. "North Metro Church and Pastor Lovett will help me in the transition all they can, even try to help me find a place to stay. But I'm thinking it would be a lot easier if the children and I could just move into the house with you for a few days. Just until we know what's happening. If you think that might be okay."

"That'll be fine," he told her. "I'm hardly ever here anyway." There was no attempt to offer any emotional consolation, not even an expression of shock or surprise at what she had told him.

Rachel felt her spirits sink further. Did her dad have any desires at all to open up emotionally and was just unskilled? Or was he simply too hard-hearted to even care? If she could afford to, she would just forget him and rent an apartment on her own somewhere.

The conversation drew quickly to a close.

During the seven weeks that followed, Rachel was swept along by the momentum of the circumstances. She would never have imagined in a hundred years how the shock and humiliation of abandonment could so utterly decimate one's soul.

The ladies of the church helped her sell her furniture, helped her pack the household items she decided to ship back to the States, helped her with the children, and helped her paint a few rooms and clean the house for new occupancy.

They also brought meals to the house every day. Nevertheless, Rachel steadily lost weight, eighteen pounds at the last count.

The night before leaving Sweden, she was lying stone-faced on a borrowed air mattress and was staring at the walls of the empty master bedroom. The children were spending the night with Eric and Lena Torleif. Against everyone's wishes and offers, she was spending the night alone.

She had never cried as much in her entire life as she had cried during the last three hours. She had let the river of tears flow undisturbed down her face. Her pillow was soaked. So was the T-shirt she was wearing.

Even now, though her eyes were drained, her soul was still mourning.

It was one o'clock. Moonlight streamed through the open window. The sun, just barely below the horizon, would within the next two hours begin to spread its mellow rays over the city.

Rachel rolled to her side. She couldn't stop the onslaught of memories.

In her right hand she held a small charm attached to a gold necklace around her neck. The masculine necklace was one that Clay had bought for himself two years ago. The handcrafted charm was a helmeted Viking warrior, wielding sword and shield.

The necklace was the first and only one Clay had ever owned. He had been drawn to it in a jewelry shop one afternoon, primarily because of the unique charm. From the time of purchase, he had worn it regularly, always under his shirt, as a "symbol of the Christian's lifelong battle for truth and rightness."

On the day he first placed it around his neck, he told her that the charm was going to be a personal reminder for him to be a spiritual fighter and to never lose his heart for God.

Rachel realized now that he was involved with the other woman at the time and that the necklace must have been a reflection of his conscientious struggle to say no to the clandestine escapades.

She found the necklace three weeks ago, just before having a "walk-through" furniture sale in their home. She had pulled Clay's chest of drawers out from the wall to wipe off its rear panel. There behind the chest she spotted the gold chain at the baseboard.

Ever since, she had been drilling herself with the same questions. Had Clay removed the necklace with the intention of never wearing it again, dropping it purposely behind the chest as a sign of defeat? Or had it been accidentally knocked off the chest and Clay had been unable to locate it?

She wanted to believe the latter. She wanted to believe his heart was still trying to fight for his God and his family. She wanted to believe he would be coming back to her.

She closed her eyes and squeezed the small Viking warrior in her palm.

Her love for her husband was deep. But so now was her bitterness. How could she ever forgive him for what he had done? How was it possible that he could have chosen to be so heartless? To be such a deceiver? Such a betrayer?

She reached around her neck and unlatched the necklace. She gathered it in her open palm and stared at its dark outline in the moonlight. As she gazed at it, powerful memories continued to surge relentlessly through her head. Sucked to the bottom of another emotional wave, she clutched the necklace in her fist. Cocking her arm, she started to hurl the little Viking, with all of its symbolism, against the wall. But with her hand hoisted in the air, an explosion of maddening guilt ravaged her. Her raised arm slowly descended, quivering.

The reason for the betrayal couldn't be just one-sided. It just wasn't conceivable. She had to be partially at fault. She had failed Clay somehow. It had to be.

But how? Why hadn't Clay attempted to spell it out for her?

Did she at some point stop satisfying him visually? Or physically? Did she not perform sexually according to some secret desire he possessed? Did she fail to uphold him emotionally? Did she not tell him often enough how great he was, or how much she loved and valued him? Was she too much of a disappointment recreationally? Socially? As a mother? Did she not stimulate his intellect? Was her support as a pastor's wife insufficient?

She pulled the fisted necklace to her chest. "If you had just told me what it was!" she screamed, bursting into a tearless cry. "Was I, at least, not worth that much?"

Drawing air through a raw throat and watery nose, she rolled onto her back and screamed the same question at God. If He cared as much about her marriage as He was supposed to, then why hadn't He revealed to her where she had been failing as a help-meet? Would that have been too much to expect from a loving God? Would it have been too much of a demand on His busy schedule, on His omnipotence?

For weeks, the endless questions had played havoc with her sanity. They had stalked her like devouring beasts. They were now louder and more frightening than ever. Still looming, still unanswered, raping her soul pitilessly on this eve of her departure. She honestly didn't know how much longer she could survive.

She threw her arms to her side and screamed again. Her body contracted into a rigid fetal position. Her moans continued through untracked time. Then faded. Until, from sheer exhaustion, she finally fell asleep.

Her sense of urgency awakened her about three hours later. Sunrise was already well under way.

She and the kids were scheduled to board their plane at 7:00 A.M. They would fly SAS Airlines nonstop to New York City. There they would change airlines for the final leg of their journey to Atlanta. The full trip, including the three-hour layover at JFK International Airport, would take approximately fourteen hours.

She got off the air mattress and folded the tear-stained sheets. Eric and Lena, who were temporarily holding one of the house keys until the interim pastor and his family arrived next week, would come by later in the morning to collect the sheets, the mattress, and the few other items she had borrowed.

As she dizzily made her way toward the shower, she thought about her own household goods: four bicycles; a cherished secretary made of Scandinavian pine; and sixty-two cardboard boxes filled with clothes, toys, dishes, kitchenware, pictures, whatnots, books, and linens. Packed into a wooden crate with the help of Bengt, Sten, and some of the other men, it sailed from the Stockholm harbor eight days ago. If everything was going according to plan, it would now be more than halfway across the Atlantic on its way to a receiving dock in Charleston, South Carolina.

Everything else she and Clay had collected through the years, including all their furniture and 220-volt appliances, had either been sold or given away. The money she had earned—equivalent to 4,800 U.S. dollars—would help furnish an apartment in Atlanta when the need arose.

Bengt, however, was keeping the 1981 Volvo station wagon for her. To sell it had been a part of Clay's original furlough plan, so that's what she had attempted to do, until she learned that Clay's name was the only name on the title. She discovered that the complications of legally selling the car without Clay's signature would not be quickly resolved.

To help her out, the church voted unanimously to "buy" the car without official papers for 4,000 U.S. dollars. Bengt would keep the car in his garage. If Clay showed up within the next month or two, the church would return the car to him. If he didn't turn up within that time, Bengt would work through the necessary legalities to have the title transferred to the church, and the church would sell the car on the open market. If the car sold for more than 4,000 U.S. dollars, everything above that amount would be wired to Rachel's bank account in the States.

As Rachel stepped into the tub and closed the shower curtain, she tried not to dwell on the fact that this would be her last shower in this tub. At this address. In Sweden.

Oh, the memories. Nine years' worth! Fresh tears crested her lower eyelashes as she turned on the faucet.

As hot water sprayed her body, she bathed herself and forced her brain to concentrate on her last-minute checklist. All the funds in their Swedish bank account had been withdrawn and exchanged for dollars. She couldn't officially close the account without Clay's signature. All their Swedish bills, including the telephone and utilities, had been paid in full. Their health, automobile, and house insurance, along with their telephone and electric service, had all been terminated. The inside of the house had been thoroughly cleaned, thanks to Rita Holcomb, who had stayed in the country until two weeks ago, and to numerous volunteers from the church. She and the kids were registered out of the country. Their suitcases were packed, along with tickets, passports, and money. They had said their good-byes to the church congregation and their closest friends at a farewell fellowship two nights ago.

She rinsed the soap from her body and slowly turned off the water. She stared awkwardly around the tub, down at her feet, and at the flowery shower curtain she had sewn by hand a little over a year ago. She leaned into the corner of the wall, pressing her hands and forehead against the light blue tiles.

It took several minutes for her to pull herself away. Trying to conquer the emptiness, she finally got out of the tub, dried herself with a borrowed towel, and dressed.

◆   ◆   ◆

The numerous travelers scattered throughout the Arlanda International Airport were bustling around in early morning quietness.

Rachel headed toward her gate, accompanied by Eric and Lena, who were helping with the children and carry-on luggage. Rachel held Holly's hand and carried a large shoulder purse. Just minutes ago, she had relinquished seven bulging suitcases to the personnel behind the check-in counter.

Lena carried Justin in her arms.

Eric, leading the way, pushed a baggage cart bearing three child-sized backpacks filled to capacity and a small suitcase. Summer walked reluctantly at Eric's side.

Operating on motor skills alone, Rachel was suddenly taken by surprise when she looked ahead and saw a group of thirty or more people from the church standing at her departure gate.

Continuing to put one foot in front of the other, she choked up as Bengt stepped out from the crowd and invited her into his arms, followed by Merlene, Ingela, Sten, two of the church elders, and others.

As she walked first into Bengt's embrace, she felt her soul wanting to go limp, wanting to collapse and rest in the arms of her friends. Their demonstration of love was overwhelming.

For the dozenth time in the last couple of weeks, she wondered if moving back to America was the right decision. As one person after another tearfully hugged and encouraged her, she realized that since Clay's disappearance her Christian brothers and sisters here in Sweden had treated her with nothing less than dignity and understanding. To the contrary, Dr. Ed Brighton, the mission board, and Pastor Bill Reese were continuing to treat her with cold disfavor, as if she were the carrier of a defiant disease that might threaten the welfare of their entire denomination. Even Pastor Lovett in recent weeks had seemed purposely distant. The only person from her stateside camp who had shown her any real affirmation was Rita Holcomb.

Rachel didn't understand. Why were the Swedes treating her better than her own countrymen? Why were they more accepting and less reactionary? Why were they virtually without offense? Was it because of their society's notorious liberal thinking and propensity toward tolerance? Or did it have something to do with true spirituality and genuine love?

A female voice over the loudspeaker announced that the flight gate was now open for boarding.

Rachel wanted to change her mind about leaving. But, for every reason she could think of, it was already too late. Within a few minutes, all the hugs and good-byes were over, for both her and the children.

All the other passengers were filing into the jetway. Summer, Holly, and Justin, assisted by some of the ladies, tearfully slipped on their backpacks and prepared to board.

Rachel picked up her small suitcase. Was she in a nightmare? Would she wake up in a few minutes? As she faced her dearest friends and tried to wave a final good-bye, she noticed through glazed eyes a blurry but colorful Viking caricature on one of the men's T-shirts. She groaned involuntarily.

She turned to face the jetway, closed her wet eyes, and reached up to touch the gold Viking charm dangling over her pounding heart. Holding on to the necklace, she slowly started walking.

For the millionth time, she directed her bitter-filled thoughts toward Clay. She wondered where he was, and what he was feeling right now.

17

Clay McCain didn't want to have to contend with his present thoughts. Not at such a peaceful and relaxing moment. But the overpowering thoughts, like the undertow of a storm-driven surf, churned him helplessly in their grasp.

From his reclined position at the edge of the private pool, he looked down across the hard, stunted shrubs and white, sandy beach out into the blue waters of the Mediterranean. The sun, noon high, was blistering the Spanish island with its golden rays.

Having just been in the pool to cool off, he was letting his tanned skin dry beneath the smoldering sun as he waited for Anika to return from the kitchen with sandwiches and Cokes.

He ran his hand through his sandy blond hair, now sun bleached, then shook his head, slinging water in all directions.

He looked toward the back of the large stucco house, toward the open backdoor that provided a clear view into the kitchen. He saw that Anika was still preparing their lunch.

He turned and once again focused on the one-meter-high concrete block wall separating the property of the house from the public throughway leading down to the beach. The image of the two native Majorcan children, both girls, seemed to remain imposed in the air along the top of the wall.

It was the girls' laughter, less than ten minutes ago, that had lured his attention. Dressed in bathing suits and carrying towels, the girls had appeared to be around six and nine years old, the same ages as Summer and Holly. The younger one had been precariously leading the way along the top of the white paint-crusted wall. The older one had been holding the younger one playfully from behind, by the shoulders.

Clay had shouted at them in English to get down.

They had both turned and, for a second, confronted him with looks of innocent hurt, then jumped off onto the rocky trail and ran off toward the beach, giggling.

The childish expressions, the spontaneous mischievousness, the limber movements, and the carefree snickering had all crystallized in his head. Except that the facial images were now those of Summer and Holly.

He continued to stare at the wall, attempting to squelch the hounding memory.

He inhaled deeply, tears quickly filling his eyes.

Standing in Justin's bedroom doorway, he stared at the blond-headed two-year old through the semidarkness of the early morning.

Rachel, Summer, and Holly were sound asleep in their rooms, oblivious to what he was about to do. So was Justin, lying diagonally across the twin bed with his tiny legs uncovered.

Lifting his pain-filled eyes from his son, he looked across the room into the pine-framed bedroom mirror. With frayed emotions, he felt his head, shoulders, and arms start to shake as he became absorbed with the shadowy image that stared back at him.

The athletic physique. The exceptional good looks that had been pointed out to him since childhood. Those physical qualities, combined with his outgoing and winsome personality, were finally going to destroy him.

He impulsively squeezed the doorframe with his right hand. How can I do this to my family? he heard his brain shout at his heart. How can I do this to my church? To my friends?

He had tried to win against the temptations. God knew he had. He had tried daily to deny this part of himself, ever since that fateful afternoon three years ago when he engaged in his first extramarital affair.

But the passion that possessed him had become too great. His will, his energy, and his strength to do what was right had all been sapped.

He tried to straighten his back as he felt his knees slowly start to buckle. He braced himself against the doorframe.

Since the beginning, he had wanted to contact his pastor and the directors of his mission board in America, rip off his mask, and cry out to them that he was struggling and needed help.

But he had kept postponing because deep in his heart he feared them. He feared the judgment and condemnation that he had repeatedly witnessed to be their never-ending approach toward anyone who was less than perfect.

To avoid being the recipient of such treatment, he had tried to work secretly through his problem. He had tried hard. With occasional victories.

But it was over, and he had lost. A once-powerful force on the side of truth and decency, he had now been totally paralyzed by sacrilege and deceit. The erosion process, like a solid clay wall slowly eaten away by the nonstop pounding of the ocean surf, had reached its lonely climax.

The remains of the strong man he used to be were now only distant memories.

Gasping, he wiped away the tears washing down his cheeks.

Riddled with the inexplicable pain of breathtaking guilt, he was drawn back to the bed. To touch his son one last time.

Moving to the bedside, he tried for the thousandth time to deny the personal and lifelong hell that his son, along with his wife and daughters, was about to enter into.

He leaned over the sleeping child and mouthed his final words in a heart-wrench-

ing whisper. "Forgive me, Justin...I...uh...I..."

He wanted to say more, but the words wouldn't come.

And then, with the last bit of goodness left in his heart, he slowly brushed the boy's blond bangs off his tiny forehead and held them to one side. As if trying to turn back the calendar, he performed what at one time had been a nightly bedtime ritual between him and his son: He kissed the soft skin above the boy's eyebrow and told him he was special.

He strained to prolong the moment. Strained to the point of physical pain. And then, like a helpless marionette suddenly manipulated by the strings of an unseen and overpowering force, he turned away and walked out of the room.

He moved silently down the wooden stairs toward the front door of the house, glimpsing sideways at the framed portrait of his family made last Christmas. The blond and brown-headed images stared back at him.

Rachel, the bride to whom he, as an innocent and naive young man, had promised his lifelong love and commitment. Summer and Holly, his cherished daughters. And Justin, his only son. All in their beds, asleep. And unaware that their lives were about to change. Forever.

A new stream of tears ran down his cheeks. He tried to counteract the thoughts of those life-sharing relationships and responsibilities and push them out of his head. Permanently. The decision had been made. For over a week.

Approaching his loaded mountain pack in the entryway of their two-story house, he used the sleeve of his leather jacket to viciously wipe the tears from his face.

Hating himself, but not finding the strength to care anymore, he swung the eighty-pound pack onto his back. With quick and jerky motions, he threaded, tightened, and buckled the straps.

When the backpack was positioned and secured, he grabbed the handle to the front door.

Then paused.

He stared at his hand clasping the metal lever. The hand was covered with sweat. He was shaking.

He fought the urge to turn around one final time and visualize the family memo-
ries that had taken place within these walls during his family's nine years in Sweden.

He closed his eyes and swallowed hard. Finally overruling the temptation, he took
a deep breath and then, with the voices of his wife and children beckoning to him
throughout the deep recesses of his mind, he opened the door to the early morning
quietness and disappeared out of their lives.

Continuing to stare at the concrete wall, Clay tried to shake the memory. But the details, as if only moments old rather than two months old, wouldn't go away. Every day since he had walked out of his home, the thought, the memory, the abandonment had stalked him like a nightmare.

He tried not to think of how Rachel and the children were now hurting. Of how their lives were completely destroyed.

As a gospel preacher for twelve years and a foreign missionary for nine, he had always loathed men in the ministry who succumbed to sexual immorality, had despised them for the massive hurt they caused. He never thought he would be among their number. With Rachel at his side, he had vowed repeatedly—both in his heart and from his pulpit—that he would never be found guilty of such a heartless sin.

And now he had committed the most hideous sex-related sin of all.

Ever since his initial affair with Anna Gessle, he had progressively and beyond his comprehension lost his heart for everything that was good. For being a husband. For being a father. For being a spiritual leader. He still didn't understand how his heart could become so base.

He was legally married to one of the most attractive, good-hearted, faithful, and loving women he had ever known. Yet, against logic, his love for her had grown cold and died. A love that at one time was so intense he had walked twenty miles, after an engine blowout along the road left his car inoperable, to keep a date with her. She was still the same fun-loving and wholesome woman to whom he had said "I do" thirteen years ago. She had not changed. She had not given him any reason or excuse for what he had done.

He was the guilty one. He was the one who had changed. Had he simply become too bored with that which was familiar, lured by the carefree lifestyle of the beautiful and lustful Swedes and their liberal culture? Had he fallen to the bottom due to an unchecked midlife crisis? Was it because he had become spiritually fatigued after living a disciplined and pure life for the last seventeen years and, thus, found it somehow enticing to revert to the unregulated lifestyle of his pre-Christian years?

Or was it due solely to the depravity of his human heart? Or a lethal combination of all four reasons, or perhaps some cause not yet contemplated? He was convinced he would never know the answer and that it wouldn't make a difference now even if he did.

"What are you looking at, Mr. McCain?" Anika's voice suddenly split the air with lightheartedness. She was moving toward him, carrying a tray loaded with open-face egg-and-cheese sandwiches, along with salads, drinks, and cookies.

Clay quickly turned to face her. "Uh…nothing in particular. I was just…enjoying the sun on my face, Miss Wiberg." He forced a smile as he sat up and helped her place the tray onto the umbrella-covered table at his side. "Yum, looks good," he added.

Anika, standing there in her gold bikini, eyed him seriously as if she were going to accuse him of changing the subject. But suddenly, she broke into one of her magnificent smiles and said, "The food? Or me?"

Clay chuckled in relief. Impulsively, he pulled her into his lap. The touch, feel, and smell of her long dark silky hair mesmerized him without fail. So did the feel of her body.

He pulled aside her hair and kissed her on the neck. "Why don't I just say that I'd prefer to try the sandwiches after they sit a while."

"You do, huh?" Anika responded, kissing him on the forehead. "Well, in that case, I think you'd better get up and take me into the house."

In one strong, fluid movement, Clay gripped her securely in his arms, stood to his feet, and headed toward the dwelling. As he maneuvered around the corner of the pool, he glanced one more time at the concrete wall. And one more time he tried in vain not to think about his atrocity.

As he stepped into the shade of the stucco house, he wondered for the first time since leaving Stockholm if Rachel and the children could ever forgive him, should he decide to go back.

 **PART 2**

WINTER AND SPRING 1990

18

Listen to me, people!" the fifty-year-old, partially bald evangelist shouted. "I don't care if you're the president of a local bank or a carpenter or a schoolteacher; if you don't accept what I'm telling you this evening, you're going to be completely *ineffective* as a Christian! Do you *hear* me?"

The man paused, pulled a white handkerchief from his suit pocket, and wiped his brow.

"God pity your soul if you don't." He groaned and, with his free hand, lifted his sermon notes into the air. "I hope you understand that God is going to use this message to *judge* you. He's going to hold you accountable for what you're hearing tonight.

"So what are you going to do? Are you going to develop some spiritual fortitude and decide to be holy? And please Him? Or are you going to spit in His face and play the fool by deciding that holiness is not a relevant issue in this day and age, by thinking that you can merrily go your way disobeying His commands without invoking His wrath?"

He returned his notes to the podium and once more wiped his forehead. Then explosively shouted again, "This is not a game, folks! This is..."

Sitting twelve pews from the front, in the Saturday night revival meeting crowd of eight hundred people at North Metro, Rachel was sure she could see the veins protruding from the evangelist's neck.

She squirmed restlessly. After four consecutive nights of meetings, the man's constant shouting—like Pastor Lovett's and every other preacher's in this denomination that she was familiar with—had become unnerving. In years past, she had enjoyed this style of preaching. But in the last seven months, it had become overbearing, almost insufferable. Feeling nauseated, she wanted to stand up and leave.

After working eight tedious hours a day this week at her job as a bank proof-operator, plus cooking, washing, and trying to give each of her children what time she had left, she didn't even know why she was here. Except that Pastor Lovett, who had become more intimidating to her by the month, had told her he expected her to be present in every service.

But why did she even care? She was hurting so deeply that she was sure nothing would ever again make any sense. Not life. Not church. Not her Christianity. Not even God. Christianity, with its flagrant promises of "rightful guidance," "progressive sanctification," and "bonding brotherhood," had come to seem like a monstrous hoax.

Rachel flinched as the wooden podium suddenly cracked beneath the evangelist's pounding fist.

"I can't believe how some of you are sitting here with such nonchalant looks on your faces!" he yelled. *"Especially* some of you teenagers."* He pointed to a large group of high schoolers sitting together, midway to the back. People throughout the auditorium turned and looked.

The evangelist continued to stare at the youngsters. "I don't believe you're hearing a *thing* God's trying to convey to you tonight! Is that because you're deaf? Ignorant? Or is it maybe because you're fooling yourselves and you're not really Christians at all?

"Is that too tough for you? Well, let me really get tough then!" He loosened his tie and picked up his leather-bound Bible. "If you don't have an automatic inclination toward holiness and purity," he proclaimed in the direction of the teenagers, vigorously waving the Bible in the air, "then don't for *one moment* even *think* you're a Christian! Because *you're not!*"

He lowered his voice. "Shall I make it even plainer? All right, I'll make it real plain," he announced, as if the majority of the teens nodded eager consent. "If any of you young men ever find yourself alone with a young lady in the backseat of a car and cannot and will not say no to devouring her as if she were a free piece of candy, then don't shame the name of God by calling yourself a Christian! Because you will be lying, both to yourself and to God! And if you, young ladies, allow yourself to be put into that kind of situation and encourage the guys with little or no resistance, then you're equally deceived.

"Real Christians, my friends, will not permit that kind of unholy behavior! Why? Because they're motivated by God's Spirit to…"

Rachel dropped her head and inwardly groaned. She couldn't believe what she was hearing. Propelled by seven months of suppressed anger, bitterness, and disillusionment, she fantasized about jumping up, throwing one of the thick green hymnals at the man, and calling him a pompous idiot, then marching out of the church to never come back.

She quickly thought that maybe she should just throw a hymnal at the whole crowd!

Since she had returned to Georgia, the entire North Metro congregation, with the sole exception of John and Rita Holcomb, had treated her as if she were a discarded mannequin, a lifeless, worthless, unneeded piece of refuse. Even Pastor Lovett had grown more distant toward her. Except in his "official" role of spiritual potentate.

She did not understand how the North Metro people could treat her this way. One of their own. One who needed love and help more now than she had ever needed it in her life.

Apart from Rita and John Holcomb's regular inquiries about her and the children's welfare and about the latest news from the Swedish police—Rita did baby-sit for her sometimes as well—not a single person had attempted to encourage her. No phone calls. No visits. No heart-to-heart conversations. No fellowship. Only an occasional stiff and condescending nod to acknowledge her presence.

It was as if she had single-handedly betrayed the congregation and as if they, in return, had placed her in social quarantine and declared her off-limits. There had been no one with whom she had even been able to share the exasperation of her and the children's reverse culture shock.

As the evangelist shouted his way to the conclusion of his sermon, Rachel's anger-induced thoughts replayed other ways North Metro had contributed to her disillusionment.

Three weeks after returning to the States, she received the message via pastoral letters from her supporting churches that due to her family's "moral travesty" and "forced resignation from the mission board," all of her and Clay's monthly support would be immediately terminated.

Out of desperation, she responded shortly thereafter to an announcement that the church was looking for a new, full-time secretary. Upon applying for the job, she discovered that she was one of only two ladies in the church who pursued the position. The other applicant, a Mrs. Esther Chamblee in her midforties, had only a high-school education, had no children, and was supported by a husband who had worked for nearly twenty years as a well-paid electrician.

Rachel was sure, considering her dire circumstances, that Pastor Lovett would give her the job.

He didn't. Instead, he rebuffed her during the interview.

"What you need, regarding your relationship to the church," he told her firmly from behind his desk, "is to sit passively in all the meetings for an indefinite period of time and try to heal. So I've decided to give the secretarial job to Mrs. Chamblee. Besides, it will be better for the testimony of Christ if, as soon as possible, you start supporting your family through a nonchurch-related job." He explained that North Metro would continue to give her their normal missions support for another three months to help her make the transition. After that time, the monetary support would be canceled.

"As an extra affirmation of our concern," he added with little emotion, "we'll let your children attend the school here for the next year without payment, based on the absolute understanding that you're willing to conform to the standards of both the church and the school."

Founded twenty-six years ago by North Metro's former pastor, Reverend Jason Faircloth, the school was one of the church's most recognized ministries.

Rachel agreed to the school offer. To do so had at the time seemed the safest and simplest decision regarding her children's education. To place the kids in an educational environment where they were known, she reasoned, would be worth making a few changes in their family's outward appearances: knee-length dresses for herself and the girls when attending school and church, a short and tapered haircut for Justin, and a King James Version of the Bible for each of them.

The decision required the purchase of new wardrobes and Bibles, but those expenses equated to only one month's tuition at the school for three children.

She had since convinced herself, however, that Pastor Lovett's gratuitous decision concerning the free schooling had been for no other reason than to bring her and the children back into conformity with the church's long list of dos and don'ts.

In the same conversation, Pastor Lovett had made clear his grave disappointment in her family's loss of convictions while living in Sweden. "The pants, the pop music, your associations with people of liberal denominations that you've told me about were all a blatant disregard for Christian standards," he expressed sharply. "And don't think for one minute that those compromises, and the patterns of behavior they created, didn't seriously contribute to your family's moral breakdown."

A week after he denied her the secretarial job, he wouldn't even give her a "pastoral recommendation" needed to secure a teaching position at a neighboring Christian elementary school.

On her own, she finally found the proof-operator job at a local bank. The salary was not substantial, but it was enough to put food on the table and pay the rent on her frugally furnished three-bedroom apartment.

Rachel looked down at the King James Version now lying open

across her burgundy knee-length cotton skirt. She thought about Summer, Holly, and Justin, who were attending the children's church service in the main annex building. She thought about their hardships as a family and about the changes that had been forced on them in order to be "spiritual."

Rachel pulled a facial tissue from her purse.

She had adhered to the church's expectations and had sat passively, and alone, for nearly seven months. She had been present for nearly every service—Sunday morning, Sunday night, and Wednesday night. Still, she wasn't healing. Neither were Summer, Holly, and Justin. The whole situation, especially regarding Pastor Lovett, had left her disillusioned and resentful.

She used the tissue to dab moisture from her eyes.

She and the kids needed love and friends, not stupid and irrelevant "religious" rules! Couldn't anybody understand that?

The evangelist, lowering his voice a few decibels, suddenly asked everyone to stand for a public altar call.

The pianist, organist, and music director quickly moved into place. Pastor Lovett and Pastor Reese stepped down from the platform, where they had been sitting, and stood at the head of the red carpeted auditorium to pray and counsel with those who would come forward.

As Rachel closed her Bible and stood with the crowd, her anger faded into a hopeless depression. She regretted that she had ever left her friends and church in Sweden. Leaving them, she believed now, had been her greatest mistake. For both her and the children.

She opened a hymnal to the announced hymn of invitation. When everyone started singing, she let her hymnal droop to her side. Her heart felt heavy enough to crush her. She didn't know how much more of the isolation she could tolerate.

She sat back down on the edge of her pew and propped her arms and head, facedown, on the back of the pew in front of her.

Swallowed up in her pain, she lost track of her surroundings till someone called her by name and tapped her on the shoulder. She sniffled, looked up, and saw Pastor Reese standing at her side. Everyone else, she noticed, was mingling around. The crowd had been dismissed.

Bill Reese eyed her autocratically and said, "Pastor Lovett wants to meet with you in his office tomorrow evening, about twenty minutes before the service. There's something he needs to talk with you about." He started to walk away, then stopped. As if trying to simulate concern, he turned and asked, "Has the Swedish congregation still not heard anything from him?"

Rachel shook her head and whispered no. She didn't say it, but she was certain now that Clay's abandonment was permanent, that none of them would ever hear from him or see him again.

Bill Reese left her without saying anything further.

As Rachel retrieved her children in the cold night air and drove through the winter darkness toward home, she wondered for the first time if family suicide would be a welcome escape for them all.

19

At 6:35 the next evening, Rachel escorted Summer, Holly, and Justin to their regular Sunday evening classrooms at the North Metro Church of the Bible complex. A light rain, mixed with some sleet, was falling.

At 6:40, Rachel stood outside Pastor Lovett's office door trying unsuccessfully to control her nervousness. Though she had searched her brain exhaustively, she had no idea why Pastor Lovett had requested the appointment. She was trying to be optimistic.

She smoothed out her dress and knocked. On each side of the office door was a floor-to-ceiling smoked-glass panel. Through the glass, Rachel saw a blurry image move toward the door.

She was surprised when Bill Reese opened the door, looking extremely businesslike. He nodded for her to come in.

Rachel saw Pastor Lovett across the room, sitting behind his desk in his high-backed chair. She saw a third man sitting on the couch along the wall perpendicular to Pastor Lovett's desk. The man was Ronnie Johnson, one of North Metro's longtime and outspoken deacons.

Rachel felt disconcerted and knew that her face showed it.

"Good evening, Rachel," Pastor Lovett said, rising to his feet. Ronnie Johnson likewise stood. Pastor Lovett motioned with his hand toward a cushioned chair in front of his desk. "Have a seat," he said.

Rachel wondered if the three men could hear her heart thumping as she walked across the room and sat down.

Except for a few coats of paint, the room had changed little during the last seventeen years. Two of the four walls were covered with walnut bookshelves. The three or four shelves that weren't filled with theology books displayed family pictures, diplomas, and decorative knickknacks.

Years ago, when Rachel was new to the church, Pastor Lovett's office represented a whole new world of fascination for her. The hundreds of volumes had given the room an ambiance of specialized enlightenment. Rachel was now numb to everything in the room except the disillusioning memories the place evoked. And to the three men, dressed in conservative suits and ties, now sitting around her.

She watched as Pastor Lovett and Ronnie Johnson took their seats. Bill Reese joined Ronnie Johnson on the couch.

Rachel stared ahead at Pastor Lovett.

"Something came across my desk a couple of days ago that needs to be dealt with," Lovett announced as if his patience was pushed to the limit. "It seems that one of the ladies in the church has seen a picture of you that's quite incriminating."

Rachel almost stopped breathing.

"I'll not reveal the lady's name," Lovett proceeded, "but one of her non-Christian relatives is employed at your bank. When the two of them were together recently, the relative pulled out some pictures taken a few weeks ago at the bank's Christmas party. The church member recognized you in a couple of the photographs. She was so disturbed by what she saw that she felt obligated to report to someone in church leadership. For practical reasons, she contacted Ronnie who, in turn, has passed the report along to me. It seems, according to the photographs, that there was liquor and champagne flowing quite freely at the occasion. Is that true?"

Fragments of the evening's memories flashed into Rachel's head. She hung her head like a tired fighter as she groped for a response.

"I won't deny that," she uttered slowly, her heart racing.

"Do you drink, Rachel?" Lovett asked tersely.

Rachel felt anger intermix with her hurt. "The only alcohol that has ever touched my lips is wine. On three, maybe four occasions in Europe I took a couple of sips. Nothing more."

"Are you saying you believe God supports occasional or social drinking, then?"

"I believe He's against drunkenness," she answered, trying to exhale slowly.

"That's not what I asked. I asked if you believe He supports *drinking.*"

Rachel rubbed her palm on her forehead. "I believe the Bible makes it clear that he's against *drunkenness.*" Although she wasn't looking at Bill Reese and Ronnie Johnson, she was certain she could feel their heated stares.

Lovett shook his head. "When you and Clay left here to move to Sweden nine years ago, Rachel, you were some of the strongest Christian young people I'd ever known. I never thought I would see the day when either of you would be deceived into surrendering your God-honoring and Bible-based values to such an openly sinful society as Sweden's.

"And now," he emphasized with disbelief, "on top of your blatant compromises in the areas of clothes, music, and ecclesiastical associations, you're participating in pagan parties where the devil is destroying lives with booze. And you don't even think it's wrong!"

Lovett leaned forward over his desk. "I believe you need to know and hear it said, Rachel, that somewhere along the way you've failed. Instead of influencing and changing the Swedish culture like you and Clay were sent out to do, you both let the culture, with all of its blatant ungodliness, influence and change you."

Lovett leaned back to an upright position. "I care about you, Rachel, and I care about your family. Despite the fact that you're no longer an active missionary, I'm mercifully letting your children attend the school and the after-school day care program free of charge. But I explained to you from the start that you would be held accountable for submitting to the standards of both the school and the church. And in case you don't remember, we at North Metro Church of the Bible believe that the consumption of alcohol, or any kind of association with it, is a transgression against almighty God."

Lovett looked at his watch. "Even though I care about you, Rachel, I care equally about the testimony of this church. And I will not stand by and allow this church's reputation to be ruined because of its generosity to a former missionary who is living in opposition to our convictions.

"Consider this to be your last warning. If there's one more violation of any kind, then our mercy comes to an end. At that point, your children's free tuition will be terminated. Is that clear?"

Rachel managed, just barely, to nod.

Pastor Lovett looked toward the other two men. His face had

the appearance of chiseled consternation. "Bill, do you or Ronnie feel a need to add anything? If not, we three need to pray together before the service starts."

Both men shook their heads no.

Rachel was promptly dismissed.

The next morning at work, Rachel was still reeling from the humiliating treatment she received from Pastor Lovett fourteen hours earlier.

Sitting in her second-floor bank office at her proof machine, surrounded by nine other operators, she picked up a customer check made out for $53.27. She keyed in the amount of the check on her numbered keyboard and punched the debit key. She then dropped the check into the document-entry area, where it was encoded and conveyed to the machine pocket.

She felt hatred overtaking her heart. Hatred for Pastor Lovett. For Pastor Reese. For the deacons. For the whole church.

Would she—could she—keep passively concurring with their rules and attitudes while continuing to be treated like a spiritual leper?

She thought of Summer, Holly, and Justin. They were just now, after seven months in the States, showing minute signs of adjusting to the North Metro school, their teachers, and their classmates. Could they survive the upheaval of transferring to a different school and starting over again?

The journal printer on her proof machine printed a notification, signaled by a beep, to let her know the item-count pocket was full.

Feeling as if her heart were literally going to explode, Rachel tore off the twenty or so pages of proof tape and emptied the machine pocket of its checks. She then placed the bundle of proofed checks, along with the proof tape, in the wire basket atop the machine.

She hung her head and closed her eyes. She then pushed herself from the machine, grabbed her purse from the floor, and moved directly to the ladies' rest room and hid inside a stall. She leaned against one of the partitions, feeling pressure building painfully in the lower part of her forehead.

She had to stay at North Metro, didn't she? She had to cooperate for the children's sake. For their stability and emotional welfare.

If she could manage to pay the school tuition on her own, she would call the church office and demand that they withdraw her church membership within the hour. And Pastor Lovett and his heartless congregation would never see her, or her children, in any of the church services again.

She pulled some tissue from the dispenser roll and wiped her nose. Placing hope in them had been a wayward fantasy. She never would have believed it was possible that one treacherous nightmare in life could be followed so quickly by another.

She opened her purse and stared at a recently bought medium-sized bottle of aspirins. More than a hundred tablets.

She thought about her Christian heritage. God, during the greatest pain of her life, was not providing her with any consolation. Neither was the Bible. Even though she had opened its pages many times out of desperation during the last several months, its words read like wasted and unproved rhetoric from an ancient grave.

It was all a beastly lie, wasn't it? A person's life unfolded by nothing more than chance, didn't it? Faith and goodness were simply illusionary supports.

She unscrewed the top of the aspirin bottle. Even her own dad, by his physical and emotional absence, had failed her during the last seven months. For someone in her situation, maybe death was truly the only consolation.

She poured a pile of aspirins into her hand. How many would it take to kill her? Sixty? Eighty? She lifted the handful of aspirins to her face and stood there staring at the tablets, mesmerized.

Seconds passed, along with the numbing silence.

"Are you planning to attend Margaret's baby shower this weekend?" a female voice suddenly resonated off the walls as the restroom door swung open.

Rachel flinched.

"I didn't know about it until yesterday," a second voice followed the first. "And I've already told Joyce I would go with her to the craft show. So…"

Rachel dumped the handful of aspirins, along with the bottle, into her purse. She flushed the toilet, then left. Back at her proof machine, she realized she was clammy with perspiration.

She looked at the wallet-sized school pictures of Summer, Holly, and Justin taped to her machine and fought back tears. She reached over and pulled a new check from her stack of work and entered it into the machine.

Grayson Cole had just finished a brief consultation with one of the other proof operators three machines away. Exiting the area, his eyes singled out Rachel.

He had been the assistant manager of the branch for less than three weeks. He had noticed Rachel the day he was introduced to the staff. Since that first day, he had wanted to talk to her one-on-one. His initial workload, however, had thus far preempted such leisure.

He noticed, as he had on a couple of other occasions, that she appeared to be deeply distracted by something.

He looked at his watch. And decided that today would be the day.

20

Two or three minutes after her lunch break started, Rachel was in her winter coat, sitting alone behind the wheel of her Toyota with the engine running. Within a week of her arrival back in the States, she had purchased the four-year-old, metallic brown car from a used-car dealer she found located five blocks from her dad's residence.

Idling the car in its parking space on the far side of the lot where all the bank employees parked, she leaned her head on the wheel and passed in and out of alertness.

She finally sat upright and tried in vain to remember the errand she needed to run.

She pulled a Kleenex from her purse and blew her nose. Wondering if the hurt in her heart would ever go away, she decided to just drive.

Before shifting the transmission into reverse, she looked at herself in the rearview mirror. Her eyes were bloodshot and pink. Her skin was pale, her cheeks sunken. She had continued to lose weight because of an almost nonexistent appetite. No longer motivated to keep up her "attractive" appearance, she had even cut her shoulder-length wheat blond hair into a short wash-and-go style. Her hair looked greasy.

She was lost in her feelings of self-deprecation when a knock on the driver-side window startled her.

A female coworker stood outside the car door. Wearily, Rachel lowered the window.

"Rachel, I'm sorry to bother you," the lady said, her breath visible in the cold January air. "But Mr. Cole sent me out to tell you that he needs to see you in his office before you get away for lunch."

Mr. Grayson Cole had been transferred to their branch from one of the bank's branches in Savannah, on the Georgia coast. He had formally introduced himself to Rachel and all the other employees on his first day at the bank, about three weeks ago. Rachel had not spoken with him since. There had been neither the occasion nor the need.

"Okay, thanks."

Not wearing a coat, the lady excused herself and hurried back inside.

As Rachel got out of the car, she started to worry. She assumed she was going to be reprimanded for some kind of oversight or failure in her work.

As she covered the breadth of the parking lot and went back into the building, she tried to convince herself to be brave. She walked past the tellers and the crowd of customers directly to Mr. Grayson Cole's small glass-walled office, and knocked.

Mr. Cole waved her in as he finished a phone call.

Rachel entered the gray-carpeted room. Silver-framed abstract paintings hung on the one and only wall that was not glass. Grayson Cole, with his stocky and medium-sized frame, motioned for her to take the seat in front of his desk. By the time Rachel sat, Grayson had concluded his phone conversation and was hanging up.

"Excuse me, Rachel, for intruding into your lunch hour," he announced as he rose to his feet and leaned over the desk to shake her hand, "but I would like to talk with you for a few minutes." His voice sounded smooth and professional. His thick black hair was stylishly cut.

"All right," she answered, trying to appear at ease.

Grayson sat back down. "How long have you been working here as a proof operator?"

"For only about six months."

Grayson leaned back in his chair and relaxed. "Please don't jump to any conclusions about what I'm going to say, but I've noticed for a week or so now, according to the department log, that your volume of work is consistently, and sometimes substantially, outpaced by all the other operators in your department. As you can probably understand, this is a concern to management."

Grayson paused as if his statement had been posed as a question.

When Rachel didn't respond, Grayson continued. "I wonder if this is something you would care to talk about? I mean you don't appear to be the kind of person who's lazy or incapable of being competitive with the other ladies. I'm assuming, therefore, that something's distracting you and making it difficult for you to concentrate.

"Again, please don't misunderstand. This is not a rebuke. Your employment here at the bank is not in jeopardy; it's just that I would like to offer my help. I would like to make your job a little easier or a little more comfortable for you if I can. If you're being distracted by something inside the office, such as the seating arrangement or the lighting, then I'll do what I can to make some changes."

In spite of Grayson Cole's effort to be congenial, Rachel still felt the sting of reprimand. She understood, however, that his remarks about her job performance were true. She did lack competitive zeal. That had been true since day one. But no one in management had highlighted it as a problem. Until this moment. Why now?

Didn't it count that she had not failed once to accomplish her daily quota? What was she supposed to do? Check her broken heart in at the door every morning, forget about it for eight or nine hours while she focused on setting speed records at the proof encoder, then reclaim it again on her way out? And what could Mr. Cole do? Wave a magic wand over her head and make all of her pain just disappear?

She wanted to scream at him and inform him that in light of her circumstances she was performing the best she could.

But she also wanted to keep her job. She couldn't afford to be out of work for even a few days.

"I'll...uh...try to be more focused," she finally uttered.

"You didn't say if there's anything I can do to help."

Rachel closed her eyes and softly shook her head. "The seating...the lighting, they're not a problem."

"But there is a problem of some kind, isn't there?"

Rachel hung her head. "Things in my life are just a little tough right now, that's all."

Mr. Cole sat quietly for a moment. "You're not being abused or anything like that are you, Rachel?"

Rachel winced as if a rock had struck her. "I...uh...no, I mean..."

Mr. Cole leaned slightly forward in his seat. He waited.

Rachel eventually declared, "My husband is *not here* to abuse me. He walked out on my children and me nine months ago when we were living overseas. He left us for someone else. As you can understand, this has made my life somewhat complicated. This is the problem I'm struggling with. It's difficult right now to concentrate on anything else." She had not shared these facts with a stranger before. She revealed them now only to clarify her dilemma.

"I'm assuming you're receiving some kind of moral support to help you through this?"

Rachel spoke barely above a whisper. "To be honest with you, no, I'm not."

"You sound as if you've somehow been isolated."

Rachel looked down at the floor. "Maybe I have."

"Are you telling me that all of your friends are leaving you alone to fend for yourself?"

"I'm not sure I have friends anymore. Not here in Atlanta, anyway."

Mr. Cole folded his hands together and rested them at the base of his stomach. "Have you considered sharing these things with a professional counselor?"

Pastor Lovett's warning throughout the years suddenly replayed in Rachel's head. *Psychiatric counselors, including those who practice "Christian" counseling, are repulsive humanists. They deny a personal need for God by teaching either directly or indirectly that people can heal their own hearts and minds if they can just learn to use the right mental keys. Stay away from them. They are blind leaders of the blind. They'll only make matters worse for you.*

Rachel rubbed her forehead with her fingers. "My background as a Christian has discouraged me from seeking that kind of help, but maybe that's what I need right now." Her admission of faith was only the second time at the bank that she had associated herself with Christianity. She had not talked to many of the other employees about anything, much less her faith or former missionary work. She simply reported to the bank, did her job, and went home. Her reputation of being a loner was firmly established among her colleagues.

Mr. Cole asked, "Am I being presumptuous, or is it a church that's turned its back on you?"

Rachel gave him a bewildered stare. "Yeah...that's what has happened. But how did—?"

Mr. Cole looked at his watch. "There's a story I'd like to share with you, Rachel, but I have an appointment with a customer in about five minutes, and after that I'll be busy for the rest of the day." He picked up his daily planner and turned a page. "Where will you be eating lunch tomorrow?"

She shrugged. "Uh...I...I guess at The Salad Bar, at the I-75 exit." The restaurant was located about half a mile from the bank.

"If you don't mind, I'll join you there for a few minutes at about twelve-thirty. I think you might find a little consolation in what I have to tell you."

Throughout the rest of the lunch break and the afternoon of proofing checks, Rachel experienced a slight taste of curiosity. What could Mr. Cole tell her that would give her consolation? She eventually concluded that it didn't matter. Just the fact that he had not been condescending or threatening, but rather concerned, was cause enough for an upward shift in her attitude. At least someone had made an effort, albeit minor, to reach out to her.

The minimal boost helped sustain her for a few more hours...until she stopped by the after-school day care center at

North Metro to pick up the children. There she was met in the school hallway by Mrs. Baker, one of the day-care facilitators. Mrs. Baker had Summer at her side, sternly holding her hand. Summer was staring angrily at the sky-gray linoleum floor.

Rachel noticed immediately that Summer's upper lip was swollen. She also saw the red scratch on her neck, just above her dress collar. Rachel closed her eyes, hoping that when she opened them again she would be welcomed by a more favorable sight.

Mrs. Baker signaled a greeting with the bob of her head. Her seriousness was pronounced. "I'm sorry to have to ruin your after-noon, but we've had a little problem. About forty minutes ago, Summer and Matthew Johns, one of the boys in her fourth-grade class, got into an argument. Before any of the supervisors could step in and put an end to it, Summer went into a rage and started hitting him. Matthew hit her back."

Summer was still staring downward as Rachel took her hand from Mrs. Baker.

"Both of them," Mrs. Baker continued, "were made to apolo-gize to the supervisors and to each other and were then sent to Principal Strickland's office. After talking with them, he decided to suspend them from school tomorrow. He wanted me to let you know. He also told me to remind you that if a student receives three one-day suspensions during a school year, her grade level for that year will be dropped a point. He said if you want to talk with him, he'll be in his office until six."

Rachel was repulsed at the thought of being preached to by Mr. Strickland, another of North Metro's key leaders. She decided to ignore his invitation to talk. She was convinced that nothing she could say would change his choice of punishment anyway. He was as rigid as Pastor Lovett and the rest of the North Metro chieftains.

Rachel politely thanked Mrs. Baker and led Summer by the hand down the hallway to collect Holly and Justin.

When they had taken only a few steps, Summer jerked her hand from her mom's and began to run. "I hate America!" she cried. "And I hate this school!"

Rachel started after her.

"I want to go home to Sweden and look for my daddy!" Summer's voice rang up and down the hall.

Rachel had Summer confined in her arms within seconds. Bending over, she turned her daughter's face toward hers. "I know, honey. I know you do." Her head pulsated in rapid harmony with her lungs as she tried to think of something helpful to say.

Summer laid her head hard on Rachel's shoulder. "Matthew said that Daddy is an evil man and that he hates me and you and God and everybody. And that he deserves to go to hell."

"It's okay," Rachel tried to tell her. "Everybody has his or her own opinions. But it's *your* opinion, and what you believe, that counts. You've got to understand that."

"I hate him," Summer said.

Rachel didn't know if Summer was referring to Matthew Johns or Clay. She didn't ask. And she didn't try to stifle her daughter's feelings. Instead, she put her arm around Summer's shoulders and continued down the hallway to pick up Holly and Justin.

Collecting her mail that evening, Rachel discovered amid the sweepstakes announcements and advertisement leaflets a letter from Eric Torleif.

Nowadays, the letters from cold and wintry Sweden brought the deepest warmth to her heart. She wished for the thousandth time that she had not left her beloved Scandinavian friends quite so readily.

While the kids watched television, Rachel sat at the small dining room table and opened the envelope. She slowly unfolded the letter, as if to savor the moment, and saw that it consisted of two typewritten pages.

Dear Rachel,

Greetings from Stockholm, from all your brothers and sisters who think of you often. I know that Lena and some of the other ladies in the church have written to you recently, but I felt like it was time for me to communicate with you again as well.

I wanted to let you know that Bengt finally managed to sell the Volvo. Unfortunately, he was able to sell it for only $400 more than what we gave you when you left. Tomorrow, he plans to wire the $400 to your U.S. bank account. If you haven't received the money by the time you get this letter, please let me know. We truly wish the amount could be more.

Our hearts break every time we think of the cruel and unbelievable way Pastor Lovett and his congregation have treated you. I don't understand how the man can call himself a Christian leader and then ignore, even forsake, you during this time when you have so many needs. It just doesn't make sense. In fact, it's one of the most non-Christian things I've ever heard of. I become angry every time I dwell on the matter.

Please know we are praying with all our hearts that the man will quickly see his gross misconduct. If he doesn't change soon, however, I would urge you to seek out new friends at a church where some semblance of God's love is practiced. After all, at this point what would you really be losing if you left North Metro?

Know that we love you and are praying every day that God will give you new strength, energy, and hope.

Neither we nor the police have yet heard anything, directly or indirectly, from Clay. His silence still lingers as a heavy burden for us all. Our church, in spite of diligent efforts, still hasn't recovered from the shock of it all. The healing process is much more complicated and painful than any of us ever dreamed. We can only imagine that it must be a hundred times worse for you and the children.

As we pray earnestly for you, please pray for us as well.

As Lena told you, another family—the Stenlunds—recently left the church, primarily because of disillusionment. That's now a total of seven that have left. Only two new families during this time have been added. I share this, only because I know you want to stay informed.

Pastor Kendall's dry and tactless leadership is simply not sustaining us very well. The elders have already clashed with him on two or three occasions. We are talking seriously about asking him to step aside. We are even thinking of dismantling all our associations with the PCCGE mission board due to all the philosophical differences.

Please know, however, in light of all that I'm reporting, that everyone here, both those who remain as a part of the church and those who have left, still hold you in the highest regard. You are a very, very special lady. Don't ever forget it.

Give our hugs and kisses to Summer, Holly, and Justin. Tell them I pray for them by name every single day.

We love you all.

May God somehow miraculously embrace you till you once again feel secure.

A brother who truly cares,

Eric

With tears, Rachel read the letter two more times. For several minutes afterward, she sat with the pages in her hand and tried to extract life-giving energy from Eric's spirit of love and support.

The letter rejuvenated her hate for North Metro. She wanted more than anything to break her connection with that group, as Eric suggested. Additionally, she wanted to abandon *every other* church, just as Clay—and God—had abandoned her. With her Christian beliefs now shattered, what difference would it make?

But once again, it was the children and their familiarity with North Metro School that kept her from following her urges. In spite of the incident involving Summer a few hours ago, the three children had finally adjusted to their teachers, had made a few school friends, and were showing signs of academic achievement.

If she chose to keep living, then she wanted to protect her children from any further upheaval. She couldn't justify forcing them so quickly into another stressful change.

As much as she was sickened by North Metro, she found herself willing to sacrifice her own needs and endure church-wide scorn in order to try to provide her children with an element of stability.

Having no one else to turn to for help, she called Rita Holcomb later that evening. Rita agreed to let Summer stay at her house tomorrow during Rachel's work hours.

21

Rachel was sitting alone in one of the front booths at The Salad Bar. The multilevel wooden restaurant, "the meeting place with ambiance" its sign proclaimed, was crowded to capacity, mainly with middle-aged businesspeople.

Rachel picked at the last few bites of a small tuna salad. She looked at her watch: 12:38. She wondered if Grayson Cole's request to meet her here and share his "story" had been nothing more than an overly hasty and ill-planned idea that was easily forgotten. Just as she thought of requesting her bill, she saw Mr. Cole walk through the front door, dressed in a suit and long, dark overcoat.

He quickly scanned the room. Rachel motioned with her hand when he looked in her direction.

Rachel laid down her fork as he approached the table.

"Please forgive me for running late," he said as he took off his overcoat and slipped into the booth on the opposite side of the table. "But I was tied up with a land developer borrowing a large sum of money for one of his business ventures." He reached over to shake her hand.

Rachel shook his hand, shrugging off his tardiness. "I had just finished my meal. I still have about twenty minutes before I have to be back."

Grayson looked at his watch. "Okay, I'll go ahead and talk," he said, catching his breath, "and I can order my lunch after we're finished."

Grayson looked briefly down at the table as if he needed to gather his thoughts then looked back up at Rachel. "I, of course, don't know the details of what you're going through, but it's obvious that you're hurting. Based on the little information I heard yesterday, my heart goes out to you. To some degree, I'm sure I can even empathize."

Rachel's curiosity was instantly piqued.

"A little over three years ago," Grayson emphasized, "I was the teacher of a men's Sunday school class in a small church just outside Savannah, the same church that the majority of my friends attended. My wife and I had been married sixteen years at the time. Not many of our friends knew it, but at that point our marriage was not much more than a facade. It seems that over the long haul, we had unintentionally grown cold toward one another. She blamed me, saying I was a workaholic and couldn't keep my work at the office. I felt she was at fault because she was a perfectionist and idealist, and I could never measure up to her demands. She became a habitual complainer, and I emotionally withdrew. We were staying together, it seemed, only for the sake of our two sons.

"Eventually, however, that became more than she could bear, and she started begging me for a divorce. I tried to persuade her to go to a marriage counselor with me, but she refused, saying that if I wouldn't file for a divorce, she would. So I consulted a lawyer. The man advised me strongly to go ahead and file on the grounds that my wife was verbally abusive. He claimed the court would view me as a victim and give me better visitation rights with my boys. Maybe I—"

A red-headed waitress stepped up to their booth to take Grayson's order.

"Yeah, can you bring me a large glass of sweet tea," he told her with the briefest of eye contact, "and then give me another fifteen minutes before taking my food order?" Grayson then turned to Rachel. "Is there anything else you would like?"

Rachel shook her head.

As the waitress hurried away, Grayson proceeded with his story. "As I was saying, maybe I acted too hastily, but I went ahead and filed according to the lawyer's advice. It's not really what I wanted to do, but I didn't want to lose my kids, so I did it to ensure my visitation rights. And that's when the bottom fell out. The news about our divorce quickly spread to our church and to all of our friends. My wife twisted the story, saying I was the one breaking up the marriage. Within a week's time, the pastor asked me to give up my Sunday school class. Gossip started circulating that I wanted a divorce because I was seeing another woman. Almost immediately, all of the men in the class started avoiding me, the very group of guys I had been teaching for three years. There was never one word of thanks or any kind of appreciation. I was just cut off. From there, things only got worse, until eventually almost everyone in the church, including those I thought were my best friends, stopped associating with me. To be honest with you, Rachel, I thought I was going to go crazy. The divorce, the move out of my house, the rejection by my friends just about left me devastated. That feeling of being all alone in the world nearly destroyed me." Grayson paused then asked with a bit of uncertainty, "Is any of this sounding familiar?"

To be sitting in the company of someone who had experienced a similar pain nearly brought tears to her eyes. "Yeah," Rachel sighed. "It is."

Grayson's visage suddenly showed optimism. "I thought the loss—"

"Did you stay in the church or leave?" Rachel interrupted.

"Well," he backtracked, "I became so upset and angry with the way I was treated that I left. I not only dropped out of *that* church, I dropped out of church altogether."

"And what about these days? Are you attending anywhere?" She wondered if it was possible for anyone in his shoes—or hers—to ever forgive and achieve reconciliation.

"No, I'm not. After learning to survive on my own, I never had a desire to get involved again. I just don't feel a need anymore. Actually, that's my point for wanting to tell you this story. I want you to know from someone who's been there that the human spirit is very, very strong, Rachel. Stronger than you're able to imagine right now. I just want to remind you that in spite of who, or how many, have turned their backs on you—even if it's a group of sanctimonious Christians—you're going to rebound. You're going to make it. Your life *will* eventually be stable again."

Rachel shifted her eyes from Grayson and stared across the crowded room. "There were times in my life, before Clay left me," she mumbled, "when I would have believed what you're saying. But I'm not sure what I believe…about anything anymore."

"How long were you and Clay married?" Grayson probed.

The waitress approached and placed Grayson's glass of iced tea on the table.

In that moment of distraction, Rachel looked at her watch. "Excuse me," she said to the waitress, "can you go ahead and bring my bill, please?"

Grayson reflexively checked his watch and became aware of the time situation. "That's okay," he said to the young redhead. "You can include her bill with mine; I'll take care of it."

"All right. I'll be back in a few minutes to take your order."

Rachel started to dig into her purse. "Here, let me give you some money to cover that."

"I don't want to hear any more about it; it's already settled."

Not having the desire or the energy to argue, Rachel thanked him. She then answered his question about how long she had been married and wondered out loud if maybe they could talk further.

"Yeah, of course we can." Grayson retrieved his electronic pocket-organizer from the inside pocket of his suit. "If your situation is anything like the one I was in, then you *need* to talk." With a slight pause, he keyed up his schedule for the week. "If you think it'll encourage you, I'll be glad to tell you more about my story and try to share some insights with you. Or, if you just need someone to listen while you vent your hurts and frustrations, I can do that as well." He looked at the organizer's miniature screen. "I have some available time this Friday at twelve. We can meet here again if you have that slot free."

Rachel didn't fully understand the disappointment that swept over her, but she preferred not to wait three more days to continue their talk. She seriously needed this type of honest, nonthreatening, and therapeutic exchange. She needed to hear from someone like Grayson Cole, who was intelligent and neutral, that she was indeed being treated horribly, that she was not insane, and that there was light beyond the consuming darkness. She needed to hear a sympathetic heart, in addition to her Swedish friends, articulate that what was happening to her was the height of injustice. She just needed to know that someone else, someone nearby, believed it.

But she decided not to be presumptuous and ask for an earlier meeting. If Friday at lunch was the time he was offering, then she would wait. And in the meantime, she would just be thankful that he was even willing to reach out to her at all.

"I'll plan to be here," she told him. She knew she would not need a reminder, but she made a written note of the appointment anyway.

On the way back to work, she felt a little less depressed. At least she now had something to look forward to over the next few days.

Waiting on the chicken salad he'd ordered, Grayson felt gratified. He had obviously been successful in encouraging Rachel, even if the encouragement was minimal. He hoped he would be able to help her more, once he knew the details of her story. He would certainly try.

As he took a sip of iced tea, he did not, for one instant, try to resist the attraction he was feeling.

22

S o, thirteen years of marriage; that's quite a while," Grayson expressed at the offset of the conversation, commencing where they had left off three days ago.

The Friday lunch crowd at The Salad Bar was so large it had forced him and Rachel to sit on tall bar stools at one of the few two-person tables. The table was a minimum-sized plank protruding out of the wall. The setting provided a feeling of coziness, but not without the sacrifice of comfort.

Ignoring the menu in front of her, Rachel pursed her lips and squinted an affirmation. "Long enough to never get over."

Grayson nodded his concurrence. "What about the children? How many, and what are their ages?"

"Two girls and a boy. Summer, our older daughter, is nine. Holly is six. And Justin, our son, is two. And how are they? I wish I could say they're going to be okay. But I...uh...honestly don't see how they're ever going to outlive something like this.

"Summer is carrying around enough pent-up anger for three or four people and has become distant and noncommunicative toward everybody. Holly, on the other hand, is so full of sensitivity that she doesn't even involve herself in child's play anymore. Instead, she spends her time trying to reassure and rescue me. Otherwise, she just sits like a zombie in front of the television. And then Justin"—Rachel swayed her head in lament—"you've never seen a child so confused, clingy, and insecure. He's almost three and, because of the trauma, he's still not even toilet trained." Rachel looked Grayson in the eye and tried not to cry. "It doesn't sound very hopeful, does it?"

Grayson slid his hand to the middle of the table as if wanting to reach over and touch Rachel sympathetically. "I'm sure it's not as permanent as it seems. Their response is only normal. And if they're like most kids, they'll survive and eventually turn out quite ordinary." He retracted his hand. Rachel removed a tissue from her purse and swiped at her eyes. "How about your sons? How have they coped?"

"Well, they're now fifteen and fourteen, and both live with their mother. Mark, the older one, is a star player on his junior-varsity basketball team. Alex is the vice president of his ninth-grade business club and is very involved with computers. Like your oldest daughter, both of them initially carried a lot of anger, but they eventually worked their way through it. And now they're very normal teenage boys." Grayson reached over as if wanting one more time to offer a consoling touch. "Your children will fight back as well. They're stronger than you think."

"I don't know. I just don't have that assurance," Rachel replied. "Kids who suffer through a divorce at least have the element of certainty on their side. It's certain, for example, that the marriage is over. It's certain where the mother will be living, where the dad will be living. It's certain which parent has custody, and on which days the other parent has visiting rights. Those certainties give the family something concrete to work around and to build on.

"In our case, none of those certainties exist. My husband and I

RANDALL ARTHUR ◆ 188

are *not* divorced. The children and I don't know *where* he is. Or *who* he's with. We have no idea if he intends to ever come back. For nine months, there has been nothing but silence. The only reason we know he's alive is that about a week after he left us, a couple of people responded to a police report in the newspaper. One of those witnesses claims they had inside knowledge that he left town with a mistress. And the other witness claims he actually saw him with the lady in her car on the morning he disappeared.

"So, it's like being the family of a soldier who's missing in action. There's no final chapter, no foreseeable climax to the whole painful thing. There were no good-byes or last wishes before he left. And there hasn't been any communication since. There's no corpse. No burial. Nothing.

"Nothing but day-by-day *whats* and *what ifs*. Just endless waiting. And to be honest with you, the waiting, with all of its darkness, has filled my life with hate, bitterness, and hopelessness, even fantasies about...cutting my life short.

"I don't know; maybe we would all be handling the situation better if he had died and we had seen his body put in the ground. There have been times when I've prayed, even begged God, that we'd get a call notifying us that he's been found dead somewhere. Just so we can have a little bit of the certainty I talked about. Just so we can establish some kind of fixed direction for our lives."

Seeing and hearing the intense sincerity of her analysis, Grayson chose not to argue or disagree with what she said. Instead, he responded with a simple, "I don't believe anyone in the world would challenge the validity of your feelings. At the same time, though, you can't just stop believing in yourself and in your children. Convincing yourself that there's no hope for your family is like waking up one morning, discovering that all the grocery stores have been permanently closed, and concluding you're going to starve to death. You could starve, or you could fall back on the inner strength and ingenuity of the human spirit and learn to survive off the land. It wouldn't be comfortable, convenient, familiar, or easy, but it could be done.

"How do we know it could be done? Because since the beginning of time, millions of our ancestors have done it." Grayson paused to let his logic sink in. "I'll be the first to admit that your situation is far more complicated than mine, but I'll also be quick to emphasize that thousands of women and children around the world have for centuries lost their husbands and fathers to mysterious and unknown fates. Yet, using their God-given nerve and fortitude, they've fought back and overcome. They've carved out their own certainties."

Grayson placed his fingers on the back of her hand. "You're made up of the same spiritual fiber as everybody else in your shoes who has won against the odds." He slightly squeezed her hand. "Just keep reminding yourself of that fact."

Rachel pressed her eyes shut. A couple of seconds later, she opened them again, a frail grin taking shape on her lips. "You sound like a high-powered motivational speaker."

Grayson pulled his hand away as a waitress approached their table. "It sounds to me as if a few good motivational speeches are what you need right now."

"Well, I haven't been graced with very many during the last few months, that's for sure."

After ordering, Rachel answered his questions about where overseas she had lived, and why. At his prompting, she went on to tell about Clay, about their ministry in Stockholm, and about North Metro Church of the Bible and its dominant and longtime role in her life.

When their salads arrived, she told him about the shocking way North Metro was treating her and about the unmitigated disillusionment she was feeling toward God and Christianity.

Grayson urged her to dismiss the religious rejection by North Metro as nothing more than psychological perversion. "They're the ones who are sick, sicker than they know," he stressed.

The hour was quickly over.

After paying for their meal, he pulled one of his business cards from his coat pocket and jotted down his home phone number on the back side.

He slid the card to Rachel. "I know it won't be easy, but try not to let yourself get sucked down any further into the isolation trap. Whenever you need encouragement, or just need someone to vent your frustrations on, give me a call. I can try to be a cheerleader for you. I mean it."

Rachel placed the card in her purse. "Please know that I'm grateful for your company. And for the fact that you've been willing to listen. It means more to me than you realize." She sighed. "And I might very well take you up on your offer."

Grayson nodded in acknowledgment of her gratefulness. "It's the least I can do."

"No man, having put his hand to the plow, and looking back, is fit for the kingdom of God," Pastor Lovett quoted loudly into the microphone to compete with the thunderous rainfall that three or four minutes ago started pummeling the church roof.

The medium-sized Sunday evening crowd was scattered throughout the auditorium. The breaking storm was sparking continuous waves of eye contact all around the room between spouses, parents, friends, and even strangers. Pastor Lovett, nearing the end of his message, was losing his audience.

Rachel sat alone eleven rows from the front, next to one of the outside aisles. Instead of focusing on Pastor Lovett, she found herself watching the glances, voiceless mouthing, and other expressions of silent communication taking place among the people.

Lovett bellowed even louder and suddenly deviated from his outline to try to regain the people's attention. "To illustrate the overall point of my message, and in order to make it personal, I'm going to give you a name. I'm going to give you the name of someone who in the past has been a part of this church. Someone who epitomizes putting his hand to the plow and then looking back. Someone whom God says is not fit for His kingdom." Lovett paused for effect and to see if his strategy was working.

It was. Almost every pair of eyes was now looking in his direction.

Rachel not only pivoted her full attention to what Lovett was saying, but she felt the whole of her insides knot up. *No, you couldn't...you can't!*

"The person I'm talking about," Lovett persisted, "served in a high-profile position. He's a man in whom a great number of people here at North Metro trusted. They believed in him and in his ministry, to such a degree that they supported him with their hard-earned dollars. Today, however, according to God's assessment, the man is nothing more than a spiritual misfit. He's a man who for the rest of his life will carry the stigma of betraying both God and the brotherhood of this ministry. His name?"

Rachel braced herself. Her anger toward Pastor Lovett piqued at his brazen insensitivity. She determined not to slump at the public declaration of Clay's name. She would keep her back straight and head held high.

"His name," Lovett announced dramatically, "is...Reverend Jason Faircloth, my predecessor as pastor of this great church. He..."

Rachel stared above the podium at Lovett's moving lips. Her mind, having felt the vivid stillness before the storm, did a retake, went numb, and then exploded with relief all in a matter of seconds.

It wasn't Clay's name, she whispered silently. She slowly released her breath, allayed almost to the point of tears that she had been spared the public beating.

But as she continued to look straight ahead, a different kind of anger pounced on her heart, an anger that made her wonder about her denomination's proclivity toward character bashing. *Our leaders relish it, as if it brings them some kind of sadistic joy,* she mentally scathed, *as if they believe they're God's divinely appointed inquisitors.*

She had been too naive, too trusting. Clay had been right all along. The shepherds of their denomination didn't try to empathize with people's inner struggles. They expected the wounded and fallen to immediately heal themselves and treated them like vile pagans if they didn't.

As Pastor Lovett finished his tirade about Jason Faircloth, Rachel couldn't help but wonder why it was that Faircloth, in

Lovett's words, had *looked back*. She had heard his name mentioned five or six times in years past, always by North Metro leaders and always in a severely negative context, as if he had been one of Satan's major followers. She personally had never met the man. He had resigned his pastoral position at North Metro seven or eight months before she came to the church. For the first time, though, she wondered if he had been a transgressor as accused or a victim like herself. Had anybody ever tried to help him? Or to touch hearts with him? Or had he simply been cut off like herself, and like Grayson Cole?

Such questions added both to her anger and to her confusion. She suddenly wanted to leave the premises and get away from everybody around her.

After the dismissal prayer, she got up and hurried toward the exit. She collected the children, getting drenched in the process. She fought the blinding downpour on the drive home and was nearly sideswiped along the way by a pickup truck that hydroplaned out of control. At home, she tried to listen to Holly, who asked, in the light of her evening's Bible lesson, why God had not answered their prayers about Daddy.

By the time the three children were lying silently in their beds, Rachel felt as if she had spent the whole evening battling a tireless monster.

She needed to talk with someone. She removed Grayson Cole's business card from her purse and stared at it. She struggled with the decision through two bowls of cereal, then finally yielded.

She felt awkward when Grayson answered. She tried to explain why she was calling. "Maybe it's a female thing for me to need to talk through my feelings," she told him.

Grayson, with his assured manner and positive spirit, quickly put her nervousness at ease.

Emboldened by the emotional linkup with a sympathetic peer, Rachel told him, in controlled exasperation, about the upsetting sermon illustration Pastor Lovett had so piously used and how it had become another source of provocation for her.

Grayson listened patiently to her story, then entered into the conversation with clear interest and desire. His welcoming attitude became a springboard for her to unload everything else that the evening's events had piled onto her soul.

When she finally hung up, she saw, according to the kitchen clock, that Grayson had listened to her deluge of thoughts and feelings for more than an hour.

The last conscious thought she had before falling asleep an hour later was of gratitude for her newfound friend.

The next morning, Grayson waited an hour or so before he approached Rachel at her proof machine.

"I'd really like to share some additional thoughts with you, if you have time," he told her. He asked if she would again like to join him for lunch at The Salad Bar and listen to what he had to say.

"I think I can handle that," she answered humbly, stressing her heartfelt gratitude for his availability yesterday evening.

Grayson smiled. Thankfulness abounded in his heart as well. "Good. I'll plan to meet you there shortly after twelve."

Rachel, with lassitude lingering in her eyes, nodded and returned a genuine smile.

23

By mid-February, rendezvousing for lunch and conversation at The Salad Bar developed into a regular once or twice a week event.

For Rachel, Grayson's company—his listening ear, unconditional acceptance, and persuasive exhortations—became a strong medication that helped dull the pains in her life. She credited his friendship with single-handedly dissuading her from any attempts at fulfilling her suicidal wishes. For the first time since moving back to America, modest laughter occasionally crossed her lips. She had pulled back the curtain of her heart and had made herself vulnerable. And Grayson Cole had proven to be a trustworthy confidant. Repeatedly taking a risk and opening his heart as well, he quite innocently became a best friend.

The awkwardness of the situation didn't escape her, she being a married woman and he being a divorced man. She even learned that he was not, and had never been, a Christian who professed to know Christ intimately as his personal Savior. Her Christian camp, she knew, would condemn the friendship on all points.

Despite the fact, however, that she had lost all respect for every leader in her denomination and had grown cold in her own faith, the ever-growing friendship with Grayson heckled her with periods of guilt. She did not know if the guilt was induced by her wifely conscience, by God, or, as she strongly suspected, by her legalistic Christian heritage. She tried not to think about it, or even care.

After all, no one this side of the Atlantic, other than Grayson, had shown the decency to reach out to her. Even John and Rita Holcomb's occasional assistance had been kept, for whatever reason, at an emotional distance.

She couldn't help it if Grayson was the only friend she had.

Rachel's sessions with Grayson at The Salad Bar did not go unnoticed. A Sunday school teacher for a group of junior high girls at North Metro, a twenty-five-year-old single lady who worked in the office of a North Atlanta—based insurance company, frequented The Salad Bar with coworkers for lunch as well. She had witnessed Rachel on at least two occasions sitting with Grayson, engaged in "friendly" conversation. She was sure the conversations were more than just business related. She was convinced by the hand touching, the relaxed spirit of both parties, and the prolonged intimate eye contact. Concerned that the North Metro leadership know what was possibly going on, the young lady reported the eyewitness accounts to Pastor Bill Reese.

Pastor Reese, in turn, passed along the report of the trysts to Pastor Lovett.

Caught up in the momentum of emotional intimacy through the next several months, Rachel eventually reached the point of feeling sexually vulnerable in Grayson's presence.

The feeling was unexpected and brought confusion and fear to her heart. But she was convinced that severing the friendship after so many months of help and support would be almost unbearable for her. Not seeing Grayson anymore was not a step she was ready to take.

She tried to convince herself that she was still strong enough to keep the relationship purely platonic. She failed to understand, or to admit, just how vulnerable she was until Memorial Day weekend in late May.

On the Friday afternoon before the three-day weekend, she was busy at her proof machine when Grayson walked by and left an envelope on her desk.

Rachel looked up from the machine as Grayson nonchalantly walked out of the area. She then emptied the item count pocket of the last batch of checks, placed them, along with the slips of corresponding proof tape, into the holding basket, and picked up the envelope.

She removed a one-page handwritten note and read its message.

Dear Rachel,

As you already know, in a few hours I'll be driving to Savannah for the weekend to visit my sons. I'm planning, however, to be back in Atlanta on Monday evening in time for a seven o'clock concert at the Fox Theater. A pianist from France, one of my favorites, will be giving a performance.

I know it was presumptuous of me, but yesterday when I ordered my ticket, I decided to order one extra, hoping you might join me. I would be thrilled to have your company. It would be a great evening. I would love to even take you out to eat afterward.

*Don't make a quick decision. Take the weekend to think about it. If
you decide you would like to come along, just leave a message on my
answering machine sometime on Monday and I'll plan to meet you at
the Fox ticket window around six-thirty. If your answer is no, I'll completely and sincerely understand. I mean it. I'll just simply try again
some other time.*

    Grayson

Rachel saw a smiley face at the end of the last sentence.

She lowered the paper. Her eyelids closed as she tried to corral
her thoughts. Part of her wanted to chase Grayson down and say,
"Yes, I'd love to spend Monday evening with you!" Another part of
her felt pressured to step back and cautiously think through the
situation.

Outside of her lunch meetings with Grayson at The Salad Bar,
she had been together with him only one time. Three weeks ago, at
her request, he had followed her after work to an auto repair shop
a few blocks from her apartment where she had to leave her car
overnight for the installation of a new muffler.

From the auto shop, he had driven her to John and Rita
Holcomb's, where she had arranged to borrow a car for the
remainder of the day.

During the fifteen-minute drive to the Holcombs', he had
asked if he could drop by the apartment later in the evening and
visit with her after the kids were put to bed. "We can just sit outside
and enjoy each other's company," he told her.

He had been careful to suggest an outside location and a time
of evening that would protect Summer, Holly, and Justin from
seeing or hearing anything that might provoke twisted thoughts

and stress-filled questions.

To Rachel, the idea had sounded like a fun and innocent way to end the tiring day. Plus, the weather on that day had been gorgeous and had lifted her spirits. She had been in a rare optimistic mood. "Sure, I don't see why not," she smiled. "As a matter of fact, it sounds quite nice."

They ended up spending three hours or more that evening sitting in lawn chairs at the side of the apartment-complex pool. For a late-night snack, they called out for pizza and Cokes. Their time together, in the nighttime glow of the underwater pool lights, had been relaxed and immensely enjoyable and had even included a few cherished moments of hilarity.

There had been only one unsettling moment in the whole evening. As Grayson was getting ready to leave, he told her how much he was starting to like her and then, without forewarning, kissed her on her cheek, close to her lips. Rachel tried to ignore the advance, but the act of intimacy had left her feeling guilty and confused. Yet, in the secret part of her soul, she appreciated the reaffirmation of her womanhood.

As she reflected on that particular evening, Rachel folded the note that was in her hand and placed it back in the envelope. She looked around the room. Grayson was nowhere in sight.

She wanted to say yes to his invitation. The truth was, she needed him. Needed his company. His conversation. His acceptance. His encouragement. His laughter. His optimism. And even his male attraction.

Her luncheons with him during bank hours had been a safe forum for her. Meeting with him outside of that environment clearly presented some risks as the kiss had demonstrated.

Did she really want to maneuver into such risky territory? Should she? Did she possess the motivation and the strength to maintain clear boundaries?

She desired to do what was right. So why couldn't, and why wouldn't, she strictly supervise their private moments together?

If it wasn't that simple, then maybe she should decline his invitation, and all his future invitations as well.

But that was not the decision she wanted to make. After a complete year of living as an abandoned wife, and knowing the full scope of pain that accompanied that status, she craved the therapy of close adult friendship. And her hunger for such friendships was more paramount now than ever.

She sighed with frustration as the myriad conflicting thoughts settled on her mind.

She reached down and placed the envelope inside her purse. For the remaining two hours of work, she found it difficult to give adequate concentration to her proof machine. Her mind would not stop grappling with how she should respond to Grayson's note.

That evening, Justin, now an insecure and introverted three-year-old, started behaving as if he were not feeling well. Rachel placed her hand on his brow and found it fevered. She took his temperature. The thermometer read one hundred and one degrees.

Rachel gave him a couple of children's Tylenol and put him to bed. For more than thirty minutes, she lay by his side holding a cold washcloth to his forehead. She tried to quell his whimpering by singing lullabies. He finally closed his eyes and relaxed.

When Rachel was convinced he had fallen asleep, she got up to clean the dinner dishes and to interact with Summer and Holly.

Her hands had been in the dishwater for less than five minutes when she heard Justin, in his room, throwing up. By the time she reached him, he was sitting up in his bed with vomit puddled on the sheets around his buttocks and legs.

Rachel lifted him out of bed and took him to the shower, where she pulled off his messy pajamas and washed him off. "Mommy's going to stay right here with you and help you, honey," she kept reassuring him. She then dressed him in a clean pair of pajamas and took him to her bed.

She positioned him under the covers and told him he could sleep in her room for the night. She placed an empty, plastic trash can on the floor at the bedside. "Lean over and use this if you feel like you're going to throw up again," she explained.

He did, about an hour later. And at least four more times throughout the night.

Rachel nursed him all day Saturday, along with attending to her other household and motherly duties. By evening, she thought he was getting better, but his fever quickly returned. During the early hours of Sunday morning, he vomited twice more. And then, just as suddenly as the fever had come, it vanished.

Rachel explained to the children at the breakfast table that, in order for them to rest up after Justin's two days of sickness, they would spend the morning at home and not attend Sunday school or the worship service.

"But today's the day the special clown team is going to be there for all the kids," Summer protested. "Holly and I *want* to go!"

After thirty minutes of being pestered nonstop, Rachel finally consented to take the girls and go to church. Rachel's dad was in town for the weekend, so she called him and arranged for Justin to stay for a few hours at his place.

Once at church, Rachel, due to fatigue, fought in vain to stay awake during both the Sunday school hour and the preaching service.

From his chair on the platform, Bill Reese looked out over the congregation as he listened to Pastor Lovett preach a special sermon on the need for massive sums of money to repave the church parking lot and recarpet the church auditorium. His eyes eventually fell on Rachel, who was sitting in the audience with her eyes closed.

Was she asleep? She was, wasn't she? Instantly, Reese felt perturbed.

Did the lady think that just because she was a poor, ruined mother she was exempt by God, or anyone else, from shouldering her part of the church's financial load? Was she so blatantly indifferent to her church's needs?

Through the remainder of the sermon, Reese continued on and off to look at her. He saw that she dozed heavily, seemingly without shame. He wondered if she had been up till the early morning hours with her new man friend. *If I only had evidence!* he thought, feeling his disgust being torqued even further.

He looked at her again. *Something has to be said,* he decided.

Rachel walked heavy-eyed to the annex building, got the girls, and led them to the car. She wanted to get home, put lunch behind her, and lie down for an hour or so.

She started maneuvering her Toyota out of its parking space when deacon Ronnie Johnson walked up alongside her car and knocked on the driver-side window.

Rachel stopped the car. When she saw who was standing there, she felt a stark surge of adrenaline spread through her body, followed by an unwanted shortness of breath.

What had she done wrong this time? Was she going to be reprimanded again?

Do they still think I'm a closet alcoholic? she wondered sarcastically as she rolled down her window.

"Pastor Reese asked me to make sure you got this before you left," Johnson announced with authority, sticking a folded piece of notebook paper through the open window.

Rachel started to ask what it was before she took it. Instead, she slowly lifted her hand and allowed Johnson to place the paper in her grasp.

With no additional words, Johnson stepped away from the car. Rachel backed out of the parking space and drove away.

"What is it, Mother?" Summer wanted to know.

"Just a note from Pastor Reese," Rachel said as she pulled out of the church parking lot and headed toward her father's house to pick up Justin. She stuffed the sheet of paper into her purse.

She removed the note to look at it only after she had served lunch, cleaned the kitchen, and was in her bedroom alone. The children were watching a cartoon channel on television and were told to stay there until she finished her nap.

Rachel set her alarm clock to beep in a little over an hour.

Sitting on the bed, she unfolded the paper and read the handwritten message.

I don't know what kind of extracurricular activities are going on in your life to make you so tired, but church is not the place to catch up on your sleep. Seeing you nap throughout the service this morning really irked me, especially in light of the advance emphasis given to this special fund-raising effort. The impression you continue to give is that you couldn't care less.

As far as I'm concerned, the lack of heartfelt progress that I've witnessed in your life is a disgrace to the cause of Christ. I seriously wonder, Rachel, if you're really even a Christian.

Pastor Reese

Reese's words, as if they were pickax handles, explosively slammed at Rachel's heart until she realized she was lying on the bed with her hands covering her chest.

The only thoughts that would come into focus for her were thoughts of hate and anger. She suspected that she would have tried to hurt Reese if he were standing in the room with her right now.

One thing, though, was certain: She would never, *never* dignify this defamation with a response. As far as she was concerned, the man could rot a hundred times over in his self-righteous ignorance.

With emotion oozing from every pore in her body, she looked toward heaven and shouted, "And so can *You!*"

Within minutes, she was punching in the telephone number to her dad's. It took only seconds, once she had him on the line, to pressure him to keep all three kids tomorrow evening and tomorrow night. She offered him no explanation except that she needed time for herself.

She then called Grayson. His answering machine clicked on.

"This is Rachel," she said. "My answer is a definite yes. I'll meet you at the Fox ticket window at six-thirty tomorrow night. I'm looking forward to it."

24

Clay McCain took a slow bite of the juicy melon he was holding. Sitting alone on a towel on a small, deserted, sandy beach, he stared eastward over the greenish-blue waters of the Caribbean Sea.

Less than a hundred yards behind him stood a lush rain forest. The terrain was famously typical of Costa Rica. The smell in the air was of humid flora. From atop the trees, exotic birds sang and chirped by the hundreds. Howler monkeys could be heard squealing their high-pitched noises.

Clay spat a couple of melon seeds onto the sun-baked sand.

He scuffled with his weighted thoughts.

Perhaps coming to Costa Rica with Anika Wiberg instead of returning to his wife and children had been a mistake. But was it too late to reverse his decision?

He thought of Stockholm, the Swedish city spread across fourteen tightly clustered islands on the Baltic coast, the Venice of the North, the place that continued to hold his conscience prisoner to his past, to the unrequited memories of Rachel, Summer, Holly, and Justin.

Had it really been a full year since he cut his family out of his life and left them marooned to a devastating fate?

His mind began to sift through recollections of the last twelve months, a period of time that had pushed his pastoral occupation of the past into the realm of another world, a world that was now foreign to him and seemingly beyond reach. Of his own volition, he had allowed himself to be catapulted into a life of unrestrained lust.

Fueled by his eagerness, Anika had introduced him in a grand way to the "good life" of seizing selfish dreams and tasting endless pleasures.

In Majorca they had become proficient at scuba diving and jet skiing and had acquired elementary experience at skydiving and parasailing.

Here in Costa Rica, since their arrival three months ago, they had white-water rafted, motorcycled, and explored volcanoes and were learning the art of sportfishing. The automobile they were driving was a black 1966 427 Shelby Cobra. It, along with a Costa Rican mansion, was one of the items Anika's father, a steel-manufacturing tycoon, had left behind in his grandiose will.

In addition to all the sporting activities, parties, material luxuries, traveling, and opulent freedom, there was the incessant and unabated sexual feasting. Feasting of every style, twist, and preference, including occasional orgies.

Yet, as exhilarating as all the desired fruit had been, his heart was empty.

But the dark side of his nature had long since been his conqueror. He was addicted.

There was a part of him that could now see the folly of it all, a part that truly wanted to stop, that wanted to return to his family and beg for forgiveness, restoration, and healing. But like any other addict, he could not seem to grasp the needed power or ability. He was captured in a counterfeit paradise where there were seemingly no exits.

He set the melon down and thought of Anika. Perhaps more

than being addicted to the lifestyle she had provided, he was addicted to her. The sight, feel, smell, and taste of her still intoxicated him and left his heart hungering helplessly for more. She was a twenty-eight-year-old goddess of sensuality whose intelligence, charisma, and thirst for life were additional hooks in her overall allure. Their chemistry together, even after a year, consistently produced carnal highs that lifted him above his ability to reason.

That's why he had followed her here to Costa Rica, the country where her parents, for climate and tax reasons, had built their retirement home. It was the country where Anika had spent her late teens and early twenties. It was a country that offered all the goods and services of modern society, yet where rural charm was still prominent and where the people were extraordinarily friendly. It was a place where one could walk out of the modern cities and see coffee and banana plantations, jungles, caverns, volcanoes, even giant sea turtles. It was a place that Anika loved.

He liked it here, too, but the rising complications in his heart and soul, which he had been trying to deny, were now crippling his ability to pretend he was okay with himself and with life.

He suddenly picked up a handful of sand and slung it hard into the air.

Before he left Stockholm with Anika, he had revealed to her his marital status, his fatherhood, and his occupation. She had listened thoughtfully. But she had never brought up the matter in conversation since. Neither had he.

Up until now, he had kept his feelings of oppression hidden from her. But how much longer could he conceal those feelings? Should he not even make the effort anymore? Or should he continue to secretly battle the emptiness and try, contrary to what he knew was true, to deceive himself into believing he could beat it?

He picked up another fistful of sand and wondered again about Rachel, Summer, Holly, and Justin. He was sure they had returned to the States by now.

He wanted to pray for them but was afraid. The idea of a fallen worm like himself trying to communicate with a holy God smacked of mockery and vanity of the highest order. He feared that if he dared lift his head heavenward, especially on behalf of the very wife and children he had erased from his life, God might be provoked to physically punish him.

Just as he had turned his back on his wife and children, he was sure that God had turned His back on him and had cut him off from any kind of divine mercy. He tightened his grip around the sand, then let it sift slowly from his fist.

The ongoing sense that he was a traitor and an enemy of the almighty God he once served was too frightening and unnerving to think about. "Maybe I'm already in hell and am just the last one to know it," he whispered to himself in a broken voice.

With tears seeping from his eyes, he lifted his head and again looked out over the ocean. He was glad he and Anika would be attending a big party tonight.

He would medicate his conscience with a rediscovered painkiller, one that had been familiar to him in his teens--a good round of drunkenness.

Twenty minutes later, he was in the Cobra headed for the mountain roads leading to the country's Central Valley, toward the capital city of San José, the location of Anika's mansion.

With the wind whipping his hair, he found his thoughts again drawn to his wife, two daughters, and son.

25

Rachel was wearing a new, conservatively stylish maroon dress when she walked through the Peachtree Street entrance to the Fox Theater's lobby at precisely 6:30 P.M. She spotted Grayson across the room, standing beside a colorful wall poster detailing the evening's concert.

The two of them made eye contact almost immediately. Rachel simultaneously caught sight of the solitary long-stemmed red rose he was holding. She felt her heart rush ahead of her mind toward steps of surrender.

She and Grayson both smiled and started making their way toward each other. Grayson, focusing on her and her alone, looked ecstatic.

As they came together, Grayson clasped her hand in his and, as before, kissed her on the cheek at the edge of her lips.

Like a faithful messenger, Rachel's Christian background bellowed that such intimacy was not proper for her. Yet her skin, more now than ever in her life, was thirsty for touch and affection. She flinched slightly, but offered no resistance to Grayson's advance.

"I'm absolutely thrilled you could make it," Grayson said. He let go of her hand and extended the rose. "I know it might not be the most practical gift for the occasion—but sometimes a rose is the best way for a man to prove his sincerity when he looks at a woman and says, 'You're special, and I care for you.' "

Rachel took the flower and tried to control her emotions. "Thanks," she whispered. "I appreciate...both the flower and the words...more than you realize." She lifted the bloom to her face and sniffed. "It'll not leave my sight," she promised him.

Grayson inhaled with a joyful sigh. "I want to thank you, too, just for being willing to join me."

For a couple of seconds they stood still, staring into each other's accepting eyes.

"Shall we?" Grayson finally said, holding out his arm to her.

Rachel took the inside of his elbow as he escorted her into the great hall of the famous old theater.

The concert that evening by the young, internationally acclaimed French pianist, accompanied by a symphonic orchestra, was far more spectacular than Rachel had expected. The array of well-known music—from classical to movie themes to romance—was majestic. Enhanced by a dazzling display of lighting and smoke effects, the experience was unforgettably moving. For Rachel, it was ointment for the soul.

After the performance, she and Grayson talked about the event for a solid thirty minutes as they sat in a nearby posh restaurant and waited for their meal.

As they talked, Grayson moved the vase of flowers from the center of the table over to the side and held Rachel's hands atop the red linen tablecloth. Rachel soon felt their legs touch. The contact was slight and went unmentioned. From behind her part of the conversation, she stared at Grayson's friendly face and tried to deny her growing feelings.

She was just about to repeat for the third time that the "French pianist was absolutely magical" when Grayson, as if he could read her inner desires, interrupted out of the blue and said, "What if Clay never shows up again?"

"I'm sorry, what? What did you say?"

"I'm curious. Have you set yourself a time limit?" Grayson suddenly sounded as if Rachel's marital predicament had been the focus of their conversation for the last hour. "How long are you going to wait before you file for divorce?"

Rachel artificially coughed, attempted to say something, and then went silent.

"I apologize," Grayson said. "That was insensitive of me. It's just that I... Look, let's just try to forget that I mentioned it."

But neither of them could.

Grayson changed the subject, asking if Rachel had considered leaving North Metro after the kids' school year ended. The ensuing conversation branched off into a variety of topics, but Grayson appeared distracted throughout the remainder of the dinner.

After their meal, Grayson drove Rachel to the parking garage a few blocks away where she had left her car. He parked his automobile on the street at the side of the parking deck. He got out, opened Rachel's door, and started walking her hand-in-hand to her Toyota located on the second level of the complex.

"I just want you to know that this evening has been very special for me," Grayson told her. "I'll hold it in my memory for a long time to come."

Rachel squinted as she watched Grayson's face.

As they headed up the ramp to the second floor, Grayson slowed their pace in the dimly lit garage. "It's more than just the concert and the food that makes it memorable. It's the company."

Grayson stopped and prompted Rachel to face him. He took both of her hands in his. "It's you, Rachel. It's your beauty, your intelligence, your personality, your strength, your tenderness. It's everything about you. It's...it's the way you affect me. Not just now, but ever since I first met you. To be honest with you, I'm completely captivated by you. More than I've ever been by any other woman." Grayson paused, his eyes locked onto hers. "What I'm trying to say is: I like you a lot, Rachel. I care about you. I...love you."

Rachel closed her eyes, trying to absorb what she had heard. Her heart and soul greeted Grayson's feelings with the fearful joy of an orphaned child. But her mind fogged with rebutted logic. She again opened her eyes and stared into Grayson's face. How could this work out? She was still a married woman. She...

In that moment of silence, Grayson pulled her into his arms and kissed her on the mouth. Without thinking, Rachel tightened her arms around him and hungrily returned the kiss.

As the kiss intensified in its duration, depth, and passion, Rachel lost all sense of time. All she knew was that she had burst into a torrent of tears.

During the next eight days and nights, due to Grayson's initiative, Rachel and Grayson's contact with one another dramatically escalated. So did their physical intimacy.

Rachel's sense of right and wrong, and her guilt about what she was doing, were overridden by her yearning for acceptance and belonging.

The confusion roaring through her soul, however, became irrepressible.

26

Y ou saw them go where?" Pastor Frank Lovett resonated
from behind his desk.

The junior high girls' Sunday school teacher was sure she
could see Pastor Lovett's upper lip curl as he enunciated the question. She felt her neck and shoulders stiffen with uneasiness. She
suddenly wished she had never gotten involved. *But it's for the cause of
Christ and for the purity of the church,* she kept telling herself. Pastor Bill
Reese, currently out of town on a family vacation, had even under-
girded that belief when he listened to her describe what she
witnessed at The Salad Bar five months ago. He had then encouraged her to inform him of anything else regarding Rachel that
appeared to be morally corrupt, and even to follow up discreetly
on any clues that presented themselves for public scrutiny.

Trying to convince herself again of the rightness of her cause,
the young lady gathered her wits and looked Pastor Lovett in the
eye.

"Yesterday," she stressed, backtracking to give more information, "I was in my car getting ready to return to work after an early
lunch at The Salad Bar. I normally eat there a couple of times a
week. Anyway, I had just started to back out of my parking place when
I saw Rachel. She was with the same man I've seen her with there at
the restaurant several times before. I've explained all this to Pastor
Reese. He said he was going to tell you about it. I assume he—"

Pastor Lovett offered a barely perceptible nod.

"The only reason I've been concerned," she told him, "is that every time I've seen them together, they've been holding hands, whispering intimately across the table. I've even seen the man kiss her on the forehead once or twice. I don't know, this just seems terribly out of place for a Christian woman who's married. Even if her husband isn't around. I mean it's still possible that her husband could come walking back into her life at any moment.

"Anyway, yesterday I saw the two of them together in the man's car. They passed right behind me, heading for the parking lot exit. I was a little surprised because I hadn't even seen them inside— probably because the lunch crowd was so large. I drove up to the exit half wondering about them, when I noticed that they had turned toward Cobb Parkway, the same direction I was going. When I pulled out into the traffic, I was only about three cars behind them. A minute or so later, I saw them pull into the far left-hand lane at the Cobb intersection and signal to turn. I honestly got a little nervous because I had to make the same turn.

"I never intended to follow them at first, I swear. But then I saw Rachel lean over and put her head on the man's shoulder. I was only a couple of cars away; so I knew I wasn't just seeing things. At the same time, I realized they were going in the opposite direction of the bank where she works. Everything I was seeing sent up red flags. Before I knew it, we were less than a half mile from my office when I saw them turning left onto the South Marietta Parkway, headed back toward I-75.

"It was totally unlike me, but I felt this obsession to keep following them. At least for a bit more. Maybe God was trying to direct me. Anyway, I turned onto the South Parkway behind them.

I realized after turning, though, that they were probably going to get on I-75, that maybe they were headed into Atlanta for a business meeting or something. At that point, I decided to go no farther than the I-75 ramp. But right before the I-75 interchange, they pulled into the parking lot at the Hampton Inn. They drove up close to the office and parked."

Pastor Lovett sat rigidly in his high-backed leather chair. "And you're telling me that you saw them get out of the car and go into a hotel room together?"

The lady nodded. "I pulled into the parking lot of the office center across the street and watched from there. I don't think I've ever been as nervous in my whole life, but I felt I was doing the proper thing. That's the only reason I stayed. I saw the man get out of the car and go into the lobby by himself. He came back out a few minutes later, got back in the car with Rachel, and drove around to the other side of the building. I waited for about ten minutes. Then I drove across the street and drove slowly around the hotel. I was so tense I could hardly drive. But then I saw their car, parked behind the building, up next to a row of rooms. The car was empty; there was no doubt about it. I then left and hurried back to work."

"And you're sure the car you saw parked on the backside of the hotel was the same one you'd been following?"

"It's a big car, teal green, with bumper stickers. It was definitely the same car."

"And you're certain it was Rachel McCain you saw in the car?"

"Absolutely no doubt whatsoever."

Lovett stopped talking for a few seconds as he thought about what he was hearing. He then broke the silence. "Who else knows

217 ◆ Brotherhood of Betrayal

about this?"

A look of guilt suddenly appeared across the lady's countenance. "I...uh"—she cleared her throat—"I did tell a Christian coworker of mine. But the lady goes to another church. She doesn't even know Rachel. It was just that—"

"Anyone else?" Lovett interrupted.

"No," she whispered, "just that one friend."

Lovett leaned toward the desk and spoke emphatically. "You've done the right thing to bring this information to me. From this point onward, just make sure you do not share it with another soul. Not with anybody here at the church. Not with your friends. Not even with your own mother. I don't want any of this to get back to Rachel before I have a chance to decide on a responsible course of action. Do you understand?"

Noticing that the stiffness in her neck and shoulders had spread to her lower limbs, the woman nodded her cooperation and looked at her watch.

"Before you go," Lovett told her, "there's one more thing I need to know. As exact as you can be, what time was it when you saw their car parked at the hotel?"

The lady closed her eyes, then looked at her watch again. "It was about twelve-thirty, the same time that it is right now."

Pastor Lovett thanked her and stressed again the need for her to keep her lips sealed.

Before the lady had left the church building to return to work, Pastor Lovett instructed his secretary not to let anyone disturb him during the next quarter of an hour. He then called directory assistance, got the telephone number of the Hampton Inn, and punched in the number.

"Hello," he began when a male clerk picked up, "I'm calling to find out if any seminars or business parties took place yesterday in any of your conference rooms between the hours of noon and 4:00 P.M. Can you give me that information?"

"Hold just a minute, please," the male voice responded.

As Lovett waited, he removed a gold ballpoint pen from its holder and wrote across the margin of his desk calendar the words: Hampton Inn, Monday, June 4, 12:30, teal green car, RM.

"The only conference or meeting held here yesterday," the clerk's voice was suddenly saying, "was at 9:00 A.M. It was for the state's disabled World War II veterans."

"Do you know what time that meeting was scheduled to be over?"

"Another moment, please." The silence over the line lasted for less than twenty seconds. "Eleven o'clock," the clerk's voice returned.

"And there were no other meetings of any kind?"

"Not yesterday."

"All right. Thanks for your help."

Lovett placed the phone back in its cradle and leaned back in his chair. The more he thought through all the factors and their obvious conclusion, the more disgusted he became. Looking back at the words he had written across the margin of his calendar, he exhaled a breath of air like a riled bull.

After several minutes of heated contemplation, he knew decisively what had to be done, what *would* be done.

27

Ten minutes before the meeting, the attendance at North Metro's midweek worship service looked as if it was going to be above average. Two of the church's favorite singing groups—an all-male quartet from Birmingham, Alabama, and a mixed trio from south Georgia—were going to present a full evening of music.

About seven hundred people, lighthearted and talkative, were already present in the auditorium. Anticipating an exciting time, clusters of people continued to make their way into the building.

The two singing groups were on the platform making last-minute adjustments to their array of mikes, instruments, and sound equipment.

About five minutes before starting time, Pastor Frank Lovett, along with the church's nineteen deacons, entered the auditorium through the doorway down beside the platform. Lovett walked directly to the front of the platform and climbed the steps. Trying to detach himself from his thoughts concerning the just-held deacons' meeting, he stepped over cords, moved around mikes, and rallied the leaders of the two music groups.

"Are you about ready to start? Is there anything else you need?" he questioned them.

The two men assured him that they had everything they needed and that both groups would be ready within the next two or three minutes.

Lovett briefed them once again on the order of the program. "And at the end of the service, after I give the altar call," he added, "I'm going to take a few minutes to deal up front with a church matter that needs immediate attention. The less disruptions, the better. So just plan to stay in your places till I'm finished."

The two leaders nodded their compliance.

Lovett looked at his watch. "We'll begin in three minutes." He then turned and went to his chair on the platform.

When he sat, he placed his well-worn Bible on his lap and gazed out over the multitude of faces. His eyes eventually found and focused on Rachel.

He sighed. His eighteen years of leading the people here at North Metro had been marked by unquestionable stability. Called from a medium-sized church in Augusta, Georgia, to be North Metro's pastor, he stepped into the role and salvaged the church after it had been severely disillusioned and crippled by the former pastor, Jason Faircloth, who the people said had "suddenly lost his heart for everything that was right and walked out."

From day one, he, Pastor Frank Lovett, had fought to secure the church's reputation for truth and decency and to restore to the people their faith in pastoral leadership. And to the honor of God, he had succeeded.

He knew that most of the people here felt indebted to him. He received their affirmations regularly. And he equally cared for and appreciated them. He had taught their kids. Performed the marriages of their young. Regularly nourished the souls of the whole flock. Eaten in their homes. Visited their sick. And buried their dead. He had been as committed and loyal to his people as a spiritual leader could be.

Through the years, however, a handful who were either too blind or too hard-hearted had refused to submit to his care, expertise, and authority. And those people, from his point of view, had lost their way in life and were now suffering outside the church fellowship because of it.

He hated that Rachel—a former missionary, pastor's wife, and premier lady of the church—now had to be added to that list. But he had tried everything he could to help her. Overseas aid. Free school tuition for her children. Counsel. Enough Bible preaching to convert and make straight an entire army of pagans. Repeated warnings.

But she had thrown it all to the wind. And now, with her eyes open, she had crossed the boundary of church grace.

He was definitely being fair. He was sure of it. She had forced his hand and had left him with no other recourse.

He again looked at his watch. He then clutched his Bible, stood, and moved toward the podium.

Rachel, near the rear of the auditorium, sat with her eyes closed. She tried to relax and hoped the lively evening would boost her spirit.

Normally she dreaded the hours spent here on these pews, but tonight, without any preaching on the agenda, she welcomed the opportunity to just sit and listen to music. And for a few minutes, not to be called on as a mother, as an employee, or as a friend.

In order for her to survive another day, it was imperative that she try to let her mind slip into an off-duty mode. She was weary with deciphering her behavior of the last four days, dealing with guilt, and trying to make sense of what was happening. She would never have believed that her life could become more chaotic. She wouldn't have thought it possible. But it had. And right now, all she wanted was just to escape for a few moments.

She heard Pastor Lovett's voice speak into the microphone. She opened her eyes and looked toward the front of the auditorium.

"I want to welcome everyone to this special evening of good old-fashioned God-honoring gospel music," Lovett began. "I'm looking at a message that was just put on the podium by one of my ushers. It says that the attendance tonight is already close to nine hundred and fifty. And people are still coming in. Well, praise God that in our day of spiritual indifference there are still a few people left who have enough moral fortitude to break away from their VCRs and televisions after a long day of work and gather together at the house of the Lord to be blessed."

A few hearty shouts of "Amen" and "Glory to God" erupted across the audience.

"And I assure you that you *will* be blessed. Well, due to the large number of visitors who've joined us from other churches this evening, I'll not take time to recognize every individual and group by name. But I would like to ask all the visitors to stand so that we at North Metro can see who you are."

Throughout the crowd, individuals and small groups began standing.

Rachel watched as at least seventy to eighty people rose. She wished she could rejoice over their presence, but she could only see them as faceless bodies, eclipsed by her own need to lay hold of the blessing that Lovett was so sure was forthcoming.

"You're our guests," Lovett emphasized. "And we welcome

you. Thanks for coming. Our people here at North Metro will give you a warm greeting at the end of the service."

He then instructed them to be seated and added, "For those of you who have babies or small children, we do have a nursery and a children's church in the building next door to my left. I already hear one baby crying somewhere in the back. I'd like to ask the parents of that baby to be considerate of the rest of us and go ahead and take the child next door. The baby will be well taken care of by a professional staff. One of the ushers standing in the back will help you."

As Pastor Lovett made a few announcements for the North Metro people, Rachel saw a large, physically intimidating usher walk to the end of one of the back pews. He waited there till an embarrassed mother collected her baby, diaper bag, purse, and two small children and awkwardly worked her way to the aisle. The usher then led the woman and her children out of the auditorium. Rachel was mortified for the lady.

When the commotion settled, Pastor Lovett led the people in a lively opening prayer, asking God to visit their meeting with His divine presence, to anoint the singers with the power of the Holy Ghost, and to use the service to make everyone there a little more like Jesus.

Upon finishing his supplication, he said there was one more important announcement he wanted to make.

"As several of you have already heard through radio and newspaper advertisements, the former pastor of this church—Jason Faircloth—is scheduled, beginning this evening, to lead a Bible conference at a church just a few miles from here, a church that reeks of hellish liberalism. I trust that none of you are secretly planning to make a nostalgic visit to see or hear this preacher-turned-apostate. If you are, then as your spiritual leader, I'm telling you to cancel your plans. I know that's strong, but I intend for it to be.

"Just two days ago, I was able to speak to the man for the first time in my life. He called here at the church asking me if he could attend one of our Sunday services and publicly apologize for walking out on the congregation nineteen years ago and perhaps share what's taken place in his life since that time. Folks, if I'm certain of anything, I'm certain of the two spiritual gifts God has equipped me with to carry out my ministry—those of preaching and discernment. After questioning Faircloth for less than five minutes, my spirit of discernment cringed at his spiritual decrepitude. He has literally sold out—lock, stock, and barrel—to religious ecumenicalism, the end-time movement of Satan.

"I told him, and I'll tell you, it would have been better for the cause of Christ if he had stayed out of the ministry than to now masquerade as a gospel preacher with his present beliefs. The man is dangerous. He's hurt this church once. I'll not let him hurt it again. He will not be speaking from this pulpit.

"And if I hear of any of you from North Metro sneaking off to hear him at the other church, I'll call you into my office and question *your* beliefs."

Lovett smiled and said, "Trust me on this one, folks."

Rachel watched Pastor Lovett then lead the congregation in several choruses. To take her mind off her own problems, she replayed the oft-repeated fantasy of starting a mutiny and happily ousting the pastor-dictator from his citadel of spiritual authoritarianism.

She also wondered again about Jason Faircloth. Why was it that he generated such spite from the leaders at North Metro? Could they not even forgive the man if he wanted to apologize for the past?

"All right," Lovett suddenly proclaimed, "I believe we're ready to let loose and glory in God's abundance. Amen?

"Even though it's been a while since they were last here, they need no fancy introduction. We know them well. Prepare to be raptured. The Jericho Four and The Gospel Accents!"

Applause thundered throughout the auditorium. The seven singers, in the midst of the boisterous hand clapping, exuberantly took their places behind the stage mikes. Without any preemptive words, the two groups launched into a vivacious rendition of "All Hail the Power of Jesus' Name."

At the completion of the song, the trio from south Georgia returned to their seats on one of the front pews. The quartet went directly into the next song. For thirty minutes the four men entertained the crowd with their tight four-part harmonies.

The trio then replaced the quartet on the platform and for another thirty minutes pleasured the people with their musical expertise.

Rachel's emotions were lifted to a glorious high. The hour of music was the most inspirational church service she had experienced since returning to the States a year ago. Maybe it was the songs' hope-filled lyrics. Or maybe the meeting had simply distracted her from her other thoughts. She tried to savor the moment regardless of the reason.

When the trio was finishing the last note of their last number, the congregation was on its feet and applauding wildly. Shouts of

"Glory" and "Hallelujah" filled the hall.

Both groups, with Pastor Lovett's approval, returned to their mikes for one more number each and for another combined performance as the grand finale.

Pastor Lovett then stepped behind the podium to draw the service to a close. "Well, praise God! There's one thing for sure. If we can ever get a taste of heaven on earth, then we've had it tonight. Honestly, if you haven't been blessed by the musical feast just put before you, then I'm not sure you'll ever be blessed by anything."

He turned and faced the seven singers now standing at the rear of the platform with sweat glistening on their foreheads.

"On behalf of the congregation, I want to say a sincere thank-you for setting this evening aside to be with us here at North Metro. And thanks for letting God use you. Our hearts have truly been uplifted."

Following his cue, the congregation gave another round of riveting applause.

When the applause finally subsided, Lovett announced into the podium mike, "At this time I'm going to ask the pianist and organist to take their places at their instruments. And I want all my ushers to come forward. We are going to collect a special love offering to help cover the groups' traveling expenses. I know everyone will want to give generously to show your appreciation.

"I also want eight or nine of my deacons to come to the front and be ready to assist in an altar call," he added.

He waited for just a moment while the instrumentalists moved into place and the ushers and deacons gathered at the foot of the platform. He then led the congregation in prayer. He thanked

God for the splendid evening and prayed that the offering would be a good one, one that he, their pastor, could be proud of.

"In just a moment," he announced to the audience upon completing his prayer, "after the ushers finish moving down the aisles, I want anyone who feels a need for counsel or prayer to come and take the hand of one of the deacons. They'll be prepared to give you direction from God's Word and pray with you. If God has spoken to your heart tonight and is nudging you forward, then cooperate with Him. Determine in your heart not to let this opportunity slip by you. All right, let's stand."

As the pianist and organist started playing, Lovett took one of the hand-held mikes and moved down onto the main floor.

The ushers busily moved down the rows with the offering plates.

Rachel opened her purse to remove a ten-dollar bill.

"Rachel McCain," she suddenly heard her name spoken over the sound system, "will you join me up front, please?"

For a split second, Rachel froze. Then quickly looked up. Did she hear correctly? Or did her mind misinterpret? Her heartbeat and her breathing instantly accelerated.

She stepped slightly to her left until, around a hodgepodge of shoulders and heads, she acquired Pastor Lovett in her vision.

He was looking in her direction. The mike was raised to his mouth. "Rachel," she saw him say, "come up front and stand with me."

Lovett saw bewilderment on Rachel's face. He watched as she slowly and haltingly shuffled her way past the people to the aisle.

Lovett had not expected to feel this way, but as he watched her make her way up the aisle and saw the cowardice in her eyes, he felt overtaken by a certain element of hostility. By the time Rachel was standing face-to-face with him and questioning him with her eyes, he had lost any sympathy for her that he might have earlier possessed.

He turned from her for a few seconds and looked out toward the audience. "As the organist and pianist continue to play, I invite those of you who need prayer or counsel to come to the front. Go ahead and step out. Let God have the victory in your heart tonight."

Lovett saw an old woman and a young man head up the aisles to deal with burdened hearts.

He then returned his attention to Rachel. He lowered the mike to his side so that his voice was heard only by her. "Just stand right here with me," he instructed. He then motioned for one of the deacons already standing at the front to come and stand at Rachel's opposite side. The deacon joined them.

Just when Lovett thought Rachel was about to open her mouth, no doubt to ask what was happening, he began.

"I have something I want to read to you, Rachel."

He laid the mike on the communion table behind him and removed a folded sheet of paper from his sport coat's pocket. He captured Rachel's eyes with his and then, loud enough for only Rachel and the deacon to hear, he quoted from memory the words written on the piece of paper.

"Hampton Inn," he emphasized slowly. "Monday. Two days ago. June the fourth. Twelve-thirty in the afternoon."

Lovett saw panic rip through Rachel's eyes. He had already told the deacon to take her by the hand if she attempted to flee and to try, without risking any kind of judicially liable maneuver, to encourage restraint. The deacon stood ready.

Lovett continued. "Teal green car. A man who is *not* your husband. You're guilty of adultery, aren't you, Rachel?"

Lovett waited for an answer. He saw Rachel's eyes slam shut, almost instantly squeezing out tears. He then heard her try to muffle a high-pitched groan as her shoulders trembled and slumped.

"You *are* guilty, aren't you, Rachel?"

He saw Rachel struggle for a breath. The scene was intensified by the seconds that lapsed. And then her eyes flashed open. Lovett was suddenly staring into a pair of eyes that penetrated him with pure contempt. Lovett felt himself flinch. He immediately hated himself for such a reaction. With equal speed, he recomposed himself.

"Your silence betrays you, Rachel." He stiffened his neck with repugnance. "You're a reproach and a disgrace. You're a reproach to Christ, to this church, and to everything that is Christian. Therefore, my warnings to you have expired. In accordance to a decision made unanimously by the deacon board just prior to this service, the patience, mercy, and help that have been extended to you from this congregation have now ceased. As of this moment, your membership at North Metro is nullified. So is your children's enrollment in our school. So, what I'm going to ask you to—"

"No!" Rachel snapped, erupting into a sob. "You're not going to ask me to do anything! You and your—"

Lovett felt his jaw tighten as he aggressively steeled himself.

The deacon at Rachel's side took her by the arm.

Rachel threw the deacon's hand away and yelled, "You will leave me and my family alone! Do you understand? You—"

Lovett motioned for a couple of deacons to come and help bring her under control. He caught a glimpse of a few people standing in the front rows, images of shock frozen on their faces.

The two deacons responding to Lovett's summons hurried to where Rachel was spewing disjointed words through her sobbing. One of the men placed his arm around her shoulders and was about to sternly whisper into her ear to calm down.

Just as the man opened his mouth, Rachel flailed her arms, pushing the guy's arm off her shoulders. "Get away from me!" she shouted. "All of you!" Before Pastor Lovett or any of the deacons could say anything or do anything to manage her, she pivoted and started running down the aisle toward the exit. "None of you understand, *none* of you!" she wept loudly.

The organist and the pianist stopped playing.

The eyes and ears of the entire audience were now riveted to the scene.

A deacon moved out to try to stop her.

"It's okay. Let her go," Lovett ordered. "Just follow her and make sure she and the children leave the church grounds. And make sure she collects all of her children's belongings from their classrooms."

The deacon nodded and hustled down the aisle.

Pastor Lovett mounted the platform steps. Ignoring the trio and quartet members who were standing a few feet away, he went directly to the podium.

"Everybody just relax," he said into the podium mike, patting the air with his hands. "Everything is in order." The occasioned speech he had already prepared began to flow autocratically. "As you know, our church has gone out of its way over the course of the last year to give Rachel McCain and her children special help. We've given her financial assistance. We've given her counsel. We've given her a supportive community. Overall, we've done our best to steer her in a right direction.

"Yet time after time she has shown an unwillingness to cooperate with our guidelines. She has refused, even after several warnings from the church leadership, to live a life separated unto God. And it has come to light in the last three days that her moral standards are far lower than any of us ever expected.

"As a result, the deacon board and I decided earlier this evening, with much regret and with much pain, that some of her most recent behavior merits the severest form of church discipline: publicly expelling her from our membership. In addition, although there are only two days left in our school year, we've decided to withdraw her children immediately from the school roll.

"I'm sorry that it's come to this; all of our leaders are. But in situations like this, where gross immorality is involved, we cannot afford to take sides with the transgressor while that person insists on taking sides against God and against His body, the church.

"As the pastor, it's my divinely appointed responsibility to safeguard this church from corruptive influences. And with God Almighty's help, that's what I'm going to do. I've been diligent as your pastor to carry out this responsibility in the past. And don't think for one instant that it's not my full intention to keep doing so. *Whenever, however,* and with *whomever* the need arises. Let tonight's lesson simply be a reminder of my unwavering commitment to this high calling."

After a few more words, Lovett finished the altar call and had his people give a warm handshake and word of welcome to the first-time visitors. The meeting was then dismissed.

Before leaving the premises, Lovett was already convincing himself with pastoral pride that the entire evening had been a great success.

28

ow? How had they known she and Grayson had been at
the hotel?

Gasping feverishly, Rachel stumbled into her apartment
and slammed and locked the door behind her. She was so filled
with hate, anger, humiliation, and hopelessness that her throat
tightened beyond measure, as if it might push through her skin.

Squinting tears through burning eyes, she bashed her fist
against the door. Should she rush back to the church and scream
the truth to them? That she and Grayson had not consummated
their relationship. That she, in fact, had hesitated in the last
moments before undressing. And that Grayson, expressing an
ever-deepening love for her, had with great strength halted their
actions. That he had promptly reversed their direction and
checked them out of the hotel. Should she scream to them the
exact words Grayson proclaimed to her in the hotel room? "I care
for you too much to push you into something that will violate your
conscience and your self-respect. Let's get out of here." Or should
she remain silent and let them all believe what they wanted?

All she knew was that she could never trust anybody again.
Never! Not a man. Not a woman. Not a congregation. And not any
so-called divine deity—especially the Christian God, whose existence she doubted now more than ever.

She threw her purse and keys across the floor and fell onto the living room couch. She buried her face in the cushion and screamed.

She had a flash image of Summer, Holly, and Justin, whom she had just dumped off against their tearful protests at her dad's. She hadn't even taken time to tell her dad that she might never return.

And then she thought of Clay. "I hate you!" she started yelling, cursing him to hell.

She screamed, gasped, and convulsed so much that she felt like she was fighting for air in the vicious downward swirl of a colossal whirlpool.

With sweat-soaked clothes, she lost herself in a kaleidoscope of darkness upon darkness upon darkness, and eventually, after what seemed to be unyielding hours, into the blackness of exhaustion and jerky, intermittent sleep.

By the early hours of morning she was lying motionless in her bed, unaware of when or how she got there. Her breathing was barely perceptible but steady. She stared at the closed curtains as the light of daybreak highlighted the floral design in the fabric.

Visually tracing the outline of one of the flowers, she decided— with the same detachment used to decide between chicken and hamburger for dinner—that there was no reason for her to keep living.

The method for her final escape came to her in those still moments. Boric acid.

She remembered that the exterminator servicing her dad's house a few weeks ago had warned him that the white crystalline powder he found in jar caps beneath the kitchen sink was highly dangerous.

"I'm serious. A couple tablespoons of that stuff will kill a person deader than a stuffed hen," the exterminator had told him.

Her dad had retorted, "Yeah, and it's doing a dang good job of killing the roaches too. Much better than that stinkin' mess you've been spraying all over the place during the last five months. As a matter of fact, it's doing so good that after today your services won't be needed anymore."

Rachel decided that the powdery acid would be the simplest and best choice. A whole box of it could be purchased at any grocery store. It could be stirred into a glass of juice and gulped down in a matter of seconds. No permit. No prescription. No waiting period.

She continued to lie in stillness. After uncounted minutes, she got up and put on a fresh change of clothing. She ignored the ringing of the phone. She was sure it was her dad.

When she finished dressing, she walked into the living room and retrieved her purse and keys from the floor. She quietly walked out the door, got into her car, and headed the Toyota toward a twenty-four-hour grocer about five miles away.

Only when she thought about her children again, and about the contents of the suicide letter she needed to leave for them, did her eyes release a new surge of tears. She was still crying, sniffing, and wiping at her face when she parked in front of the grocery store. She noticed the clock on her dashboard—7:02 A.M. She stayed in the car and waited for about twenty minutes until she thought she had herself under control. Then she got out and walked across the few yards of sunlit asphalt into the store.

Once inside and confronted by smiling people and a large birthday-cake promo picturing a boy about Justin's age, she was jerked back to a perspective of normal life. She attempted to dismiss the picture, but the effort was futile. The placard of the laughing birthday boy created an influx of mental images of Justin, Summer, and Holly, images of them skipping in their socked feet through the house, laughing together in the car, tickling each other on the floor, kicking a ball in the backyard, jostling in the hallway, and living for the childish anticipations that life, in general, so richly provides.

She started to cry again.

As she wandered up the aisles, the memories continued to come. School projects. Easter egg hunts. Christmas mornings. Birthday parties. Vacation adventures. Dentist visits.

She stopped in the middle of the aisle and grabbed her head with both hands.

What am I on the verge of doing? After hammering the question into her brain a dozen or more times, she started walking again. *What is this going to do to the children? To the life they still have left? To their sanity?*

She scanned the items on the shelves but failed to register what she was seeing. She suddenly felt like she needed to sit down somewhere. She placed her hand on one of the shelves and steadied herself.

I just need to get it over with! she yelled inside her head. *Acid. Boric acid. That's what I'm here for. So just find it. And then do what has to be done.*

She pushed herself to move. This time she concentrated as her eyes searched the myriad shelves. She drove herself from one aisle to the next, determined not to give up until she found what she came for.

After a mad search, she finally found the acid in the aisle with the cleaning supplies. One hundred percent boric acid in a hard plastic cylinder-shaped container. For less than four dollars.

Feeling as if she were announcing over the store's intercom system what she was intending to do, she lowered her head and avoided eye contact with the two shoppers in the aisle with her. She picked up one of the containers and read the warning label on the back: "A hazard to humans and domestic animals. Life threatening if swallowed."

She held on to the container and went straight to one of the cash lines. She paid with a five-dollar bill.

When she crawled into her car, she laid the boric acid on the passenger seat. She then squeezed the steering wheel in her hands and pressed her head against the wheel's rigid surface.

Where are You, God? She gritted her teeth and wept. *And where are Your people? The ones who are supposed to love...and...and...* She pressed her head harder into the wheel. *It's not supposed to be this way!*

She started the car.

"Betrayal," she whispered through the tears clinging to her lips. "You and Your people are nothing but a brotherhood of betrayal!"

She shifted the transmission into drive and made her way through the parking lot. At the exit to the street, she waited for a string of traffic to pass. As the Toyota idled, Rachel caught a glimpse of a bank building diagonally across the street. The thought clipped her brain that she was supposed to be sitting at her proof machine in an hour or so. She didn't let the reminder do more than flash in and out of her head. But her thoughts were diverted for a few seconds toward Grayson Cole. The intimacy she had shared with him had been treasured, but it had been a mistake. She was sorry she would be leaving him to hurt this way. He was one of the few people who did not deserve such treatment.

A car horn honked behind her. She put her foot to the gas pedal and pulled out into the street.

A half-mile from the grocery store the name Jason Faircloth grabbed her attention. She saw the name when she stopped for a red light at a major intersection. The name, in large black magnetic letters, was on a church signboard announcing the Bible conference Pastor Lovett had warned his people about. An arrow on the sign pointed toward the church, down the street to her right.

Conference now in progress: *June 6–10*

Guest speaker: JASON FAIRCLOTH

Theme: *Spiritually Abusive Leaders*

Times: 8:15–10:00 A.M. *Wednesday, Thursday, Friday*

11:00 A.M. *Sunday*

7:30 P.M. *nightly*

CROSS-LINK COMMUNITY CHURCH

Pastor Wray Montgomery

The subject matter of the conference went unnoticed by her. It was Jason's name, along with the serious curiosity it had created inside her head in recent months, that penetrated her thoughts.

She also glimpsed the time of the morning sessions. The traffic light turned green. As if her arms were suddenly operating under their own will, they maneuvered the car into a right-hand turn.

29

I'm not losing interest in you!" Anika yelled defensively, her voice slightly slurred by the alcohol in her blood. The emerging light of sunrise revealed the signs of sleep deprivation in her body from the all-night party.

Clay, contending with a hangover, sat behind the wheel of the Shelby Cobra, now stopped and idling just off the shoulder of the road. "Then why, for over a week now, have you refused to let me do more than just barely kiss you?" he yelled back. "You make up excuses every time I come near you. Yet, you didn't offer any resistance this morning to Miguel, or whatever his name is. As I saw it, you were even the one doing the seducing."

Anika turned to face Clay as much as the bucket seat would allow. Her already short red skirt climbed even higher. "This is an open relationship!" she snapped. "You've been with as many different women as I've been with men! So why are you all of a sudden playing this jealousy game?"

"Because for the first time you're resisting me, that's why!"

Anika tried to give a stern look through her drunkenness. "How many other men besides you are *living* in my house and in my bedroom? How many other men besides you am I providing a livelihood for?"

"Oh, so that's it! You're paying my way; therefore you think you have the financial right to just turn off your affection whenever you grow tired of me, without any regard for my feelings!"

"You're being ridiculous!" she barked, jerking herself around to face forward.

He cursed. "I'm not being ridiculous! I left my wife and three children because of my love and desire for you!" He paused to catch his breath, then reached out and touched her hair. "Look," he said, lowering his volume, "I don't mean to raise my voice. It's just that I can't tolerate the idea of you starting to use me like a joker in a deck of cards and shuffling me arbitrarily in and out of your emotions. We've come too far to regress to that kind of child-ishness. Don't you *understand* that?"

Anika continued to face forward and gave no reply.

"Don't you understand how much I want you; how much I *need* you?"

Still looking straight ahead, and with her arms folded, Anika finally retorted, "What I understand is that right now you are just overly tired."

Clay leaned closer to her. He took her chin in his hand and coaxed her to turn and look him in the eyes. "I need you, Anika." He removed his hand from her face and placed it on her leg. "And I want to be with you. Now. This morning."

Anika stared at him without expression. Her silence and her stiffness lasted too long.

Without comment, Clay tensed to a point beyond return. He then lunged out of the car and slammed the door.

He strode about a hundred yards up the road when Anika pulled alongside him in the Cobra. Clay kept walking.

Anika drove the car to match his pace. "Are you going to get in or are you going to walk all the way?"

"I believe I need to be alone for a while," he growled.

"We're fifteen miles from home, for heaven's sake!"

"I believe I can handle it."

"Look, I'm sorry…I—"

He angrily waved her on.

"All right, forget it," she said. "Do it your way."

Hesitantly she pulled away and left him.

He spotted the pay phone at a Gasotica gas station. He stopped a few feet from the phone, sat cross-legged on the ground, and agonized further about his decision to make the phone call.

For over two and a half hours he had pounded his way along the curvy and hilly two-lane road. He was now at the outskirts of San José and only three or four miles from the house. His shirt was wet with perspiration. The morning was still young, but the temperature had already climbed to around eighty degrees, the humidity to about 90 percent.

He started to shake. How, in the name of reason, could he do it? What could he possibly say that would be convincing? Could he really promise anything? Would it make a difference even if he could? Maybe if he could just hear their voices. Maybe that would be reason enough.

He started rocking. He argued with himself not to go through with it.

He was lost in a dark cave of emotion when he gradually realized, as if emerging from a dream, that a toothless old man was watching him through the window of a rusty pickup parked a few yards away.

To break the distraction, Clay stood and slowly walked to the phone. He reached into his pants' pocket and removed a two-colones coin and a telephone credit card from his wallet.

As hard as he had sometimes tried, he had never been able to forget the telephone number. The number was now drumming unyieldingly inside his head.

He deposited the coin and lifted a trembling finger toward the keypad. Slowly he punched in the code for the international operator. Within seconds he was quoting to a faceless voice the all-consuming number.

As the operator made the connection, Clay tried to remember the opening statement he had rehearsed so many times.

He heard the ringing on the other end. He felt his throat go dry.

This is never going to work! he shouted to himself.

Fighting rapid breathing, he willed his eyes shut and tried to visualize the four faces. But the images had grown less exact with the passing of time.

He inhaled deeply and held his breath, then opened his eyes and stared at the phone cradle. After a few seconds he started to pull the receiver away from his ear.

The ringing suddenly ceased when a distinct *click* sounded over the line. Someone had picked up.

"Hello," he heard a man's voice say. "The Kendall residence. This is Pastor Harlan speaking."

Clay was still not breathing.

"Hello," the man said again. "Can I help you?" More silence. "Hello! Is there someone there?" There were six or seven additional seconds of silence, and then the line went dead.

Clay shakily returned the receiver to its cradle. After expelling the air from his lungs, he bent over and threw up onto the asphalt.

As he had suspected, they were no longer there. Probably no longer even in Sweden.

30

Only when the Toyota approached the Cross-Link Community Church parking lot did Rachel's reasoning catch up with her actions. She realized that one of the final things she wanted to do was to see the man whose entire denomination turned against him. To see what kind of beast he was. And to perhaps see a hideous reflection of herself from the "good" Christians' point of view.

It would also bring her twisted pleasure to defy Pastor Lovett's demand that no one from North Metro attend any of Faircloth's meetings.

Maybe her last act on earth would be to call Lovett and give him a detailed report of the meeting.

She drove into the nearly empty lot, then glanced at the dashboard clock—7:50. The meeting was not scheduled to begin for twenty-five minutes.

She parked several rows from the sanctuary.

Her homeward momentum, she realized, was being delayed. And that disturbed her. But she promised herself that her plan for self-extinction was not in jeopardy. She would simply wait, go inside, defy Lovett, satisfy her curiosity about Faircloth, and then leave. Her ultimate escape would be postponed by only an hour or so.

Nevertheless, she still argued with herself about the delay. Two or three times over the next fifteen minutes she cranked the car to leave. But each time, she turned off the engine.

As her thoughts and emotions battered one another like wind-thrown chaff, she opened the glove compartment and removed a pen and a piece of paper.

She started writing.

Dear Summer, Holly, and Justin,

Please know that each of you is the greatest gift any parent in the whole world could ever be blessed with. You are more special and more wonderful than all—

Her hand started shaking so badly that her next few words became illegible scribbles. She laid the pen and paper on her lap and leaned her head back onto the seat.

She needed to leave. She started the car once again and shifted the transmission to reverse. She moved the pen and paper over to the passenger's seat.

She saw three people walking together across the parking lot toward the auditorium. After watching them disappear around the corner of the building, she sat for another two or three minutes staring toward the church's front lawn.

She finally switched off the ignition, got out of the car, and went into the building.

It was only the second time since becoming a Christian eighteen years ago that she had attended a church outside her own denomination. The other time had been in Sweden. She and Clay had attended a Christmas concert a few years ago at a Swedish state church. They had concealed that fact from the mission board; attending churches of other denominations had always been against mission policy.

When Rachel entered the Cross-Link worship hall, she saw that all of the pews across the rear half of the fan-shaped auditorium were roped off. She took a seat just in front of the rope, on the last row possible. She sat next to the aisle and avoided eye contact with everyone, especially the few men and women sitting near her. She kept her eyes closed and feigned prayerful meditation.

She remained that way for four or five minutes until the meeting started.

"Good morning. Welcome to Cross-Link Community Church," a man's mature voice spoke into the microphone.

Rachel looked up.

"I'm Pastor Wray Montgomery, and I want to welcome each of you to this session where we'll once again examine the issue of spiritual maltreatment, or spiritual abuse. I see a number of new faces this morning. I want all of you who are visiting to know that I'm thrilled you're here with us. I trust that God will truly minister to your hearts.

"Well, the theme of our conference, Spiritually Abusive Leaders, has definitely struck a nerve. A lady who was a longtime victim of spiritual abuse came to me last night after the service and said she wished it were mandatory for every preacher in her former denomination to attend a conference like this where this information"—he paused for a second and grinned—"was force-fed to them.

"Well, there are hundreds of pastors perhaps in many, if not all, denominations who need to face these truths. But if just…"

Rachel lost track of Montgomery's words for a few seconds as the term *spiritual abuse* punctured her attention. She had never heard the expression before. The question of whether or not spiritual abuse was what had been happening to her hit her like a chilling winter breeze.

"And I can't think of anyone," she heard Montgomery continue, "I'd rather hear address the subject than Jason Faircloth. He's a man who brings an extraordinary amount of experience to the topic. And he's one of the few men in the world I truly respect. In the area of human and spiritual insight, I look up to him as a mentor. I'm honored that he's chosen to take time from his ministry as a pastor in New York City to be here with us." With those words, he gestured toward one of the front-row pews for Jason Faircloth to come up to the lectern.

As Faircloth moved toward the mike, a dozen or so people throughout the auditorium stood and applauded.

Rachel was struck by the paradox. She found herself stretching upward to get her first look at this man who was accused by one church of being a devil and was now being recognized by another church as someone very special.

The man she saw approaching the podium, though, was a surprise. Instead of having a conservative, professional appearance as she had assumed, the man looked as if he had come straight to the meeting from leading some kind of archaeological expedition overseas. He looked to be in his mid to late fifties, and nearly six feet tall with a sinewy physique. He was wearing a beige, short-sleeved pullover shirt and a pair of khakis. His arms and face were tanned. His face was covered with white stubble, and the best Rachel could detect, he had his white hair pulled back into a nubby ponytail.

Rachel thought, *Pastor Lovett condemned the man from a moment of limited contact just over the phone. What would he say about the man if he appraised him on the platform at this instant with his eyes?*

Just to defy Lovett, perhaps, Rachel's own judgment of the man's unconventional image was positive.

And strangely enough, she thought she could actually see meekness in the man's walk, a rare and potent quality that in her mind was far more important than a ministerial look.

Faircloth took his position behind the lectern, slightly lowered his head, and didn't immediately say anything.

A calming silence, combined with an aura of strength, exuded from his presence.

Rachel wondered if Faircloth was even aware of the placid stillness. He appeared as if he were in his own world. Was he making some kind of final decision regarding his talk? Was he trying to focus the people's attention? Was he praying?

He finally looked up and inhaled. "I was never convicted by a jury of my peers or held in custody by a court of law, but during the sixties and early seventies I hideously and repetitiously abused my wife." He stopped and inhaled again. "I also abused my teenage daughter, my only child. As a result of my abuse they both died within a few weeks of each other.

A riptide of quietness blanketed the auditorium again.

"They're both buried not very far from here. I killed them, not by physical abuse, but by *spiritual abuse.*" He paused to let the words sink in.

"The tragedy is amplified by the fact that I was a pastor at the time."

Brokenness resonated in Faircloth's voice. Rachel was sure she could see it in his eyes as well. She had never before seen brokenness in a pastor, in any pastor. Neither had she seen such honesty and vulnerability. Something deep inside her was touched. She was immediately drawn to the man.

"Why do I talk on this subject? Because right now, all across America, and other countries as well, there are an untold number of pastors, evangelists, missionaries, Sunday school teachers, elders, deacons, and youth pastors who are inflicting injury on their congregations and followers through spiritual abuse. The same kind of mistreatment with which I killed two people. Many of these leaders are abusing their people unknowingly, but the destruction they wreak is not partial to intent.

"What are the marks of these leaders? First of all, to recap yesterday's lesson, these people are identified by a know-it-all, authoritarian approach to ministry. Their public attitude—sometimes blatant, sometimes subtle—is that they and *they alone* have authority in their group. And that they and *they alone* are theologically right. Anyone, inside the leader's group or out, who takes a differing position is not just different but blind, ignorant, and wrong."

Rachel had never before heard this kind of presentation. She was transfixed.

"Second—and this is the point I'll discuss this morning—since dictatorial, abusive leaders believe they are the only ones in their group who have the God-given intelligence to provide true leadership, they *fight* to protect their position. Thus, they are marked by a twisted compulsion to squelch, rebuke, discredit, silence, punish, or eliminate anyone who challenges their authority with dissenting views or behavior. They feel that they and they alone must be in control. 'Do what *I* tell you to do, and believe the way *I* tell you to believe, *or else'* is their creed."

For the next ten or fifteen minutes, Faircloth explained that these leaders subsequently find it necessary to control their people through the suppressive elements of fear and guilt. Through fear, by threatening them with God's severe judgment to get them to cooperate. And through guilt, by making them feel damned and worthless whenever they are less than cooperative.

"This type of leadership possesses several inherent dangers," Faircloth emphasized. "One of those dangers is that it drives people to withdraw into silent and listless obedience. It stifles the natural learning process of questioning, disagreeing, debating, and discussing. It likewise dissuades people from openly sharing their real thoughts and feelings about life, about God, and about themselves.

"And when people are driven to this kind of muteness, they become close-range, standing targets for Satan and the personalities of darkness. We know from both Scripture and observation that Satan's goal is to kill, steal, devour, and destroy. If God prohibits him from devouring and killing a person's physical body, then Satan will try to destroy the person mentally, emotionally, socially, and spiritually.

"His primary weapon for achieving this destruction is his lying. I repeat, his primary weapon is his lying. In the words of Jesus, Satan is the father of lies. He is utterly devoid of truth. This is an invariant."

Faircloth paused. Rachel saw that his eyes were inflamed with experience-born conviction.

"And Scripture and observation make it exceedingly clear that Satan's lies are far more effective if he and his demonic ranks can isolate their victims geographically, socially, emotionally, mentally, or religiously and barricade them from hearing what is *true*.

"We see this fact exemplified with Eve when she's alone in the Garden of Eden. We see it with John the Baptist when he's isolated in prison." Faircloth took the time to read the accounts in Genesis 3 and Matthew 11.

"Therefore, if a person is in a church structure where there is no freedom to express one's thoughts and feelings, but is instead driven to a prison of silence by a menacing, insecure leader, that person, even though he or she is part of a congregation of one hundred or five thousand, will become dangerously isolated. He or she will be alone with the enemy and his lies. Consequently, many such people end up believing long-term lies about themselves, about life, about Christianity, and about God.

"Authoritarian leaders who force people into this situation are playing right into Satan's ploy. And the severity of the situation is even compounded if the leader, unchecked and unaccountable, is unknowingly believing the enemy's lies himself and then teaching them to his people."

Faircloth paused. His countenance hinted at unpleasant, but necessary, thoughts.

"I'll give you an example from my own life. During the sixties, I, as a pastor, followed my denomination's epidemic practice of building my preaching around man-made, denominational-made, and culture-made rules. There was a standard list of these rules that we, supposedly under divine guidance, boldly amended to the Scriptures. We zealously twisted the Bible to accommodate those rules. And then we imposed those rules universally—not in the name of our church, our denomination, or our culture, but *in the name of God.*

"Rules such as these: Christian men had to have short, tapered haircuts and could not wear beards. Christian women could only wear knee-length or longer dresses, never pants. All Christians had to be clean and well groomed. They could use only the King James Version of the Bible. They could never attend a movie theater. They could not play board games that included dice. They could not listen to pop music of any kind. They could never question the pastor. They had to attend church services a minimum of three times a week—Sunday morning, Sunday evening, and Wednesday evening. A pastor must always preach in a suit and tie. Only pianos, organs, and trumpets could be used as instruments in the worship services, never guitars or drums."

Rachel felt a sudden repugnance rise in her soul. For her, the list was all too familiar. She listened intently as Faircloth continued.

"Holding up these, and other, extrabiblical rules and demanding that they be obeyed as a measure of genuine spirituality became my focus as a preacher. In my thinking, these rules became a dividing line that separated the righteous from the unrighteous, the authentic Christian from the dubious Christian.

"Adherence to this all-important list of man-made standards was actually judged to be more significant than the genuine fruit of the Spirit. If a person measured up to this list of dos and don'ts, then it was a moot point if he or she were filled with so much anxiety that they had to use drugs to put themselves to sleep at night, or were racist, or had a critical tongue that scourged everyone who was deemed unworthy, or had an impatient and abrasive temperament that hurt family, friends, and strangers.

"On the other hand, those who failed to measure up to this

man-made list, regardless of the truly spiritual qualities in their lives, were rebuked and condemned as people who were out of God's will and who brought shame to the Christian faith."

Faircloth removed the mike from its holder and walked with it to the side of the lectern.

Rachel had blanked everybody else out of her vision. What Faircloth was saying was like a medicinal ointment. He had actually put into words, and made sense of, all the loose and scattered ideas about Christian legalism that had besieged her soul in recent years. The irony did not escape her, however, that she was hearing it articulated and confirmed during her last hours, when it was too late to be of any help.

"As an abusive leader, I believed an atrocious lie," Faircloth said softly, yet painfully. "And I preached it to my people in the name of God. Because of my horsewhip tactics, I frightened my people into silent submissiveness. Most of them accepted the lie. I'll never know the full extent of the spiritual, emotional, and mental injuries I caused.

"I do, however, know what I did to my wife and daughter. With a steel-trap demeanor, I never gave my daughter, for example, the freedom to question my convictions. I forced them on her every day of every week of every month. I cut her short every time she tried to argue or reason with me, and that was regularly. Because of her resistant attitude, I repeatedly told her that she was a disgusting excuse for a pastor's daughter."

Faircloth slightly lowered his head. "At the age of sixteen, Hannah ran away from home. I had pushed her to a breaking point. My wife and I didn't know her whereabouts for a year and a half, until we received notification of her death. She had died in

Miami, six hundred miles from home, while giving birth to a baby girl.

"My wife...died a few days later."

Rachel found herself rubbing her thigh with anger. She was not sure if she was reacting to the story of Faircloth's family or of her own family, or both.

"Hannah, my only child, despised me so much that her feelings of repulsion even took root in the heart of the young man she married. When she died, the young husband, although he had never met me, decided he didn't want his surviving baby girl ever to be in my presence. He did everything possible to carry out that wish. He even moved across the Atlantic and lived in Europe for a while. My desperate attempts to find them or make contact with them always ended up in vain.

"I met my granddaughter, Daytona, for the first time just seven months ago. She was turning eighteen. She was a prostitute and heroin addict who was in a New York City hospital recovering from a suicide attempt. My son-in-law, whom I finally met one time, died at the age of forty-three from the effects of alcoholism. Daytona and I are the only surviving members of our immediate family.

"I say from the experience of one who stands guilty: Religious leaders who have the mentality of a know-it-all master and who are focused on and driven by lies *are not innocent people*. They are debilitating parasites.

"And the sad fact is there are thousands of these leaders, both nationwide and worldwide, who perpetrate massive hurt and disillusionment. Their victims number in the tens of thousands."

Rachel found it strange that the man now speaking from the

pulpit had been Pastor Lovett's predecessor at North Metro Church of the Bible. But why, she wondered, had it taken the tragic deaths of his wife and daughter to force him to trade his scepter for a heart? Were extreme and lethal measures the only way to break such leaders?

Rachel grimaced.

In a few hours, when North Metro heard about her suicide, maybe Pastor Lovett, Pastor Reese, and the entire congregation would bear some of the guilt for *her* desperate demise. Maybe they would reflect on their cruel behavior, as Faircloth had many years ago reflected on his. Maybe they would realize how they had dehumanized her.

Maybe. But probably not.

Maybe she deserved what she had gotten. She pressed her fingers against her temples.

She heard Faircloth cite another danger of authoritarian leadership. "It squelches diversity," he claimed, "and, therefore, destroys the possibility for overall balance in a group." He elaborated the point and continued to hold Rachel spellbound for another half-hour.

Faircloth concluded the morning session by announcing with great joy that his granddaughter, Daytona, was with him and would share her miraculous story of redemption later in the evening service. At his request, and to the pleasure of the crowd, Daytona—medium-height, blond, blue-eyed, and effervescent—stood to be recognized and then sat back down. Rachel could detect the pride and love that existed between the young lady and her granddad.

"And tomorrow morning," Faircloth told them, "I'll highlight another mark of spiritually abusive leaders: Instead of following

Christ's example and being servants to people, they manipulate people to serve *them*. Not just them, but *their* programs, *their* ideas, and *their* visions. And, at your pastor's request, I'll also briefly tell you how God used a multinational church and a wise old man in Oslo, Norway, to salvage my own broken life."

Oslo, Norway? Did Rachel hear the words correctly?

Her mind reeled. Was Faircloth saying he had *lived* in Oslo, the capital of Norway? Less than nine hours by car across the southern part of Sweden from where she and her family had lived in Stockholm?

The idea was uncanny, but she was certain that's what she heard.

When had he been there? How long had he stayed?

Rachel felt that the coincidence of their both having ties to North Metro church and ending up in Scandinavia, that sparsely populated and almost secret northern corner of the planet, was simply too striking to be ignored.

She decided, against all inner protests, that she had to linger for a few minutes and speak with the man.

31

Rachel intended to ask Faircloth two quick questions: "How did your wife die?" and "When were you in Norway?" And she wanted to share two facts of camaraderie: "I was a member of North Metro for eighteen years" and "I served as a missionary in Stockholm." She also wanted to tell him to never stop delivering his message about the ugliness of religious tyranny. And then she would go straight to her apartment to spend her final moments alone.

She had been waiting patiently for about twenty minutes at the front of the auditorium to talk to him. Eight or nine other people had gotten to him first. The last of those people was now conversing with him at the foot of the platform.

She kept her head lowered as she waited, occasionally looking up. She tried not to think or feel.

When she lifted her face again, she saw him looking at her. There was no one left between them. She was now staring into the eyes of the man who for the last eighteen years had been listed by his former denomination as a person to avoid. Because, reputedly, he was dangerous to the faith.

After only a second or two, however, he broke eye contact with her. He turned around, picked up a Bible and leather briefcase from the edge of the platform, and started walking.

Rachel was completely taken aback by the awkwardness of the

moment. It looked as if Faircloth was going to walk away and leave her standing there. As Rachel's feelings geared up for a response, Faircloth walked to the front pew and sat down, facing her.

"Take a seat," he said, pointing to the scarlet-padded pew. "You look tired."

Rachel looked him in the eyes again. She slowly took a seat.

"I'm glad you waited," Faircloth told her. "I'm glad you didn't leave before you had a chance to talk."

Rachel's thoughts stumbled over one another. She heard her voice stutter with emotion. "I don't understand. You must be confusing me with someone else... I..." Her voice faded.

Faircloth's gaze seemed to pierce all the way to her soul. "I could see the longtime hurt in your eyes. Even as you were making your way to the front. It's not the kind of pain you want to carry around alone."

Rachel's eyes grew wider. *How...?* Then she wanted to cry. She stayed the tears and sighed an admission. "I'm...I was a pastor's wife," she whispered. "I'm just curious to know how your wife died. And if there was anyone who ever knew she was hurting, or anyone who cared?"

Faircloth's eyes remained steady. Yet there was something there—a slight twitch, a minuscule lift—as if he read volumes between her words. "What's your name?"

"Rachel."

He tenderly shook her hand.

"I was a very insensitive marriage partner, Rachel. I was not only a dictator as a pastor, but I was equally dictatorial as a husband. I destroyed my wife emotionally through years of criticism, unreasonable demands, and too little affection. My wife was just an empty shell by the time our daughter ran away from home. At that point in time, my wife's sole purpose for living was to fulfill her role as a mother. When word reached us that Hannah was dead, my wife literally lost her will to live. She went into shock and became physically ill. Neither medical technology nor medicine was able to sustain her. A few days later she died. Did anyone know that she was languishing emotionally and spiritually?"

He paused.

"It's doubtful. As you know, pastors' wives usually don't have the freedom to reveal their negative feelings about their life and marriage without, to some degree, risking their husband's reputation. They're under an enormous amount of pressure to uphold their spouse's public image of being a model husband and father. So they become extraordinarily proficient at concealing their personal struggles from the public eye. From their children as well. Even, sometimes, from their husbands.

"Pastors' wives are consequently some of the loneliest and most bottled up people in all of Christendom. If a lady's husband works as a salesman or an accountant, and the man is a lousy marriage partner, the lady can talk freely about his disappointing character and performance wherever, whenever, and to whomever she wishes. And the man's career will not be put in jeopardy.

"A pastor's wife who's in a bad marriage, however, doesn't have that liberty. If she talks openly, even if it's for therapeutic purposes, she knows her husband could very well lose the respect of the people, along with his job and the family income. She knows that with a forced resignation on his record, her husband's popularity as a candidate for another pastoral position would plunge to around zero. To speak up about her unhappiness thus affects her

RANDALL ARTHUR ◆ 260

financial security. Even minimizes her chances for sufficient alimony if she pursued a divorce.

"So, as was the case with my wife, she buries her feelings and dies alone on the inside. More often than not, no one knows she's hurting until she reaches a breaking point—till, for instance, she has an affair, till she stops functioning and needs medical or psychiatric help, till she finally throws her fear and caution to the wind and runs to a divorce court, or till she attempts to end her life."

Rachel suddenly realized she was as motionless as a bronze statue. She was also aware that Faircloth had stopped talking.

She wanted to respond, but didn't know what to say, didn't know where to begin.

"How close are you to that breaking point, Rachel?" Faircloth asked.

It was those nine words and the penetrating heart of the man behind them that breached the dam of her soul. She leaned her upper body toward her knees and thought of the boric acid sitting on the front seat of the car.

"I've been there for longer than anyone knows," she confessed with wet eyes. With that difficult declaration, an outpouring of her soul quickly followed.

She started by telling him why she had come to hear him. And then for the next hour, she told him her story. She told him about her eighteen-year connection with North Metro Church of the Bible, about her conversion under the ministry of Pastor Frank Lovett, about her engagement and marriage to Clay, about her and Clay's move to Stockholm to be church planters, about the three children born to them, about her and Clay's progressive shift from the hard-core legalism of their denomination, about Clay's

eventual withdrawal and mysterious behavior, about his abandonment of their family and the discovered cause, about his
still-unknown whereabouts, about her and the children's move
back to Atlanta, about her dismissal by the mission board, about
the cold and rigid treatment by the North Metro congregation,
about her loneliness and suicidal wishes, about Grayson Cole,
about her progressive intimacy and near adultery, about her public
expulsion from North Metro's membership in last night's service,
and about the boric acid right now in her car.

"The bitterness, the depression, the guilt—it's all too much to
handle," she said in summation, slumping in the seat. "I feel that
my only solution is to end it all." She wiped her eyes with a handkerchief that Faircloth had given her near the beginning of her
tale. "I fully intended to go straight to the apartment from this
meeting and put myself to sleep. And never wake up."

She had now completely emptied her heart. Faircloth looked
as if he had absorbed everything. Including the pain. And especially the humiliation of her confession of emotional intimacy with
another man. Not once while she was speaking had his attention
strayed. He had not even peeked at his watch.

"Where are your children?" he asked.

Rachel explained that they were with her dad and took a few
minutes to tell about her dad and his virtual noninvolvement in
their lives.

Faircloth briefly closed his eyes, looked heavenward for a
second or two, then reconnected with Rachel's gaze. "Will you give
me permission to be your friend and helper, Rachel?"

Rachel squinted. She was touched, as unexpected as it was, by
Faircloth's concern. But how could anybody, even this man, help

her now? "I…I just don't have the strength… I—"

"I would like to be your strength for you."

"I don't understand," she sniffled.

Faircloth gave her the most selfless, yet most assured and understanding, look she had ever witnessed. "To my regret, I helped build the ministry that condemned you. It would be a real honor if you would let me now embrace you with grace, the same kind of grace with which others embraced me." He told her how in 1975, while searching for his grandchild, he ended up in Norway as a prodigal with a broken faith, and how God used a wise old Burmese pastor and an international congregation to salvage his life. "I was at one of my lowest points ever, and those people, with God's help, became my strength for me. How? They accepted me. They listened to me. They fed me. They provided me with employment. They gave me their time and friendship. They gave me themselves and thus protected me from the dangers of isolation. I've gratefully tried to pass along that help ever since. Especially to those like yourself who are ravaged and left alone."

Rachel wasn't sure if she fully grasped what Faircloth was offering. In one sense, it sounded abstract. In another sense, it sounded very concrete. Either way, it sounded too surreal. Yet, almost against her will, she felt her heart responding, as if to some kind of spiritual or emotional CPR.

But it was too late for any true or lasting help, wasn't it? Didn't she *want* it to be too late? Didn't she just want to go home, close her eyes, and die? Wasn't that the simplest? She sniffled and leaned her head back.

She heard Faircloth's voice: "What are the telephone numbers to your dad's and to the bank?"

Was she going to awaken in her bed in a few moments and realize she was just dreaming? She heard a voice, sounding like her own, speak up and give him the numbers.

For Rachel, the next few hours became a blur.

Faircloth first introduced her to Pastor Montgomery and told him an abbreviated version of her story. Faircloth was careful, however, not to give specifics about her emotional affair. He simply referred to that part of her story as a "behavioral choice" that had caused her home church to publicly sever their relations with her before they had gathered all the facts.

Faircloth canceled his afternoon plans to hike to the top of Stone Mountain with a group of single adults and managed to secure the Cross-Link's guest quarters, the former church pastorium located on the church property, for Rachel's use for the next three or four days.

Accompanied by his granddaughter, Daytona, he then drove Rachel to her dad's house to pick up Summer, Holly, and Justin.

Upon their arrival at the house, Rachel numbly listened to her dad reveal his impatience with her, claiming that he had sacrificed a profitable truck run because of her morning disappearance. She then had to deal with the children's questions about missing school.

Faircloth returned them all to the church building and showed them into the guesthouse, where a couple of smiling middle aged ladies, recruited by Pastor Montgomery, were already in place to help take care of the children for the day. Take-out hamburgers, fries, and Cokes had just been placed on the table for lunch.

Rachel could not bring herself to eat. So, while the children ate, Faircloth walked her to the church office and called Grayson Cole at the bank. Faircloth, without presumption, introduced himself and told Grayson why Rachel had not reported to work that morning, explaining what had happened to her during the last sixteen hours. He explained that he, his granddaughter, and several people at Cross-Link Church would, with everyone's agreement, make themselves available over the next few days to provide Rachel and the three children with meals, company, and moral support.

Grayson wanted to talk to Rachel.

Rachel took the phone. When she heard Grayson's voice, she broke into tears. All she could manage to say between sobs was "I'm really...sorry...that I've complicated your life so much."

Grayson told her that he would not for one moment entertain such a pointless apology. He was just thankful that she was still alive. He then asked with great alarm and concern if staying at the Cross-Link Church was what she truly wanted. If not, he would immediately come to get her.

"If it weren't for these people," Rachel choked out, "I'm afraid I would already be gone. If they really want to help me, then I think I need to stay. I just don't have the energy to work right now, or to be responsible for the kids. I just—" She started crying again, so hard that she couldn't talk anymore.

Grayson told her he would like to come to see her as soon as he left work. She managed to squeak out an okay and then gave the phone back to Faircloth, who gave Grayson the church's address.

Faircloth turned to Rachel. He saw that she was still very jittery. "It's a beautiful day outside. Would you like to go for a stroll around the church parking lot and talk some more?"

Rachel was surprised that Faircloth was willing to sacrifice another portion of his day for her. She was deeply moved by the offer. She nodded her desire to accept the invitation.

"Please tell me again why you're doing all this," she said when they were outside.

Faircloth gazed at her with eyes of sympathy. "During the four years following the deaths of my wife and daughter," he related, "I battled my way through the normal disillusionment, confusion, and anger. I eventually became very exploratory and very liberal in my behavior. I was quite wayward by the time I landed in Norway in the winter of '75.

"That made it improbable for the judgment-prone Christian to see the emptiness and the search for God going on inside my heart. As you know, humans tend to pardon or condemn, based strictly on their view of a person's actions. Christians especially, because of our moral expectations, look so closely at a person's conduct that we often forget there's a life going on inside that person's heart.

"Those who condemned you, for example, focused totally on your emotional involvement with another man and your assumed physical affair. They failed to recognize or even look for—much less appreciate—the intense struggle inside your soul as you tried for weeks and months to resist the temptation of such intimacy. They failed to see the fear, the agony, the crying out, the restlessness, and the guilt.

"In Norway, I was fortunate in that I was engulfed by the friendship of a discerning old man who made the effort to see the wounded and searching heart beneath my callous exterior. The fact that he incorporated my heart into his overall opinion of me reflected the love of Christ and taught me a lesson I will never forget. I'll be indebted to him for as long as I have breath.

"So why am I stepping into your life and offering acceptance, friendship, and help? Because I can see and feel your heart. It's a confused and lonely heart that just wants to be loved and to do what's right. And because I want to. Because I care."

Rachel fixed her eyes on Faircloth as she shuffled across the asphalt. "I hear you..." she gulped down her reply, "but I'm afraid."

Faircloth looked at her but kept silent.

"I'm afraid to trust again," she told him. "And I'm also afraid to hope again. For anything. Besides, if I accept your help for the next three or four days, what am I supposed to do when you leave and return to New York? I've already proved to myself that I can't cope in my current situation. It's...it's all useless." Her throat constricted. She coughed to alleviate the awkward pain.

Jason thought carefully before he responded. "What I'm about to share with you, Rachel," he began with the hint of a reverent grin on his lips, "is, I believe, more than just a coincidence. Six months ago, I was getting ready to return to Norway for a long-term stay. I had just completed a two-year ministry commitment with the Liberty International City Church in New York City. It was in those remaining hours when Daytona and I providentially found each other.

"Because of her urgent needs, I altered my plans and decided to stay indefinitely in the States. I ended up buying some real estate, a triplex to be exact. Daytona and I share one of the apartments. The other two I bought to share as rent-free shelters or places of refuge for people in need. A young couple who lost their home and two young children in a house fire last Christmas are living in one of them. The other one, fully furnished with three bedrooms, has been empty for about five weeks. Daytona and I have been praying that God would bring us into contact with someone who would be truly helped if the apartment were made available to them, someone in dire circumstances whose options and resources are all spent. Someone who stands in need of friendship and encouragement.

"I understand that it's difficult for you to believe in people again, Rachel. I've been there. So has Daytona. But I'm sincere when I say that you and your children are welcome to go with us to New York and use the apartment.

"It would be no problem to incorporate the support of the Liberty International congregation of over fifteen hundred people, with all of their energy and resources, to provide the long-term help you need."

Rachel stopped walking and buried her face in her hands.

"You can live in the apartment rent free," Faircloth promised. "In addition, I'll personally be willing, for four months or so, to cover all of your family's food, clothing, and travel expenses. That way you can be free from any financial responsibilities for a while and focus on your children. And on your own recovery as well."

Rachel stood speechless.

Sounding as if he could feel the weight of his proposal and the added turmoil it pushed onto Rachel's life, Faircloth whispered, "I realize you're drained, too drained to think quickly through such a decision. But if you want, you, Daytona, and I can talk about the idea over the next three days."

Rachel, still speechless, lost herself and wept on his shoulder.

32

Grayson arrived at the Cross-Link Community Church around five-thirty that evening. He was outraged at North Metro Church of the Bible and Pastor Frank Lovett for what they had done to Rachel the night before. Even as he greeted and hugged Rachel and was introduced to Jason and Daytona, his feelings affected his composure and his speech.

He spilled over with questions of suspicion toward Faircloth. He wanted to know who Faircloth was. He wanted to know the man's motive for inviting Rachel and the children to spend the next three days at the Cross-Link Church. He wanted to know just how the man expected to help.

Within five or six minutes, though, Grayson began to calm down. Faircloth's controlled and mature manner, along with his straightforward answers, stifled Grayson's aggressiveness. The information that mellowed him the most, however, was Faircloth's history with North Metro Church of the Bible. Grayson then better understood the quickness with which Rachel had trusted the man. Rachel and Faircloth's linkage with North Metro and their similar journeys out of the same legalistic web had created a bond between them.

After another ten minutes of conversation and being touched by Faircloth's purity of spirit, Grayson understood even further Rachel's response to the man. He learned more about Faircloth's role as the teaching-consulting pastor for the fifteen pairs of copastors who led the fifteen congregations of Liberty International City Church spread throughout New York City. He learned additionally that Faircloth was sixty-one years old and a widower.

Grayson then listened as Rachel told him how Faircloth had helped her over the last ten hours.

Wanting Rachel to receive the care she needed, Grayson finally concluded that perhaps it would be best if she indeed placed herself and the kids for the next three days under the care of Faircloth and the Cross-Link Church. He was persuaded, both by what he heard and by what he saw, that Faircloth was a man of integrity.

Grayson finally ushered Rachel into a children's Sunday school classroom where the two of them sat in private facing each other in miniature wooden chairs.

Grayson noticed for the first time how rundown Rachel appeared. Her hair was oily and uncombed; her eyes were milky gray with deep crimson blotches.

He reached out to take her hand, but drew back when he saw no reciprocation. With emotion, he began speaking. "I wanted to be alone with you to tell you how sorry I am for my actions and for the humiliation I've caused you. I blame myself for what happened to you last night. I should've known better than to put you in that situation. But whatever has happened, or is going to happen, you've got to believe me when I say I love you and that I feel the hurt with you. As a matter of fact, I would like to—"

"He's invited me to take the children and move to New York," Rachel spoke up softly with little expression in her eyes.

"I'm sorry, he's what? Who's *he?* What are you talking about?"

"Faircloth. He's invited the children and me to go to New York with him. He owns some apartments, and one of them is empty. He's saying we can stay there without paying rent and that he and his granddaughter and the church he helps pastor will all pitch in to help us out."

Grayson's growing optimism vanished. "I, uh...I don't understand. Why would you—"

"Maybe that's what the kids and I need. A fresh start in a different city." She looked into Grayson's eyes. "I know you say you love me. And I believe you. But I'm not sure about *my* feelings. I'm just not certain about anything right now. Maybe I've just used you to medicate all my other hurts. I...I just don't know."

Grayson wanted to shout: *I know you've been nearly pushed over the edge, but you can't be serious about running away to New York with a stranger. You're not being sensible. Just give yourself a little time. I'm certain you'll realize that you love me. In the meantime, you and the kids can move into the house with me. I'll take care of you. It would be an honor.*

Instead, he said, "Just don't rush into anything, okay? Take the rest of the weekend, along with three or four days off work next week, and think through all of the ramifications of what you're saying. And get some rest. If you don't feel that you can go back to living alone, then maybe with the help of this church we can find another single mom or a single lady who can share the apartment with you until you're back on your feet again. If we can't find someone, then you're welcome to move into my house. I've got plenty of room."

"The kids," she said without blinking. "It would never work out. They haven't even met you. It wouldn't be right."

"At least think about it," he said, shifting positions and leaning back in his chair. He then asked if she felt like telling him, in her own words, what had happened last night.

Looking newly trampled, Rachel told him what she could remember. For about thirty minutes, they talked about the whole ordeal.

Grayson wondered aloud how Lovett—"the disgusting man"— had even known about the hotel. "Did he have someone following us? I need to march right on over there and make clear to him that—"

"I don't think I want to talk about it anymore right now," Rachel suddenly interrupted.

At that point, she excused herself to go explain to the children what they would be doing over the next three days.

Grayson, with his mind left mulling, then went and confronted Faircloth about the wisdom of inviting Rachel and the children to move to New York City. If Rachel did decide to accept the invitation, didn't the risks of such a move far outweigh the benefits? What if she couldn't find work; how would she stay afloat financially? What if her kids, who needed as much peace and security as possible, ended up in an oppressive school? What if Rachel, or any of her three children, was not able to adjust to a new city and a whole new way of life? No disrespect intended toward Faircloth, but was he sure he was able to keep his promises of a rent-free apartment and a safety net of wonderful new friends? What if Liberty International City Church simply failed to perform according to his expectations? If Rachel made the move and the choice proved to be detrimental, wouldn't the odds of her recovery plunge completely off the bottom end of the scale?

Faircloth answered each of the questions thoughtfully and truthfully, acknowledging that risks indeed existed. He shared, however, that the move would provide Rachel with three things she urgently needed: number one, distance from the North Metro congregation that lived throughout the area, some members even using the bank where she worked; two, unencumbered time from the pressures of a forty-hour-a-week job and from the pressures of her relationship with Grayson in order to focus solely on her healing and the healing of her children; and three, the friendship of objective people who could understand her pain and who could give her the emotional, spiritual, mental, and physical support necessary for her recuperation.

Grayson knew he was sitting in the presence of a secure individual when he heard Faircloth say graciously, man-to-man, that he, Grayson, was not a healthy element in Rachel's life right now. He knew also that he was in the company of a resourceful person by the fact that Faircloth was willing and able to cover Rachel and the children's expenses for the next four or five months. He stared at the older gentleman.

"If she chooses to go," Faircloth presented in a fatherly tone, "is it possible for you to guarantee her a continued position at the bank in the event she wants to return shortly?"

As Grayson looked into the man's face, he found that he could not readily refute or deny the old pastor's overview of the matter. He finally answered, "I think I can guarantee that, *if* she chooses to leave."

"I was raped by my father on my sixteenth birthday," Daytona said nervously to the Cross-Link crowd that had gathered for the evening service. "I had always hated him because of the way he physically abused me throughout my childhood and teen years, but on that night, the night he raped me, I wanted to kill him."

Having chosen to stay for the meeting, Grayson sat in the center of the auditorium separated from Rachel, at her request. His attention, along with everyone else's in the hall, was now pinned to Daytona's story.

"But instead of killing him," Daytona said somberly into the mike, "I ran away from home. I ran from Buffalo, where we were living at the time, and went to New York City." She went on to tell, with rising intensity, how she dropped out of high school and became a streetwalker in order to survive. How, for over a year and a half, she progressed from using marijuana to becoming a heroin addict. And how she regularly drowned herself with alcohol. "I became so physically wasted that I was repulsive to look at. I started losing money as a prostitute. My pimp eventually beat and raped me and removed me from the street. So, to support my habits, I became a shoplifter and a thief." After illustrating that point with a specific episode, she proceeded to tell that she then learned she was pregnant. "I didn't know who the father was, but the little life inside me became my reason for living." She then told how she miscarried when she was running from a couple of gang members who spotted her witnessing one of their drug-related executions. In her escape attempt, she fell from a wall and was left unconscious. When she came to, she lost the baby and was alone in a harborside junkyard. "After the miscarriage, I decided I wanted to die. So I threw myself in front of a taxi. But instead of killing myself, I only managed to get myself hospitalized with some broken ribs, a punctured lung, and a brain concussion."

It was during her depressing recovery, she explained, when Jason Faircloth, assisting a pastor friend at the hospital, started talking to her. "Why? Because he said I looked like I didn't have a single friend in the whole world." Faircloth befriended her and started visiting her daily in the hospital. Because of him and his Christian witness, she learned for the first time that God loved her and had penalized His own Son for her moral crimes. And that God, through His Son, wanted to cleanse her heart and her conscience and give her a new life.

Awestruck by such a message of hope, she humbly pleaded for God to somehow redeem her soul. And He did.

She was so affected that she made a trip home to Buffalo to forgive her dad, face-to-face, for raping her. Her dad, a longtime alcoholic, was dying from cirrhosis of the liver. She told him of her life-changing experience and about Jason Faircloth, the man who had helped her. She discovered amazingly from her dad's dying words that Jason Faircloth was her grandfather. She rushed back to New York City and broke the news to Jason as he was preparing to fly back to Norway. An unbelievable celebration rocked their lives. "That was six months ago," Daytona declared. "For my sake, my granddad canceled his plans to move back to Norway and ended up buying a house for us in New York City. He's helped rebuild my life. He's now tutoring me and helping me earn my high school diploma. Because of him and his willingness to reach out to a stranger, my life has been forever changed. Without a doubt, he's the greatest person I've ever known. It's my prayer and my hope that one day I'll be a wise and loving teacher like he is, that I'll be a person who can help hurting people find a path to God. Just like I was helped."

The power and intensity of Daytona's words stilled Grayson. It seemed to him that everyone around him had been equally arrested. He noticed a couple of ladies wiping tears. He understood why. He too had felt the reprehensible sting and the august gratification of the young lady's story, a concert of emotional extremes, all with a grand and miraculous climax that left a person believing that there indeed must be a God who graces the halls of human affairs.

The portion of Grayson's heart that bowed to true goodness was convinced beyond any reservations that Faircloth and his granddaughter were the genuine articles. He realized he had not even offered up a proper thanks to the gentleman for stepping into Rachel's world and saving her from a sure suicide attempt. *At the end of the meeting,* he told himself, *I've got to tell him how grateful I am.*

However, in spite of his appreciation, he still did not see a need for Rachel to follow the man to New York. He still hoped that Rachel's rational mind would prevail over her impulse.

But in the event Rachel acted unpredictably and was swayed by whatever reason to make the move, he was leaning toward the resolve not to take it personally or interfere with her decision. After all, considering the scope of what she had been through during the last twelve months, she deserved the freedom to pursue any means of healing that became available to her.

He would miss her if she relocated. About that, there was no doubt. Her absence would leave an aching void in his life that simply would not be soothed. But if he had *ever* loved anybody, he knew now, more than ever, that he loved Rachel. Therefore, he would simply endure the loneliness, without begging and without manipulating. Until she returned.

If, on the other hand, she elected to remain in Atlanta, then he would go out of his way to grant her the distance she needed in their relationship and the space to search and know her feelings for him. And whenever they were together, he would make sure to restrain their intimacy.

Either way, if she left or remained, one thing was certain: She now dominated his heart.

By eleven that night, all was dark and quiet inside the Cross-Link guesthouse. Stretched out between clean sheets on one of the beds, Rachel for the first time in weeks felt a tinge of cherished tranquility. Justin was in a deep sleep at her side. Summer and Holly were asleep in the adjacent room.

Daytona and an older lady, volunteering to be on call through the night, were in the bedroom across the hall.

As Rachel entered the first phases of sleep, her thoughts drifted to words that Daytona had spoken to her earlier in the evening. "I know I'm just a teenager, but I'll be your friend. I'll accept you for who you are, no matter what. Even if you can't come to New York with us, I'll still stay in touch with you by letters and by phone calls." Rachel thought about the others: Jason, Pastor Montgomery, and the ladies who had helped with her children. She felt her soul sigh with needed release.

The last thought she remembered, a thought that fused into a brief dream, was that she had been whisked away on a gurney and miraculously rescued by a team of soul-saving paramedics.

33

Clay McCain, dressed in expensive sports clothes, sat at the bar at San José's exclusive Hotel Camino Real. He was waiting for his and Anika's late-night table reservation at the hotel's Mirage Restaurant. Anika, however, had decided at the last minute to stay home, claiming she was overly tired from the previous night's party and wanted to go to bed early. As Clay sipped his drink, he tried to put Anika out of his mind. But the problems rising between them played havoc with his ability to relax and focus on anything else. The tension in their relationship had throughout the day escalated to new proportions.

"Are you holding this seat for anyone?"

Clay looked up. He eyeballed the face behind the deep, rich voice. A tall, dark-haired man dressed in a suit and tie stood there waiting for him to answer. Clay offered a nonchalant twist of the head to signal that the stool next to him was available. Clay then turned his attention back to his drink and to his thoughts.

The dark-haired man settled onto the stool and ordered a martini. Then he looked at Clay and said, "I'm not even sure why I travel anymore. I've only been here in Costa Rica for three days and I'm already so bored I can hardly stand it."

Clay eyed the man again. His expression said, *I'm sorry; are you talking to me?*

The man, without hesitation, repeated his statements.

Clay puffed a whatever-you-say response.

"My name is Klaus Leitner," the man said, "from Germany." He extended his hand.

Clay grunted his lack of interest, but briefly shook the man's hand. His eyes immediately reverted to his glass. Live music suddenly reverberated from a hotel nightclub.

"I'm a doctor." Klaus raised his voice. "An orthopedist."

Clay did not respond, but that did not stop the man.

"I have more money than I know how to spend." He paused and waited this time for Clay to face him.

Clay turned and looked at the guy. The face, behind a stylish pair of glasses, was handsomely rugged. The complexion was ruddy and smooth, with only a couple of wrinkles beneath the eyes. It was the kind of face often seen on television commercials.

"I'm thirty-eight and single," Klaus added when he saw he had Clay's attention. "I have all the toys a man could ever want—an upper-class apartment in Berlin, a hundred-year-old renovated farmhouse in the Bavarian Alps, a Porsche 911. Yet, I can't find any real happiness in life. So, what do I do? I travel. I get six weeks of holiday every year, so I try to chase happiness. I've been on every continent. I've been around the world literally one and a half times." Klaus shook his head in apparent frustration. "And I've finally come to the conclusion that traveling is not the answer. After a while, one place just blurs into another."

Clay was not sure how he should respond. This was the first time since abandoning the ministry that he had been on the receiving end of a stranger's gut-spilling purge. He just kept quiet.

"And then there are the ladies," Klaus continued. "I've been with so many through the years that I've lost count. Blondes, redheads, brunettes. I've been with some of the most beautiful and erotic women who can be found. Some of the relationships lasted a month or two. One of them lasted for over a year. But most of them lasted only a few days, some for just one night." Klaus's voice grew quieter, almost introspective. "I think I've tasted everything life has to offer. And it's all left me empty. There's just one thing that has eluded me. It's the one thing that I believe would make life worth living."

Clay's ears were now tuned to what the man was saying.

"If I could find one woman whom I would truly love and commit myself to for a lifetime...and if she would in return love me, really love me and only me...and if we could have children and pass down to those children our love and all grow old together..." Klaus sounded almost desperate. "I know this probably sounds unsophisticated, but if I could just have an old-fashioned family, to me, that would be worth more than all the money, toys, women, and places in the whole world."

Klaus issued a few more related remarks. But Clay did not register them. The few words he had already heard were suddenly punishing him with the vengeance of a harpoon. He turned away from Klaus. The German finally stopped talking.

Clay lingered a few more seconds, then left the building. In the open night air, he tried to shake off the impact of the German's comments. But he had already learned too well their haunting truth.

Clay walked the depth of the dimly lit parking lot. Why had the man assumed he would even listen to such personal matters? And how had the man known to speak English to him? Clay had not revealed to the stranger his name, his nationality, or anything else about his identity. He had not spoken a single word in the man's presence.

At the end of the parking lot, Clay stopped and stared up into the cloudy sky. Was the man a secret angel sent from heaven to paralyze his soul with additional guilt? Or was he a demon sent from the darkness to mock him and to pillage what was left of his sanity? Or was the meeting just an aberration of unbelievable odds?

Clay wanted to pray. But all he managed to do was droop his head and mourn his fate.

34

"Will Grandma get in the pool with us again like she did the last time we came to see her?" Holly raised her voice above the road noise and asked from the backseat of the Toyota.

Rachel started to answer from behind the steering wheel when her eyes caught sight of the huge green sign marking the state line. "Look, everybody! We're crossing over into Florida right...right...right...*now!*"

The three children celebrated the moment with shouts of glee.

"Only three and a half more hours to go," Rachel announced.

It was a lighthearted instant in the midst of a somber time. Rachel realized she was smiling.

"Will she, Mommy?" Holly posed her question again.

"She's still recovering from her broken hip, hon. So I don't think she's going to be able to. So don't get your hopes built up, okay?"

As the car clip-clip-clipped its way across the ribs of the interstate pavement, Rachel played one of the children's favorite audio cassettes, a condensed version of songs and dialogue from a popular feature-length animated movie.

As the children sang along with the tape, Rachel turned up the air conditioner a notch and tried to let herself feel good about the decision she had made to accept Jason Faircloth's invitation.

The pivotal point that helped make up her mind had come two days ago, on Sunday afternoon, the closing day of the Cross-Link conference.

Sitting alone with Grayson in his car in the church parking lot, she had told him that, in spite of her fears and all the risks involved in a cross-country move, she felt more and more inclined to accept the offer. She explained that Jason Faircloth had already earned her respect and trust quicker and more substantially than anyone she had ever met. It was not, however, only because of the saving manner in which he had treated her, as if she were a beloved daughter, but also because of the way he treated people in general. She illustrated the point by describing to Grayson the Sunday morning service that he had missed. Jason, after tracking down a black family who had been victims of his ministerial abuse during his North Metro years, brought the family to the church service at Cross-Link. There he apologized publicly to them for refusing their request twenty years ago to be baptized by him simply because of the threat the color of their skin posed to the unity of the North Metro church. He asked them to please forgive him for his bigoted and non-Christlike attitude and for any disillusionment, pain, and humiliation he had caused them. They did, with hugs and smiles.

"I've never met a pastor like him," she told Grayson.

And besides, she reminded him, Faircloth had assured her that if she got to New York and did not like the setup, he would pay to have her and the children flown back to Atlanta at any time she chose.

Plus, she explained, Summer and Holly, to her surprise, both had expressed a readiness, almost an eagerness, to live someplace new.

After listening to her views, Grayson stressed how much he loved her and how fearful he was that he might lose her. Nevertheless, he had decided that he wanted what was best for *her*, and that she knew better than anyone what she should do. He then promised her that there would always be a job waiting for her at the bank.

That elemental promise had given her the last bit of courage she needed.

Within an hour after the conversation with Grayson, she had told Faircloth her decision. She told him that before she flew to New York, though, she wanted to spend a week or so with her in-laws in St. Petersburg, Florida.

Yesterday morning, four round-trip airline tickets to New York were placed in her hands. They would leave Atlanta for New York on June 21, just nine days away. The return tickets were open-ended and could be validated anytime within the next twelve months.

Yesterday afternoon, she had withdrawn the $700 in her savings account and paid her July rent in advance. She had $160 left, which she was now carrying in her purse.

She asked Grayson to keep an eye on the apartment and the car during her time in New York. When she returned from Florida next week, she would leave him the keys to both.

She looked out the window at the passing Florida palms drenched in sunlight and again tried to convince herself that it was okay to feel positive about the whole situation.

"I got to pee pee!" she suddenly heard Justin break away from his singing and squeal from the backseat.

She promptly started looking for an exit.

◆ PART 3

FIVE YEARS LATER

1995-1997

35

Clay was awakened suddenly out of his sleep by the vicious thrust of his stomach muscles and the burning vomit at the back of his throat. He jerked upright in the bed.

He quickly remembered the plastic bucket on the floor at the bedside and heaved himself toward the pail as he disgorged the elements of beer and bread. Most of the mess splattered into the target. Some of it spewed onto the misshapen planks of the gray wooden floor.

With one hand on the floor, he held himself steady over the bucket as he retched one more time.

His nose and throat were burning as he used his free hand to wipe the residue from his face. He rolled back over onto the mattress. He groaned and slowly placed a hand on his forehead. The fever was still substantial.

What was happening to him? He had been fighting the fever, along with diarrhea, for two consecutive weeks. The small quantities of food he had tried to eat just would not digest properly. There was no scale in the two-room shack, but he was certain he had already lost fifteen to twenty pounds. He had initially suspected that the cause of his condition was some kind of food poisoning. Now, he didn't know what to think.

He had resisted going to a doctor, convinced he could fight through the sickness on his own. He was still determined to keep trying.

He grimaced and rolled onto his side, facing the wall. His eyes wavered for a second or two at the framed photograph hanging from a nail right above the bed. It was the only personal photograph he possessed—a picture of himself, along with fifteen strangers, all outfitted in colorful wet suits and scuba gear. They were posed on the stern of a fifty-four-foot dive boat anchored on the beach of a Nicoya Gulf island five miles from Costa Rica's mainland.

The picture, now two years old, had been taken a year after his and Anika's relationship had unraveled.

After splitting up, Anika had returned to Europe. Clay, carrying too much shame and self-deprecation to hope any longer that he could reconcile with Rachel and the kids, had stayed in Costa Rica and found employment as a nighttime waiter in an upperclass hotel restaurant in the Pacific port town of Puntarenas. During the days he had attended several advanced scuba classes and eventually earned a dive master's certificate, which qualified him for hire as an underwater tour guide at scuba centers worldwide. After attaining the permit, he quit his job as a waiter and worked full-time for the dive center that trained him.

The photo on the wall commemorated one of the first groups of divers that had been entrusted to him. The pictorial record of the event had initially been an attempt to remind himself that he, unlike most others, dared to chase his dreams, no matter what the cost. Now, the picture was nothing more to him than an icon of derision, a self-portrait of a broken piece of humanity who epitomized absolute debauchery.

The part of his conscience that still functioned haunted him with the endless and ever-stronger reminder that he had been an asinine wretch as a husband, as a father, as a pastor, as a man, as a son, as a Christian, as a friend, even as an immoral lover, and most recently as an employee. The grandiose divemaster job had not even lasted two years. He had been fired a month ago following unheeded warnings from the owner of the dive shop that he cut back on his alcohol consumption. He was finally released from his position when he showed up so drunk for a scheduled dive one morning that he could not manage to pull himself into his wet suit. The boss sent him out the door with one final paycheck, claiming he was an irresponsible and hopeless alcoholic.

He was now forty-four years old. All alone. Impoverished. Living in a filthy, stinking shack in a poor and dirty town.

He was considered unemployable because of his losing battle with booze, and he did not deny the characterization any longer. He could not. Piles of empty beer cans were scattered everywhere throughout the dwelling, and his small refrigerator was crammed with unopened cans waiting to be downed.

He closed his eyes and tried to put the photograph out of his mind.

The sweat of his fever trickled down his brow. The late-morning sun, combined with the ninety-degree weather, simply added to his discomfort, heating up the tiny wooden structure like a nonventilated outhouse.

He kicked the sheet off his legs. He twisted and turned for a few minutes until he found a position that presented the least amount of discomfort. And then he tried to blank out all thoughts and reenter the painless and welcomed state of sleep.

36

Rachel unfolded the letter and emitted a sigh of deep reflection.

Before directing her concentration to the letter's handwritten script, she looked up from the couch, where she was snuggled on an afghan, and slowly looked around the room.

It was nine-thirty Saturday evening, December 9.

Summer, now fifteen, and Holly, twelve, were spending the night with friends. Justin, a strapping eight-year-old, was upstairs in his room asleep.

The tiny white lights on the Christmas tree blinked lazily. A log fire burned in the fireplace. Stockings for the children were suspended from the old mantel. An advent wreath, holding four thick red candles, sat atop the coffee table's Christmas runner. Hanging low on the wall opposite the fireplace, the family's handmade Swedish Advent calendar—with its twenty-four pockets—held small and inexpensive presents for each of the children for the remaining fifteen days till Christmas.

Rachel looked out the window. A moderate snow had fallen earlier in the day. The yards, trees, and parks throughout the neighborhood were covered in sparse patterns of white. The bit of snow in the trees brightened up the night with reflected moonlight. She could not think of any other place she would rather be.

She had grown to love the locale, mainly because of her dear friends from the Liberty International City Church who lived all around her. Her job as a fourth-grade teacher at a local private elementary school, the school Holly and Justin attended, was making it possible for her to afford the three hundred dollars each month for the duplex. The remarkably low rent, especially for Queens, was a gift of mercy from her seventy-year-old landlady, Mrs. Tempie Hunter, a gracious and loving widow who lived in the other half of the house and was a member of the Liberty International Church.

Aunt Temp, as Mrs. Hunter was affectionately known, had, because of the regular attention she gave to the three children, become a surrogate grandmother to the McCain household. To Rachel, she was not only a grandmother, but also a dear friend.

Rachel looked back to her lap at the open photo album containing pictorial and written records of the last five years of her life, the album in which the five-year-old letter in her hand had been kept.

She sighed again, with gratefulness. Life was good.

With both hands, she lifted the letter to eye level. It was a photocopy of one of the first letters she had written to Grayson after moving to New York. Jason Faircloth had encouraged her to make copies of all her letters during those days to help gauge the progress of her inner healing. It was this healing process she was now dwelling on.

She was gearing up for tomorrow night. She was scheduled to tell her story at Liberty International's quarterly joint service, a time when the church's twenty-one congregations gathered from all over the city to worship under one roof. About four thousand people normally attended.

In recent months, she had shared her testimony with three of the congregations, at the request of the pastors. Jason, having heard extremely positive feedback from the listeners, encouraged her to talk to all the congregations combined.

A part of her was excited about the prospect of knowing that God could use her words to impart hope and inspiration to others who might be on the verge of giving up.

But a part of her was also nervous. She figured it was partially because of the sheer size of the crowd. And also because Grayson would be in the audience. He had flown up from Atlanta yesterday evening.

During her first year in New York, Rachel had communicated with Grayson only a few times by phone and letter. Recently, however, the frequency of their letter writing and phone conversations had increased. They now communicated at least once a month. But his presence in New York this weekend marked only the third time since she left Atlanta that she had been in his company. The limited visits had been at her request. She had needed for her concentration on her and the children's recovery to be unfettered by any face-to-face pressure.

Grayson, because of his love for her, had graciously honored her request. She was more appreciative of his cooperation than he would ever know. His love, to say the least, had truly been felt in the matter.

After so many years, though, of rebuilding her life without Grayson, she felt to a strong degree that, if she wanted, she could completely cut him off and walk healthily into the future. Yet, at the same time, she felt wooed by his love, a love placed under self-restraint for her sake. She knew he longed for her as a companion and was waiting patiently and loyally for her to decide what she wanted.

She thought about him in his hotel room and about how far she had come in her life during the last five years, and then read the letter.

Dear Grayson,

Where do I begin? The last few weeks have opened my eyes more and more to just how drastically I've needed emotional rest. With no outside responsibilities, the kids and I have slept in till about nine or nine-thirty every morning. We've spent our days sitting around the table and talking about each other's needs, exploring the neighborhood by foot, and walking in the nearby parks. It's as if for the first time in over a year we've been able to come up for air. It's been unspeakably wonderful. We have even laughed together. I feel like a million-ton weight has been lifted off my back.

I don't know yet how long we'll stay, but coming here when we did was the best possible decision I could have ever made.

Our life is filled with free and open-ended time so that we've been able to give our full attention to each other. Our house is filled with groceries. And, because of the Liberty International City Church, our lives are filled with the kindest and most helpful group of people I've ever met in the United States. We've already been invited into people's homes three different times for a meal. It's like we are a part of the human race again.

I'm still overwhelmed, to the point of tears, by Jason Faircloth's graciousness. He's one of the most Christlike men I've ever met. In spite of his busy schedule and all the help he's given us, he has gone out of his way to give special time to Justin, to give him some adult male interaction. He even took him for a "men's day out" to the zoo one afternoon.

Justin loves the man and has started calling him Grandpa.

In a way, I'm afraid we're all living in a dream and that it will be taken away from us before we're ready. I try hard not to dwell on that thought. I keep reminding myself that I should just accept that each and every moment we've experienced here has been a gift unto itself and that we've already been granted more than we could have ever hoped for.

Well, among all these other things, I'm attending church again. If you think you're surprised, I'm even more so. It's just that the church here is so different. It's difficult to explain, except to say that it's a church that practices Jason Faircloth's kind of love and forgiveness, the kind without which I could not live another hour. I'm of course talking about the Liberty International City Church, the one that Jason helps lead. It's set up like no other church I've ever seen. It's a group of about 1500 people who have divided themselves into 15 congregations. Whenever one of the groups reaches a steady attendance of around 120, that group purposely splits up and forms a new assembly.

The congregation I'm meeting with, numbering about 70 people, is pastored by a twenty-eight-year-old man named Dan Shaw. He's actually a pastor-in-training. Jason is the one working with him and instructing him.

A couple of weeks ago, Dan preached a short sermon on the subject of giving to the poor. He then did something I'll never forget as long as I live. I think surely some of the attendees must have known about it in advance. He directed us out of the worship hall—a former Chinese restaurant—and onto the city streets. He told us to roam the area and give away our Sunday morning offering hand-to-hand to some individual or some family in need. He asked us to gather back at the meeting center within forty-five minutes to share reports of what happened. Since Daytona attends the same congregation, I walked with her. I only *had a couple of dollars I could give away. We were outside for no more than twenty minutes when we came across an old man in a wheelchair. Both of his legs were missing. He looked as if he had not had a bath for weeks. He was delightfully surprised, to say the least, when we offered to buy him a lunch and escorted him into a small restaurant. We bought him a twelve-dollar steak meal. He thanked us a couple of times with a look of disbelief, as if no one had ever done such a thing for him before.*

The experience was very gratifying. I can't believe that I had never, in all my years as a professing Christian, given to the poor hand-to-hand like that. I got the impression that Daytona is not a stranger to this type of personal giving. Anyway, when everybody regathered, about twelve or thirteen people told about their charitable episodes. It was a touching conclusion to the whole morning experience.

During the last year, as you know, I've doubted the validity of the Christian faith more and more. But I'm seeing a side of Christianity here that's causing me to backtrack and reconsider all over again. If there indeed is any element of authenticity in the Bible message, then what I'm witnessing here surely must be it.

Last Sunday, Jason spoke in the church service and began a series called "one anothering." He highlighted all the New Testament verses where the words "one another" are used. He then shared his observation that the typical church, when assembled together, very seldom, if ever, puts these verses into practice. He quoted, for example, a verse that tells us to pray for one another He spent only about ten minutes teaching the verse, then he placed four folding chairs in the middle aisle. He had every family, every single adult, and every person who was alone (child, teenager, spouse, or divorcée) each take a turn sitting in the aisle chairs. As they took turns, the rest of the congregation stood around them and prayed for them out loud by name.

When I was asked to sit in the circle and listened as eight or nine people zealously prayed for me, I broke down and cried. At North Metro, despite my roots and despite my broken home, I was never prayed for in public by anyone, not a single soul.

Jason says that next Sunday he's going to focus the service around the verse that teaches us to "comfort one another." I keep wondering with anticipation what such a meeting will be like.

I know I've said it before, but Jason is the most insightful and compassionate person I've ever met. It's because of him that my trust in humanity and my belief in a personal God hasn't completely and permanently vanished. I've asked him several times what motivates him to give so much to so many. He says simply (and from the heart, I might add) that he's a debtor to all men. He's definitely an exception, even to the better people I've met. The rare power that advances through him must be that of God. Man alone, I'm convinced now, is incapable of generating his kind of goodness. I'm just humbled that the kids and I are currently some of the objects of his kindness.

Anyway, I've probably babbled on for long enough. And I'm wondering now if I should even put this letter in the mail to you. I know you say you love me, and I believe you, but I think that, for the time being, frequent and regular correspondence between us would not allow either of us the room we need to clear our heads. And for me personally, to find a clear head will, I think, take a while. I'm asking you for this distance, not because of any negative or offensive feelings I have toward you, but simply because of my own confusion. If I'm going to be able to sort through and make sense of my life, I've got to carry a lighter load emotionally, that's all.

Thanks for your listening ear and your supportive spirit during the last half year. And for your love. I owe you.

I'll talk more about my request for distance the next time we converse by phone.

Your complex friend,

Rachel

P.S. Please forgive me again for having complicated your life, first by my intimate involvement, which I now see was wrong, and now by my withdrawal and need for space.

P.P.S. Thanks for taking care of the September rent for my Atlanta apartment. I promise I'll repay the money as soon as I can.

Rachel lowered the letter.

Grayson had paid the Atlanta rent for her not only in September of that year, but for October and November as well. He had even offered to continue paying it through the winter months. But she had decided to cancel the lease on the apartment and remain indefinitely in New York.

As soon as she had found employment and started working, first as a teacher's assistant and then as a teacher, she attempted, in small amounts, to return the money to Grayson. But each time, he had sent the money back, telling her to keep it.

Again she thought about him, lodging at this very moment in a hotel room nearby. She wondered how many other men, knowing her circumstances, would have so lovingly and patiently held out for her for the last five years, especially after hearing her expressed conviction that their earlier intimacy had been wrong.

According to typical standards, he definitely measured out on the high side. But did she really want to surrender to his love and risk giving her and the children's lives away to someone who was just simply "above average"? Her head told her that she had come too far to take such a gamble, especially when she was now strong enough and capable enough to live on her own. Besides, she had taken so many substantial strides forward in her spiritual life that she wondered if she and Grayson would now be able to relate to one another regarding that all-important aspect of life. Yet, her heart had been softened by his demonstrative love, and she did not want to just coldly ignore the fact.

Summer, Holly, and Justin, even though they had known about Grayson for a couple of years, had met him for the first time today. They had all spent the morning and a part of the afternoon with him touring Ellis Island.

"I like him, Mother. Are you thinking of marrying him?" Justin blurted out with a grin after Grayson left them and they got back to the house.

Rachel thought about Justin's remark, wondered how he really felt, and finally smiled. She folded the letter in her hand, returned it to its place in the album, and turned to the next page, continuing her preparation for tomorrow night's presentation.

37

S omeone asked me the other day if I ever think about Clay anymore," Rachel said softly as she approached the end of her forty-five-minute testimony.

Grayson sat three rows from the front in the concert hall that Liberty International City Church rented for this once-a-quarter gala. He hung on Rachel's every word. He saw Rachel lean closer to the stage mike and watched as she paused and closed her eyes for a moment.

"I think about him almost every day," Rachel said. "But I have accepted what has happened. And with God's help and the help of Jason Faircloth and this church, I've finally, during the last couple of years, been able to let go of it all. And I've been able to forgive. I've decided that a full recovery is not only possible, but it's actually within sight. I'm now looking hopefully to the future as opposed to morbidly staring at the past. The second half of my life will..."

Grayson felt his eyes grow teary. He could not have been more proud of anyone than he was right now of Rachel. He had watched the transformation that had taken place in her life. And he was touched. He knew, based on what she had already told him, that when she spoke of forgiveness she was referring not only to the forgiveness in her heart toward Clay, but equally toward Frank Lovett, Bill Reese, the entire North Metro congregation, and Dr. Ed Brighton and the PCCGE mission board. And he knew that the forgiveness had come gradually with no great ease.

The changes in her heart had for two or three years now incited Grayson to reflect on his own life. He could no longer deny the unpleasant things he was finding. Most obvious were the deeply buried bitterness and lack of forgiveness he still held toward his ex-wife and ex-church friends because of the false and malignant gossip they allowed years ago that crippled his life and reputation. He realized that for almost a decade now he had used that bitterness as an excuse to discredit the Christian faith.

In truth, though, he had never, not even during his churchgoing years, been possessed in his heart and soul—like Jason, Daytona, and Rachel—by the life-nurturing presence of God. He now understood that his religion, when it existed, had been nothing but words.

The gradual recognition of his spiritual pauperism, in the stark light of Rachel's life, had stirred in him a realization of need and longing. In the last couple of weeks, he had actually prayed for the first time in years. He had prayed that God would somehow grant help to his empty soul.

He stared at Rachel with admiration as he concentrated on her closing sentences.

"So, what I've learned, and am still learning, is that pain does not have to be wasted. If we can be taught, with the help of God and others, to review our pain and learn from it rather than to fritter away our life regretting it, we will discover that pain, like no other source, can supply our heart and soul with compassion, mercy, and understanding for the hurting world around us. My pain has changed my life forever. And I'm determined that a great deal of that change will be for the good.

"Please don't stop praying for me. And especially for my two daughters, Summer and Holly, and my son, Justin. Although the effect of being abandoned by their father six years ago isn't as evident in their day-to-day lives anymore, they still carry the hurt deep in their hearts. Occasionally that hurt surfaces in a sob, an outburst of anger, or an expressed hope that Daddy will someday still return. Just pray that they will continue to find healing and that they too will become more sensitive to others because of what they've faced."

Appearing grateful for the opportunity to have shared her story, Rachel looked out into the audience with sympathetic eyes and said, "Thank you."

A light applause erupted as Rachel turned from the crowd of approximately four thousand faces and headed across the stage to a chair where she had sat earlier during the opening minutes of the service. The clapping, like a crescendo of music, progressively peaked until it became a standing ovation.

Grayson clapped harder than anyone. In those moments, he felt a strong and holy presence fill the hall. It was a presence he could attribute only to God.

In the midst of the audience's display of emotion, Grayson saw an Asian lady make her way to the microphone. The lady stood and waited. When the ovation finally subsided, she gave a slight nod to the conductor of the orchestra positioned to her distant left. The orchestra instantly commenced a musical introduction, and the lady began singing. The lyrics of the mellow but intense song echoed Rachel's testimonial. The words extolled God's historical reputation for providing hope and sustenance to those who humbly and contritely recognize a need for Him.

Grayson Cole bowed his head for a few seconds and then looked upward as if he could see through the ninety-foot-high ceiling. Craving the source of life-altering strength he had witnessed working in Rachel's life and was now hearing about in the lady's solo, he sustained his upward glance and sighed, *I need You. I need You...don't I?*

When the woman concluded her song, Jason Faircloth took the lady's place at the mike. "Will the twenty-one senior pastors, or at least a leader from each of the congregations, please come and line up across the foot of the stage." Jason waited patiently while the group of multiracial men slipped out of their places and moved down front.

When the church leaders—some dressed in suits and ties, others in jeans and sweaters—were in place, Jason proceeded. "I've been touched by the extremely heartfelt and compelling words I've heard tonight. I'm sure many of you have been as well. It's therefore very likely that some of you feel a need for prayer or perhaps realize you have a need for guidance or encouragement regarding your spiritual pilgrimage. If that's the case, then after our dismissal prayer in just a few seconds, I invite you to come to the front and meet with any of these pastors. They will take as much time to pray with you or converse with you as you need." Jason paused thoughtfully. "If you do not have a personal relationship with Christ, then please know that the God who has demonstrated His immense and personal love for Rachel McCain cares about you with equal passion. He wants to close the distance between you and Himself and be your divine companion. He was crucified, placing Himself on the punishing end of His own justice for your shortcomings, and then resurrected from the dead to make possible His reconciliation with you.

"If you wish to know more, or if you need for someone to walk with you through your decision to accept God's offer of redemption, then please, I implore you, talk to one of these men before you leave tonight. They will be here waiting to help.

"Now, Dwight Sosby, the newly appointed overseer of our homeless outreach ministries, will come and dismiss us in prayer."

Grayson, over the course of the next minute or so, did not hear a single complete sentence of the benediction. Suddenly knowing what he should do—had to do—he gave his attention to trying to bring his nervous breathing and increased heart palpitation under control.

When the prayer was over and the crowd burst forth in movement, Grayson opened his eyes, released a deep breath, then moved toward the stage.

He needed to talk with one of the pastors. Preferably Jason Faircloth.

38

D addy?" a little boy's voice shrieked.

The child's cry, along with the bright morning sun in May, sizzled through Clay's head like a lighted dynamite fuse. *Justin!* his brain shouted at him deep inside.

The young child's petition rang out a second time. And a third.

Clay moaned and tried to open his eyes wider. He saw fuzzily that he was facing some kind of concrete wall, only inches from his nose. He tried to turn over. He needed to see his son.

With near panic, he fought his dull-headedness until he managed to roll over and face the opposite direction. He barely succeeded in lifting his head off the ground as he strained to focus amid the blinding sunlight.

He saw a young boy run by him at a distance.

"Justin?" he tried to call out. The word came out only in a mutter. He felt saliva run down the week-old stubble on his face. "Justin?" he whispered again.

"Just because I'm a few steps ahead of you doesn't mean I'm leaving you, Bryan!" a man's emphatic retort pierced the air.

Clay saw the boy fifteen to twenty yards away reach up and take the outstretched hand of an adult male.

"Don't be such a baby, son!" the man barked, turning and leading the boy away.

Clay lowered his head back to the ground and grimaced with confusion. It took him three or four minutes to figure out his whereabouts. He was lying beneath an almond tree on a three- or four-foot strip of ground running between a wall and a cobblestone plaza near one of Puntarenas's large ferry wharves.

He looked out toward a moored ferry. "American tourists," he muttered.

He tried to sort through how he had gotten here. Slowly, bit by bit, he remembered the tug-of-war decision he had made yesterday morning. The acute nervousness surrounding the decision had enticed him, while en route to catch an afternoon bus to San José, to stop at a bar and calm his nerves with a drink. He had promised himself midway through his first shot of tequila that he would strictly limit his alcohol intake and board the bus in a respectable state of mind. But his chemical dependency, which had reached unprecedented depths during the last six months, had mocked his pathetic determination to stay in control.

His drunken wanderings, he concluded, had brought him here to the plaza, where he had fallen asleep in a stupor and spent the night curled up at the foot of the plaza wall.

Yesterday's decision again bounded to the forefront of his thoughts. He tried to argue against the decision's sensibility, but his arguments, with all their different angles, proved insufficient, the same as yesterday. The decision was now irreversible. It had simply become necessary for his survival.

He went over it again. He would travel by bus the two hours to San José and find the American pastor of the English-speaking church. He had heard about the church through the social grapevine during the two years he had lived in the city with Anika.

He knew that the church operated for the numerous American retirees residing in the region. He had driven by the building many times. He would seek out the American pastor, look the man in the eye, and confess everything. He would stress his utter brokenness and his undiminished desire to return to his family. He would ask outright for the man's advice...and would hold his breath while he waited for an answer.

Clay was self-conscious in such close confinement with so many well-dressed travelers. He knew that his alcoholism was irrepressibly manifested in his eyes, odor, and posture. And although he had bathed, shaved, and put on fresh clothes before taking his seat on the bus, he knew his ragged clothes still carried an odor. His hair was long and unkempt, and he had never regained the weight he had lost seven months ago during his sudden and mysterious illness. He was six-foot-one and weighed a sickly 155 pounds. All of his clothes were now a couple of sizes too big. The excess folds in the clothes he was wearing were so numerous that they hung in piles.

He was glad that only three-quarters of the seats on the bus were occupied. He did not want anyone to have to sit beside him.

As he stared out the window, he saw the first drops of what appeared to be the onset of a major rain shower. The annual rainy season in Costa Rica had begun right on schedule a few weeks earlier.

Watching the rain, he contemplated his visit with the American pastor. He felt his hands start to shake with nervous apprehension. He clasped them together and held them on his lap to keep them steady.

Was his plan too idiotic? He kept pounding the reminder into his head that if he failed to carry through with this initiative, the final bits of desperate hope that lingered in his soul would die with him. And that demise, he was sure, would be much sooner than later. In the last seven months, he had sunk from being a sick, unemployed alcoholic to a drunken, scavenging bum who slept on the streets. And he was convinced by this slippery and unabated plunge that if he continued to remain alone and estranged from his wife and children, there was no reason why he would even try to keep living.

God was right, he rubbed in the rebuke for the thousandth time: *The lawless man will die because he does not control himself; he will be held captive by his own foolishness.* And he, Clay McCain, had proved it by brandishing one of the most defiant and out-of-control spirits of hedonism possible to man.

He wiped at his runny nose and leered at the reflection of his skinny face in the window. He then squeezed his eyes shut, wishing he had a full bottle of tequila in his hand.

He glanced once again at the large clock hanging on the wall across the hallway from where he was sitting. It was 4:15 P.M.

He had been sitting and waiting for an hour and fifteen minutes. He felt as if he could not sit anymore. Yet, he did not trust himself to get up and pace because he knew he might yield to the urge to exit the building and walk to the nearest bar. And he had already fought through too much inner resistance to reverse directions now. He forced himself to stay seated.

An open door to the church secretary's office faced him across the hall. He could see the secretary's arms and hands working at a computer keyboard. He could occasionally see the lady's face when she leaned forward. The lady appeared to be an American in her mid- to late fifties. Twice, since he arrived on the premises and requested to speak with the pastor, the lady had stepped out from behind her desk to make sure he was okay and to explain that the pastor should be free at any moment.

Clay got the impression that the lady was uncomfortable with his presence in the building, especially just outside her office. He noticed that about ten minutes after his arrival the lady had paged a man, apparently the church custodian judging by the man's tool belt and work clothes, and whispered a few words to him. Ever since, the man had not been far out of sight. He was currently working inside the ladies' lavatory, with the door propped open, just a few yards down the hall.

Clay began counting the concrete blocks from which the surrounding walls were constructed. He counted all the blocks he could see from his seat. He then looked at the clock again: 4:22.

For the third time in the last hour, he picked up a three-month-old religious periodical lying on the seat next to him. He forced himself to read an article about America's declining church membership, a page of ill-fated church humor, and an annual financial report for the magazine's denomination.

He once more focused on the clock: 4:38. He leaned his head backward against the light green wall and started to panic.

Then he heard a door open inside the secretary's office and a man's voice fill the room. Clay sat upright.

Within seconds, the man came out into the hallway offering a greeting with a distinct Texas accent. "Good afternoon, I'm Pastor

Joe Glenn."

Clay stood to his feet, accepting the man's extended hand. "Clay McCain."

"I apologize that you've had to wait so long, Mr. McCain, but I was tied up in a phone conversation that demanded urgent attention, and I just couldn't break away."

Clay was looking into the face of a man only two to three inches shorter than himself, a man with short pumpkin-colored hair and a nicely groomed mustache to match. The man, about fifty, wore a tan suit and cowboy boots. Clay was immediately disarmed by the man's broad, genuine smile.

"But I'm free now, so come on into my office and you can tell me what's on your heart."

Clay, with bunched lips, nodded his consent and followed the man through the secretary's office into a spacious study decorated with richly colored Latin American fabrics, four or five large tropical flowers, and a potted palm tree.

"Have a seat," Glenn said, directing Clay to a cushioned chair. He pulled a folding chair from behind the door, plopped it open, and sat down facing Clay. His manner was relaxed and inviting.

"So, what can I do for you?"

Seated with his legs crossed, Clay was aware that his whole upper body was shaking. He saw Glenn trying not to stare.

Clay pursed his lips again. "I've...I've got a slight alcohol problem," he began with difficulty. "It's been a full day or more since I've had anything to drink. That's why I'm...shaking."

Glenn gave a look of concern and bobbed his head.

Clay cleared his throat. "But the alcohol problem is not really why I'm here. I'm here because..." He paused to try to overcome the knot that was suddenly tightening in his throat. "I'm here because I need some advice." He had not used the word *need* aloud with anyone for over five years. Neither had he knowingly been in the presence of a pastor or minister during that length of time, probably longer. And he had not been in a church building since he left Sweden. He suddenly found that Joe Glenn's presence, as a representation of God and universal purity, caused him again to doubt what he was doing. His feelings of sinfulness and hideousness thundered anew throughout his being. He suddenly wondered if God might not strike him down on the spot and impatiently thrust his soul into hell. He started rocking back and forth in his seat. He grabbed his forehead and then coughed to work through the lump in his throat. "I...uh...I..." He sighed through a trickle of tears. "I'm a real bad man, Pastor Glenn. I...and right now I'm thinking I shouldn't even be here."

Glenn hesitated for just a second or two. "Pardon me for disagreeing with you, Mr. McCain, but at the moment, this is probably the one place in the whole world where you should be."

Clay shook his head. "You don't understand. I just don't think God will ever forgive me for the things I've done. I can't..." The words faded into a wheezy groan.

Glenn scooted his chair closer to Clay and touched his shoulder. "It's okay. Tears are oftentimes necessary. They help release some of the pain. But in response to your statement, I want to assure you there's nothing you've done, or could do, that's so bad that God would be provoked to withhold His forgiveness from you. He majors in forgiveness, Mr. McCain. That's His specialty."

Clay grappled with unbelief at the age-old message, a message he had once taught many times to many people. He wanted to believe. Oh, how he wanted to believe. But forgiveness for him was not possible, was it? How in the name of decency and justice could it be? He rose to his feet. He felt that he should leave.

Pastor Glenn remained seated on the edge of his chair. "I think God has gotten your attention and is speaking to your heart. You should listen to what He's saying, Mr. McCain."

Clay was caught off guard by Glenn's words. Was God trying to talk to his soul? The thought seemed to stretch the realm of the absurd. How could even the inference be entertained? How was it possible that the holy Creator God would reach down to the absolute base levels of willful, human reprobation and have any interest in erasing his, Clay McCain's, guilt? Yes, God was forgiving, but surely He would not, could not, allow His purity and His patience to be mocked by the blackened heart of such a defiant sinner.

"You've waited for more than an hour to talk. Why don't you sit back down?"

Clay realized he had been standing motionless, lost in his thoughts.

Glenn looked Clay in the eye and nodded toward the empty chair. "You said you need my advice. Why don't you at least tell me what's troubling your heart? We're here. We're undisturbed. We've got time."

Clay looked at the chair and then at the door. He closed his eyes for a second or two. He then opened his eyes and slowly returned to the seat.

"Why don't you just start from the beginning?" Glenn suggested. "I'll listen. And then I'll give you my honest and best advice."

Clay looked at the floor. With his eyes focused downward, he replied with a dry and weak voice, "All right. I'll tell you the whole story."

And he did. For forty-five minutes he told about his conversion to the Christian faith as a twenty-year-old, his unshakable commitment to his new beliefs, his Bible college training, his marriage to Rachel, his ordination as a gospel minister, his and Rachel's move to Sweden as missionaries, their three children, the Swedish congregation, his progressive shift from far-right conservatism, and then his friendship at the fitness studio with Anna Gessle.

"I only saw it later in retrospect," he explained to Glenn, "but by the time I first met Anna I had been coasting in my life for quite a while as a pastor, as a father, and as a husband. I had been performing above average, I thought, in those roles for so long and felt capable of maintaining my performance with such little effort that the sense of day-to-day challenge somehow dropped out of sight. I had become blind and didn't even know it. Anyway, I became just bored enough to feel slightly restless."

Clay paused. His thoughts reached back to remember the truth.

"Anna was the type of woman who could instantly provoke a man toward lustful thinking. I was not exempt. Because of the humdrum that I was feeling about everything else, I allowed myself the freedom for the first time in my Christian life to entertain and savor such unbridled thoughts. And those thoughts focused on Anna. The excitement of those fantasies began to chase away the boredom that was creeping into my life. The more time I spent around Anna at the health studio, the more my fantasies were fueled. But somehow I felt safe. No one in my Swedish congregation had a membership there at the club, and I was five thousand miles from my stateside supporters and directors. Plus, Anna was a married woman and had children. I honestly thought I was strong enough to contain my wayward thoughts.

"But then we started training together. And then the flirting began. It seemed innocent enough at first. We mainly talked about her bodily assets. From there, however, our conversations grew more and more provocative."

Clay went on to tell about the subsequent touching and the eventual open door for an affair. "I resisted the infidelity for two or three months, trying to convince myself not to go the full distance, but I finally let the whole situation intoxicate me to the point of surrender.

"From that moment onward, Anna and I were together two to three times a month for nearly three years. Our spouses knew nothing about it. At first I struggled with tremendous guilt, but eventually something broke inside my conscience. I actually reached a stage where I could ignore the wrong of what we were doing.

"And that's where the tragedy of the story really begins."

Clay half-consciously hesitated in order to gauge Glenn's reaction. Glenn sat expressionless and said, "Go on."

Clay nervously moistened his lips and proceeded.

He told about his introduction to Anika Wiberg, about the development of the second affair, and about the twisted feelings of love for Anika that vanquished his sanity and his emotions. He told about his withdrawal from his family and from his church. And about Anika's eventual request that he move away with her.

"It's almost impossible to believe, I know, but—" For the first time during the telling of his story, Clay choked with emotion. He could not stop the tears from seeping. "—Like a man gone insane, I pretended to shut down thirteen years' worth of marriage. I...uh...I actually—" his sobbing became pronounced—"I coldly rejected everything I knew to be right and true and turned my back on my wife and three children and just walked unannounced out of their lives. They...they never knew what happened to me."

Still sobbing, he told about his and Anika's travels to the Spanish island of Majorca and then to Costa Rica. He told about the mansion close by in the city, about Anika's wealth, and about their life of frivolity together.

"I tried to use all the pleasure and the so-called fun stuff to drown out the reminder of my crime. But not a single day has gone by in the last seven years that I haven't thought about my wife and my kids."

Clay placed his hands against his face in an attempt to give some privacy to his anguish. He was unable to talk for a few seconds. When he did speak again, he told about his and Anika's eventual breakup, about his downward slide into alcoholism, and finally about his absolute and deadly emptiness of soul.

His voice suddenly lowered to a whisper. He closed his eyes and sounded as if he were repeating a statement he had made to himself a thousand times before. "The only desire now left in my life is to be back together with my wife and children, to tell them...I'm sorry." Keeping his eyes closed and breathing irregularly, Clay hung his head and did not move. Minutes seemingly passed.

"Well?" Glenn's voice spoke up, with an overtone of sadness.

Desolately, Clay looked up into Glenn's face and, with his eyes, conveyed his lack of understanding.

"You said initially that you've come here for advice. So, what is it that you want to ask?"

Clay dolefully inhaled. "Do...do you think I should go and find them? My wife and kids?"

Glenn sat all the way back in his chair. "You're asking me if I think it's advisable that, after all these years, you find your family and try to reenter their lives?"

Clay nodded.

"And they have no idea where you are, or that you're even still alive?"

Clay slowly moved his head from side to side.

"What you've shared with me is a heavy and complicated story, Mr. McCain. And I think the consequences of your actions have rightfully haunted you. Unfortunately, there's no simple advice that I can offer you. You've left a carnage of broken lives all around you. The whole thing is quite a tragedy."

Glenn paused. "My wife's father walked out of her life because of a divorce when she was eleven years old. To this day, she wishes that the man would show up out of nowhere and become a part of her life again. Maybe your wife and kids sit at the window every day and, in a similar fashion, hope for your return.

"On the other hand, maybe they somehow discovered your infidelity and hate you and are even praying every day that you're dead. It's impossible for me to know. But if I were forced to make a guess, I would say that by now they've come to grips with your absence, have worked through a lot of their grief, and are well on their way to rebuilding their lives. So, I really can't give you any concrete advice.

"There's a part of me that wants to tell you to get on the next plane leaving San José and rush to make immediate contact with your wife. Yet my gut feeling, considering all the years that have passed, is that you should accept your consequences and stop dreaming." Glenn paused as if to let his words find their target. He then proceeded matter-of-factly. "You're an alcoholic, Mr. McCain. And the universal odds say that you will *remain* an alcoholic. To reenter as a drunkard into your family's life would not, by any stretch of the imagination, be constructive. You would simply be creating a brand-new hell for them." Glenn slowed his words for emphasis. "And I really don't think that's what you want. Maybe for your family's long-term benefit, you should think—"

As if he had been hit on the head with a blunt object, Clay felt his eyes roll backward into his head. He continued to hear Glenn's words in the background. At some uncertain point he interrupted and whispered under his breath, a final abdication more for himself than for Glenn, "You're right, of course. I...uh...would only be creating a new hell for them. And that's not what I want." As he echoed Glenn's assessment, he knew, against every hope and dream inside him and against his deepest fears, that it was the truth.

He placed his hands on his knees and straightened his back as he fought to breathe. He stood up.

Glenn stood up as well. He placed his arm around Clay's shoulders and prayed for him. He then added, "God still offers you His forgiveness, Mr. McCain. Your sin, regardless of its magnitude, is *not* greater than His mercy. Don't ever forget that."

Clay, as he left the meeting a few minutes later, tried to determine in his heart not to forget.

◆   ◆   ◆

Over the next three days, Clay isolated himself in his shack in Puntarenas and drank himself into oblivion.

Around four-thirty on the fourth morning, he had been awake from the dead for about two hours when he made an inexplicable decision.

With an abnormal and enigmatic power of resolve, he decided, lying incapacitated on his bed in the wetness of urine and vomit, that despite his shame, despite common sense, and despite the whole accursed world, he had to see his wife and children again.

Would see them again.

39

On a Saturday morning in May, Rachel, ballpoint pen in hand, sat at the kitchen table staring down at the question: What was the approximate date of the plaintiff's last contact via mail, telephone, or any other means of personal communication with the defendant? It was the next question on the seventeen pages of Queens County divorce solicitation forms.

Seven years and three weeks had passed since that life-shattering morning in 1989 when Clay had walked out of her and the children's lives. Rachel had not heard from Clay since he had vanished. She still had no idea as to his well-being and whereabouts.

According to the state laws of New York, she now—after having been an official resident of the state for more than two years and after having recently proven to the county supreme court through an exhaustive search through military, utility company, motor vehicle department, and telephone company records that Clay McCain had no known place of domicile and could not be found— qualified for an uncontested divorce based on abandonment.

By filling out the forms, with plans to mail them on Monday morning to the matrimonial clerk at the Queens County Courthouse, Rachel was simply taking one more of the needed final steps to help bring some kind of closure to her old life with Clay McCain. She conjectured that she would soon be holding in her hands a legal attestation of divorce.

As she continued to stare at the question at hand, she fought to throw off feelings of melancholy.

"What's wrong?" Summer's voice suddenly spoke up. "You look like you're seriously having second thoughts or something."

Rachel looked up to see Summer energetically pulling a bowl and a box of cereal from the kitchen cabinets.

"No second thoughts," Rachel explained as she watched her sixteen-year-old move to the refrigerator and grab a carton of milk. "Just stalling over a few memories; that's all."

"Well, the only real memory I have of the man is that he hurt us. He certainly doesn't deserve any more patience, especially on your part. And as far as I'm concerned, he doesn't deserve any more of your special thoughts either." With those passing remarks, Summer disappeared into the den with a bowl of cereal in her hand to watch television.

Rachel, with her mother's heart, tolerated the expressed feelings. Though still negative and frank, Summer's present attitude regarding Clay was far less destructive and angry than it had been in years past.

Rachel glanced up at the ceiling in the direction of the second-floor bedrooms where Holly and Justin were supposed to be carrying out their weekly chore of cleaning up their rooms.

Her thoughts drifted to yesterday evening, when she had sat down with the three children for a family conference and announced that she would be mailing out the divorce forms on Monday morning. Summer had reacted with jubilant relief. Holly had offered a look of indecision, then reluctantly conceded, "If you really believe he's never coming back, then I guess maybe it's okay." Justin had simply shrugged with boyish innocence. "Sure!"

had been his reply.

Despite her momentary nostalgia, Rachel possessed a sure peace about the rightness of what she was doing. With that assuredness, she prayed for each of the children that God would somehow use her decision to help refortify their determination to overcome the painful pull of the past and to be strong for the future.

She then thanked God for all the gracious and sacrificial help she had received during the last six years, for the progress that had been realized in her life and heart, and now for the ability to take yet another significant step forward. She prayed, as she had done regularly the last couple of months, that God would grant her wisdom about her relationship with Grayson.

For the last twelve weeks, Grayson had been flying up to New York every other weekend to be with her and the family. She had agreed to the visits primarily because of the new heart she had seen manifested in his life following his December conversion. The transformation continued to be striking. "All those years of blindly trying to be my own god, I could never let go of the resentfulness," he expressed with brokenness shortly after his regenerative experience.

The spiritual passage had added a fresh new innocence to his life that was gradually turning Rachel's respect into a willful love. She was still resolved, however, to proceed cautiously. She wanted to make sure that her head tempered her heart. Thankfully, Grayson's interaction with her, void of any pressure and manipulation, provided her with that kind of freedom. Summer and Justin, on the other hand, were already so fond of the man that they were trying to cheer Rachel on toward a romance.

Rachel smiled as she thought about last Sunday morning's

worship service when Justin fell asleep with his head in Grayson's lap. The expression on Justin's face, even while he slept, had reflected a sense of security. "Today was the best church service I've been to in a long time," Justin had proclaimed en route to a restaurant right after the meeting. Rachel chuckled quietly and shook her head.

With that release of emotion, she again read the question she had paused over. What was the approximate date of the plaintiff's last contact via mail, telephone, or any other means of personal communication with the defendant?

Resisting the lure of further nostalgia, she proceeded to answer the question along with the dozens of others that followed.

On her way to school on Monday morning, Rachel mailed the completed forms to the Queens County Courthouse.

40

A re you sure you want to pay the full amount now?" the lady travel agent asked across the desk in a Spanish unique to Costa Rica's western coast.

"Yes, that's what I want to do," Clay said in the most intelligible Spanish he could manage.

"December the twenty-sixth is still four months away, though." The lady stared dubiously at Clay in his dirty jeans and T-shirt as if he were not thinking sharply.

"I know," Clay replied in an effort to validate his right-mindedness for the lady. "Today is August the twenty-eighth. December the twenty-sixth is four months away. I want to pay the whole amount up-front, now."

"Very well, then." Without further comment, the lady finalized the reservation for a one-way ticket for December twenty-sixth from San José, Costa Rica, to Atlanta, Georgia, aboard Aero Costa Rica flight 1100. Less than a minute later, she handed Clay a printout of the flight details. "The total price is 120,000 colones."

Clay removed the money from his pocket and counted out the amount, which equaled six hundred U.S. dollars. He had worked and sweated harder for this money than for any money he had ever held in his hands. In order to earn it, he had fought for three and a half months now—102 days—to stay sober. He had managed the feat only because of his fighting and consuming emotional preoccupation.

By day he had cut grass and trimmed bushes for 260 colones, or $1.30, an hour, an amount slightly above Costa Rica's minimum wage. In the evenings, he had washed dishes and cleaned toilets in a small family-owned restaurant where the pay had been even less.

He looked at the money with a sense of pride and relinquished it to the lady. As the lady counted the colones, Clay sighed and felt on the brink of tears. He had been so afraid that he would not be able to earn the money. He still weighed around 155 pounds and had continued to suffer from recurring nausea and a depletion of energy. All of the yard and restaurant work had been painstakingly slow and tedious. But he had earned it. And now that it had left his possession, it could not be squandered on a possible alcohol relapse. When the lady handed a receipt to him, he clutched the slip of paper protectively. One of the tears, poised at the brim of his eye, spilled over. As he stood to leave, he heard the lady tell him, "You can pick up your ticket around the first of December." He lifted his hand to show that he understood.

When he was outside, standing on the sidewalk of one of Puntarenas's main streets, he paused with gratitude and then tried to psych himself up for his second wind. He now had to work steadily for four additional months so that he would be able to purchase basic necessities upon his return to the States: a very cheap used automobile, gasoline, food, and two or three sets of new clothes. But primarily he needed the additional time to try to maintain his sobriety and to prove to himself that he was seriously on his way to overcoming his alcohol dependency. He was determined with every pitiful bit of strength he had left to not go back to the States as a drunkard.

If he arrived on American soil under these hoped-for conditions, he would first make contact with his father-in-law in Atlanta and find out where Rachel lived. He would then attempt to reunite with his mother and father in Florida and possibly use their house for his lodging and base of operation. He was convinced, however, that the odds of his father-in-law and parents receiving him with joy and offering quick and total forgiveness were against him. His failures as a son-in-law and son were eclipsed only by his inhumanness as a husband and father.

As he started walking back to work, a new tear followed the first one. He wanted to pray that God would forgive him. He wanted to believe Pastor Joe Glenn's words that God's mercy was greater than his—Clay McCain's—abhorrent sins. But he was afraid. Afraid of the probable silence.

Entering the grounds of the old Queens County Courthouse from the boulevard entrance, Rachel passed through the gate of the iron fence and up the steps between the giant stone pillars.

Once inside the building, she asked the security officer stationed in the foyer for directions to the records room. She had received a postcard two days earlier from the clerk's department notifying her that a verdict regarding her petition for a divorce had been rendered and that she could pick up a certified copy of the judgment in the records room of the courthouse.

Having arranged for a teacher's aide to fill in for her during the last period of the school day, she had left her classroom an hour early in order to get to the courthouse during office hours.

With an underlying nervousness, she followed the security officer's directions to room 106 in the basement and was soon standing behind seven or eight other people waiting in line in the records section.

She tried to pinpoint the reason for her nervousness. Was it because she was in a place of governmental power, a place she was unfamiliar with, a place that was somewhat intimidating? Or was it because she was almost certain that the court had ruled in her favor and that the Clay McCain file in her life was about to be officially closed forever?

She realized that she could not rule out either of the two reasons, especially the latter. Deep in her heart, she had never been able to completely dispel the hope that Clay would return. She could not deny that a small portion of her heart still loved him and probably always would. As she bided her time in the waiting line, she whispered a special prayer for him as she had done frequently in the last couple of years. She prayed that, wherever he was, whatever he was doing, and whomever he was with, God's redeeming and sustaining grace might somehow touch his life.

When it was her turn to be served, Rachel stepped up to the counter and removed the court's notification postcard from her purse. She laid the postcard on the counter along with her New York driver's license and her old passport. One of the messages on the postcard explained that she was required to bring with her to the records office some form of picture ID.

The gray-haired lady behind the counter looked dutifully at the documents, then at Rachel. She typed something at her computer keyboard and stared at the monitor. "Just a moment," she stated flatly. She pushed herself from her desk and went to a file cabinet. She soon returned with the original copy of Rachel's court judgment and a release form. "In order to acquire a certified copy of the document, you have to sign here, please." She pointed to the line on the release form where Rachel was to sign her name.

Rachel used the pen attached by a small chain to the counter to write out her signature.

The lady took the signed form and handed over to Rachel the original one-sheet record of the court's decision. "Take the original," she instructed mechanically. "Make your copy there in the corner to your far left. Bring both the original and the copy back to me."

Rachel took the legal page, moved to the row of copiers and lifted the cover of one of the dingy, well-used machines. Before she placed the document facedown on the glass plate, she held the paper at eye level and searched the script. Losing awareness of everybody around her, she chewed lightly on the inside of her cheek as she started reading. The statement she had anticipated vaulted off the page at her:

The marriage of Clay Alexander McCain and Rachel Ilene Ward, effectuated in Marietta, Georgia, on June 26, 1976, is hereby—August 22, 1996—dissolved by reason of abandonment.

The document, six days old according to the date of authorization, bore the notarized signature of the Honorable Joseph Pallock.

Rachel would have been surprised had the court rejected her requisition. She would have also been mildly upset because of the time-consuming hassle of facing and going through the appeals process. On the other hand, she had not in any way expected that a favorable judgment would cause her to be emotionally jostled. Yet, a mild wave of sadness swept over her. The significance of the moment as a final good-bye simply could not be diminished.

She stood transfixed amid a montage of memories. She exhaled deeply. After a few moments, she made her copy and was sent upstairs to the clerk's office where the copy was released to her for an eight-dollar fee.

Upon her arrival home, Rachel reported the finalization of the divorce to the kids. That evening, in the privacy of her locked bedroom and without any notable fanfare, except for an emotional, instrumental tape playing in the background, she removed her wedding band. She placed it in the bottom of her jewelry box among jewelry she rarely used anymore. She sat in sentimental silence for about twenty minutes in honor of Clay's memory and in honor of all the good times they had shared together.

Then, around eight-thirty, she called Grayson in Atlanta. Although Grayson was planning to fly up for the weekend, he had requested to know the court's decision as soon as Rachel found out.

"Well," Rachel breathed solemnly into the phone when Grayson picked up on the other end, "it's finally over. I'm holding in my hand a certified copy of the court's official judgment."

Rachel listened to Grayson's reaction, then answered with a tired but earnest smile, "Yes, Mr. Cole, I am now a free woman. And yes, I will gladly let you take me out for a grandiose dinner on Saturday night."

She then listened with a grateful heart as Grayson, with the kindest and choicest of words, expressed his love for her.

"I love you, too, Grayson," Rachel said. This was the first time she had spoken those words to Grayson. She now knew in her heart that she unequivocally meant them.

Her breathing skipped a beat as she heard the tearful joy in Grayson's response seven states away.

41

Clay sat alone on a bus-stop bench, eating a traditional Costa Rican Christmas tamale, a *tamal navidenos,* made of corn flour and mashed potato dough layered with rice, pork, sweet peas, and carrots and wrapped and boiled in a banana leaf.

He had just earned a little extra money doing some inside painting at the home of his restaurant employer, and he was now waiting for a midevening bus to take him to the restaurant, where he was expected to be on dishwashing duty in about an hour.

As he slowly chewed, he saw a large delivery truck drive by. Pictured across the entire side panel was a Christmas advertisement for a major grocery chain. The colorful scene portrayed a well-dressed man sitting at Christmas dinner with his family and friends, having responsibly provided for this family with the best food products available.

The memories of Christmases past flashed into Clay's mind. He thought about his own family gatherings when he was a dependable and trustworthy husband and father. He also thought about the fun and hectic church parties he wholeheartedly directed, which had always earned him the free-flowing approval of his people, about the December church services where he stood before large crowds as a respected leader and heralded the good tidings of God's Christmas story, and about receiving gifts of appreciation from his Swedish congregation. His life in those days had been filled with a righteous purpose, an influential platform, and a positive notoriety. But most of all, his life had been saturated with people—friends, supporters, coworkers, ministry colleagues, a wife, and children.

Clay looked down at his paint-spattered, dirty old jeans. His life now bore no value, claimed no respect, and knew no friends. Even the people who employed him kept their distance from him. Only one driving force had helped him sustain his sanity and his sobriety through the last few months: the dream of once again being with his wife, his daughters, and his son.

Clay looked up. All around him, adorning the shop windows and city grounds, were signs of the Christmas season: colored lights, nativity sets, fake snow made from cotton balls, lighted Christmas trees, figurines of Santa Claus, and decorative displays of pine branches. People with Christmas packages scurried along the streets.

The joyful season only highlighted his aloneness.

He took another bite of the tamale. He had to hold on for only two more weeks. The one-way ticket to the States was in his billfold. So was enough money to purchase his initial stateside needs.

Lingering on the snow-covered sidewalk, en route from the Christmas party to the car, Rachel looked at Grayson, caught her breath, and stared again at the diamond ring that had just been placed between the tips of her fingers. Even through her breath, the ring sparkled in the glow of the neighborhood lights and the full moon.

She again looked at Grayson. The words "will you marry me" lingered in his eyes and on his lips with priceless anticipation.

The proposal, resounding majestically in Rachel's ears, was something she had been eagerly expecting. For two or three months now, she and Grayson had discussed issues relevant to a life together—issues such as spousal expectations, temperament differences, conflict management, spiritual nurturing, future dreams, money, careers, parenting philosophies, additional children, and home location.

Wanting with every strand of life she possessed to make a right decision about marrying Grayson, Rachel had even asked Jason Faircloth for special counsel and advice. Through the six and a half years Jason had been a part of her life, his shared insights had always, without exception, earned her deepest respect and trust.

Some of Jason's offered words as a mentor still hung in the forefront of her thinking. *Teaching us versus teasing us,* he had highlighted for her just a few days ago, *is a biblical principle that needs to be remembered.* He had illustrated the point with biographical accounts from the Scriptures then emphasized with sensitivity, *God does not playfully place us in circumstantial mazes to see if we can entertain Him by figuring our way, by trial and error, to the end. Rather, he uses His Word and the circumstances of life to educate us with solid, insightful lessons so that, based on faith in His supreme knowledge, we can take clear and decisive steps into the future.*

Rachel became teary as she returned her eyes to Grayson's. One definite lesson she had learned during her years in New York was that it was okay, even healthy, to risk trusting and loving people again. More and more, she had taken steps to implement this lesson on a social and friendship level. And the fruit had surpassed all of her expectations. She knew now that it was time to imple-

ment the lesson on a matrimonial level. She had definitely prepared for the moment patiently, cautiously, and wisely.

"Grayson," she responded splendidly, "if I searched the world
from continent to continent, country to country, I honestly don't
think I could ever find another man who would be so loving and
supportive toward me as you've been. And," she added with a big
smile, "so determined to win my heart." She tightly embraced
him, as much as their heavy coats would allow. With her chin
buried in his wool scarf, and with her cheek against his, she whispered, "God knows I mean it when I say, 'I love you as my friend.'
He also knows I mean it when I say, 'Yes, I'll now love you as my
husband.'"

There was a split second of stillness. Rachel then gasped as she
felt herself being squeezed and lifted off the ground as Grayson
exploded into a robust and joyous hoopla. Rachel lost herself in
the ecstasy of the moment as Grayson twirled her, kissed her, and
shouted unintelligible sounds of overwhelming glee.

When Grayson finally put her down, he giddily danced a few
steps, then picked her up and whirled her again. As the two of
them locked in a passionate kiss, Rachel was sure she felt Grayson's
tears mingling with her own.

Then she thought she heard the sound of applause. She was
certain the noise was not just imagined. As she turned her head
toward the clamor, she saw about thirty people standing out on the
porch of the house from where she and Grayson had just left the
church-sponsored party. Standing in the gazing crowd were Jason
Faircloth, Daytona, Aunt Temp, Pastor Dan Shaw, and dozens of
others who had become her dearest friends. Everyone was indeed
clapping. Even whistling and cheering.

As Rachel blushed and felt her eyes grow big, she heard Grayson shout toward the approving audience, "Did you hear it? She said *yes!* She said she's going to marry me!"

"Yeah, we already kind of caught that!" someone from the porch quipped, followed by another round of hoots and whistles.

"Grayson!" Rachel whispered emphatically, grinding her fist lightly into his ribs. "How long have they been standing there?"

"Oh, just for a little while," he beamed.

Caught by the additional surprise in the rapturous moment, Rachel rolled her eyes, then waved and smiled coltishly to the crowd.

With his face glowing, Grayson slipped the engagement ring onto Rachel's finger, then took her by the elbow and led her to the car.

Before he opened the passenger door for her, he said, "Believe me when I say, I love you more than anything else in the whole world." Then he added as he pulled open the door, "Even if you hadn't said yes, you would still deserve every single one of these."

The dome light lit up the car's interior.

What Rachel saw took her breath away. The entire backseat, from window to window, was literally stacked to the top of the seat's headrest with long-stemmed crimson-red roses. Hundreds, thousands of them. The air was filled with their sweet fragrance.

Rachel looked at Grayson, then back at the flowers. Her senses were completely overwhelmed. Such an expression of adoration was unequalled to anything she had ever experienced. Her hand moved to her forehead. "Grayson, I don't know what to say. I...I..."

Grayson took her by the shoulders and kissed her. "When you said you'd marry me, you said everything I could have ever hoped to hear for one night. Nothing else has to be said."

"But, Grayson, this…this is—"

"It's okay." He put his finger over her lips. "Just enjoy them. Let them make you feel like the desired and cherished lady that you are."

Stirred by the power of his words, Rachel squeezed him and wept.

Intertwined in the viselike hug, Grayson waited for a few seconds and then whispered into her hair, "What do you say we go and break the news to the kids?"

Rachel bobbed her head in agreement.

Within the hour, the children, especially Summer and Justin, were frolicking with delight over the news that Grayson was going to be their new dad.

While Grayson and Justin made frequent trips out to the car to haul the flowers into the house, Rachel, Summer, and Holly busily filled the few available vases and then started tying the remaining flowers in arrangement-sized bundles. The bundles were then placed throughout the house: across the top of the fireplace mantel, in the Christmas stockings, on the Christmas tree, onto the stair railings, atop the refrigerator and microwave oven, on the living room end tables, on top of the television set, on all the win-dowsills, on the back of the toilets, on bedposts, atop dressers, and even hung to the light fixtures and lamps.

The sublimity of the occasion, along with the illustrious floral display and the profuse fragrance of the thousands of roses, created an unforgettable evening.

The emotional high continued throughout the next day as Grayson and Rachel discussed a wedding date.

To accommodate and expedite their new life together and to assure long-term stability for Summer, Holly, and Justin, Grayson decided to give up his position at the bank in Marietta, Georgia, put his Atlanta house on the market, and find employment in the New York banking industry. His own two sons had long since moved out of the South anyway. His older son, now twenty-two, had joined the navy two and a half years ago and was stationed at a naval base in California. The younger boy, twenty-one, was in his sophomore year at a major university in Indiana. There was no longer any binding reason for Grayson to stay in Georgia.

By late afternoon the next day, two days before Christmas Eve, the marriage date and locale were settled· Saturday, March 8, 1997, just a little over two months away. In New York City, at the Liberty International City Church.

42

Wearing new clothes and displaying a fresh haircut and a clean-shaven face, Clay McCain exited the jetway and stepped into the international terminal at Atlanta's Hartsfield International Airport on the afternoon of December 26. He found himself breathing uncomfortably in short, quick bursts. The emotional and visual impact of walking on American soil again after an eleven-year absence was both immediate and jarring.

He walked slowly through the concourse carrying all his belongings in a cheap carry-on sports bag. Starting to shake uncontrollably, he stopped and leaned against the wall of the spacious corridor. People passed him as he placed his bag on the floor between his feet.

He looked around. He was actually at the airport in Atlanta.

Atlanta! The place of his roots. The place he called home.

Trying to control his breathing, he allowed himself to be pulverized by an overload of images and memories.

Memories of his childhood: Riding his pushcart down the leaf-covered hills of Grant Park. Roasting marshmallows on sticks with his Boy Scout troop in a lakeside campground at the base of Stone Mountain. Enjoying the warm, humid evenings and the juicy hot dogs at the Starlight Drive-In Theater. Eating his mother's homemade whole-wheat pancakes.

Memories of his high school years: Fretting over pimples. Playing on the varsity football and track-and-field teams. Learning to drive his parents' new 1966 baby blue 350 Chevy Impala in the parking lot of an old Moreland Avenue shopping center. Sitting with his dad in the upper level of Fulton County Stadium watching his first live major-league baseball game. The night of his high school graduation.

Memories of his early adulthood: Spending two years at the technical institute in downtown Atlanta. Becoming a Christian and experiencing such a drastic change in his thinking. Joining North Metro Church of the Bible and studying under Pastor Frank Lovett. Rachel Ilene Ward.

Rachel Ilene Ward.

It all happened here. In this city.

A tremor gripped his shoulders and neck. He forced himself to pick up his bag and start walking. He attempted to distract himself by taking in the fresh sights of the airport. He was quickly reminded of the American affluence so rightfully perceived around the world. The massive and opulent building undeniably mirrored that fact to him.

Willing himself to keep moving, he followed the rest of the passengers through the customs checkpoint and then out into the international arrival hall.

A huge number of people were gathered on the arrival floor bearing flowers, placards, and looks of anticipation. Many were already greeting their parties with hugs and laughs. Some with tears.

Clay wove through the throng of people celebrating their reunions and descended one of the lengthy escalators to the underground airport train. He there joined a cluster of people waiting for the next train to transport them to the main terminal and exit point. Clay realized for the first time that he was standing in what must be a new addition to the airport, concourse *E*. He idly wondered if the Atlanta airport was still the largest airport in the world.

An automated voice announced from overhead speakers that the next train was approaching. Within seconds, the computer-operated train halted in place, its doors sliding open.

Clay boarded the vehicle and took hold of a vertical pole for balance. He was starkly revisited with the realization, based on the Americans he was obviously seeing and hearing in the packed space, that the typical American was not only more affluent than most everyone else around the world, but was also louder and fatter. Distastefully so.

As the train accelerated, Clay tightened his jaw and rebuked himself for making such a derogatory judgment. How could he, a freakishly underweight deviant, pretend even for one second to be offended by anyone else's lifestyle or appearance? He reminded himself that most of the Americans around him probably had families and were loyal to them.

As the tram proceeded to concourses *D, C, B, A*, and the *T*-gates, allowing even more people to cram into the car, Clay tried to corral his thoughts and concentrate on the business at hand. He first needed to find an airport bank where he could exchange his colones for dollars and then find a rental-car office.

The electronic voice, emitting from the onboard speakers, announced that the train was approaching the baggage claim area and exit terminal. In less than a minute, Clay, clutching his sports bag and still breathing irregularly, followed the crowd up the escalator and into the heart of the airport's main building. At the top of the escalator, an overhead green poster proclaimed "Mayor Bill Campbell welcomes you to Atlanta, home of the 1996 Centennial Olympic Games."

Almost immediately as Clay passed beneath the welcome sign and entered the huge hall, he found a row of six or seven rental-car offices and then a bank. He first exchanged his money. With the 220,000 colones he was carrying in his pocket, the sum total of his hard-earned cash, he purchased $1,065 dollars minus the deduction of the commission fee.

He swallowed hard with appreciation.

After counting the money, he buried the bills deep in his pocket and walked over to a car-rental agency whose name implied cheaper-than-average prices. All of the agency's uniformed representatives were busy helping customers, so Clay took a spot in line and waited. He saw a poster on the counter advertising subcompact cars for as low as thirty-four dollars a day. He tried to calculate how many dollars he would have left after paying the thirty-four dollar fee, plus taxes, and ten dollars' worth of gas.

"Can I help you, sir?" a tired but friendly female voice spoke up with a prominent Georgia drawl.

Clay saw that the young lady behind the car-rental counter was looking at him. He stepped forward and told her he needed the least expensive car for no more than twenty-four hours.

"I'll need to see your credit card and driver's license, please," the lady replied, placing onto the counter a pamphlet that explained the various deals the company offered.

"I'll be paying with cash." Clay reached into his pocket to

retrieve his newly acquired international driver's license and some of his money.

"I'm sorry, sir, but we only take payments through credit cards."

"You don't accept cash?"

"Only credit cards. It's company policy. We're in the business, sir, of releasing fifteen- to thirty-thousand-dollar automobiles to complete strangers. A credit card assures us that a customer has an acceptable credit rating. Plus, it provides us with trace information such as the person's address and state of residency. It's all for security reasons."

"And for those like myself who don't have a credit card?" The last credit card he'd owned was when he lived in Sweden. He had left that one behind with Rachel.

"Sorry, sir, it's a company rule."

"And what about the other agencies?"

"It's a rule, sir, that's applied industry-wide everywhere in the country."

Frustrated by the impediment to his plan, he wanted to raise his voice at the lady and ask her to please stop saying "sir" in every sentence, despite the freshly recalled fact that both "sir" and "ma'am" were as prevalent in the South as grits and black-eyed peas. Instead, he turned and walked away. He stopped at the desks of two other car-rental companies and inquired about cash payments just to make sure that what the young lady had told him was true. It was.

At a momentary loss for direction, Clay strolled past a newsstand, souvenir shop, and flower boutique decorated with Christmas candles and Christmas holly and sat down in the atrium of the airport to reflect and to revise his plan. He felt irritated, almost embarrassed, about the credit card issue and wondered if, after such a substantial hiatus from the States, he was going to be completely out of sync with his native culture. He finally resolved to take one step at a time and be patient with himself. He then walked out of the building into the fifty-five-degree weather and found a taxi.

"I need for you to take me to the nearest section of town where there are several car dealerships within walking distance of each other," he told the cabdriver, an African-American man with a lot of gray showing in his hair and goatee. "*Used-car* dealers," Clay quickly appended.

"Used cars, you say. Hmm, let me think a moment. I 'spect your best bet would probably be there in Forest Park, right on Forest Parkway. It's only about seven or eight miles from here. I can think of at least five dealers in less than a mile, a mile and a half, from each other. And there might even be more."

Within fifteen minutes, Clay was paying a cab fare of twenty-two dollars and getting out at a Chevrolet dealership in Forest Park.

By seven-fifteen that evening, after scouring the lots of the Chevrolet dealer, a Toyota dealer, a Dodge dealer, and three small independent dealers, Clay was back at the first independent dealer handing over seven hundred dollars to the salesman for a drab 1980 white Buick LeSabre. The car's odometer registered 177,523 miles. The windshield was cracked badly on the passenger's side. The fabric covering the driver's seat was ripped down the seam, with dirty foam rubber showing. The right rear fender was dented and scraped. Two tires were bald; the other two were tread-worn enough to also merit replacements.

Even though the engine regularly misfired and dense gray smoke spewed out of the exhaust pipe, the two test drives revealed that the V-8 engine started every time on the first try, that the transmission shifted steadily, albeit roughly, through the gears, and that the brakes gripped adequately.

The salesman handed Clay the bill of sale. "You do understand that it's illegal in the state of Georgia to own and operate an automobile without insurance, don't you?" Clay had already admitted, at the man's inquiry, that he did not have an insurance policy and was not able at the moment to afford one.

Clay acknowledged the reminder and signed his name to the car title.

"And I'll need your address for the registration," the man declared.

Clay recited his father-in-law's Marietta address, hoping he remembered it correctly.

"All right," the man told him, "I'll get the title over to the Department of Motor Vehicles to be reissued in your name. When it's ready, it can either be mailed to your address or you can pick it up here in about six days."

"I'll just pick it up here," Clay said.

The salesman handed the two sets of keys over to Clay. "Don't forget, you've got until May first to transfer the tag over to your name."

"I'll remember."

Clay drove immediately to a gas station and was honestly surprised to discover that gasoline in the States could still be purchased for around a dollar a gallon. He topped off the tank then added a quart of oil to the engine and checked the air pressure in the tires.

Minutes later, he guided the car north onto Interstate 75. His next stop would be at his father-in-law's in Marietta, just north of the city. He hoped dearly that Mr. Ward would tell him the current whereabouts of Rachel and the kids.

43

Clay drove northward in the dark past the new, well-lit, red-brick Olympic stadium and then through the heart of Atlanta on the downtown connector. He was amazed at how massively the city's skyline had expanded—both upward and outward—during the last eleven years. Even the interstate had been enlarged to six, and sometimes seven, lanes in each direction to handle the increased traffic of the city's ever-growing population.

To Clay, the changes seemed to loom as a concrete-and-steel manifesto declaring the irreversible and consequential power of time. The strength of eleven single years collectively strung together hit him with fresh impact.

He now wondered anew about the seven and a half years that had elapsed since he had forsaken Rachel and the children. After such a vast period, was his quest for reconciliation insane? Was his hope single-handedly upholding all that was foolish? He squelched the uninvited thought and pushed onward.

He finally found himself slowing the car on the exit ramp at Marietta. He relied on his memory of the roads and of a few enduring landmarks to guide him to his father-in-law's house.

Because of the reconfiguration of a major Marietta intersection and the newness of a gargantuan commercial development, he became confused and nearly missed a turn. Otherwise, he drove without mishap directly to his father-in-law's mailbox and parked at the curb.

The sight of the three-bedroom brick house, even at night, evoked nostalgic memories. Fighting to keep the memories from distracting him, he decided that if Billy Allen Ward was in town, then he was most likely sitting in the house watching television.

The first bad sign, though, was the presence of a car in the driveway instead of Billy's everlasting Chevy pickup. The second omen was the tall grass and overgrown hedges. Both were distinctly silhouetted in the backdrop of the surrounding house lights. Ever since Clay had known him, Billy had religiously kept his grass cut to within an inch of the ground and the shrubs trimmed back to the nubs.

Clay got out of the car, approached the front door, and knocked on the aluminum frame of the outer screen door. He knocked again. As he waited, he realized that, without a jacket, he was shivering in the cold air of the early darkness of December.

He winced as he was suddenly bathed in the brightness of the overhead porch light. As the front door opened, Clay held his breath. The person appearing on the other side of the screen door, however, was…definitely not Billy Allen Ward.

"Whooo are you and whaaat do you waaant?" a male voice asked with a slow and heavy slur.

Clay saw that he was looking into the face of a thickly built, middle-aged man with Down's syndrome. Before Clay had a chance to reply to the question, he heard a woman's voice.

"I thought I told you a thousand times, Mickey Joe, not to open that door until you first know who's there!" The woman, at least in her sixties, marched into the room where the young man was standing. "Get back into the kitchen right now. Do you hear me?"

The man turned and raised an open hand as if he were going to strike the lady. He then mumbled some words that Clay could not understand and hesitantly shuffled past the woman into another room.

"Now, who are you, and why is it you're here, mister?" The curtness of the question matched the lady's steel-eyed, don't-take-any-garbage-from-anybody appearance. She was tall, with short gray hair and bad teeth. And she was chewing tobacco.

"I apologize for interrupting your evening," Clay said, "but I'm looking for a Mr. Billy Allen Ward. He's my father-in-law. He lived here in this house for over thirty years."

"Don't live here no more."

"Ma'am?"

"The man don't live here no more, I said. Don't you understand English?"

"When did he move?"

"'Bout three years ago."

"Would you happen to know where he moved to, or where I might be able to find him?"

"Don't know nothin' else 'bout the man 'cept he moved. Don't even know if he's still alive. So, if you don't mind leavin' my property, I'd feel a lot less tempted to grab the pistol that's sittin' right here on the shelf behind this door."

Gosh! Welcome to America, Clay told himself. He lifted his hands in a show of nonaggression. "Ma'am, I'm not here to threaten anybody. I'm just simply trying to locate my wife's father. Can you please just relax for a moment and try to remember if Mr. Ward, before he left, mentioned the name of a particular street, a certain part of town, or maybe even another county where he might have been moving to?"

"You really don't hear English very well do you, mister? I'll repeat my statement one more time for your thick head, and then I'm gonna give you to the count of five to start backin' off my porch. I say again, I don't know nothin' about the man."

Clay saw the lady indeed reach for something behind the door and heard the metallic *click* of a firearm being cocked. The lady, with her gun-bearing arm blocked from view, looked him in the eye and started counting.

Clay threw his hands up in disgust and left.

Uncoiling from the unexpected and unpleasant confrontation, he drove to a nearby gas station and at the service counter looked through an Atlanta phone book. Billy Allen Ward was not listed. He searched for Rachel's name and noticed that his hands were shaking. Her name was not listed either.

He went outside to the pay phone, called an operator, and requested the code for directory assistance. After receiving the three-digit number, he called and asked for the telephone numbers of Billy Ward and Rachel McCain.

There was a listing for a Bobby Ward, a Buck Ward, and a Buddy Ward, he was told, but no Billy Ward. Not even a William Ward. Rachel McCain could not be found either.

Hanging up, Clay brainstormed but could not think of a single person he could call who could possibly tell him Billy Ward's new address. Billy did not have any brothers or sisters, and Rachel was his only child. Billy, of course, had friends and associates. Clay remembered a few of the people, but he could not remember their full names or addresses.

After further thought, though, Clay did remember the name of the business where Billy worked. He called directory assistance again. He spelled out the name of the trucking company where Billy Ward had been employed for more than three decades and asked for the firm's number. He felt victorious as he jotted down the 800 number. Seconds later, he punched in the number, only to hear an answering machine tell him that the office was closed and would not be open for business again until eight o'clock tomorrow morning.

Clay stood there by the phone and stared at the traffic passing by on the main street. With two or three hours of evening yet facing him, he argued with himself about whether or not to call his parents in St. Petersburg. He elected not to. If in the next couple of days he did not uncover Rachel's place of residence, he would drive to St. Petersburg, call his parents within a few miles of their home, and then be in their presence within minutes after the contact. Even if they did not receive him with welcoming arms, surely they would at least tell him where he could find his wife and kids.

He crawled back into the old Buick, turned on the heater, and just sat for several minutes. Then he drove a few blocks to a super-sized twenty-four-hour department and grocery store complex he had seen earlier in the evening. He had to buy a winter coat.

While strolling the aisles of the superstore, he found himself overwhelmed by the boundless selection of goods. There was an entire aisle just for breakfast cereals of every imaginable kind, a few of which only eccentrics could have imagined. There was another long row of shelves stocked with just pet foods. Animal food, for heaven's sake! While millions of toddlers around the planet were in the throes of starvation. Seeing the wastefulness and the spoiled frivolity of the American culture, especially in the light of his recent poverty, affected him so strongly that he hurried himself along to the men's clothing department and bought the cheapest coat he could find. Then, unable to brace his mental nausea, he fled the consumer carnival.

He drove the Buick around to the backside of the store and parked beside a row of Dumpsters. Wrapped in his new coat, he curled up in the backseat and slept overnight in the car. Or at least tried.

"Retired three years ago?" Clay stood in a hallway, speaking with the personnel manager of the trucking company.

"Yeah, ol' Billy finally called it quits," the manager confirmed from behind his cup of morning coffee. "Said he'd seen the country streaking by the windows of his big rig at deadline speeds for thirty years and that it was about time he started enjoying it leisurely from behind a stack of old back-road maps and fishing poles."

Clay tried to relax the rigidity of his face muscles. "So you believe he's on the road somewhere?"

"All I know is that he talked about buying a nice camper and living out of it while he traveled around for a few years."

"Do you know if he maintains any kind of residence here in Atlanta?"

The manager wrinkled his brow and took a sip of coffee. "I'm not positive, but I can make a phone call and find out for you." He motioned for Clay to follow him, then moved down the hallway and into his office. "Come on in," he told Clay when he entered his work area.

Clay obliged. As he stood and observed, the manager used the phone at his desk and eventually penned something onto a piece of paper before hanging up.

"Well," the manager reported, "according to the office that mails out the pension checks, your father-in-law does have a local address. But it's a P.O. box." He handed Clay the paper on which he had just written the address. "I guess, if nothing else, you can reach him by letter."

Clay thanked the man for his help.

Back in the Buick, Clay stared at the address. He had no earthly idea where Billy Ward might be right now or how often he collected his mail at this particular post office box. Every week? Once a month? Once a quarter? Or just whenever he happened to be in town? If he was indeed living on the road all the time, was there a probability that he was even using other post office boxes in other parts of the country?

Clay placed the address in the inner pocket of his coat. Should he stake out the local post office and wait for Billy to show up? Or search for him through alternative avenues?

Feeling as if he were peering into the mouth of a labyrinth that, if entered, could cost him precious energy and time and possibly prove to be a dead end, Clay decided to switch his focus to St. Petersburg, Florida, to his mom and dad.

He drove to a grocery store and bought a bag of Golden Delicious apples and a ninety-nine-cent highway map of the eastern United States. He estimated that he would be in St.

Petersburg, barring any unexpected delays, by late afternoon.

As he was leaving Marietta, he made a last-minute decision. He drove a couple of miles out of his way and, in a slow pass, viewed the facilities of North Metro Church of the Bible. He saw on the church's marquee that Pastor Frank Lovett was still the presiding pastor. Even after the passing of so much time, Clay could still envision the man standing ramrod straight in the pulpit purporting himself and his denominational peers to be the exclusive beacons of God's will and God's laws. Even though Clay had been sensitized in recent years to the rightness of God's ways by the destructive experience of his own wrongdoing, he was still convinced that Frank Lovett's perception of righteous living and righteous leadership had been off target and dangerously misleading.

As the North Metro building filled the car's rearview mirror, Clay wondered if Frank Lovett was still a dictatorial legalist or if he had possibly evolved into a more tolerant and seasoned man, tutored and changed by the stretching-rack of time. Clay could only envisage that the man was just as judgmental as ever. It was his bygone observation that men with Lovett's type of bulldogged posture seemed only to petrify with age.

Most importantly though, Clay wondered if Rachel was still a member of North Metro and was thus living in the immediate vicinity. If she was no longer a member of the church, then Clay was reasonably sure that Pastor Lovett would still know or could easily find out the proximity of her whereabouts. But one of the least desirable prospects of Clay's life was to stand as a "traitorous" and "fallen" missionary in the presence of Frank Lovett. Even if only to make a simple request.

Clay concluded a dozen times over that he would rather face

the unbearable humiliation of standing before his parents. Approaching Lovett for help would be a last resort.

With his hopes now fully on St. Petersburg, Clay traversed the nearest route to Interstate 75. Wondering if the Buick's thin tires would survive the long and high-speed journey, he turned onto the expressway and headed south.

44

C lay sat in his car while it idled at the main gate of the Golden Sands retirement village in northwest St. Petersburg. He was waiting for the young security guard in the fortified gatehouse to ring Lloyd and Hester McCain's villa and receive confirmation that he was welcome to enter through the sliding iron gate.

Clay had tried to call his parents from a drugstore a few miles back up Highway 19. He called seven or eight times over a period of fifteen minutes and continually received a busy signal. Then finally the phone rang, but no one answered. He tried twice more, only to hear someone pick up and be immediately disconnected by what sounded like an electronic glitch. In one last effort, he had heard the line successfully connect again yet give another busy signal. He gave up and decided to contact his parents in person.

He felt like a punching bag for nervousness as he now watched the security guard flip through the registry of the residents' numbers. The tension caused by the heavy rush hour traffic he had endured for the last hour and the frustration he had tasted throughout the day because of engine problems were now dwarfed by the imminency of seeing, and hopefully being embraced by, his mother and father again.

It had been seven and a half years since he had spoken with

them. Eleven years since he had seen them. He had never even seen their home here in Florida. Now that he was just yards away, he felt that he wanted to approach their front door crawling on his belly.

He suddenly thought that it might be more gracious of him to turn around and drive away. But his hope, now rising like a giant hot air balloon, refused to be restrained.

"I'm sorry, did you say their name is spelled M-C-C-A-I-N?" the security guard wanted to know.

"Yeah, that's right."

The guard corked his head back and forth. "The name is not in my directory. You must have the wrong address."

Although Clay had never visited his mom and dad at this site, he had spoken with them several times by phone during the first year and a half they had lived here. He knew he was not in error about the name of the development or its location.

"Is there another retirement village in the vicinity with the same name?" Clay asked.

"No, I wouldn't think so."

"And every name of every Golden Sands resident is on your list?"

"Every name is here. The list is updated twice a month and even more often when it's necessary."

Clay, trying to sound congenial rather than desperate, explained to the guard that he had been living overseas for the last eleven years and had been out of touch with his parents for quite a while. They had at one time lived here in the Golden Sands community, but had obviously moved. Clay then asked if he could speak with the resident manager and try to find out when they had moved and to where.

The guard rang through to the resident manager's home and passed along Clay's request.

Within a quarter of an hour, around sunset, Clay was sitting in a sales office housed in the garage of one of the retirement community's model homes.

"And so you're telling me you're the son of Lloyd and Hester McCain?" the older man—Mr. Aldrich—asked after hearing the basic details of Clay's circumstance.

Clay nodded softly, suddenly wondering how much the man had heard from his parents about his maligned history as a missing family member.

"Can you show me some proof of your identity?"

Clay extended his international driver's license and his passport.

The man studied both documents carefully. "Mr. McCain, I'm sorry to have to break this news to you. But when I began my employment here in May, I'd been moved into my house for less than twenty-four hours when a Mrs. Hester McCain, a widow in villa 19-A, passed away with a heart attack. It was my understanding that her husband, Lloyd, had passed away about a year or so earlier."

Clay instantly froze then gasped as if a giant twister had dropped suddenly out of the sky and sucked all the air out of his body. He squeezed his eyes shut and saw only black haze. "No, they...can't be dead. That's not—I mean—"

He leaned backward, stretching his abdomen to rush air into his lungs. He pictured his dad, who for years assayed to remain positive, even cheery, in the face of his degenerative nerve disease.

A man who always refrained from using his handicap as an excuse to impinge upon others. A man who used his walking stick and his walker as resourcefully as a carpenter used a hammer and a measuring tape. A dignified and gentle-hearted man who, at the minimum, deserved a loving and attentive son. He visualized his mother, a simple but tough-spirited lady who was made beautiful by the virtue of her good-heartedness. The lady who nursed him, changed his diapers, cradled him in her arms when he was a baby. The lady who had assisted him with his homework and regularly drove him to and from school when he was a boy. The lady who always expressed an undiminished pride in her son. The lady who had shown him nothing less than perpetual love and honor throughout his entire life.

And now, both Mom and Dad...gone!

"Hester and Lloyd McCain? Shell Drive, 19-A? That can't...can't be right."

No! Please no. Not before he had a chance to fall at their feet and plead for their forgiveness, to offer some kind of restitution, to say a last word, a final good-bye. Not before they could know that he had realized that they and everybody else were right and he was wrong, and that he was finally trying to find his way home.

But the resident manger affirmed his previous statement. He then said, "I'm sorry, Mr. McCain."

Clay bent over, feeling as if every muscle inside his skin were tightening and placing him in a punishing vise.

He posed a few additional questions, hoping that what he was hearing was a case of mistaken identity. Was the man sure that the Mrs. McCain who died was the same Mrs. McCain who was in her late seventies, who with her husband purchased their Golden

Sands home in 1987, and who had possibly still been driving a 1988 pink Cadillac?

The older man, with a steady reply, did recall the pink Cadillac, which was parked at the Shell Drive address at the time of Mrs. McCain's death. Second, the sales information showed that Mr. and Mrs. McCain had indeed bought their villa in 1987. And yes, the Hester McCain who died last May looked to be in her late seventies.

Clay's strained thoughts shattered into a thousand useless pieces. He was half sure that he heard his voice muddle out a mechanical inquiry about the location of the burial. "I'm sorry, I don't have that information," was the answer he thought he heard. The rest of the conversation was lost in the chaos of shock. He barely remembered leaving the man's company and getting back into the car.

As if prompted by an ancient homing instinct, he dazedly searched for and found the house at 19-A Shell Drive. He parked for a few minutes at the curb. The name Houghton was on the mailbox. The McCains were truly gone. Clay stared at the lighted windows. He miserably and hungrily tried to picture the final years of his parents' lives behind those walls—their activities, conversations, joys, and hardships and, no doubt, their maternal and paternal depression caused by the fact that he had raped them of their parental pride and dignity and had discarded their needs and feelings as if they had been total strangers.

With self-hatred mounting in his soul by the millisecond, Clay finally drove away.

Through the night and into the early morning, he sat fixed at a table in a darkened corner of a low-class bar and stared with self-pity at a full bottle of Jack Daniel's.

At about four in the morning, he took the unopened bottle outside and bashed it over the roof of his Buick. He then paced up and down the sandy shoulder of the street and screamed and wept.

At around nine, he found a pay phone and called a half dozen or so cemetery offices until he found the graveyard where his parents' bodies had been buried. He wrote down the name of the cemetery and the plot number.

In less than thirty minutes he was walking across the manicured lawn in the Everlasting Garden section of the Pinellas Memorial Cemetery. There were no tombstones. Instead, each grave was marked by a flat bronze plate on which raised letters identified the name of the dead along with the person's date of birth and date of death. Behind each plate stood a matching bronze flower vase, which could be laid over into a groove for lawn mowers to pass over. The plot number of the grave was inscribed on the foot of each vase.

Clay searched until he found plot 49. And then, without allotting himself any transition time, he read the markers.

Lloyd Alexander McCain   Hester Johnson McCain
January 3, 1914–January 27, 1995   March 6, 1917–May 15, 1996
Perpetual rest   *Beside the still waters*

When he finished reading and assimilating the facts, he turned and tramped away. He took about six steps then stopped and turned around. As if his legs were suddenly sheered from beneath him, he dropped to the grass. He started beating himself with his fists, repeatedly striking his legs, face, and ribs. When halted by exhaustion, he collapsed prostrate onto the ground.

Pressing his face into the sod, he cursed himself for his consuming selfishness, a selfishness that had allowed his own mother to live her last year and a half of widowhood and motherhood all alone.

Starting to sob, he pulled himself across the grass and lay at the side of the graves. "Forgive me. Please, I never wanted to hurt you."

But even as the words flowed from his lips, he could not rid himself of the accusatory inner voice that blamed him for contributing to the deaths of the two precious people at whose graves he now lingered.

Feeling as if his soul were about to explode, he clenched his fists and screamed. He then dropped his head to the ground again and fell quiet. He just lay there in the direct morning sun. He stayed there for minutes. For hours. He eventually slept.

Awakened a short while later by a familiar sickness in his stomach, Clay slowly lifted his head off the grass. He gripped his belly with one of his arms and moved to a sitting position. He felt woozy and realized he was feverish.

Before he could establish his equilibrium, he heaved the contents of his stomach onto the cemetery grass. He spent the next ten minutes on his knees dry heaving. He then lay back down to try to be still and to rest, but the pain building inside his head refused him that comfort.

He made his way to the car, drove to the nearest convenience store, and bought a small bottle of aspirin.

By the time he paid the cashier and returned to the car, he was trembling all over with the chills. He put on his jacket and zipped it up to the neck. He jostled three aspirin into his hand and started to pop them into his mouth when his stomach tried once more to vomit up contents that were no longer there.

When he finally straightened again, he swallowed the aspirin and drove back to the cemetery. He wanted to stay at his parents' side for a while. He wanted to kneel in their presence as he grieved. He wanted them somehow to see the anguish that was punishing his soul, to know how much he thirsted for their forgiveness. He wanted them to believe him as he tried to persuade them of his miserable and pathetic love.

But as he parked the car, his headache became so intense that he had to lie down in the backseat. For the next thirty-six hours, he staggered back and forth between the car and the burial site as he battled relentless waves of nausea, chills, and fever and, at the same time, tried to survive the undertow of guilt and despair.

By the early hours of Monday morning, when his bout of sickness had run its course, his clothes were spotted with sweat, stomach bile, and grass stains. He reclined in the driver's seat of his car and ate one of his apples. Then once again fell asleep.

When he awoke around lunchtime, he drove the streets of north St. Petersburg and found a cheap motel for fifteen dollars a night.

Upon entering his room, he immediately stripped down and bathed. Afterward, as he stood in front of the room's half-length mirror, he was shocked at his appearance. Judging by the skeleton pressing against the skin around his hips and ribs, it looked as if another ten pounds had disappeared from his frame.

What was going on inside his body?

He decided for the first time since he started losing weight fourteen months ago that it was mandatory he be examined by a doctor. He determined that he would make a medical appointment a priority as soon as he could earn the money to pay a doctor's fee.

He pulled back the bed covers and stretched out on the bed. It was the first time in four days he had lain on a mattress. He crawled under the sheets and stayed awake for less than a quarter of an hour. During those few brief minutes, he realized that he would now have to contact Pastor Frank Lovett. He was no longer concerned about the possibility of being humiliated by Lovett's judgment or reaction. In the amplified shame of his current circumstances, he no longer felt that pride, even in the smallest quantity, lived anywhere in his spirit. Even the success of his sustained sobriety now appeared to be bereft of any noteworthiness.

As he faded into a deep sleep, he did so with hazy questions slipping through his brain, questions about how he would approach Frank Lovett, about who had acquired his parents' house and property, and about the horrid possibility that Rachel had remarried and was living in Atlanta with a different family name.

And then, for sixteen hours straight, he slept.

When he awoke, it was Tuesday morning, New Year's Eve.

Unhurriedly, he dressed and drove to a grocery store, where he bought a loaf of bread and five bananas and got six dollars' worth of quarters. He sat in his car in the store parking lot and ate two of the bananas and about a third of the bread. With his stomach satisfied, he then wrote out a course of action that he would follow, starting tomorrow: (1) He would call Pastor Frank Lovett from a pay phone and ask for Rachel's address; (2) if Pastor Lovett was out of his office or out of town, he would seek help from the church secretary; (3) if he was unable to obtain his needed answer from anyone on the staff at North Metro, he would call Dr. Ed Brighton at the PCCGE mission board and try to find his answer there; (4) before he left St. Petersburg, he would randomly call a lawyer listed in the local phone book and ask how to obtain information about what had happened to his parents' belongings and financial holdings. He reviewed the points, then added a fifth: (5) If he passed through Atlanta again, he would pick up the title to his Buick.

He put the list aside, vowing to give it his attention the first thing tomorrow morning. He then drove around until he found a florist shop. He perused the store's stock of fresh flowers and finally requested an arrangement of red carnations, fern, and baby's breath.

He drove again to his parents' gravesite. There he placed the carnations inside the bronze vase at the head of the name markers and reproved himself for not giving flowers to his mother more than two or three times during her life. With the sun to his back, he sat at the foot of the graves and ceremoniously and tediously confessed to his mom and dad the details of his missing years, from Stockholm to Majorca to Costa Rica, apologizing with tears once again for his pernicious behavior. He told them how much he missed them and offered up the final good-byes that he had not been around to give during their dying hours.

Not knowing when he would be back again, he sat dutifully at their side through the remainder of the day.

When midnight approached, and with it the new year of 1997, Clay made a vow to his parents. He would do all within his power, he told them over and over again, to ensure the well-being of their daughter-in-law and their grandchildren.

45

When Pastor Frank Lovett stepped out of the shower on New Year's Day morning, he was greeted by the smell of a hearty breakfast cooking in the kitchen—scrambled eggs, fried sausage links, grits, homemade white-flour biscuits, and black coffee. On this particular holiday, he planned to do nothing more than indulge himself in twelve straight hours of eating favorite meals, relaxing, and watching televised football games. He shaved and dressed and then made his way to the dining room as his wife, Pauline, laid the hot food on the table.

His wife could see his invigoration of the last two or three days still showing in his eyes. "Are you just overjoyed because of the free day ahead of you," she questioned, "or are you still on a high because of the success of the conference this past weekend?"

"Both," he replied, sitting down at the table. "I just keep remembering, as the conference confirmed over and over, just how privileged we are to be part of a group of churches that represent God's last real bastion of truth." He shook his head in amazement. "It's an extraordinary honor that makes me unbelievably proud."

When Pauline sat down, they thanked God for their food, cut into the biscuits, and talked about specific highlights of the conference.

The conference, an annual three-day event, was hosted by a different church each year and normally drew between four and five hundred of the denomination's pastors, evangelists, and missionaries. The purpose of the meeting was to rally the ministers to be ever faithful to their heritage of right-wing conservatism. This year's conference, hosted by North Metro, had been coordinated around the theme "No Retreat; No Compromise." One of the unforgettable memories for Frank was that on Sunday morning in a brief but noted portion of the program he had been publicly recognized by the president of the association as one of the *"great defenders of the faith"* for his generation.

Frank was gratified when his wife chose to comment proudly on that segment of the meeting. He stifled a grin.

After several more helpings of food and more conversation, Frank moved to the den to his reclining chair. The first football game was not scheduled to be broadcast for another two to three hours, so with the weekend conference still fresh on his mind, he popped a tape of the Sunday morning service into the tape deck of his entertainment center, put on a set of headphones, and cued the cassette to the part where the president of the association extolled him with rousing words of praise.

He lay back in his chair and basked in the accolades.

He allowed the tape to spool onward and into the first few minutes of the sermon that had been delivered by the pastor of one of the largest and most prestigious churches in their denomination.

"As we approach the New Year," the man declared with his sharp and distinct voice, "we need to admit that many of the churches in our camp are experiencing a significant decline in numbers. And if your church is one of those, then I say, 'Don't lose heart.' The seepage of people from our ranks is, in many cases, due to the admirable fact that most of you men have refused to tailor your ministries according to the world's ever-deteriorating standards, to the fact that you've refused to entertain the notion that we should dilute and contemporize our Christianity. You have vigilantly held high the banner of God's immutable morality. And for that, my brothers, you should never, never, never lose heart."

There was an outburst of boisterous amens around the auditorium.

"What I truly believe we're seeing is the fulfillment of the great apostasy that the Scriptures tell us will occur in the last days. We're seeing the nonbelievers in our churches, those who merely profess the name of Christ but do not possess the nature of Christ, being seduced by the doctrines of demons.

"And instead of fretting over their exodus, I'm convinced we should welcome it. We should view it as a healthy and necessary cleansing. As a matter of fact, I want to challenge you today—for the spiritual safety of the genuine believers in your church—to go back into your pulpits and preach harder than ever, to be tougher than ever, to be bolder than ever. I want to challenge you to *assist* the ongoing purge! To flush out the impostors in our ranks.

"And once they have left us, I challenge you to take every precautionary measure to ensure that they do not find their way back in. Remember, their apostasy has been prophesied. God has given them over to a seared conscience. They are immune to Spirit-filled preaching and to the Holy Spirit's wooing. They are outside the fold and always will be..."

At that instant, Frank Lovett saw his wife walk suddenly into his space and strongly mouth the word "telephone." A look of awkward and intense unbelief filled her eyes as she extended the cordless phone. Her gestures, in uniformity with her eyes, said that she had just been yanked out of her holiday cheer.

Just as Frank grabbed the phone, he thought he saw his wife silently and dazedly pronounce the words "Clay McCain."

Clay waited for Mrs. Lovett to transfer the phone to her husband. He felt as though every muscle, bone, organ, and corpuscle in his body were condensed into one big, collective knot.

He stood in a phone booth on the far side of a seafood restaurant's parking lot. He had just minutes before called the office of North Metro Church of the Bible, only to be told by an answering machine that due to the holiday the church office was closed. Quickly he had called directory assistance and acquired Pastor Frank Lovett's home telephone number. With his pile of quarters on hand, Clay had wasted no time entering in the number.

Astonishingly, Mrs. Lovett had reacted to his call in an extremely normal and neutral manner, as if he were no one more unusual than a local meat cutter she had talked with at the store on a few occasions.

Was it possible that the passing of so much time had numbed people's doubtless hatred toward him? Had he wasted an hour or more this morning pacing and trying to build up his courage to pick up the phone? Dare his hope resurrect from its deathbed?

"Hello, this is Pastor Frank Lovett," a voice spoke cautiously and coldly over the line.

Hearing the well-known voice of years gone by, Clay immediately experienced a renewed intensity of horrific guilt and shame, as if he were caught in his sin for the very first time and stood naked and without excuse before a holy rector.

Clay tightened his grip on the phone. "Hello, Pastor Lovett," he began shakily. "This is…Clay McCain. I realize this is an unexpected and maybe even shocking phone call. And I know that after all the years I've hidden in silence I…I don't deserve for you to be merciful to me in any way or even to listen to anything I have to say. But for the first time in eleven years I'm back in the States and…I'm calling…to…uh…to ask a favor."

There was a period of prolonged silence.

"Years you've hidden in silence, to ask a favor," Lovett finally echoed in a whisper. The voice then immediately transposed to the slow, deep tone of an angry father. "Well, are you back with your family, Clay?"

Clay could hear his heart beating. "No, I'm not yet back with my family. But that's why I'm calling. I'm standing here in Florida where I just found out that my mom and dad passed away a year or so ago. I came here hoping they would be able to tell me where I could find Rachel and the kids. But…" He started clearing his throat and then burst into a sob. "I'm a broken and ruined man, Pastor Lovett. I just want—"

"In God's name," Lovett interrupted, "do you have any earthly idea what kind of devastation and disillusionment you inflicted when you ran off into your little world of lust and perversion? Do you even *begin* to know how many congregations and families all over this country were hurt and betrayed by what you did? Have you ever for one moment thought about how deep those pains were felt, especially by those who supported you with their hard-earned dollars and who looked up to you as a spiritual hero? Can

369 ◆ Brotherhood of Betrayal

you even slightly answer just one of those questions? In the name of God, I just want to know!"

Clay's head drooped, tears sliding down his cheeks. "Thousands of times, Pastor Lovett. I've thought about those I've hurt thousands of times. And I know that what I did probably hurt them more than I can ever imagine." Clay hesitated. In the semi-quietness, he was sure he could hear Lovett breathing. The breathing sounded pushed by anger. "I know that what I did was wrong. I was a blind and selfish fool, and, despite what anybody might think, I've suffered hell almost every day of my life because of it."

"Well, you're a fool all right, Clay. And as far as your personal suffering goes, I think everybody who knows you from the past would agree that whatever kind of suffering it is you're experiencing right now, you deserve every last bit of it."

Clay felt his soul recoil at Lovett's words. Did Lovett think he was going to be given only three or four minutes to talk and no more, and therefore felt compelled to quickly unload seven years' worth of vindictive feelings?

"I have no doubt that you're right," Clay conceded. "I'm sure I deserve, as you say, every bit of it, and even more. In the meantime, though, I'm trying to find my wife and my kids. I'm wondering if you know where they are. And if so, will you please tell me how I can reach them?"

"I'm afraid your wife proved to be as untrustworthy as you did, Clay," Lovett answered, his tone still harsh. "The deacon board and I were forced to discipline her out of the membership of the church about six years ago. I haven't heard from her since. So I have absolutely no idea where she might be right now. And even if

I did, I'm honestly not sure I would give you that information. After what you've done, I'd say you probably need to face your consequences a bit longer. As a matter of fact, if I know anything at all about the character of God, I'd say you hurt His church so greatly that He's going to judge you all the way to the grave and then right on into the lake of fire."

"Is there no forgiveness and restoration allowed in your Christianity, Pastor Lovett?"

"Not for Judas Iscariots. I'm sorry, Clay. You made your choices. You'll have to live and die with them."

Clay made one more attempt to acknowledge the depth and enormity of his sin and to offer an apology, but he was only confronted by another diatribe of condemnation before Lovett hung up on him.

Clay had believed earlier that he no longer had any pride left, but he was mistaken. For the first time in his life, he had just felt the bitter sting of being officially classified by the organized church as an unacceptable human being, even for as little as trying to dialogue with his former pastor.

He had been certain, of course, that Lovett, North Metro, and probably the entirety of his former denomination would refuse to associate with him when he reemerged. It never occurred to him that they would disdain even his *admission* of wrongdoing. But it had just happened, and it hurt in a new and unexpected way.

He quickly tried to make himself believe, however, that the excessive repudiation, even though unforeseen, was rightfully deserved, along with every other pain his wickedness had generated.

He shuffled out of the phone booth, sat down on the curb, and faced the newly added layer to his already abject loneliness. At the same time, he felt an uncharted ache for Rachel overcome his heart as Lovett's remarks resounded in his head: "Proved to be as untrustworthy as you... Were forced to discipline her out of the membership of the church... Haven't heard from her since."

Those disturbing words comprised the one and only report Clay had heard about Rachel in seven and a half years. Clay ground the asphalt with his shoes. He had tried to handle his guilt all along by denying that Rachel's life, after the abandonment, would become unmanageable, but Lovett's report ripped through his delusion. A dozen fearful questions about her welfare and stability newly pounded his soul.

"I've got to find her," he whispered to himself.

He went back to the phone, rang through to directory assistance in South Carolina, and obtained Dr. Ed Brighton's home phone number in Greenville. Clay took a deep breath and called the number.

Clay wondered when he heard the first ring if he should be more forthright and less apologetic than he had been with Pastor Lovett. But there was no answer. Even after fifteen rings. He waited five minutes and called again. Still no one picked up.

He hung around the booth for the next hour and called the Brightons' number several more times, without reaching anyone. Realizing the Brightons were probably away for the holiday, he decided to make use of his time by putting a particularly nagging thought to rest, a thought that had been pestering him for nearly twenty-four hours now. He got into his Buick and drove back to the Golden Sands retirement village.

The security guard on duty at the gatehouse was not the same man who had helped him six days ago. Clay again explained his story, asking if he could please speak with the resident manager one more time.

The guard phoned the resident manager's house, spoke for less than a minute, then passed along to Clay the manager's instructions. "Mr. Aldrich is just getting ready to leave for the day. He says he'll give you about ten minutes. He'll wait for you at his driveway." The security guard pointed to the main street on the other side of the gate. "When you drive through the gate, just follow the street to the second intersection. Turn left and drive all the way to the cul-de-sac. You'll find Mr. Aldrich's house there at the end of the street. It's house number twenty-eight."

"Thanks." As the gate opened, Clay drove through and made his way directly to Aldrich's house. Mr. Aldrich was in the driveway loading a couple of golf bags into the trunk of a Lincoln Town Car.

Clay parked his ratty old Buick on the street.

Aldrich broke away from what he was doing. "Did you manage to find your parents' burial site?" he asked, walking down the driveway to meet Clay.

"Yeah, I did," Clay answered heavily and then apologized for disturbing the man on a holiday. He then asked the question that was on his mind. "Can you tell me if the Mrs. Houghton who moved into my parents' house is a middle-aged lady? Attractive? Blond? Has three young children?"

Aldrich replied with questioning eyes, "I wouldn't call Mrs. Houghton unattractive. But no, she's definitely not middle-aged. She's at least in her late sixties. And if she has any children, they don't live at home with her. Why do you want to know?"

Clay's bothersome question was answered; the Mrs. Houghton

living in his parents' house was not Rachel with another married name. Clay shook his head to dismiss the issue. "I'm just curious," he went on to change the subject. "If the Houghtons are not kin to me, how did they end up with my parents' house? I mean, wouldn't the house have been willed to someone in the family?"

"I guess to get answers to those questions," Aldrich said, twiddling his car keys in his hands, "you'll have to talk to the executor of your parents' will."

"I never saw their will. I'm embarrassed to say that I have no idea who the executor might have been. How can I find out that information?"

"You might need to talk to an attorney, but I think the county courthouse keeps a copy of all the wills that are probated inside the county. If you can go there and indeed see a copy of the will, it'll give you the name of the executor. Plus, it'll tell you who inherited what, including the house."

"Yeah, of course," Clay said, more to himself than to Aldrich. "I'm grateful for your help. It's appreciated more than you know."

By the time Clay started his Buick, he had already decided that he would go to the courthouse the first thing tomorrow morning when the state offices reopened after the New Year's holiday.

As he headed back toward the main gate, he impulsively took a slight detour and, for the sake of solidifying a needed memory, once again passed his parents' retirement house. As he came to a near stop in front of the eloquent gray brick structure, he passionately reiterated his promise to his mom and dad that he would do everything within his power to reestablish the well-being of Rachel and the children.

Upon exiting the gated community, he found another pay

phone and inserted a handful of quarters to call Dr. Brighton. Brighton's phone still went unanswered. Clay called directory assistance in South Carolina to verify that he was calling the right number. The number was correct.

Back in the driver's seat of his automobile, Clay sat for a few minutes rubbing his temples and his forehead. The time was a quarter past noon. With his needs holding him in St. Petersburg for one more day, he headed back toward the motel where he had spent the two previous nights. En route, he stopped by an auto parts dealer and bought four quarts of motor oil, an oil filter, and eight spark plugs.

Once at the motel, he registered for another night's stay, paying cash up-front.

In his room, he counted his money. He had $178.45 left of his original $1,065. He decided he would start sleeping in the car again or else try to find a bed in a downtown mission that ministered to street bums and derelicts. And when the need for more money arose, he would simply have to find work. He remembered when he worked for a construction company during his high school summers, the foreman often hired one-day laborers from an organization called Manpower. Perhaps he could find day-to-day work through such an agency.

He refolded his money and placed it back into his billfold. He then went to the motel manager, a thin man from India who smelled strongly of coriander and curry, and borrowed a set of wrenches.

Taking advantage of the warmest part of the day, Clay parked his car at the edge of the motel property and lifted the hood. He retrieved a one-gallon plastic milk jug from the motel Dumpster and cut it to use as a catch bucket. He then spent an hour or so changing the car's oil, oil filter, and spark plugs. Afterward, he returned the wrenches to the front desk, went back to the room, and bathed. He then used the phone at the side of his bed and tried Brighton's number again. The unanswered rings seemed to be a parody of cruelty. He slammed the phone down and sighed. He just wanted to find his family! Why couldn't something fall into place for him?

Feeling tension building in the back of his neck, he fell backward onto the bed and tried to relax. He lay there and daydreamed about his three children. He tried over and over to picture the details of their faces. But it was so hard to remember. He fantasized, the best he could, about holding each child in his lap and weeping and embracing and beginning the relationships all over again. Holding them to his chest. Stroking their hair. Getting to know them again with words of confession and longing.

The fulfillment of such fanciful dreaming was not beyond the reach of possibility, was it? He could not give himself permission to believe that it was. As the hope-inducing images filled his head, he dozed off into an afternoon nap, the hint of a smile etched somewhere on the backside of his lips.

By the time his eyes opened again, evening was approaching. He sat up for a few minutes, then stood and slapped cold water onto his face. He checked the time. It was five thirty.

He sat back down on the edge of the bed and picked up the phone. He punched in Brighton's number, this time from memory.

"Hello," a male voice answered after only two rings.

Clay inhaled a diminutive breath and puffed a short burst of air. "Is this Dr. Ed Brighton, European director of the PCCGE mission board?"

"This is Dr. Ed Brighton, *general* director of the PCCGE mission board."

"Dr. Brighton," Clay began, not missing the emphasized promotion, "I know this might be difficult to believe, but this is Clay McCain, former missionary to Sweden. I'm calling from…"

"I've been expecting your call, Clay," Brighton interrupted with a cold and forbidding voice. "Pastor Lovett has already spoken with me. He told me all about your conversation with him. And I want you to know without the slightest bit of doubt that we're both absolutely appalled that you think you can just show up out of nowhere after six, seven, eight years of silence and start asking for instant grace and favors. That's not the way it works, Clay.

"As a matter of fact, and I want you to listen to me very carefully on this, we've decided that if you want our help—*any* help from *any* of us who were your past supporters and associates—then you're going to have to play the game the way it's supposed to be played. I'll spell out in exact terms what that's going to mean for you.

"To begin with, if you want to talk, then we'll do it in person, not over the phone. And it will not be a one-on-one meeting. It will be in a setting with a plurality of witnesses, namely Pastor Lovett, his assistant pastor, and the entire North Metro deacon board, along with myself and two other directors from the office here in Greenville. At that meeting, you will, in the presence of all the witnesses, make a complete and unequivocal admission of guilt regarding your adultery, your abandonment, and all other vile actions you've been guilty of.

"You will then publicly agree to place yourself under the spiritual authority and leadership of Pastor Lovett. You will agree to undergo three to four months of extensive pastoral counseling, during which time you will be required to attend all of North Metro's church services, to be completely silent in all those services, and to be strictly accountable at all times to the North Metro pastoral staff. This, and nothing less, is the way the game will be played.

"Starting tomorrow morning, we will begin contacting every church and every individual who has ever supported you financially. We'll also contact every church on the general roster of PCCGE supporters. We will tell everyone that you've resurfaced, and we will tell them about the offer that's been extended to you. If you accept the offer, we will tell them of your cooperation. If you refuse the offer, we will tell them of your unrepentant heart and of the moral and spiritual risk they will be taking if they try to renew any kind of association with you. In other words, you will be blacklisted around the country in all of our churches. No one will open their doors to you. No one will grant you any favors. You'll be completely shut out as, in my opinion, you will deserve."

As Clay listened to the verbal lashing that he was sure he merited, he started gnawing on one of his fingernails. Maybe their proposition was truly a gesture of justice and thoroughness. But all he was seeking was a simple answer as to where he could find his wife.

"I'm just calling to find out if you can tell me where my wife and children are. That's all I—"

"You heard the offer, Clay. It's clear, straightforward, and final."

Clay moved off the bed and knelt on the floor. "But what

about my wife and children?"

"Until you've first been helped, Clay, you're going to be a walking detriment to anyone and everyone, including any of your family members, you attempt to get close to."

Clay tightened his grip on the phone. "I'm not trying to disagree, but a lot of time has lapsed since I ran away from things. My heart and my life have been broken, Dr. Brighton."

"Have you been through any long-term pastoral counseling since reality has caught up with you, Clay? Have you made yourself accountable to an acceptable Bible-believing church somewhere?"

"No, but—"

"Then it's time you received help. That's the most self-evident thing in the world. You've been given an offer, a very gracious offer in my opinion. And you've got to make a decision. You have my number. I'll be here for the rest of the evening if you decide to call back and accept what I've laid out for you." Before the call ended, Brighton added, "This might be the last chance God will ever give you, Clay McCain. If I were you, I would think real hard before I turned my back on it."

After the call, Clay remained kneeling.

Maybe he's right about everything he said, Clay agonizingly told himself over and over again. *I'm just not certain I—*

He pounded the mattress. *Three or four months!*

Now that he was back on American soil and especially since finding out about Rachel's publicized expulsion from North Metro, he felt more restless and more of a need than ever to find and rescue his family.

During the next two or three hours, Clay paced and struggled to make a decision. He reached for the phone several times to call

Dr. Brighton, but no matter from how many different angles he analyzed the offer, Clay just could not bring himself to accede to it. Regardless of how deeply he looked, he could not find the will to allow himself to be purposely decommissioned for another three or four months while Pastor Lovett, Dr. Brighton, and whoever else monitored his every response and decided if he was worth redeeming.

Was such a decision really theirs to make anyway? He slapped the mattress again and moaned. Was following their prescribed route the only choice he had if he wanted to be reunited with his spouse and children?

Was he sure he was even ready to reestablish ties with the organized church, particularly with the same group that had ousted his wife? Besides, hadn't Pastor Lovett already stated dogmatically that there was no open door for reconciliation at North Metro for Judas Iscariots?

Well, was there an open door or wasn't there? Was there a major rift between Lovett's position and Brighton's position? Or had Pastor Lovett, during his telephone tirade, simply been speaking impulsively? Was he in actuality willing to stoop to such compromising depths and work to rehabilitate a Christ-betraying jackal?

Clay finally grew weary of the mental bantering and gave up. He chose not to acquiesce to Lovett and Brighton's unbending procedure. In silently ignoring the offer, maybe he was making another horrendous mistake in his life. But consenting and then waiting around for another four months before continuing his search for Rachel and the kids just was not an acceptable option for him. Even if his former church friends did blacklist and stonewall him.

At least when the news got out that he had resurfaced and should be avoided as a walking malady, perhaps Rachel would somehow hear about it. Perhaps she would even try to make her whereabouts known to him.

Clay stepped outdoors. He went to the motel's solitary vending machine and bought a bag of roasted peanuts for his evening meal. He pledged to himself that regardless of Lovett and Brighton's collaboration, he would think of other ways to locate his spouse and offspring. There were at least two other resources, albeit long shots, that might be able to assist him in tracking down his family: the Atlanta Police Department and the Stockholm Independent Bible Church, especially Bengt Wennergren.

He could speak in person with a detective at the Atlanta Police Department within the next two or three days. As he thought of Bengt, he looked at his watch. The time in Sweden, six hours ahead of Eastern Standard Time, was around two-thirty in the morning. He would call Bengt the first thing tomorrow morning.

46

*After payment of my just debts and funeral expenses and any taxes
occasioned by my death, I, Hester Johnson McCain, give and bequeath
all my property, real, personal, or mixed, which I own at the time of my
death in fee to my one and only child, Clay Alexander McCain.*

Clay winced as he read his name, the name of a reprehensible
and undeserving son listed as the primary beneficiary in his
mother's last will and testament. He was sitting in the File
Management Department of the Pinellas County Courthouse in
downtown St. Petersburg. The probated, twelve-page legal document was lying on the table before him. He was reading his way
slowly and thoroughly through its paragraphs.

Slammed beyond words by the revelation of his mom's unconditional love, he laid his head on the table and in a few minutes of
tearful quietude drank in the extraordinary acceptance.

He then felt repulsed by a sudden and intrusive thought: *How
much did she leave me, and where is it being held?*

He tried to dismiss the mental query as a desecration of his
mother's sweet memory. He looked up and tried to distract
himself by gazing around at the montage of people and activities
surrounding the service counter.

He eventually lowered his head and continued to read.

In the event that my son, for reasons of absence or neglect, does not present himself to receive the said inheritance at the time of my decease, then all my said properties, real, personal, or mixed, will be designated as the TRUST ESTATE. Such TRUST ESTATE shall be held in my son's name and shall continue to be held in my son's name unless there has been official verification of my son's death or unless my oldest grandchild, Summer Leena McCain, is twenty-one (21) years old or older. In either said case, the TRUST ESTATE shall immediately be apportioned in equal parts for the use and benefit of each grandchild of mine born to the marriage union of Clay Alexander McCain and Rachel Ilene Ward.

As to all or any portion of the TRUST ESTATE that shall be in trust hereunder for the benefit of any grandchild of mine under the provisions of this Article V, such share shall be relinquished in equal proportion to each grandchild on his or her twenty-first (21) birthday.

If my decease occurs prior to the date of my oldest grandchild's twenty-first (21) birthday, the TRUST ESTATE will be held in my son's name until the said date of my oldest grandchild's twenty-first (21) birthday. At such time, if the TRUST ESTATE has not been claimed by my son, the TRUST ESTATE shall be apportioned in equal parts for the use and benefit of each grandchild of mine born to the marriage union of Clay Alexander McCain and Rachel Ilene Ward and shall be relinquished in equal proportion to each grandchild on his or her twenty-first (21) birthday.

Clay stopped reading. He felt an immense gratitude that his mother's loyal love for him as an only child was counterbalanced by her prudence.

He then tried to digest the will's subsequent and lengthy article that minutely outlined the general powers, duties, obligations, restrictions, and conditions governing the executor and trustees designated to handle and distribute the trust.

Four articles and seven paragraphs later he uncovered the prime piece of information for which he was combing. His mother had named the First State Bank Trust Department as the executor and trustee of her will.

Even though Clay could not satisfactorily dictate to himself the definition of a bank trust department, he knew he was staring at the name of the party that could give him answers about his parents' property.

The legal document drew to a close after another two paragraphs. The will was signed and dated in his mother's handwriting, accompanied by the signatures of two witnesses, an Oscar Kensington and a Pearl Eaton. An affidavit was attached legitimizing the witnesses and their signatures. A notary seal alongside the signature of the notary public made the document official.

Equipped now with the identity of the executor, Clay felt charged to meet and speak with the individual, or group, as soon as possible. He returned the will to the service counter and paid for a photocopy.

On his way out of the building, he saw a pay phone in one of the hallways and was reminded of his plan to call Bengt Wennergren in Sweden. He had called earlier from the motel room and had been frustrated to hear nothing but unanswered rings. Since establishing communication with Bengt was a current priority for him, he sidestepped to the phone and easily made the transatlantic connection. But the rings of the Wennergrens' phone still went unattended. Clay then called the First State Bank and learned that the Trust Department was located at the bank's central

RANDALL ARTHUR ◆ 384

office in midtown.

After hanging up, Clay entered the men's rest room down the hall. He washed his face, buttoned his shirt collar, and dampened and combed his hair. Within the next thirty minutes, he found his way across a quarter of the downtown's commerce area to the main office of the First State Bank. There he followed a receptionist's directions to the third floor, where he stood facing another receptionist in the lobby of the bank's Trust Department.

He waited while the fair-skinned, red-headed lady sitting at the desk forwarded four consecutive callers to their appropriate parties. At the lady's beckoning, Clay introduced himself, displayed the copy of his mother's probated will, and explained that he wanted to speak to the will's executor.

"Have a seat, and I'll arrange for an officer in the Estate Group to speak with you," the lady instructed.

Clay took a seat and began to skim through an investment magazine. Shortly thereafter, a tall, slim, elegantly dressed lady appeared from the hallway behind the receptionist's desk and approached him.

"Good morning," the lady said, extending her hand. "My name is Gloria Dodson. I'm one of the estate administrators here in the Trust Department. How can I help you?"

Clay stood and shook hands. He repeated to her what he had told the receptionist. He showed her a copy of the will and added that he was the primary beneficiary and wanted to know what had happened to his parents' house, car, land, and money.

The lady quickly glanced at the paragraphs identifying the names of the benefactor, beneficiary, executor, and trustee.

"All right," she told him. "Come with me, and I'll find the

385 ◆ Brotherhood of Betrayal

administrator who's been assigned to this particular trust."

Clay followed her and soon found himself sitting on a moreen upholstered chair watching the lady from the other side of a solid oak desk as her fingers blitzed a computer keyboard.

"Okay, what I'm seeing here," Gloria Dodson said to him while referring to the monitor, "is that Mrs. Sally Hargrove was the originally appointed administrator of the McCain trust. However, she left the bank about a month and a half ago. The administrator who took over Mrs. Hargrove's accounts is Gerald Fields." Dodson shifted her focus from the computer screen to Clay. "So what I'll do is turn you over to Mr. Fields."

Gloria Dodson picked up a phone, called Mr. Fields and outlined for him Clay's situation. She then led Clay down the hall and around the corner to Gerald Fields's office, where there was another round of introductions, including the presentation of a young, bookish man named Skye Willoughby, an administrative assistant. Mrs. Dodson then dismissed herself.

"Well, welcome to my second home, Mr. McCain," Fields said with a tired smile. "Have a seat." At Fields's lead, all three men sat down.

Gerald Fields studied the copy of the will, then scooted to his computer and punched up information about the McCain trust. After several seconds, he looked at Clay and said, "All right, Mr. McCain, I need to see a couple of pieces of ID with your picture."

Expecting at least this step in the protocol, Clay took from his jacket his passport, his Costa Rican driver's license, his international driver's license, and his expired U.S. driver's license and laid them on the desk. "I've also got a Social Security card and an old worn-out copy of my birth certificate." Clay pulled them from his wallet and added them to the assortment.

Fields picked up the official documents and scrutinized each one, especially the U.S. driver's license and passport.

Clay explained that he had been living overseas for the last several years, which was why he was just now attending to the business of his mother's will.

Fields listened perceptively then instructed Willoughby, "Make a copy of each of these pieces of ID and then go to the vault and pull the microfilm for the McCain trust. Take Mr. McCain's copy of the will and run a comparison with our files to confirm that there's no reason for either party to question the will's original integrity."

Willoughby gathered up the documents and left the room.

"Perhaps Mrs. Dodson already told you," Fields rerouted his attention to Clay, "but you need to know I'm not the administrator who was initially assigned to this trust. The initial caretaker for the estate was Mrs. Hargrove, a lady who very likely was personally acquainted with your mother. As the current administrator of the trust, however, I can only tell you what has happened with your mother's properties and moneys from an impersonal perspective."

Clay acknowledged that he understood.

"For security reasons, as you can understand, I have to run an authenticity check on your passport. If everything's in order regarding your ID, it's then going to take an hour or two for me to review the history of the trust in order to provide answers to your questions. It'll take at least that long as well for Mr. Willoughby to complete his examination. So, you're welcome to sit and wait, or if you prefer, you can come back at one-thirty, and we'll be ready to present to you some facts and figures."

Clay told Mr. Fields that he would go out for a bite to eat and would return at one-thirty.

Sitting at one of the microfilm readers in the workroom just outside the vault, Skye Willoughby scrolled the film of the McCain file to the introductory page, prepared by the First State Bank Trust Department. He noted the following:

- The date of Hester McCain's death;
- The date Hester McCain's Last Will and Testament was probated;
- The name of the primary beneficiary of the will—Clay Alexander McCain;
- The address of the primary beneficiary, coded as currently NA;
- The appointed sequential beneficiaries—all the children born to the marriage union of Clay Alexander McCain and Rachel Ilene Ward;
- The address of the known sequential beneficiaries—listed as Forest Hills Avenue, New York, New York. The house number, along with a telephone number, was specified.

As Skye read the New York City address, his thoughts were instantly imbued with memories of his first trip to Manhattan just seven months ago. He had spent a week of summer vacation visiting a best friend. Skye had been shocked when he learned that his buddy was paying nearly one-half of his salary to cover his rent and utility costs.

"What I pay," his pal volleyed without the slightest hint of insincerity, "is average for a New Yorker; besides, it's simply one of the joyous sacrifices that one makes for living in such an exhilarating city."

After only three days of living under the intoxicating influence of the city's alchemic spirit, Skye began to understand his friend's sentiment. Even though the expensiveness of the city had drained his bank account to a balance of zero, by the end of his seven days, Skye was a convert to the unforgettable city.

New York.

He would definitely plan to go back one day.

Skye adjusted his glasses as he scrolled to the title page of the will and resummoned his concentration for his work.

"Your identity has been verified," Gerald Fields pronounced to Clay when the three men reconvened around a conference table at 1:40 P.M. Stacked on the table were newly printed sheets of data. Fields handed Clay the top sheet. "So the next step is to let you know what happened to your mother's property. As you can see on the paper you're holding, which was copied directly from your mother's will, the trustee 'shall have full discretionary power to manage, rent, sell, invest, and reinvest any and every item of money and property now or thereafter owned by any trust hereunder.'

"Thus, according to the file history of the trust, Mrs. Hargrove, the original administrator of the trust, started liquidating all your mother's property—her house, her land, her car, her furniture, her jewelry, her household goods, her clothes, all her physical assets—about four and a half months after your mother's death.

"As you can understand, we as a financial institution cannot maintain physical properties, like houses and cars, indefinitely. The overhead cost would simply cut too deeply into the trust money itself. So liquidation is the normal procedure in a situation like this."

Fields handed Clay five more sheets of paper, which itemized the properties that were sold and for what price.

"All of your mother's possessions were sold over a two-month period at very competitive prices to a variety of buyers. As the effects were liquidated, the earnings were placed into a diversity of mutual funds. At the present time the total sum of money is spread throughout twelve different funds." Fields slid twelve more sheets in Clay's direction. "These are reports for each of the funds. On each of the reports you'll find the name of the fund, the principal deposited into the fund, and the current balance."

Fields lifted one more sheet from his pile and presented it to Clay. "This shows the balance of all twelve funds combined. The dollar amount highlighted in the bottom right-hand corner, which has been adjusted to show the deduction of the bank's maintenance fees and all dividend and capital gains taxes, is the holdings that currently belong to you, the primary beneficiary."

Clay stared for a second or two at both Fields and Willoughby, then leaned forward and took the paper. He fixed his eyes on the bottom-line figure.

He clamped his bottom lip between his teeth and closed his eyes. When his eyes opened again, they were damp with liquid guilt. The number reflecting in his retinas was $248,366.21—

nearly a quarter of a million dollars.

"We can start the paperwork for the transferal process right now if you'd like," Fields said.

At the end of a wordless stupor, Clay finally managed to loosen his tongue. "Can I...uh...have a few minutes just to think through some things?"

"Certainly. Take as many minutes, hours, or days as you need. And keep in mind that if you need any financial advice, we're here to provide you with that service."

Clay decided he needed more than just a few minutes to think through the colossal decision suddenly filling his thoughts. He told Fields he would contact him tomorrow and left the bank. He returned to the motel and, in the midst of emotional sensitivity and fuzzy-headedness, spent the next four or five hours juggling numbers and staring at an assortment of figures. By eight o'clock that evening, he had made his decision.

The next morning, he arrived at the bank within minutes after the front doors were unlocked to the public. Gerald Fields welcomed him into his office and offered him a cup of coffee. Clay accepted. Skye Willoughby soon joined them.

"Well, shall we start the paperwork?" Fields asked, looking at Clay.

Clay cleared his throat and tried to appear sane. "Is it possible for me to just take the $8,366 off the top and leave the rest?"

A question of uncertainty instantly took shape on Fields's face. "I'm not sure I understand. Are you saying you want to leave $240,000 in the trust?"

Clay nodded.

"Are you disclaiming the inheritance, then?" Fields picked up a copy of Hester McCain's will from his desk and flipped to the document's penultimate page. "Because if you are, I'll have to require that you do so in writing. The will dictates in article eleven that 'Any beneficiary may disclaim all or any part of such beneficiary's rights in either principal or income, provided such disclaimer is exercised in writing.'"

"No, I'm not disclaiming anything. I'm simply saying that I want to take only a portion of the total. And unless I return at some future date and collect more of the money, I wish to let the will run its course. I want my two daughters, Summer Leena and Holly Fay, and my son, Justin Carl, to eventually receive the rest of the money exactly when and as my mother prescribed."

Fields pondered the unprecedented request then muddled through a few reasons why the bank might not have the freedom to divide the trust money as Clay was asking. But his reasons lacked both soundness and conviction.

Clay stuck fast to his decision.

Fields eventually excused himself, explaining that he would have to consult with the department's senior manager. Willoughby left the room with him.

Clay laid his head on the table and questioned the prudence of his resoluteness. But he quickly reminded himself that his choice of action regarding the inheritance had come only after hours of deliberation and was one that was true and loyal to his recovering heart. His thoughts then started whirling around the issues of making contact with Bengt Wennergren, soliciting the assistance of the Atlanta police to help find Rachel, renewing his U.S. driver's license, picking up the title to his car and possibly having the engine tuned up, making an appointment to be examined by a doctor, and wondering if Lovett and Brighton had already started publicizing the news that he had resurfaced with an "unrepentant heart" and was "a moral and spiritual danger" to anyone who would dare fraternize with him.

"Okay, Mr. McCain, it looks like it's going to work out for you," Fields announced when he reentered the room twenty minutes later with Willoughby close behind. "What we will do is issue a check to you for $8,366 and then assume that you will return one day in the near future to claim the remaining dollars in the trust. If for whatever reason you choose not to do that, then the moneys, as ordered by the last will and testament, will at the appropriated time be dispersed equally among all the children born to you and Rachel McCain." Fields explained to Clay that Willoughby would help him fill out the forms required by the bank for relinquishing the money, plus additional forms required by the county for notifying the probate court of the distribution. "It's going to take about an hour before we can cut the check and place it in your hands," Fields clarified. "So while Mr. Willoughby walks you through the forms, I'll start the process of getting the check ready."

Not having a bank account, Clay was suddenly struck with the thought that getting an Atlanta bank or any bank to cash such a hefty check would probably be an impossibility. He quickly cited to Fields that he preferred to receive the money in the form of traveler's checks. To be exact, eight thousand in traveler's checks and three hundred and sixty-six in cash.

Fields hesitated a moment then aloofly agreed to accommodate Clay's wishes. He made known, however, that gathering eight thousand dollars' worth of traveler's checks would take a bit longer. He then left the room.

"Have I...uh, been too far out of line with my requests?" Clay asked Willoughby, feeling as if he had offended Fields somehow.

"No, everything's fine," Willoughby said as he sat down with Clay at the table. "The traveler's checks just make the transaction a little less convenient, that's all. And as for dividing the inheritance the way you're wanting to do it, well, we've never heard of anyone else doing it that way before. But, hey, I've spent time in New York City; I know how expensive it is to live there. Your kids are going to need every dime they can get. As far as I'm concerned, they're lucky to have a dad who's looking out for them. As a matter of fact, I commend you for wanting to leave the bulk of the money to them."

Clay's thoughts excessively backtracked. *New York...your kids are going to need every dime they can get.* What was Willoughby saying? "New York," he said aloud, trying to conceal the fact that he had just been stunned. "How do—?"

Willoughby turned a light shade of red and shifted his eyeglasses. "Excuse me, I didn't mean to be too personal. It's just that I saw the address when I was reviewing the file. And I have very strong memories of New York, so..."

New York! Was Willoughby saying that Rachel and the children were living in New York City? Clay's explosive inclination was to ask Willoughby the question point-blank, but a cautionary alarm went off in his head telling him that Skye Willoughby, as a young assistant, might have just leaked information that should have remained within the boundaries of bank confidentiality. Clay rallied, "It's okay. Forget it." He nodded toward the stack of forms on the table. "Let's just go ahead and get started."

As they commenced to fill out the forms, however, Clay found it nearly impossible to pay attention. *Why would Rachel and the kids be living, of all places, so far north in the nation's most densely populated metropolis?* Had Billy Ward chosen to move to that area, and Rachel simply followed because of a heartfelt or financial need to keep the family in close proximity? Had she been lured there, irrelevant of her father's life, by a job offer? Had she cemented Clay's fear and married another man who had whisked her away to a new place? Or were she and the children really not living there at all?

Clay's burning priority was to get to a phone where he could make some calls in private. He feigned, however, a state of calm until he penned his final signature to the last form.

The arrangement was then made that he would return an hour or so before closing time and pick up his traveler's checks.

As soon as he stepped outside the building's front door and cast a shadow onto the concrete walkway, he quickened his pace, utilizing all his restraint to keep from sprinting to the car.

Once he was behind the steering wheel and driving out of view of the bank, he accelerated heavily and hustled the Buick through downtown traffic until he eyed a public phone at a parking area along the waterfront.

Within minutes of parking the car and reaching the phone, he found out the area code for Manhattan and was speaking long-distance to a directory assistant with a strong New York accent. When the telecommunications employee informed him that there was a Rachel I. McCain listed under the Queens exchange, Clay, trying to breathe evenly, confirmed that he would like to have the number. Gripping his pen extra hard to keep it from shaking out of his hand, he feverishly wrote the telephone number in the margin of his eastern U.S. road map.

"Is there a street address with that number?" he asked, his whole body trembling.

"The address," the female voice replied, "is Forest Hills Avenue." The lady then recited the house number from her public listing.

The call was over.

Clay stepped away from the phone for about sixty seconds and tried, for the sake of vigilance, to stand still and think. He stared at the information he had scribbled along the edge of his map. Before he solidified any conclusions that might be premature and might set him up for a pointless celebration, he admitted that he had only one sensible option: to call the number. Not to talk, but simply to try to listen in silence for a recognized voice. Months ago he had finalized the manner in which he would attempt to reenter Rachel and the children's world. Wanting to be accepted so badly, and thus feeling compelled to retard any rejection on their part, he had decided that the first two-way contact would be neither by phone nor letter. He wanted to walk into their presence. In person.

With his shaking partially repressed, he returned to the phone. Trying hard to keep his emotions crimped, he inserted some coins and punched in Rachel's number.

Could this be one of the first telltale moments of rectification after seven and a half years of impenetrable sorrow? Clay had to coerce himself to exhale after each of the first seven or eight rings. The call, though, went unanswered.

Two hours of restlessness and twenty calls later, he finally received an answer at the Queens residence. "Hello, Justin McCain speaking," a young boy's voice declared energetically.

All of Clay's joints and muscles, from the innermost regions to the extremities, immediately froze.

"Hello, who is it?" the young voice echoed.

In the following two to three seconds, ten years' worth of shame, guilt, regret, and longing erupted through the core of Clay's heart. Clay thought he was going to rip physically into a million different pieces. Would he ever begin to know the number of monsters he had set loose to haunt this young child's life and inner security? As he heard his son's voice, he realized his own lips were trying to move, but his vocal cords would not function.

Above the cries of his hurting soul, Clay then heard a woman's voice approach the phone in the background and ask the boy, "Who is it?"

"I don't know," the boy replied. "Nobody's saying anything."

"Hello? Hello...is anyone there?" the woman asked into the receiver.

The familiar voice, now filling the acoustic bubble of the pay phone, blitzed every pore in Clay's flesh and sounded and felt like the song of a thousand angels. It was Rachel. Rachel Ilene McCain. The only woman he had ever taken as his wife. The only woman he had ever truly loved. Clay instinctively and tenderly moved his left hand to the mouthpiece and for the first time in his existence tried efficaciously to touch someone through the phone. His lips and chin started quivering wildly, squeezed by the brute force of desperation and longing.

He then heard a click followed by a dial tone.

"No, please," he whispered tearfully into the mouthpiece, trying to keep himself from bashing his head against the inside of the phone shelter. "Don't hang up. Please! Don't hang up. I need you. I love you. I..."

Caught in a vortex of unbearable emotion, he stood there for a few minutes trying to keep his heart from racing through his rib cage. He eventually staggered back to his car and sat on the ground, leaning against a tire. He remained there until he was sure he was going to be able to pace himself and maintain his sanity.

A few hours later, with his traveler's checks and cash in hand, he was driving north out of St. Petersburg. Staring teary-eyed into the horizon beyond the Friday evening rush hour traffic, he incessantly replayed Justin's and Rachel's voices over and over again in his head and kept sobbing, "Thank you, Skye Willoughby. Thank You, God."

47

Because of ongoing engine problems, Clay was forced to make a layover in Atlanta from Saturday morning until Monday evening. He paid out eight hundred dollars for a major engine overhaul. In addition, he bought new tires, brakes, and shocks. He also picked up the Buick's title and some more clothes, including a thick winter coat.

On Monday night, when the mechanics finished their work, Clay resumed his northward journey.

Pumped with hope, he arrived in Queens on Wednesday night. Around eleven-thirty P.M., he found Rachel and the children's place of residence.

On Friday evening at six-forty-five, Clay stood in the shadows of a three-story parking deck at a Manhattan concert hall. He watched from a distance as Rachel, Summer, Holly, and Justin locked up the Nissan minivan and entered a concrete stairwell.

Justin was now nine years old. Holly was thirteen, and Summer was sixteen. The odds were that he would never have recognized them had they not been with Rachel.

Rachel was now forty-two. The last seven and a half years had only deepened and matured her resplendence. How had he ever, for one second, lost his attraction for her?

He bowed his head and pressed his brow against a cement pillar.

He was sure that the joy teasing, yet tormenting, his heart must be equal to the joy of Thanksgiving, Christmas, Valentine's Day, a surprise birthday party, and a vacation holiday all wrapped together in one sensation.

But the instant he had first seen them—yesterday morning, from his parked car, through the house windows—he had been stormed anew by his unworthiness and by the magnitude of what he had done. Those odious feelings for the last thirty-six hours had kept him from walking up to the Forest Hills Avenue door and knocking.

The four people living behind those walls were simply never going to be able to forgive him. What could he possibly do that would persuade them to give him a chance? He was sure now that for their sake he could refuse alcohol of any quantity or type for the rest of his life. But what if his presence alone, minus any aspects of alcoholism, released a whole new deluge of demons into their lives? The proliferation of such negative "what ifs" had paralyzed him.

Yet, now that he had tasted the unimaginable bliss of again being in his family's presence, he could not for one moment stand to let them out of his sight. He could not stop following. Watching. Observing. Agonizing.

Yesterday morning, after drenching his shirt with tears while sitting in his car and witnessing their images pass back and forth across the living room and kitchen windows, he had trailed them in their van as they set out to begin their day.

Their first stop had been at a corner gas station where he had watched Justin, tall for a nine-year-old and lean, pump gasoline into their vehicle. Clay's genes were imprinted all over the child, from the boy's fair hair, to his build, even to his mannerisms. Clay had sat there biting the inside of his lower lip.

The next stop had been at a large Forest Hills community middle school and high school complex where Summer and Holly, hauling school backpacks, had kissed their mother good-bye and jumped out of the van. With the strongest of nostalgia, Clay had noticed that still true to their childhood natures, Summer vivaciously moved across the school grounds while Holly, more like a lost poet, meandered as if deep in thought.

His daughters! He had wanted to leap out of the car and rush into their lives to take up a position as their infinite protector. To protect them from loneliness. From unwise choices. From lust-crazed young men. To protect them from all the destructive vices, so familiar to him, that were hidden in luring and harmless-looking facades.

His heart had been torn asunder as he pulled away from the schoolyard to continue following Rachel. He had reiterated to himself, for the sole purpose of rubbing in the pain, that if the girls had passed all their grade levels through the years, Summer was now in the eleventh grade and Holly in the eighth. Holly had not even been old enough to attend school when he abandoned her. She was now just a grade or two away from being in high school! How, he wondered, could it ever be possible for him to atone for missing out on her youth?

Crushed by the weight of those particular thoughts, he had managed miraculously to keep Rachel's minivan in sight until she finally parked at an elementary school. There he had watched as

Justin, book laden, ran into the building. Rachel followed, clad in a knee-length winter coat, toting a purse and a business satchel.

Clay had sat steadily and waited for Rachel to return. When she did not return to her van after an hour and a half, he noted the name of the school and left to find a public phone. He wanted to follow up on a hunch. He found a phone about seven blocks away, just outside a video store.

"Good morning, my name is Joe Davidson," he lied when one of the ladies at the school office answered the phone. "I'm calling to get the school's mailing address. My wife needs to send a letter to a...Mrs. Rachel McCain, one of your teachers."

"The address is P.O. Box 6000," the lady answered. She then quoted the name of the mailing district and the zip code.

"And can you tell me which grade Mrs. McCain will be teaching next year?"

"Just a moment." There was a pause of about ten seconds. "Fourth grade," the lady eventually replied, sounding disinterested.

By the time Clay had been able to say thank you, the lady was already hanging up.

With his suspicion confirmed, Clay returned to his car. He had not been surprised to learn that Rachel was a schoolteacher. Blessed with a keen mind, she had always been able to clearly expound ideas, facts, and information. A history of informal teaching for her had included working with Summer, Holly, and Justin at home, along with teaching the Bible for many years to young Swedes in Stockholm.

But why had she moved to New York to teach?

Continuing to dwell on that question, Clay had spent the rest of the morning and afternoon parked on a side street next to the elementary school's playground, comforted by the knowledge that Rachel and Justin were physically within a hundred yards or so. For one short thirty-minute period during that long vigil, he had been consummately entranced as he spotted his son enjoying a recess out in the cold with his classmates, playing a chaotic game of sandlot basketball.

Had he for one moment known with certainty that Justin would accept him and not be further scarred, he would have paid the eight thousand dollars in his possession just to run onto the asphalt court for five minutes and toss the ball with his boy.

With Justin carrying on with life right before him, Clay thought he would go crazy. Because of his complex dilemma of indecision, his insides had felt like a yo-yo being spooled mercilessly between the glories of heaven and the horrors of hell.

The feeling had been sustained, if not heightened, throughout the evening as he had remained at a distance and watched Rachel and Justin go into a supermarket, as he had watched Rachel and the three children eat dinner together around the kitchen table, and as he had watched them all settle in for the night.

Today he had posted himself adjacent to Summer and Holly's school in an attempt to snatch observations of the two girls and to establish some sense as to whether their lives displayed signs of normalcy.

He was grabbing for any substantial reason that would merit his disruption of their lives. If his daughters showed signs of extreme dysfunction, he would be quicker to give himself permission to stand on their doorstep and ring the doorbell.

What he could see, though, was extremely limited. He had only seen them get out of their van and walk to the two adjoining school

403 ◆ Brotherhood of Betrayal

buildings in the morning and then in the late afternoon board a school bus that dropped them off two blocks from their home. From there, they walked directly to the house. They had not loitered at any time before or after school, yesterday or today.

After school, they did not ride home in a souped up, packed out automobile driven by a hot-rodding teenager. Neither girl was sporting orange or blue hair or a shaved head. They seemed to be nonsmokers.

Clay could not disclaim what he saw. The girls, along with their mother and brother, appeared quite remarkably to be a fully functioning old-fashioned, close-knit family, despite the absence of a dad and husband.

This analysis, regardless of how premature it might be, lifted him to a new level of indecisiveness.

He slapped the cement pillar he was now leaning against inside the parking deck.

"Come on, man, stop stalling," he lamented to himself. "You've come this far! Just do it! Just take the risk!" Blinking to catch the tears in his eyes, he moved toward the concrete stairwell that Rachel and the children had just descended.

If only he had just one ally who could understand his breaking heart, one single friend who would forgive and accept him, one human being who would place his arm around him and help walk him through this darkness. He needed someone to listen to him, someone to pray for him, someone to advise him.

Striving to push through his loneliness, he entered the stairwell, listened to make sure Rachel and the kids were well ahead of him, then descended the steps. At ground level, he passed through a doorway into a wide, blue-carpeted corridor. He stepped through just in time to see Holly and Rachel disappear around a corner about forty yards to his right. They were definitely headed into the concert hall.

Clay wondered if he should return to his car and wait, or if he should proceed into the auditorium and experience the same event Rachel and the children were going to experience. Was he properly dressed for the occasion? Beneath his coat, he was wearing one of his new long-sleeved dress shirts along with a new pair of dress slacks, not a suit and tie like two or three other men he was now noticing in the hallway.

Attempting to appear confident, he strolled to the bend in the passageway where he last saw Holly. Ahead of him was another stretch of hallway and another bend. He continued on to the next corner, then stood facing a huge lobby. The high-ceilinged room was filled with people, most of whom were making their way into the main performance hall from the street entrance. Clay stood to the side and scanned the crowd. He did not see Rachel, Summer, Holly, or Justin.

Clay noticed then that a significant number of people were dressed casually. Whatever the nature of the performance about to take place, he decided to linger and be part of the audience. He knew now at least that he would blend easily into the crowd and not draw attention to himself.

He scoured the hallway and lobby once more and convinced himself that Rachel and the kids were not in sight. He then found the ticket windows. He was already removing his billfold when he saw that all the windows were closed. Puzzled, he gazed toward the auditorium doors to see if anyone was selling or collecting tickets. But the people going into the auditorium were passing straight through the doorways without pausing. They were not purchasing or displaying tickets, not even flashing ID badges.

Clay ambled cautiously toward the great hall, definitely not wanting to come face-to-face with Rachel or any of the children in an unplanned episode. He spotted a wide stairway leading to a balcony. He walked in that direction.

At the top of the stairs, he hastily examined the corridors to his right and left. He then stepped across the corridor into the first available balcony door. Hundreds of seats spread before him on the quarter-moon-shaped floor plan.

He stepped to his left behind the final row of seats and stood there in the shadows, leaning against the wall. Only about half the seats in the balcony were occupied. He scanned every row, seat by seat. When he was certain that neither Rachel nor any of his children were sitting in the upper level, he walked down the sloping, outer aisle to his left and took a seat at the front of the balcony, three rows from the edge. The location afforded him a comprehensive view of most of the ground floor. He noticed immediately that the lower level was nearly filled. The building was massive, with thousands of seats.

He methodically scoured one section of the ground floor, then another. After about five minutes, he had to avert his focus to ease the visual strain. He saw then that the balcony was slowly filling up. He also took notice of the stage area for the first time. The curtains were open. On the center of the stage were three or four sets of choral risers placed side by side. Positioned catty-corner to the risers was an arrangement of instruments—an electronic keyboard, a set of drums, an electronic guitar, a bass guitar, and an electronic violin. In front of each instrument stood a microphone and music stand. Seven or eight microphones were lined up across the front of the risers. An additional mike stood front and center at the edge of the stage. On each side of the stage was a giant white screen.

Clay closed his eyes for a minute or two, then resumed his effort to locate the four people who had now become his sole purpose for living. In less than five minutes, his eyes zeroed in on the thick honey blond hair that was once so familiar to him. Rachel was sitting in one of the center sections about ten rows from the front. She was leaning sideways and talking to Justin, who was in the seat next to her. Clay probed painstakingly to find Summer and Holly, but he could not pick them out anywhere. He suddenly wondered if they might be among the newcomers scattered throughout the balcony.

He slid deeper into his seat. He then asked himself whether realistically Summer and Holly would even recognize him if they were sitting within six feet of him. Had the changes in their lives during the last seven and a half years been too drastic for them to clearly remember his image? Or had Rachel kept photographs of him in the house, photographs that had kept alive their memory of his face?

He decided that the risk of being identified by his daughters was less likely if he simply remained in his place and kept still. Thus, keeping his shoulders and eyes facing straight ahead, he focused again on Rachel and Justin. As he held them steadfastly in his sight, he gave his heart the freedom to bask in the emotional rush, a depth of feeling so great that for the first time in several years he felt glad to be alive.

This one moment alone, he concluded, was worth every single

407 ◆ Brotherhood of Betrayal

minute of the last six months of menial labor, of scrounging for money, and of abstaining from alcohol. He would do it all over again in a heartbeat, would do it ten times over, just for this one unimpeded glimpse.

Why? Why had he ever allowed the pursuit of forbidden fruit to turn him into a blind, demented fool? And now that he had clawed his way back to this moment, why was he so hesitant to reach out for forgiveness? But even as he watched Rachel continue her conversation with Justin, he knew the answer to the latter question. He feared the probable rejection. And above all, he feared the risk of instigating a new hell for the ones who deserved it the least.

"Good evening, everyone," a man's voice suddenly spoke from the center-stage microphone. "Welcome to the Liberty International City Church's annual youth celebration. My name is Dennis Cook. I'm one of the youth pastors here at Liberty Church. I'm your host this evening at this long-anticipated, much-publicized, greatly prepared for blowout event where the young people of our church's twenty-four congregations have joined together to minister to each other and to celebrate the work that God is doing in our lives."

Thunderous applause with wild whistles and yells erupted from the crowd as people all over the auditorium stood.

Clay stayed seated and tried to shrink. A church meeting with people from twenty or more congregations! He felt grotesquely offensive, as if he were a pornographic poster plastered across the ceiling of the auditorium. He buried his face in his hands.

He should leave. The people would require it of him anyway if they knew his story.

"Before we begin with our celebration this evening," Dennis

Cook continued, "I want to announce that there has been a last-minute change in our program. Curtis Hart, the youth pastor who many of you know from our Williams Bridge congregation, was scheduled to give a closing fifteen-minute message. But last night during a basketball game, he broke his ankle." Fleeting moans swept through the audience. "Needless to say, he will not be taking part in our program tonight. Agreeing to speak in his place is one of our favorite sixty-eight-year-olds in the whole world. A man with the heart and attitude of a thirty-year-old. The pastor to all of our pastors. And a man who is a father figure to a great number of us. He's the only man I know who…"

Clay's attention was suddenly disrupted by someone standing at his side. "Excuse me!" a teenage girl said. Instantly thinking he had been discovered by one of his daughters, Clay jerked his head toward the voice. In one quick motion, he gulped down his tension followed by a breath of release. The girl standing at his side, accompanied by a friend, was a stranger. So was the other girl.

"Are you holding those seats for anybody?" the girl asked, pointing to two places beside Clay on the inside of the row.

"Uh…no, I'm not," Clay responded. As his heart recovered from being startled, he twisted in his seat to allow the girls to pass through.

As the girls slipped past him to the empty seats, Clay heard another round of applause. He vaguely assumed that the fusillade of approval was regarding the stand-in speaker.

Clay sat nervously while Dennis Cook next introduced and welcomed the members of the band that would be responsible for the music during the evening's two-hour program. From backstage, the all-male group hustled out to their instruments, acknowledging the crowd's third round of applause. The five young men readied themselves at their instruments, then launched into a hushed, rhythmic tune.

Dennis presented a fifty-voice choral group already approaching the risers from both sides of the stage. Dennis then exited the platform.

The choral group, dressed in red and black street clothes and made up solely of teenagers, filed onto the risers. As each singer stepped onto the first aluminum tier, he or she began singing, joining the other members already ahead of them. The lyrics of the song were unmistakably Christian.

Clay was still wondering if he should leave, but then suddenly recognized one of the singers moving onto the second tier of the risers. He was immobilized as he watched his younger daughter, Holly, singing radiantly and robustly with all her heart. She was singing a Christian song in a Christian meeting! Part of a Christian group, a Christian community.

The revelation that Holly's faith had somehow been salvaged and sustained through the years lambasted its way through Clay's soul. He remembered praying with her at the age of five, at her request, that she would be a follower of Jesus.

He whimpered deeply. The innermost desire of his heart at the moment was to stand up and clap for her. To shout to her and let her know with tears just how proud he was of her for such extraordinary strength. Fighting to batten down his yearning, he could actually feel a burning sensation spread through his heart. He was not sure how much more of the emotional oscillation he could survive. Trying to let the tension ease from his body, he remained seated.

When the choral group completed their opening song, a young man stepped out from their ranks and walked to the center-stage mike. With heartfelt enthusiasm, he led the audience in a dynamic chorus. The lyrics were flashed onto the two giant screens for everyone to follow. For twenty minutes or so, the young man led the thousands of voices in a variety of songs, some lively, others subdued and reflective.

This was the first time Clay had heard Christian music in seven and a half years. He was moved by the power and the spirit of the whole atmosphere. Especially by the emboldened and grace-filled words.

After the final chorus was sung and the young worship leader returned to the risers, the stage lights went dim. Two young guys appeared from behind the curtains and carried a park bench through the dim light to the front of the stage, where they set it down and walked away. Two girls walked into the semidarkness and positioned themselves on the bench. A spotlight suddenly illuminated the bench.

"Steve's threatening me again," one of the young girls said to the other.

"Because you won't sleep with him anymore?" the other girl asked.

The first girl sniveled. "Sleep with him. Get drunk with him. Get high with him. Everything." She wiped her eyes. "I'm really afraid, Cindy."

The dialogue continued for three or four minutes, the first girl sharing her fears and troubled life, the second girl being a concerned and responsive listener.

"Have you ever tried to talk with your parents about these things?" the second girl eventually asked. "I'm sure they would do everything they could to intervene for you."

"Are you kidding? Talk to my parents?"

"No, I'm not kidding. My parents have always been there for me when I've been in a crisis. I couldn't imagine not having them there. It might sound crazy, but about 90 percent of the time, their advice and their reasoning is right on. Believe it or not, they've actually helped keep me from a lot of heartache."

"I guess you're lucky, then. My mom and dad hardly ever talk to me. About anything. And never about anything personal or important. They never have. It's as if I honestly don't exist." There was an exaggerated pause. "Maybe that's one reason my life is so messed up."

The spotlight dimmed.

The punchy message, augmented by the dead-serious acting, left the audience silent for about four or five seconds. Then there was deafening applause.

Clay did not, could not, move.

The clapping subsided as the park bench was taken from the floor. The entire stage was again bathed in light. The choral group then sang two songs, both centered around the theme of man's innate need to be loved.

When the singers finished their final note, the band continued to play quietly. A single column of young people started pouring across the stage from the left side. The teenagers formed a line that stretched from one side of the stage to the other. A second line of young people formed behind the first. Then a third.

The background music was silenced. Dennis Cook came to the

microphone. Pointing with a sweeping gesture to the three rows of teenagers, Dennis announced, "These sixty-three precious young people standing here behind me, most of whom come from broken homes, want you to know this evening that during the last twelve months, through the various youth outreaches of our church, they have each discovered the heavenly Father's love through salvation in his Son. And to proclaim their reconciliation to God, they have been baptized, some in the Atlantic Ocean, some in the East River, some in the Hudson River, some in swimming pools, and some in church baptisteries. And their lives have all been radically changed."

The crowd was once again on its feet bestowing another booming ovation.

The potency of the scene moved Clay to free-flowing tears. He stood this time in order to blend better with the surroundings. The atmosphere was engulfing. He was sure that what he was experiencing must be the presence of God, a presence unequaled anywhere on earth, a presence he had not felt in a long, long time. And only now because of others who were deserving of God's special intimacy.

Dennis Cook waited, then motioned for the audience to be seated. "Four of these young people, two young men and two young ladies, are now going to come and share with you their personal stories."

As Clay repositioned himself in his seat, the fabric of his shirt suddenly rubbed across the back of his neck and produced a minor irritation. He reached behind his head and under his shirt to quickly massage the area and discovered a slight bump, about the size of a dime. It was indeed sore to the touch. He hastily dismissed the spot as a bug bite or a developing pimple. Almost immediately, his attention was refocused to the stage as he heard the sound of a young man's voice over the sound system.

"I've fought in street gangs and I've robbed stores, and I was never one time nervous or afraid," the young Hispanic man was saying with a smile. "But I am definitely a little nervous tonight."

The crowd responded with polite laughter.

The young man, Carlos Stellar, told of how his older brother was stabbed in the back and killed two years earlier in a gang war. Carlos had afterward spent days and weeks venting his anger through long, reclusive walks in Central Park and through aggressive basketball games on the asphalt courts of the Bronx.

"Jeff Lackey, one of the youth pastors of the Liberty International City Church, was one of the regular players on the courts at that time."

Carlos told how Jeff befriended him and got him to open up one day and talk about his anger. Carlos explained to the audience that he had grown up in a fatherless home and had always compensated by confiding in his big brother and that Jeff Lackey's sudden concern as an older guy had come at a crucial time for him. He was eventually told by his new friend that he, Carlos Stellar, was passionately loved by a sympathetic, understanding God who wanted to adopt him and be his new and eternal Father. After months of seeing God's existence so evident in Jeff's life, Carlos chose to give himself to that grace giving God. One evening eleven months ago, he had been born anew and baptized a few days later. Since then, he had left behind his old lifestyle, worked a steady job for the first time in his life, and was now facing the future with extraordinary hope and, most important, with a new and ever-present Father.

The next person to come to the mike was a Caucasian girl who shared that she had long ago concluded that organized religion was a hopeless waste of a person's time.

A year and a half ago, however, she had seen a respected friend undergo a transformation of character and outlook, a transformation the friend attributed to a newfound love relationship with Christ. The friend, who had been introduced to Christianity through one of the ministries of the Liberty International City Church, had invited her to attend last year's annual youth celebration. At that unforgettable meeting, she, for the first time on a convincing scale, had seen an authentic revelation of the living Christ, a Christ who possessed the ability to fulfill the human need for purpose, love, and security.

She started accompanying her friend to additional youth meetings. Within weeks, she had renounced the "mediocre" dreams for her life and in a life-altering conversion had chosen to be a disciple of the living Christ. Her hope was to give the remainder of her life to His service.

As Clay listened to the testimonies, he could feel the passion and the truthfulness emanating from the hearts of the young speakers. The memories of his own conversion as a teenager came back to him in full force. How was it that his earnestness for the Savior had ever been quenched? How was it that his loyalties to God and to truth had ever been misplaced?

He looked at Rachel again. Then Justin. He could not hold back the tears. If only he could live the last eleven years over again!

In the next few moments, his stomach became so knotted over the matter that he was certain he could feel the oncoming pangs of nausea.

The third testimonial was given by a disfigured African-

American girl whose face, neck, and shoulders had been severely scorched in a freak trash-fire accident when she was two. From that moment onward, her life had been marked by rejection. Consequently, she had been habitually starved for acceptance.

Seven months ago, she had visited a Sunday morning worship service at one of the Liberty International City Church congregations and had learned for the first time that Jesus had been rejected by His stepbrothers, by His community, and by His own people. As the chosen sin-bearer for the world, He had even been rejected at Golgotha by His own Father so that all of mankind could through His substitutionary execution be offered forgiveness and acceptance.

The young lady emphasized with her slight lisp, "When it became clear to me that Jesus truly understood my pain, I ran to Him with open arms. But best of all, He embraced *me* with His arms. His acceptance and His love have literally given me a new life."

The last of the four speakers was a brawny Caucasian guy sporting a ponytail to the middle of his back. He introduced himself as Sid and explained that he had grown up as a spoiled kid in the home of millionaire parents. As early in life as he could remember, he had pandered to his progressive appetites for the weird and the perverted. At the age of eighteen, at the end of a long trail of indulgent practices, he lost a girlfriend to a lethal overdose of heroin. He had been the one who introduced her to the drug and the one who shot up with her when she injected the fatal dose. The girl's death finally awakened him to his moral ineptitude. He sought out a church to try to find out if God would ever forgive him.

"I was absolutely blown away when Pastor Gossett at the Liberty congregation on Long Island showed me in the Bible that not only *would* God forgive me, He *wanted* to forgive me. And that His forgiveness was offered freely. On July the eighth of last year, I became a recipient of that forgiveness. I was baptized the next day." Sid bowed his head in humility. "God has given me a clean start in life. That's one thing my family's money could never buy."

When Sid finished, the audience clapped proudly to express their affirmation of the four young speakers. As the clapping persisted, the band launched into an upbeat tune. The sixty-three young converts then, on cue, filed offstage, followed by the choral group.

The stage lights were dimmed. As the band continued to play, a full-sized transparent baptistery filled three-quarters with water was rolled onto the middle of the stage floor and lit by a spotlight. A beam targeted the front microphone as well.

The music softened as Dennis Cook returned to the mike and glorified God for the sixty-three young lives that had been eternally redeemed. He emphasized to the audience the pricelessness of what they had just seen and heard. He specifically thanked the four teenagers who spoke, who so wonderfully mirrored the heart and soul of the other fifty-nine in their group.

He then announced with immense delight that the lives of the sixty-three young men and women that had been so revolutionized had naturally created a wake of influence. "Standing in the back wings of the stage right now," he added, "are some of their brothers, sisters, friends, and even a mom and dad who, because of this influence, have all recently turned to God for their own forgiveness and salvation. And they've all chosen to follow our Lord in baptism on this special night to publicly proclaim their new faith."

For the next thirty minutes Clay listened and watched with avid interest as fourteen people, young and old, entered the baptistery one at a time and were immersed. He watched as each person came out of the water with an expression of unutterable joy and was welcomed into the arms of jubilant, towel-carrying friends and family members.

Feelings long untouched stirred within Clay's soul. He wanted to stand up and shout at the newly baptized to never for one second stop guarding their heart, to never waste their time longing for anything more than what they were feeling and experiencing right now in the arms of those who loved them.

He deeply inhaled and exhaled a few times to stabilize himself.

When all the people, with the exception of the band members, had left the stage, the baptismal pool was rolled away and replaced with a sofa. As a couple of people moved through the shadows toward the sofa, Clay realized how overwhelmingly thankful he was that his family was connected with such an unusually blessed church.

Two young people outfitted in clothes and wigs to look like an elderly man and woman took a seat on the edge of the couch and faced one another. The teenager playing the role of the man began the dialogue.

"Forty-five years together," he proclaimed, taking his wife's hands into his. "Not bad for our generation."

Even before Clay heard the wife reply, he suddenly realized that he was looking at Summer. The makeup and short, gray-haired wig had delayed immediate recognition. But her physical movements, which he had become familiar with in the last two days, unmasked her identity.

"Forty-five years of marriage," Summer replied proudly. "That's not bad for *any* generation."

It was the first time Clay had heard her voice since she was nine.

Summer's acting partner, playing the role of her husband, squeezed her hands. "Five outstanding and wonderful children."

"And nine adorable grandchildren."

The man paused and said with utter sincerity, "Yeah, it's been good."

"Would you do it over again?"

"Wouldn't change a thing," the man vowed.

"How 'bout a few dirty diapers?"

"Huh?"

Summer smiled and shook her head to dismiss the remark. She then looked upward and outward. "Where do you think the kids would be today if we'd given up on each other during the hard times?"

The nausea that had started to needle Clay's stomach suddenly heaved bile to the back of his throat. Quickly, but as inconspicuously as possible, he made his way to the hallway. He found a men's room just before he retched. The vomiting, followed by an intense spell of dry heaves, kept him on his knees in front of a toilet for five to six minutes. Another five minutes lapsed by the time he composed himself and washed his face.

When he walked out of the men's room, he could hear extended clapping inside the auditorium.

He lightly struck the wall and cursed. He had not wanted to run out on Summer's performance or the searing message. But he had been left with no choice.

He exhaled his utter frustration. He could not help but wonder, in light of the skit's theme, if Summer had written the script, simply assisted in creating the roles, or if she had pursued the role so that she could shout to all parents the dire importance of marital commitment.

He let the frustration eat freely through his feelings and questioned if he should even go back into the auditorium. He twice made a move to head for the exit, but within a minute or two found himself back inside the auditorium leaning against the unlit rear wall. Only with strained effort was he able to acquire Rachel in his sight again. He was trying to remain focused on her when words over the sound system gradually collared his alertness.

"He could have asked for unlimited resources of gold, neverending fame, or even a steady parade of sex partners," the sprightly, older voice was saying. "But as a virile, life-loving young man, he decided not to ask for any of those tempting things. Instead, after earnest evaluation, he asked God for the rare and intangible gift of...*wisdom.*"

Clay shifted his eyesight to the image of the speaker being displayed on the two giant screens flanking the stage. He realized he must be looking at the stand-in preacher delivering the evening's closing message. The man was the only person now onstage.

Clay's immediate thought was that the man's appearance did not jell with the normal look of an American pastor. Had there been an orchestra performing, the man now speaking could easily have fit the bill of the maestro. His hair, though white and somewhat thin on top, hung straight and thick and was a little longer than average. He wore an equally white beard trimmed close to his face. His clothes were neutral colored and casual. His overall appearance was that of a sharp, free-spirited character with a strong, yet reassuring, presence. Clay was immediately drawn to him.

"I submit to you," the man was emphasizing, "that in order for this young man to have the presence of mind to ask for wisdom above everything else, he *already* had to be partially wise. So I ask, how was it that young Solomon had become so wise at such an early age?"

The man paused for effect.

"His dad," he finally answered with assertiveness. To substantiate the answer, he read Proverbs 4:3–9.

"I'll say it again," he stated after the reading, "Solomon was already insightful enough to ask for wisdom because of one primary factor: the direct and personal input of his dad. His dad— a king with prestige, authority, wealth, and fame—taught him repeatedly as a child that wisdom was a far greater possession than riches, power, preeminence, or sexual prowess. He taught him this truth from a lifetime of personal experience."

Clay was now entranced by the man's words.

"Why do you suppose Solomon listened? And remembered? Because, very simply, it wasn't just words that he heard. It was his father's heart, his father's demonstrative life. Through his father's actions, reactions, decisions, savvy, and counsel—publicly, privately, and personally—he saw this wisdom in motion. He saw its effect, its influence, its power, its profundity, its goodness, its justice, its value. He saw unequivocally that for a person to survive and flourish in this dysfunctional world, wisdom ranks as an indispensable attribute. He saw that wisdom is indeed far more valuable than gold or any earthly pleasure.

"This is why Solomon listened to his dad's appeal to seek wisdom above everything else. This is why he remembered his dad's words.

"But wait. For the sake of every father sitting here tonight whose life is marked with failure and who feels that he is an irreversible washout, I want to call our attention to another part of this Old Testament story."

Clay had stopped looking at Rachel and was staring at the face on the screen.

"Solomon's dad, King David, had earlier in his life been a thief, a liar, an adulterer, and a murderer. Do you hear the magnitude, dads, of what the Bible is showing us in this story?" The man's voice, already earnest, grew even more so. "The lesson is that as long as you and your son or daughter are alive, it's never too late to make a comeback no matter how you've failed. It's never too late to change for the sake of your child."

Clay, still leaning against the rear wall, felt the words along with the irony of the evening pound through his heart.

"King David is the proof. And Solomon, his son, is the fruit of that proof. Solomon, the child of a previously debased man, was forever influenced by his dad's salvaged and matured character. Though not without noted vulnerabilities, Solomon went on to become one of the wisest men who has ever lived.

"His legacy? A forty-year reign as Israel's king, a period of acclaimed peace and prosperity for the whole nation. And three renowned books of wisdom that God immortalized as part of the Holy Scripture, three books that have touched the lives of millions of people throughout most of the world's cultures and have become the reference points by which the world judges all other works of wisdom.

"All because his dad made a comeback."

The man repeated that it's never too late to reform one's fatherly behavior. He then pleaded with all the fathers who were parentally derailed to first seek God's forgiveness.

"David acknowledged the wrongness of his thievery, his lying, his adultery, and his murdering," the man explained, "and he became repentant. God honored his change of heart. God taught David through the consequences of his sin, yet absolved him from all condemnation, set him free from the sentencing he deserved, gave him a clean heart, and then used him as a remarkable and wise old father.

"God will likewise honor your repentance. He is, bar none, the greatest advocate for your rejuvenation."

Clay suddenly felt that he was hearing God's voice through the old man. God's voice wooing him, declaring that His almighty arms were truly open. He started to sniffle and weep.

"These kids need you, Dad," the man proclaimed, sweeping his hands before the hundreds of teenagers in the audience. "You've heard this truth stated very strongly here tonight in the dramas and the testimonies. There's simply no one who can replace you. I repeat, your kids need you. They need your wholeness. Your love. Your input. Your leadership."

Overwhelmed by the message and the sense of grace that was filling the auditorium, Clay wanted to stand indefinitely right where he was and be cleansed in the forgiveness that the old man was preaching about. He wanted to be washed of every day of the last ten years. He wanted to be clean. He wanted to know it was not too late. He was so caught up in the moment that he forgot about his sickness until an abdominal pain struck him with such intensity that he doubled over.

He propped himself immediately against the wall to keep from going to his knees. He grabbed his stomach and gritted his teeth. Panting, he tightened his abdomen muscles and tried to control the pain so he could get to the men's room, quickly.

He suddenly felt a hand on his shoulder. "Are you all right?" a man asked.

"It's okay," Clay muttered. He then left the meeting hall and teetered as swiftly as he could to the rest room. With a rising fever, he succumbed to his bodily needs, then left the building.

Facing the edified and challenged crowd, Dennis thanked everybody who contributed to the wonderful program. He mentioned several key people by name, including the evening's primary speaker, Jason Faircloth.

When Clay was finally alone in bed in a hotel room, he held a cold, wet rag to his fevered brow and decided he had to speak with the old preacher. The man's gentle, grace-filled manner was nothing less than an emotional and spiritual oasis.

Reliving the evening again and again in his mind, especially the old man's powerful words and the impression of God's willingness to forgive, Clay at some point of spontaneity maneuvered his aching body to a kneeling position beside the bed.

Trying to forget his sense of utter worthlessness and his affinity toward unbelief, he dared for the first time in seven and a half years to prayerfully enter into God's presence. Watering the sheets with tears, he lost track of time as he confessed every single immoral act he could remember ever committing. He attempted to envision God's arms opened wide. He then cried out from his heart and asked for forgiveness.

He eventually fell asleep on his knees, whispering to himself over and over that tomorrow, if he was physically able, he would walk back into Rachel's, Summer's, Holly's, and Justin's lives.

48

The excitement buzzing inside Clay's soul pushed him the next afternoon to primarily disregard his diminishing headache and fever. At around three o'clock, he parked his Buick across the street from Rachel's house. Rachel's van was parked in front of her property.

Clay was certain now that he could at least go to the front door and face Rachel and the kids in person. He did not feel necessarily like a new man as a result of the previous night's effort to reconcile with God, but he had at least come to grips with the monumental belief that God had not irrevocably abandoned him. He was still convinced, however, that before he could find consummate forgiveness from either God or himself, he would have to validate his repentance in extraordinary ways.

He looked toward the windows of Rachel's house. The cardinal question now, though, was if the woman and children living on the other side of those windows possessed any inclination to forgive. Even the slightest inclination on their part would be enough to keep him working for years, even at a geographical distance if agreed upon, to regain their acceptance.

He shifted his glance to the solitary long-stemmed red rose lying on the passenger seat. He wondered if he should take it with him to the door. Would such a symbol of love and desire be a foolish mockery, or would it successfully convey its universal message before any words could be spoken? He had wanted to buy fifty roses, even a hundred, and present them to Rachel in a giant bouquet. But such an ostentatious display of roses, even more so than one single bloom, would likely be scorned as a cheap and pitiful way to announce his return.

He started to pick up the rose. His hand was shaking like a leaf in a gusty wind. He held up the empty hand and stared. His memory, in one of those moments of erratic vagary, suddenly jumped backward seven and a half years to Stockholm, to the morning he strapped on his backpack and reached for the door handle to walk unannounced out of his family's life. His hand on that morning had trembled in the same way.

Seven and a half years!

He lowered his head and in a faltering prayer implored God to give him strength for what he was about to do. He even whispered a hope that maybe the gracious old preacher who spoke in last night's meeting could be available to help facilitate the reconciliation. He wondered if Rachel knew the man or had ever spoken with him. Clay half-consciously rubbed the swollen blemish on the back of his neck that was still causing irritation. He then opened his eyes, took a deep breath, and picked up the rose.

As he reached for the driver's door, he saw something that made him freeze. He did a series of visual retakes to make sure that what he was seeing was real. But his eyes had not blurred or misread the fact. Rachel, draped in a long winter coat, was strolling slowly down the sidewalk, approaching her yard. Side by side with a man. The man, engaging her in pleasant dialogue, had his arm wrapped around her shoulder.

Clay clamped his eyes shut. He felt his heart constrict.

He shouted inside his head not to jump to any conclusions. But it did not promote his cause when he opened his eyes and saw Justin bound out of the house, run down the walkway, and throw himself into the man's affectionate embrace.

Less than thirty minutes later, Grayson, Rachel, Holly, and Justin piled into Rachel's van.

"All right, guys," Grayson said from behind the steering wheel, with excitement in his eyes and voice. "First, we'll swing by Jeannie's to take the toothbrush to Summer. Then we'll go to the bridal boutique for the seamstress to measure the wedding gown for its alterations. And after that, *if* there's enough time left before the big game, we'll eat at the Thai restaurant. If not," he added with a joking sigh, "we'll just have to suffer and eat greasy ol' hot dogs and hamburgers at the arena."

Justin, in the backseat, clenched his fist and jerked his elbow into his rib cage. "Yes!" he hissed happily.

Rachel looked at Grayson and smiled.

Grayson, returning the smile along with a pucker and a pretend kiss, started the engine and pulled away from the curb.

Clay was about eight cars behind the Nissan van, passing through a business district, when he saw the van pull over and park against the curb. Clay immediately pulled over and parked his Buick.

With extreme edginess, he watched through the windshield as Rachel, Holly, Justin, and the man got out of the vehicle and entered...a bridal boutique. The shop's large roadside fluorescent sign poignantly identified the place.

As he'd followed them during the last twenty to twenty-five minutes, to a residential stop and now to here, he had frantically tried to convince himself that Rachel could not be married to the man. For one reason, she was still listed in the phone book under McCain. Even the school secretary who responded to his phone inquiry two days ago knew her by the name McCain. It was not rational that she would still be using his name if she was married to another man.

He had likewise tried to make himself believe that she was not living with the guy out of wedlock. Not in the presence of the children. Such an arrangement would be totally out of character with her sensitivity and devotion as a mother.

Surely then, the man must be nothing more than a boyfriend. The relationship was surely a nonbinding one. Most likely, therefore, Rachel's life would not be ravaged or broken if the relationship was tested with an unexpected interruption. Surely, in the long-term picture, the relationship might even be dispensable.

But as he saw the two adults and two children now disappear into the bridal shop, he was broadsided by the sudden implication. He tried to deny the paramount thought that stampeded his mind. He rebuffed the notion and told himself that Rachel and the man had simply gone inside to shop for a wedding gift for a friend or to make a quick pickup as a favor to someone.

A mild sleet started to fall from an overcast sky.

After fifteen minutes or so, Clay struck the steering wheel. He could not sit and wait anymore. Deciding to use the wet and gloomy weather as a cover, he got out of his car and crossed the street, opposite the boutique. He flipped up his coat collar and slowly made his way along the sidewalk. He walked until he had a straight view across the four lanes of traffic to the storefront.

The well-lit interior, made even more vivid by the predominant white, ivory, and silver colors of the store's merchandise and decor, showed only a few people moving about beyond the window's gown-clad mannequins.

Clay wiped away the beads of water that were starting to trickle down his forehead and, at the next opening in the traffic, scampered across the avenue.

When he reached the curb on the other side, he peered through the shop windows at a distance and made sure Rachel and the children were not in the front of the store near the sales counter or entryway. He then stepped closer to the building. He angled to his right to get a better view down the right side of the store's interior. He visually worked his way about three-quarters toward the rear, past two females—neither of whom was Rachel—when something odd yanked at his attention. He took another step to his right for a less obstructed view.

He squinted. He had thought the figure he was now looking at was a mannequin, but he was sure he had just seen one of its arms move. He let his eyes linger. The humanlike profile, dressed in veil and gown, was facing away from him. He saw a couple of hands suddenly tug at the bottom of the "mannequin's" dress. He saw the "mannequin" turn its veil-draped head, exposing the reflection of a face.

Clay heard the word "Rachel" rustle across his lips. The woman in the wedding dress was Rachel. The woman he loved and needed. The mother of his children.

Clay's chin dropped to his chest. Fighting with all his might to maintain some kind of orientation, he staggered to a utility pole and held on in order to remain upright. His thoughts and feelings surged too frenziedly for him to control.

In a moment of madness, he steadied himself and rushed toward the boutique's entrance, only to stop himself short. In another moment, he spotted a Coke can littering the sidewalk and kicked it twenty feet through the air, crashing it against a landscape wall that marked the shop's property line.

For five minutes or more, he huffed and puffed and paced, with sleet and rain cascading down his face. He eventually found himself back in his car, sitting behind the wheel, waiting.

And waiting.

And waiting some more.

He felt as if he were a lone journeyman in the middle of a great desert, dying of heatstroke and thirst. Unable to move but within visual range of a lush oasis, an oasis that had once been his.

When he finally saw Rachel, the children, and the man leave the building and run for the van, he felt the primal urge to roll down the window and cry out. He felt compelled to fling open the door and run and throw himself at their feet. Fighting the compulsion, he bit down on his coat sleeve and pressed his head against the steering wheel.

After the van pulled away, Clay lurched out of his car and entered the bridal shop. He walked to the section of the store where he had seen Rachel standing. He looked quickly at some of the merchandise, trying to feign a shopper's interest. He picked up a tiny photo album and approached a male clerk doing some paperwork at a nearby counter.

When the man looked up, Clay placed the boxed photo album

onto the counter and reached for his billfold. He nodded in the direction where Rachel had been standing and said with a grin, "The lady who was trying on the dress, is she getting married or was she just doing some modeling and might still be available?"

The clerk, short in stature with effeminate mannerisms, lifted his eyebrow. "I'm afraid you're too late," he responded dryly. "The man she was with is her fiancé."

Clay shrugged. "Just my luck."

Clay finished his purchase, thanked the man, and left. For the remainder of the evening and most of the night, he walked the city streets in the darkness and the rain.

49

Stretched across a hotel bed at five o'clock the following morning, Clay was emotionally and physically spent, yet wide-eyed.

It was clear now that Rachel had divorced him. But how could he possibly walk away without trying to win her back? On the other hand, how could he dare think, even for a moment, of interrupting her new dreams?

He knew he had to make a decision. And he was riddled with fear. Fear of making the wrong decision. Fear of the unknown. Fear of causing more hurt. The fear was even causing him to experience sporadic episodes of the shakes.

Approaching the light of a new day, he continued to toss and turn, and sweat and tremble.

By eight, when he suspected that at least one or two people on staff at the Liberty International City Church were at the church's office preparing for the Sunday morning service, he called the office's listed number, desperate to know how much time he had left before the wedding.

"Good morning, Liberty International City Church," a lady's voice answered cheerily, though sounding somewhat hurried.

Clay cleared his throat. "Good morning," he began without offering any kind of introduction. "I realize I'm probably calling at an inopportune time and I apologize for bothering you, but I'm in the process of booking some rooms for an out-of-state vacation and I just want to make certain I don't plan my trip during the time of Rachel McCain's upcoming wedding. Can you possibly tell me that date so I'll be sure to keep it open on my calendar?"

"Okay, just a minute," the lady answered, still sounding as if her busy pace had been unexpectedly interrupted. "I'll have to get that information from someone else. Hold on."

As Clay waited, he felt that the most consequential thing in the universe for him at the moment was to find out how much time he had left to make his pivotal decision. A week? A month? A year? Was there time to approach Rachel and establish dialogue with her? Was there time to solicit one or more advisers?

"Hello, are you still there?" the lady's voice returned after a couple of minutes.

"I'm here," Clay said, his voice suppressed.

"Okay, you're in luck. I just found out from one of our church musicians who'll be performing at the wedding that the ceremony is planned for Saturday, March 8, at 4:00 P.M."

"Thanks," Clay offered. "I truly, truly appreciate your help."

Before the lady could ask any questions, if indeed she intended to, Clay hung up.

For a second or two after the call, the date and time that had been quoted to him swam around wildly in his head. When their combined thrust finally registered, he realized that he had only two months before Rachel would give herself in marriage to another man.

By noon, Clay was so sick he could not leave the hotel room.

On his knees and clad in his underwear in front of the toilet bowl, he could feel high-grade heat emanating from his face. The unyielding ache within his head made him feel that his skull was going to split open at any time. And although it seemed minor at the moment, the sore on the back of his neck was starting to burn.

Regardless of his wretched health, though, he was sustaining his hope by leaning toward the decision of seeking out the old preacher he had heard on Friday night and asking him to be his confidant and adviser. The man, after all, seemed to possess the two qualities that were crucial for dealing with his personal circumstance: a merciful spirit and a highly perceptive mind. Plus, Rachel probably knew the man. As one of the lead pastors at Liberty International City Church, perhaps the man had even earned Rachel's trust and respect.

As Clay stood to his feet and washed his face at the sink, he meekly whispered a prayer bidding God to ensure that his eventual decisions, whatever they might be, would be only for the good of Rachel and the children.

He twisted his body around in front of the mirror in an attempt to see the irritating welt near the top of his spine. The view was awkward and strained but he was disquieted by what he saw. The bothersome sore had increased to the size of a quarter, was a rank-looking brown, and had become an open lesion.

He spotted a similar blotch, though not yet raised or opened, behind his left ear, partly hidden inside his hairline.

Clay's concern turned to alarm as he found three other such spots—one on the lower part of his back, one on his left hip, and another on the outer side of his right heel, just below the ankle. Each was the size equal to or bigger than a dime.

Again, he looked closely at the open lesion on the back of his neck. Was he experiencing an allergic reaction to something? Had he contracted some kind of skin disease? Could he possibly have skin cancer?

Not wanting to let his mind leap to the worst possible scenarios, he decided that first and foremost he needed to see a doctor. He had waited too long already to undergo an examination and find out the cause of his abnormal weight loss and enduring sickness.

He tried to relax. The doctor would most likely tell him, "It's just an intestinal parasite you picked up somewhere in Central America, either in some bad water or bad food. You should have dealt with this months ago. But the odds are that a good, strong antibiotic will restore you to a normal level of health within a matter of weeks." Turning from the mirror, he stepped out of the bathroom and went back to bed.

Now with enough money on hand to afford medical attention, he decided he would search for a physician the first thing tomorrow morning.

Hopefully, his plan to contact the old preacher would be delayed by only a few hours, or a day at the most.

Dr. Bruce Hartley, a general practitioner in Queens, made notations on a standard medical form as Clay sat on the examination table and explained his fifteen-month bout with weight loss, diarrhea, nausea, vomiting, fevers, and chills.

As a drop-in patient with no appointment, Clay had sat in the waiting room for an hour and a half before he had been invited into the examination room. He was relieved that a doctor was finally hearing a blow-by-blow account of his impaired health. He was especially comforted by the doctor's strong attentiveness.

Trying to ignore a 102-degree fever, Clay went on to tell about his recently discovered skin lesions, and leaned over for the doctor to see the one on the back of his neck. The doctor looked closely, then silently allowed Clay to finish talking.

Wanting to give the doctor as much insight into his case as possible, Clay divulged his recent history of alcoholism and light use of recreational drugs. He also stressed his long-term residency in Costa Rica. In conclusion, he explained that he had been negligent about seeing a doctor until now because he had assumed all along that the sickness would pass and because he had been focused on other imperative issues in his life.

The doctor, a middle-aged man with bags already under his eyes, withheld any upbraiding remarks. Instead, he wrote something on his sheet of paper, looked up, and asked, "Can you give me a complete list of all the different medications you've used during the last fifteen months?"

Clay had to think for only a moment. "Aspirin and Tylenol. That's about it."

The doctor started to say something, then stopped. He simply recorded the new information onto his file card. He then picked up a blood pressure cuff. "All right, I need for you to slip out of your shirt and pants just for a few minutes." Clay did as he was instructed.

The doctor then secured the blood pressure cuff around Clay's biceps and pumped it with air. After reading Clay's blood pressure, the doctor looked into his throat. He then used a stethoscope and listened to his heart and lungs. He slipped on a pair of disposable gloves and closely inspected each of the lesions, poking and pushing on them with his gloved fingers. He took a swab and collected discharge from the open lesion and smeared it onto a Petri dish.

"We'll send this over to the lab to get a culture. We'll get the results back in about three days."

Clay nodded.

"Have you noticed any blood in your stools?" the doctor asked.

"Some, especially during the last few weeks."

"Every day? Every three or four days?"

"Nearly every time I go."

"Have you noticed if it's dark red or bright red?"

"I would say more bright than dark."

"All right, you can put your pants back on." The doctor picked up his pen and paper and made additional notes.

Clay donned his trousers. He was buckling the belt and sitting back down onto the table when Dr. Hartley asked, "Any sexually transmitted diseases in your past?"

The question caught Clay by surprise. "Uh, not that I'm aware of. Why?"

"Have you ever experimented with multiple sex partners?"

Clay hesitated, then said with self-effacement, "There was a four-year period in the not-too-distant past when that was a part of my lifestyle."

"What were your practices regarding protection?"

Growing suddenly uncomfortable, not only by the nature of the questioning, but by its obvious direction, Clay tried to hold his tension in check. "Ninety-nine percent of the time I was protected. There were three or four times when maybe I wasn't. But to be honest, there's no way I can say with any certainty. I was drunk at the time."

"Any homosexual relationships?"

"No."

"Any intravenous drug use?"

"No," Clay said, his lips now barely moving.

The doctor's tone remained forthright and professional. "With your permission, Mr. McCain, I'd like to take a sample of your blood and have it tested for HIV."

Clay could not move. Only his eyeballs shifted. They rolled downward, then raised and focused on Dr. Hartley. "Are you telling me...you believe I have AIDS?"

"What I'm telling you is that you have all the classic symptoms, and we dare not take the risk of ruling it out."

For Clay, the silence that followed seemed literally to squeeze all the warmth and color from the room, leaving only a cold, ghastly gray. Like that of a tomb. After a brief period, Clay dazedly nodded his consent.

Within minutes, a nurse entered the room and had a needle stuck in his arm, drawing a blood sample. Simultaneously, the doctor explained about the lab test.

As Clay saw his blood rising in the syringe, he heard words from the doctor such as "lab technicians," "virus loads," "quantities of CD4 and CD8 cells," and "hepatitis." The words, however, were like unattached lead weights dropping sporadically onto his brain, their collective power overshadowing their individual meanings.

The doctor related during the final minutes of the visit that the blood work would be completed within a week. "Regardless, though, of what the results might be, I feel we should go ahead and additionally schedule a barium study and check out your GI tract."

Clay gave another lifeless nod.

At the receptionist's desk, Clay made an appointment to return in ten days, on Wednesday, January 22, to learn the outcome of the culture and blood tests and to undergo a barium exam.

He paid for his visit in cash.

Once he was outside, the feeling overcame him that the sub-freezing chill of the winter air paralleled the new temperature of his soul. With his hands pressed deeply into his coat pockets, he coiled up on a concrete bench and sat motionless for more than an hour. At some point, he started mumbling to himself. Drool froze to his shivering chin.

That afternoon, standing listlessly in a hotel-room shower, he decided he had to talk with someone. To do so, he told himself, was now a matter of survival. He ruled out the old preacher. He no longer thought he should speak with anyone who had probable connections with Rachel or the kids. He even ruled out Bengt Wennergren in Stockholm.

Desperate to be rescued from his isolation, he strenuously recalled the names of friends and acquaintances from his past. He needed to find someone who could forgive him, someone who could acknowledge him as part of the human race and who, with a listening ear, could grant him the simple freedom to pour out his heart. Was that so incredibly impossible?

With water pouring over his sick and feverish body, he stared at the sore on his right heel. His name search was interrupted for a moment as he replayed for the hundredth time the professional speculation of Dr. Hartley: AIDS.

He also replayed the old preacher's words from Friday night: "As long as you and your children are still alive, it's never too late to make a comeback, no matter how you've failed. It's never too late to change for the sake of your child."

He sat down in the shower stall, water spraying all around. His shoulders sagged. And then he wept.

During the sobbing a name started recycling through his head: Bryan. Bryan Lewis.

Bryan Lewis had been his roommate for five semesters at the Bible college in Anderson, South Carolina, back in the early seventies. When Bryan graduated, he had been called to pastor a midsized church in Norfolk, Virginia. That church, under Bryan's leadership, developed a keen vision for cross-cultural missions, and Clay had been one of the first missionaries the church had selected to support monetarily. The church had contributed faithfully to his work and livelihood from 1980 to 1989, up until he fled. He and Bryan had always been first-rate buddies. Clay wondered if Bryan would dare help him now.

He thought of two or three other prospects, but the name Bryan Lewis kept drumming the loudest in his thoughts.

Clay wondered if Bryan would even still be living in Norfolk. The odds were probably against it. Nevertheless, Clay found that his unspeakable need for a friend drove him to enliven the hope that Bryan was still there and would agree to talk.

By the time Clay got out of the shower, he had breathed so much life into the hope that he helplessly envisioned himself driving down to Norfolk for a few days at Bryan's request and finding open arms.

Before taking time to put on his clothes, he called directory assistance in Virginia, and quickly discovered, with a beholden heart, that Bryan Lewis was still making his home in Norfolk.

After writing down Bryan's number, Clay sat on the edge of the bed next to the phone. Pensively, he gazed again at the lesion on his foot. His mind focused on the potential ramifications the cankerous-looking sore possessed. His mind also recalled the wedding date of March 8, the point at which all existing opportunities of family contact for him would abruptly disappear.

And he could not deny what was true: Utter confusion and exhaustion, like intractable marauders, had breached all his defenses. He simply could no longer subsist, in any sense of the word, without outside help.

He fixed his eyesight on Bryan's number. He settled himself the best he could, mouthed a transgressor's broken prayer, then picked up the phone and called. Someone sounding like a young teenage boy answered on the fourth ring.

"Good evening," Clay said, trying to subdue the nervousness he felt. "I'm calling long-distance to speak with Pastor Bryan Lewis. Can you tell me if he's around?"

"Yeah, sure. Hold on, I'll get him."

Clay heard the young voice moving away from the phone, yelling "Dad!" The noise of a television program droned in the background. Several seconds passed.

The television sounds were suddenly muted. "Hello, this is Pastor Lewis."

The voice was big and energetic, just like the man it belonged to. In their college days, Bryan had been known as the Dynamic Titan. The sweet memories of those days momentarily dwarfed all the other thoughts in Clay's head. The nostalgic remembrances unexpectedly massaged him with a sense of comfort.

"Hello, Bryan. This is Clay McCain."

There was a pause before the question. *"The* Clay McCain?"

"Yeah, I'm afraid that's the one."

"Are you here in Norfolk?"

"No. I'm calling from out of state."

"Well, this is certainly not a call I was expecting on a cold Monday evening in January."

Clay felt a slight smile start to take shape across his lips. "Hey," he declared, his voice ebbing with emotion, "I'm just thankful that you're still in the same city and that I've found you at home."

"Yeah, well I do seem to stay put. It's just that I can't find any place I like better."

"It sounds like a wonderful problem. As a matter of fact, that's why—"

"Excuse me a minute, Clay. I'm going to switch over to another phone. Hang on. Give me just a moment."

Clay was abruptly breathing into a silenced phone line. His call, however, had at least been received. His hope hung in limbo.

"All right, I'm back," Bryan's voice returned. "I just needed to switch over to the phone in my study. So, to what do I owe this call, especially after so many years?"

"I need someone to talk to, Bryan. I know you've heard rumors and speculations about what happened to me. And whatever you've heard is probably true. So I'm sure it doesn't come as any surprise when I say that my life is quite a mess right now.

Actually, that's—"

"So, it's true that when you disappeared into thin air all those years ago you just walked out on your wife and kids and ran off with another woman?"

Clay closed his eyes. "Yeah, it's true." He hesitated and waited for a reply. There was none. "Anyway, like the Prodigal Son, I finally came to my senses. But…it seems that I…uh…have…" His words tightened into groans as his throat constricted.

Bryan still was not saying anything.

Clay was not sure how to interpret the delayed response. "Excuse me," he forged ahead. "I don't mean to fall apart over the phone. It's just that I don't think I'm going to make it unless I have someone who will listen to me, Bryan. My mom and dad are dead. Rachel's dad has moved; I have no idea where he is. Pastor Lovett of my home church in Atlanta won't talk to me. And Dr. Brighton at the PCCGE mission board—"

"Has given you an opportunity for restoration. I just got his letter about four days ago. He says you rejected a very gracious offer, Clay. So, what exactly is it you expect or want from me?"

Clay, still sitting on the edge of the bed, leaned over. "I just need a friend who will listen to me, Bryan. Someone who will let me explain what's happening."

Again, Bryan gave no response.

"Dr. Brighton did offer me an opportunity for restoration," Clay admitted. "But at the time I spoke with him, I was trying to find my wife and kids. I had called him simply to find out if he could tell me where they might be living. He wouldn't even discuss the matter with me unless I first agreed to undergo three to four months of counseling and to place myself under strict accountability to Frank Lovett, a man who had earlier that afternoon told me I'd burn in hell for what I've done. It just wasn't that easy, Bryan. I didn't feel at the time that I could spend one more day apart from my family, much less three or four months. I...uh...it just..."

Clay's thoughts were now running faster than he could articulate them. He paused and tried to reorder his thoughts. He heard Bryan clear his throat in the background.

"It's a long and complicated story, Bryan," Clay stressed, choosing instantly to stop and start over again. "What I'm really needing is just some face-to-face interaction and advice. You're the only friend I could even think to call, the only one I thought would even give me a chance. Do you think there might be any remote possibility that I might come and spend a couple of days with you? You see, I did find Rachel. I haven't actually spoken with her yet, and this is what I need to talk about. I've learned that she's remarrying in about seven weeks. I really need someone to help me decide if I should try to make contact with her before the wedding. Perhaps even try to make a reconciliation attempt. Plus, there's—"

"Excuse me for cutting you off like this, Clay, but I'm really not comfortable with what's happening here. I don't want to be insensitive to your situation, but to be up front with you, your actions were not just against one or two churches or a few people, but against an entire association of churches made up of thousands of members and hundreds of pastors. Instead of trying to isolate just one of those pastors and asking him to place his loyalties into question before all his peers by giving you unauthorized help, I honestly think the biblical approach is for you to go back to Dr. Brighton and Pastor Lovett. You were directly accountable to those two men. Your supporting churches and pastors placed you into their trust. And at least one of those men has offered to work with you and is willing to lead you step by step through a restoration process that would be recognized by all your former friends and supporters. So, if I were you, I would take the help that's been offered. And I would consider it a great gift."

"And if you were me, Bryan, what would you do if, along with everything else, you thought you were dying of AIDS and you were all alone in the world? Would you still go back to Ed Brighton?"

The line went quiet for a good ten seconds. "In that case, Clay, I think I would let everybody else go on with life and in my solitude try to make peace with God during the last few months or years I had left."

The previous gap of silence repeated itself.

"So, my old buddy is just going to turn me away," Clay probed quietly, more to himself than to Bryan.

Bryan sighed then spoke slower and with greater solemnity. "Your old buddy is trying to point you in the two possible directions that I think would be best for you and everybody involved. Besides, I have a wife and four children, Clay. It wouldn't be right for me to put them at any unnecessary risk, either socially from the inevitable fallout, or physically from a disease that is constantly surprising us with its uncanny ways of claiming victims."

Tiredly and silently, Clay nodded his understanding.

"I'm sorry, Clay. I'm sorry it has to be this way."

For the next thirty-six hours, Clay isolated himself in his hotel room, lying curled up in the shower basin, sitting on the carpeted floor between the two double beds, and occasionally dozing.

On Wednesday afternoon, he finally left the room. He walked to the parking lot of a nearby abandoned office building and for an hour or two slowly ambled in mindless patterns across the asphalt. By late afternoon, he had finalized his decision.

With no further delays, he drove to a travel agency and bought a plane ticket. He would be flying out of New York, and out of the United States, on Friday afternoon.

50

O n Thursday morning, Clay checked out of an American hotel for the last time. He loaded his few belongings into his Buick and drove through the early morning traffic to the elementary school where Rachel worked.

Arriving forty-five minutes before classes began, he parked his car in a spot that allotted him an optimum view of anyone approaching and entering the school building.

Thirty minutes later, the Nissan with which he was now so familiar arrived on the premises amid a major influx of other cars, parents, teachers, and kids.

With transfixed and tear-filled eyes, Clay watched as Rachel and Justin made their journey on foot across the parking area and the stone walkway to the front doors of the school. He tried to freeze their every move inside his mind, as sublime effigies to pack and carry with him in his memory.

After mother and son disappeared inside the facility, Clay sat there in his car, unmoving, for the remainder of the morning and afternoon, staring morosely at the school's outer walls.

Early that evening, in the accelerated darkness of the New York winter, Clay followed Rachel, her fiancé, and all three children in a Jeep Cherokee driven by the soon-to-be husband and stepfather.

RANDALL ARTHUR ◆ 448

Clay trailed the Jeep from Rachel's duplex to a beautiful two-story, single-family brick house located in Howard Beach, a posh section of Queens.

Clay parked the Buick about seventy yards down the street so that only the driveway of the property was in sight. He waited in the car for about thirty minutes, then slowly approached the residence on foot. Using the darkness and the abundance of shrubs and trees in the area to shield him from view, he nervously ventured up close to the house. He found a spot next to a giant tree in the backyard that afforded him a clear view into the home's ground-floor kitchen, dining room, and den. There were no curtains in any of the windows.

The house, with seemingly every light in every room shining, appeared to be mostly empty of furniture or any other type of household items. Clay could see only a card table and a few folding chairs set up in the center of the dining room, a portable television sitting in the corner of the den atop a dozen or so cardboard boxes wrapped in tape, and a few kitchen utensils the fiancé was momentarily using in the kitchen.

As the fiancé busied himself at the kitchen stove, Rachel moved in glimpses past the upstairs windows, videotaping the empty rooms. She was steadily talking, appearing as if she were recording some type of narration. Holly, engaged in conversation and smiles, was in the kitchen assisting the man. Summer and Justin were in the den building a fire in the massive fireplace.

Based on the lighthearted appearance and feeling of discovery exhibited by everyone inside, Clay was predisposed to accept what his feelings were telling him, that he was viewing the next homestead of his three children and his one-time wife. The place where they would begin a new life with a new man. In light of the upcoming wedding, just seven weeks away, the deduction only made sense.

Clay looked away from the house for a few minutes and let his eyes adjust to the darkness of the outdoors. Endeavoring to stymie the unwanted jealousy that was suddenly riveting his heart, he slowly walked the width and depth of the yard, taking in all the distinctive elements of the landscape where his kids would probably be romping, tumbling, picnicking, and partying for the next several years. Clay closed his eyes and tried to imagine the long-term noises of his kids' boisterous adolescence. He felt himself biting his lower lip.

When he opened his eyes, returned to the big tree, and peered through the windows again, he saw that they were all seated around the card table and were circulating plates of various foodstuffs, making either sandwiches or hamburgers. As they passed the food, they were all zestfully participating in some kind of group conversation.

Clay could not tell what prompted it, but at some point a spell of laughter seized everyone at the table. After a minute or so, the laughter became even greater when Justin, leaning back in his chair, fell to the floor.

Summer jumped to her feet. Her laughter became so spirited that she lost herself in a body-bending, foot-stomping spasm. The group laughter, wild and spontaneous, persisted for so long that Rachel staggered to her feet, retrieved the video camera, and shot footage of the comical affair.

In the coldness and darkness of the night, Clay felt the scarce reflex of a smile ripple faintly across his own lips. But the reflex was quickly overtaken by a surge of tears.

Clay extended his hands toward the house, grasping arduously for what would never be. He had borne the hardship of loneliness for years, but the loneliness he felt at this moment, combined with the knowledge that he was seeing his family for the final time, was the greatest he had ever encountered.

Overpowered by the moment and by the unremitting cry of his soul to be a dad, husband, and good man again, he grabbed the tree and sank to his knees.

He could not cease his crying. The tightness in his throat, pressing upward and constricting every muscle in his neck, started to choke him. With his face bent downward and one hand propped on the tree, minutes passed before he was able to regulate his breathing.

Eventually he shifted to one knee and leaned against the tree. Unable to break away from the scene, he watched the group inside finish eating dinner. He then watched as they cleaned the table and kitchen and relocated the table and chairs to the den, next to the fire.

As the group surrounded the table and brought out a board game, Clay forced himself to admit that his time to say good-bye had come. Reflecting on his long, redemption-seeking journey from the streets of Costa Rica to this backyard in New York, he pensively reached with his hand and touched the lesion on the back of his neck. He had almost made it, he told himself. Had almost made it.

Taking a full breath, he stood and stretched out his arm one more time. Lucidly closing one eye, he focused the tip of his outstretched finger against the distant outline of Rachel's face and touched her forehead.

"I …I…" The tightness returned to his throat. "I…love you, Rachel," he groaned through the pain. "I love you more…more than you will ever know."

He paused to breathe.

"The first time that I walked away, I did it…for me." The tears started to flow again, each one riding another down his thin, sickly face. "This time…I'm…going to do it for you."

Clay clenched his jaws and massaged his temples. He then kissed the ends of his fingers and placed them reverently against the smiling facial images of his three children.

"Forgive me, Summer. Holly. Justin. Forgive your daddy. Forgive me…for being the world's greatest fool. Forgive me for all the hurt I caused." He exhaled long and deep to try to diminish the physical pain. "I really do…love you. And I'm so proud of each of you."

Clay looked upward into the night sky. "Take care of them, please," he prayed.

He eventually returned his gaze to the table on the inside of the den and focused this time on the man.

"I don't know who you are, sir. But please, please love my wife and my kids…and protect them. For the rest of their lives."

Before turning and leaving, he tried with all his strength to visually retain this last vista of life as a mental trophy.

The pain in his throat spread to his chest, arms, and head. He finally turned and started to go. Then stood still. He tried a dozen times. More than a dozen times. But the pain was too great, too decimating. A muffled, high-pitched groan emanated from behind his clasped lips.

He wheeled his head around and again visually isolated each

one of his family members in the house. Rachel. Summer. Holly. Justin. The four people on earth whom he loved.

He suddenly saw them, with the man in the middle, giving one another high fives around the table. The man then put one arm around Rachel and one around Justin and jovially pulled them to his side. Everybody was smiling. Everybody was merry.

Clay slowly closed his eyes, cherishing the scene, trying to save it. He clenched his fists to his heart and looked away, then took a step from the tree. Then another.

The flashbacks started coming in sync with his steps. Rachel and the children's duplex. Rachel and Justin's school. Summer and Holly's school. Holly and the youth choir. Summer and the drama. Rachel in the bridal shop. Justin on the school's outdoor basketball court. Justin pumping gasoline. Rachel videotaping. Holly working in the kitchen. Summer and Justin building a fire in the fireplace. The laughter-filled meal in their new home. The board game. The high fives.

Clay suddenly heard his feet pounding the ground. He was running, stumbling down the street toward his car, gasping, choking.

When he fell into the driver's seat, with the door slammed behind him, he started the motor and floored the accelerator. Refusing to look back, like seven-and-a-half years earlier, he burst forth with animalistic wails.

51

A lone in her bedroom for a few minutes as the kids
watched a favorite television program, Rachel—on the eve
of her wedding—lifted her old wedding band and Clay's
old Viking charm from the bottom of her jewelry box.

She had asked Grayson two days ago how he suggested she
dispose of the items. He told her she should feel free to keep them
if she wanted. If not, she should dispense of them in a manner that
would be easiest for her.

Rachel carried the ring and the charm into the bathroom and
stood at the trash can. With a simple and earnest prayer for Clay's
well-being and a promise to herself that she would continue to
think less and less frequently about him, she unceremoniously
released the two pieces of jewelry. She watched them, with all of
their past symbolism, slip through the air and land forever out of
sight in the tissue-filled can. She truly hoped, in the event Clay
ever experienced a genuine change of heart, that he would cross
paths, as she so fortunately had done, with members of the body of
Christ who would be merciful and helpful.

She then made a phone call to Aunt Temp next door before
heading Justin off to bed.

Later that night, Rachel switched off all the lights except for
the nightstand lamp in her bedroom, and crawled into bed into a
sitting position. She was certain, although her clock showed nearly

midnight, that sleep was not going to come quickly for her.

Filled with a joyous anticipation that was beyond measure, she entertained the thought that this would be her last night to sleep apart from Grayson Cole. Within the next twenty-four hours, she would savor his bedroom embraces, the longed-for freedom of his husbandly love and companionship.

She was glad they had not set the wedding date farther in the future. The love that had solidified in her heart for Grayson had now reached proportions she never thought would be possible. She was ready, more than ready, to walk the aisle and be granted the official status of Mrs. Rachel Ilene Cole.

She reached atop the nightstand and retrieved a card from Grayson that had been delivered to the duplex in the early afternoon along with a large bouquet of multicolored tulips. She opened the card and for the dozenth time in the last nine hours read the moving and meticulously handwritten message.

PRICELESS

Seven years ago
I cast my eyes and heart on you as a journeyman
Simply because you were a rare and beautiful tune

In your soul
I heard, beneath your pain, a song that rang true and artistic

Upon becoming your friend
I, to my adventurous delight,
Even discovered that your music was magical

It taught me to dance

It provoked me to reflect and to touch my emotions

It even steadied my spirit during the rains and the darkness

Despite the recent years of distance and separation

Your music has continued to resonate with power

And has now become a symphony

A symphony that moves me like no other

Your unequaled melody

Eternally rare and beautiful

True and artistic

And magical

Has now,

On the eve of our union,

The most looked-forward-to day of my life,

Also become priceless

Priceless

Priceless

Your greatest admirer and lover,

Grayson

The card, now as before, raised Rachel's spirit to a stratum of sublimity. The strength and sincerity of Grayson's words touched places in her heart that only a man's passionate love could touch.

Rachel whispered a prayer of indebtedness to God for the way His divine goodness—demonstrated so abundantly through the lives of people like Jason Faircloth and Grayson Cole—had salvaged, sustained, and rebuilt her life.

She finally turned off the light and lay back on the bed. Her mind, however, refused to relax. Her mind started making sure that the last-minute prewedding necessities had been taken care of in full. She mentally scrolled through her list.

She had finished writing and mailing all the thank-you notes for her shower gifts. Her wedding dress, veil, pantyhose, shoes, and purse were all in place and ready to take to the church. The children's wedding outfits were also in place. The new gold wedding band for Grayson was on the chest of drawers and ready to be put into her purse. The suitcase for her honeymoon was packed with clothes and toiletries suitable for seven days in Honolulu. Aunt Temp had been given a set of house keys and would stay with the kids in the new house starting tomorrow afternoon. Aunt Temp also had the phone numbers in Honolulu in case of an emergency. The refrigerator, freezer, and kitchen cabinets in the new house were stocked with food. All the kids' clothes were clean and put away in the kids' new rooms. Schedules specifying the chores and responsibilities of each of the three children for the next seven days were posted on the refrigerator at the new address.

Confirming everything in her head several times and pacifying herself that nothing necessary had been left undone, Rachel finally dozed off.

Six time zones to the east in Stockholm, Sweden, the time was six-thirty, Saturday morning. The sun had not yet risen.

Clay, under the shroud of darkness, gazed intently toward the backyard sandbox at the house where he had lived during his nine years in Stockholm, the house where all three of his children had spent their infancy and early childhood, the house where they had been living when he abandoned them.

He stood in a public walkway that ran behind the row of houses and peered over the backyard gate.

During the last seven weeks, he had stood at this site at least once a week in the privacy of the predawn hours and just stared, sometimes for as long as a couple of hours.

He had entered Sweden seven weeks ago on a three-month tourist's visa. Upon his arrival, he had purchased four sets of baggy clothes, a pair of thermal gloves, and a large hooded coat and had moved onto the streets. To keep from freezing, he had regularly worn all four sets of clothes at the same time and had slept on ventilation grates on the city's back streets. And to keep from being spotted by anyone who might remember him, he had consistently worn the hood and had gone unshaven.

Squinting now at the snow-covered sandbox from beneath his headpiece, he again hammered the thought, pronounced it to himself till he was mentally hoarse, that he had sat and played in the sandbox with his son just one time. One measly time. He reached into the deep pocket of his coat and removed a bottle of Johnnie Walker whiskey. He unscrewed the cap and took a couple of swigs. He was now so physically weak that he considered himself fortunate to still be able to lift a bottle.

He estimated that his body weight was now down to 125 pounds. No solid foods would stay in his stomach long enough to digest, so he simply had stopped eating. The lesions on his body had become gaping, grotesque holes of rotten flesh, almost unbearable in their pain and stench.

And he compared the condition of his being to that of his

RANDALL ARTHUR ◆ 458

repulsive sores: irrevocably putrefied.

He had felt no proclivity whatsoever to reach out to anyone for any kind of aid. Not Anna Gessle, not Anika Wiberg, not even a medical institute. There had, however, been a flickering desire to contact Bengt Wennergren and possibly some other male friends from the Stockholm Independent Bible Church. But he had stifled all such urges. He had only granted himself permission, solely for the sake of nostalgia, to stand across the street from the church building one Sunday morning and watch the congregation as they gathered for their worship service. He had watched with his face concealed inside the obscurity of his hood.

Most of the people he had seen were unknown to him. Some were not: Bengt Wennergren, obviously now married, had been arm in arm with a lady and a baby; Sten Oestlund, the high school teacher, had looked balder and heavier; Rolf Nyborg, the church's best Bible teacher in days gone by, had looked the same as he did eight years ago. He had also seen Marie Blomqvist, Merlene Bildt, Ingela Sunneborn, and a few others. Conspicuously absent from the picture, however, were Eric and Lena Torleif. Clay could only wonder why.

He had just been glad to see that the church was still intact and that he had been given the opportunity to see it one final time with his own eyes. His earthly labor had produced at least something of lasting value. Admittedly, the experience of watching from a distance had been one of profound melancholy and had only intensified his feeling of aloneness in the world. At the same time, it had been a fitting moment to help bring his calamitous journey to a close.

Clay took another gulp of whiskey. He shifted his focus from the sandbox to a swing set that he had erected for Summer on her third birthday. As he steadied the apparatus in his sight, he indefatigably replayed some of his cherished father-daughter memories of backyard fun and spontaneity. He then gazed up and down the walkway where he was standing, the walkway where he had taught both his girls to ride a bicycle and where, after a heavy snowfall one November night, he had taught them to glide on cross-country skis.

His mind was embracing and nursing the remembrances when a house light in the master bedroom—the bedroom that used to be his and Rachel's—suddenly came on. People were getting up.

Clay scanned the property one last, lingering time and told it all farewell. He then pointed himself toward the center of the city and slowly shuffled away.

Sun rays shone into the church foyer through the amber-colored windowpanes and lit up the room with a brightness that paralleled the splendor permeating Rachel's heart.

As Rachel took in the setting around her on Saturday afternoon at a few minutes after four, she could hardly differentiate between fantasy and reality. She was standing with her wedding party just outside the large double doors leading into the meeting hall belonging to Liberty International City Church's mother congregation. She and those in the group were waiting for the bridal chorus to commence.

At the head of the party, nearest the door, were the two groomsmen: Corby Cross, a local husband and father who, along with his family, had dearly befriended Grayson, Rachel, and the kids; and Eric Torleif, who had come from Sweden with his wife,

Lena, at Rachel's invitation. The two men were wearing black suits, white shirts, and conservatively designed maroon and dark gray silk ties.

Next in line was Justin, now ten, the bearer of the groom's ring. Justin was wearing a suit and tie identical to those of the two groomsmen.

Behind Justin were Summer and Holly, excitedly filling the positions of the two bridesmaids. Their dresses were a stylish, floor-length silky maroon. Both girls were wearing their long hair piled fashionably above their ears.

Standing with Summer and Holly was the matron of honor, Aunt Temp. She was adorned in the same maroon color but was wearing a dress that was cut slightly different to befit her age. She was a little nervous but glowing with pride as if Rachel were her own daughter.

The flower girl was six-year-old Karlyna Skanderbeg Scott, an adopted, paraplegic daughter of a family in the church. The family had adopted Karlyna two years ago from an orphanage in the country of Albania. Karlyna, paralyzed from the waist down, was confined to a wheelchair.

And hard to believe, yet one of the biggest blessings of the day, was the man directly at Rachel's side, her father, Billy Allen Ward. He, to Rachel's surprise, had agreed without hesitation to travel across seven states to participate in the ceremony. And now here, he was even showing genuine enthusiasm for the occasion. Rachel noticed that he seemed, for the first time in years, to actually be enjoying her company. She looked at him. He was busy at the present conversing with young Karlyna. Rachel still could not believe that her dad was part of the picture.

Immediately on the other side of the doors from where they were all standing were well over three hundred well-wishers who had packed out the auditorium. Standing off to the side of the front stage and waiting for the first notes of the processional were Jason Faircloth, the officiating minister who had helped salvage her faith in God and humanity; Pastor Dan Shaw, the best man who had faithfully nurtured and challenged her during her comeback; and, of course, Grayson Eugene Cole, the man who had won her utmost love and passion and who had nearly single-handedly restored to her heart and soul a true sense of womanhood.

For Rachel, the setting was equal to that of an ethereal and euphoric dream.

She was relishing the riches of God's awesome and mysterious goodness when the bridal chorus—played at her request on a baby grand piano, a flute, a cello, and two violins—suddenly lifted the building. At the sound of the music, Jan Aaron, the wedding director, threw open the large double doors.

Daytona, Jason Faircloth's granddaughter and the bride's assistant, took Rachel by the hand and squeezed. "It's your day, girl."

Rachel returned the squeeze, smiled, and stood more erect. As her dad moved to her side, Rachel took his arm. She then turned her eyes to the front of the party. In her mind, she could easily envision Jason Faircloth, Dan Shaw, and Grayson now making their way across the front of the auditorium to the base of the platform.

It was only a minute or so later that Corby Cross, the lead groomsman, was given a hand signal to start the procession up the aisle. Rachel watched as Corby entered the auditorium, followed twenty steps later by Eric Torleif.

Advancing on cue at the same twenty-step interval, Justin went next, then Summer, then Holly. Rachel smiled a deep smile. Her children—sharp looking, intelligent, united in spirit, and as excited as she was about what was transpiring—could not possibly have made her more proud as a mother.

Aunt Temp sequentially stepped to the doorway and faced the open auditorium of three hundred people sitting with their eyes transfixed on the center aisle. From Rachel's view, the glow on Aunt Temp's face revealed that her excitement and gratification were prevailing over her nervousness. Without hesitation, Aunt Temp embarked up the aisle the moment she was directed.

Immediately in front of Rachel, six-year-old Karlyna propelled her wheelchair forward as previously rehearsed and received some final words from Jan Aaron. Secured in Karlyna's lap was a deep basket overflowing with pink rose petals. Sporting a look of sobriety, the little girl was soon rolling her chair into the giant hall.

Rachel filled her lungs with a deep breath. Arm in arm with her dad, she slowly moved up to the door.

"You're absolutely stunning," Jan Aaron announced softly. "Grayson is one blessed man, and he knows it."

Rachel nodded with a self-effacing grin. From her position, she could now see directly, without obstruction, into the auditorium. With a touched heart, she saw Karlyna scattering petals onto the carpet a quarter of the way up the aisle. She saw the capacity crowd of supportive and caring friends, the brilliance of the sunlight beaming into the big room, the exquisite floral decorations, the candelabras, and the wedding party standing in formation across the front. A tear of wonder slid down her cheek.

She then made eye contact with Grayson. From across the auditorium, across the span of three hundred heads, she could see the love in his eyes, the happiness, the gratitude, the passion, the desire. She was sure he could see the same elements radiating from her eyes as well. She then saw Grayson, dressed elegantly in his specially tailored black suit, give her the most beautiful smile a woman could ever receive. With tears dotting her face, she returned a giant, heartfelt grin.

At that instant, the sound of the piano, flute, cello, and violins stopped. Seconds later, the sound of the bridal chorus surged anew with emphatic power.

It was her time.

Everybody in the pews stood.

Rachel took another deep breath and was telling her right foot to step forward when she heard the quickly mumbled words, "I'm proud of you, honey."

Rachel turned her head sideways. The proclamation had come from the lips of her dad.

Rachel was so taken by surprise that all she could do was offer an awkward nod and a muffled thank you. As she commenced her slow walk up the aisle, with her father beside her, she could hardly believe what she had just heard. She had never before in her life heard her father say those words.

The sudden barrage of flashes from photographers' cameras, however, quickly returned her attention to the ceremony. She then heard the first "aahs" sweep through the audience. People had been telling her all day long how beautiful she looked. At this moment, she truly felt beautiful. As the lights continued to flash, she again looked across the room at Grayson. In her heart, she just wanted to be beautiful for the man she loved. Locking eyes with him, she saw his eyes grow wide as if her attractiveness were literally taking his breath away.

Her mind fleetingly envisioned the beachside bungalow in Hawaii, the honeymoon accommodation Grayson had reserved, that for several weeks now had sparked intimate and romantic anticipation for them both.

Continuing to look into Grayson's handsome face, she saw him stare fervently at her and silently mouth the words "I do."

She had to restrain herself from running the rest of the way up the aisle. Her smile was as radiant as the sunlight filling the auditorium.

52

The Swedish train engineer sat attentively at the console of the G1200 diesel locomotive. As he brought the three thousand metric tons of train and cargo into the track system of Stockholm's city limits, he reduced the speed of the train to forty kilometers per hour. The thirty-eight-car train—hauling automobiles and industrial chemicals from Germany, textiles from France, and marble and turbines from Switzerland—was being monitored by the nearby operation control center and guided by signal lights along the side of the track.

The tall, burly driver, humming an old pop tune, had taken over as engineer six-and-a-half hours earlier at the border town of Helsingborg in the southwest corner of the country, where the freight cars had been passed via ferry from Denmark to Sweden. As usual, for this particular route, he would spend the night in Stockholm. He would return to Helsingborg tomorrow, hauling a different load of freight. But after half a dozen hours at the controls, he was ready to exit the metal beast and enjoy a Monday night of relaxation and entertainment in the nightclubs of the Swedish capital.

He looked at his watch: 11:20 P.M. In about fifteen minutes, he would enter the central freight yard. The end of the line. He continued to hum as he checked all the gauges, each one glowing in the darkened cab, and verified that all operations were functioning properly.

For the next eight or nine minutes, he gave careful attention to the track ahead while taking occasional glances through the clear night air at the passing lights and buildings of the big city.

And then his heart almost skipped several beats because of what he was suddenly seeing. He jerked slightly and quickly rubbed the corners of his eyes.

Beneath an underpass about forty meters ahead, a person—a man or woman, he couldn't tell—was sitting within two meters of the track, leaning against the concrete foundation of one of the bridge piles. The driver's hands moved quickly toward the brake levers.

"Don't try anything stupid!" he whispered strongly to the character. "And please, for God's sake, whoever you are, don't make any quick moves!" The tension of the words was still lingering in his throat as the locomotive approached to within meters of the bridge.

It seemed as if the next few moments were framed in slow motion. The engineer unconsciously held his breath, realizing that all thirty-eight cars being pulled by the locomotive had to pass beneath the bridge before the trespasser would be free from life-threatening danger.

The engineer's eyes stared madly at the individual.

Brilliantly illuminating the foreground, the headlamps of the engine suddenly left no darkness or shadows around the encroacher. And what the engineer saw next sent another wave of surprise through his nervous system. The person sitting alongside the track was a man, a man whose head was leaning unnaturally sideways. A man whose arms were hanging motionlessly and awkwardly into the snow. A man whose posture was eerily rigid.

Resembling that of a...corpse.

As the locomotive rumbled past the body without incident, the engineer opened his side window and extended his head outside the train—into the zero-degree weather—to maintain visual contact with the figure.

After only a few seconds, the engineer pulled his head back into the cab, reached for his cellular phone, and called the operation control center.

Within minutes, a group of five policemen was swarming beneath the bridge with spotlights. In their ensuing search, they quickly spotted the reported personage.

Noting, and avoiding the effacement of, the single set of snowy tracks leading around the bridge embankment to where the motionless person was now sitting, they made their way to the body. As assumed, based on their dispatch briefing, they quickly discovered that the individual, a white male, was indeed dead. Sitting in six or seven inches of snow, the man was frozen.

The image, however, that unexpectedly leapt from their beams of light and seized their attention was the unusual configuration of the corpse's facial expression and hand posture, a surreal picture that none of the men would ever forget. The eyes, wide open, along with the O shape of the mouth and the strong lift of the cheeks, portrayed a dazzlement of overwhelming and breathless wonder, as if the man, whoever he was, had in the last moments of life seen or experienced something that overcame him with great power and tenderness and peace. His right hand, solidified in a semigrasp, appeared quite strikingly to have been reaching out in response to someone else's hand.

Confused, the officers looked again for an additional set of footprints. But there was none.

A thorough search of the victim's clothing relinquished no forms of identification. The only nonclothing items found on, or near, the body were a bundle of cash wadded in the front pants pocket and a stamped envelope stuffed in the coat pocket. The envelope, folded and extremely worn, bore only one visible marking: the word *Rachel*. The name was handwritten in the space designated for the receiver's address. A letter, equally as worn, was found inside.

After making support calls and summoning a crime-scene unit, the officers scoured the area for any possible clues that might enlighten the situation.

They searched in vain.

Within hours, the unidentified corpse was in the hands of medical examiners; and the cash, letter, and envelope were in the possession of forensic technicians.

The forensic lab's investigation showed no fingerprints on the letter or envelope other than those of the deceased. Not a single fruit-bearing clue was detected on any of the items, just intriguing ones. The envelope, for example, bore a costly stamp in the usual top right-hand corner, a stamp normally used for mailing letters outside the European continent. The stamp had been adhered for several weeks. And the letter itself, written by an unsteady hand, revealed a message that had been written in English. The unmailed letter had been dated five weeks earlier.

A typed copy of the document was produced for the police department.

Dear Rachel,

This attempt to take the unworthy feelings of my heart and convey them to you in a distant, handwritten letter dramatically displays my perverted and insane hope that you will dare force yourself to read what I write. If you are reading this second sentence, then I am greatly aware that you have already extended to me a measure of grace equal to that of our Creator's. Please be assured up-front that the sum total of my desire is that you simply note my brokenness and my apology. I ask for nothing more.

I just want you to know for your own deserved satisfaction that the very moment I so foolishly walked out of your life, and the children's, I started spiraling nonstop—mentally, emotionally, and physically—into a nightmarish and bottomless hell. One that I rightfully deserve.

I know you probably would not believe me if you heard me say it over and over again for a million years, but the only moments of true happiness for me since I exited your life have been when I've lost myself in my thoughts and pretended my soul was clean and I was back in our home in Stockholm holding you and the children in my arms. Laughing together. Continuing to build a life together.

I have tried a few times, in moments of daring, to reconnect with the decent side of the human race, especially the church, but it seems that only God can forgive me. That only He can see the utter destitution and loneliness of my heart.

I am not blaming anyone.

I am defenseless.

The complete and total absence of human forgiveness, however, is more difficult than can be imagined.

In addition to hearing that I've suffered dearly for my moral and social transgressions, please, please, please hear me when I say that you are the only woman I have truly ever loved.

Why, oh why, didn't I see that fact in the beginning?

And if you can ever find the ability in the dark, forgotten places of your heart, will you please forgive the day I was ever born?

The letter bore no signature.

The autopsy report, filed less than thirty-six hours later by the medical examiner's office, listed "accidental death by hypothermia" as the official cause of the man's cessation. Contributing factors were noted as "the AIDS virus and malnutrition." There were no bodily signs, externally or internally, nor any reports from the crime-scene unit indicating that the man had been a victim of any foul play. From all observable facts, the man had simply been in an unsheltered and isolated place and had frozen to death.

The identity of the male figure remained a mystery.

So did the reason for the man's extraordinary and unforgettable last expression. And outreached hand.

Epilogue

Throughout the following couple of years, the Cole family persistently matured into a solid, secure, productive family where love and commitment were prized above all else.

One of the crowning events for the whole family occurred on December 23, 1999. Rachel gave birth to a baby boy. Looking like Grayson made over, the little dark-haired fellow was given the name David Mattaniah, meaning "gift from the Lord." With the entire family present, David was consecrated to God a few days later in a special service at the Liberty International City Church.

More and more, Clay McCain became a faded memory.

About the Author

RANDALL ARTHUR served as a missionary in Europe for twenty-two years. He and his wife, Sherri, worked as church planters in Germany and Norway before returning to the United States in 1998. Arthur has written two other best-selling works of fiction, *Wisdom Hunter* and *Jordan's Crossing*. He and his wife live in Georgia with their three children.

As a missionary now basing his ministry out of the United States, Randall Arthur recruits, trains, and facilitates short-term mission teams for western and eastern Europe. For detailed information, you can correspond with him c/o Multnomah Publishers, P. O. Box 1720, Sisters, OR 97759.

Discussion Guide

1. In your opinion, why are large numbers of Christians (men and women alike) abandoning their marital commitments?

2. Do you think we fully understand the damage that is being done to the hearts and minds of children when their parents' marriage is willfully abolished? Give examples.

3. What percentage of Christian husbands and wives do you think are susceptible to infidelity and divorce?

4. Does the pursuit of happiness (at the cost of families) really set anyone free?

5. Why is it so difficult to express our wayward tendencies to the church and cry out for help? Give examples.

6. What will it take for the church to be a safe place to be real?

7. Had you been Clay McCain, what would you have done differently?

8. List several reasons why the fictitious Jason Faircloth should be a model for us all?

9. What are your feelings toward those who rejected Clay McCain? What are your feelings toward those who rejected Rachel McCain? Can you discern any differences in your feelings toward the two groups?

10. Do you treat fallen Christians in the same way Clay was treated? What do you do differently?

11. What was the most important lesson you learned from this story?

A DESPERATE QUEST...

This rerelease of Randall Arthur's bestselling novel presents the hypocrisy of Christian legalism and a man's search for the only surviving member of his family. The story's hero, Pastor Jason Faircloth, embarks on a journey that lasts eighteen years and takes him through four countries in a quest to find the granddaughter who is being hidden from him. In a process that mirrors our own spiritual journey, he discovers a rich relationship with God and the peace that finally comes with true faith.

ISBN 1-59052-259-1

VENGEANCE DEVOURS A PASTOR'S HEART

When pastor Jordan Rau accepted a position with a European missions agency, his decision was based on money, not on an opportunity to serve God. However, shortly after his family's arrival in Germany, Jordan's priorities dramatically change—his young son, Chase, is murdered, and Jordan becomes obsessed with finding Chase's killers and delivering justice. He sets out on a course of action that will destroy not only the murderers, but his own family as well—and only a miracle can stop him.

ISBN 1-59052-260-5

A FREE
"BEHIND THE SCENES"
LOOK AT YOUR
FAVORITE
FICTION AUTHORS!

www.letstalkfiction.com

Let's Talk Fiction is a free, four-color mini-magazine created to give readers a "behind the scenes" look at Multnomah Publishers' favorite fiction authors. ***Let's Talk Fiction*** allows our authors to share a bit about themselves, giving readers an inside peek into their latest releases. To receive your free copy of ***Let's Talk Fiction***, get online at www.letstalkfiction.com. We'd love to hear from you!